MURDER IN THE CHAPEL

A 1920S HISTORICAL COZY MYSTERY - AN EVIE PARKER MYSTERY BOOK 19

SONIA PARIN

ISBN: 9798860057319

CHAPTER 1

Swathed in silk and tulle

Madame Courbet's Salon

"$\mathcal{M}$adame La Comtesse's taste is exquisite, as always."

Evie stood in front of three cheval mirrors, strategically placed to capture her reflection without her needing to move around.

Shifting her gaze slightly, she saw Tom's reaction to Madame Courbet's remark, his eyes crinkling at the edges, his mouth itching to explode into a smile.

He's laughing at me, Evie thought. Of course, she didn't blame him because her taste had always been dictated by

Caro or Millicent. They both had a greater interest in fashion than she ever would. Since Madame Courbet already had her business, Evie saw no need for flattery, which she had to accept under false pretenses.

Lifting her chin, Evie asked, "And what does *Monsieur* Winchester think?"

Tom, who had hidden behind his newspaper now lowered it, albeit reluctantly. "Me?"

"Yes, you."

"I agree. You have exquisite taste."

"It's pink, Tom. *Pink.*"

"Oh, I see. I believe you are under strict instructions to steer clear of pink and select peach. Or was it apricot? And I, in turn, have been told to approve of whichever one of those two it was."

Tom and Evie turned to Madame Courbet who struggled to hide her exasperation.

Snapping her fingers in quick succession, she prompted her assistant to remove the pink silk fabric swathed around Evie. Another assistant rushed off and returned with a sample of silk fabric.

"Blushing peach," Madame Courbet declared.

Winking at Evie, Tom murmured, "Oh, yes. Much better."

Evie hummed. "The palest shade of green, with an overlay of peach."

"For a wedding gown?" Madame Courbet's eyebrows pointed upward.

Evie tilted her head from side to side. "It is not my first wedding, so I think it might be suitable."

"Pale blue," Tom suggested. "With a hint of yellow

brown. You know, like the color of leaves when they turn."

"Tan?"

"Golden tan. Just a smidgen. Perhaps as a decoration on your hair."

Madame Courbet looked at Tom as if only now becoming aware of him. Her assistant must have registered some sort of prompt because she rushed off and returned with several fabric swatches.

"That would be lovely for a suit," Evie suggested.

Madame Courbet drew out her small notebook and made some quick notes, her eyes lighting up with excitement. Excusing herself, she stepped out of the salon.

Evie noticed Tom took the opportunity to walk to the window. Drawing the thick curtain aside, but only a fraction, he looked down at the street below.

"Is she still out there?" Evie asked.

"Yes, she's keeping an eye on the front door."

Evie knew there was no point in asking Tom if it was the same woman.

In recent weeks, she had come to town twice alone to tie up some loose ends and had not sensed or noticed anyone following her. Then, since arriving with Tom, they'd both become aware of being followed.

They'd first noticed the young woman at the station. Or, rather, Evie thought, she had noticed them and, in so doing, had attracted their attention.

She'd looked like anyone else would look if they were waiting for someone to arrive, standing on tiptoes to look over people's heads and shoulders, and looking around her, as if she might have missed the person she'd been waiting for.

Her skating glance had landed on them for the briefest moment before moving on, only to swing back to them.

Later, Evie and Tom decided that had been the crucial moment when the young woman had recognized them.

It wasn't until they'd climbed in a taxicab that they'd both realized the woman had every intention of following them. As the taxicab had pulled away, her arm had sprung up to hail a taxicab.

There had been a flurry of activity outside the station with passersby weaving their way along, trying to avoid travelers coming out of the train station or going in, porters carrying luggage, and people rushing to grab taxicabs that arrived and departed in quick succession.

The young woman had looked frantic as she tried to hail a taxicab. Evie and Tom had seen her miss two and daringly jump inside one even before it had come to a full stop.

Evie held up a swatch of fabric against her. "Is she still a brunette?"

"Why wouldn't she be?"

"Tom, we've been in town for a week, and she's followed us everywhere. Either she's extremely confident or foolish."

"You're right. She should have tried to disguise herself." Stepping back from the window, Tom said, "I think it's time I have a word with her." He returned to his chair and picked up the newspaper he'd been reading. "Remind me to tell you about the article I read and, if we have time, I think I'd like to buy a pipe."

"A pipe? But you don't smoke."

"It doesn't stop me from carrying matches. I should like a pipe to…" he shrugged, "…to look pensive."

A pipe, she mused. Turning toward the mirror, Evie put on her hat and straightened her clothes just as Madame Courbet returned.

"You'll be pleased to know we have all the necessary fabrics to complete your order. You have my word it will all be completed within the fortnight and will all be sent to Halton House."

Thanking Madame Courbet, Evie and Tom made their way out of the fashion house.

"Aren't you supposed to have another fitting?" Tom asked.

"That won't be necessary. One of Madame Courbet's assistants is my exact size. Besides, my measurements haven't changed in years."

They took the stairs down and stopped at the front door to peer through the glass pane.

Tom put his hat on. Adjusting it, he grimaced. "I don't have a plan. Do you?"

"Be bold?" Evie suggested.

"Walk right up to her? What if she runs off?" He looked down at her shoes with delicate straps criss-crossing the top. "Can you run in those?"

Evie grinned. "We don't both need to run after her."

"Of course, how could I forget."

"Ready?" Evie had another look through the glass pane in the door. "We'll cross the street and then pretend to head off in opposite directions, as if we have different chores to take care of. I'll go right and you can go left. She's bound to follow one of us. What do you think of my plan?"

"It's better than the one I did *not* have."

They walked out of the Jermyn Street building, with Evie suggesting, "We should pretend we're chatting."

Tom laughed. "I just credited you with having said something wonderfully amusing."

Evie echoed his laughter. "I believe I just returned the compliment." Looking up the street, Evie said, "Perhaps we should watch out for traffic."

Tom took care of the left while Evie looked to the right. "I think we just looked rather foolish. The traffic is only coming from one direction."

The young woman did not shift from her position leaning against a lamppost. She had one foot crossed over the other and held a newspaper up, appearing to be reading it with intense focus. Although Evie noticed she had not turned the page since they'd stepped out of the building.

"I'll see you safely across," Tom murmured.

As they neared the opposite sidewalk, Evie leaned in and whispered, "There's a tearoom at the end of the street. If nothing happens, we'll meet there."

"We should walk seven paces and turn back as if we've just remembered something," Tom suggested. "That way we can see which one of us she's decided to follow."

Evie grinned. "You want to turn because you just can't bear to have me out of your sight."

"Yes, that too."

They parted ways, both walking at a sedate pace. Evie checked her wristwatch for effect and took the opportunity to glance at a store window. She just managed to catch the reflection of the sidewalk behind her and saw that the young woman had not moved from her spot.

Evie realized she'd lost track of the paces she'd taken. Arguing seven paces wouldn't be enough because she and Tom would still be within sight of the young woman, she continued walking and hoped Tom had come to the same realization.

She didn't sense someone following her. Then again, she already expected to be followed so perhaps that intuitive feeling only worked if you were oblivious of the possibility.

She'd nearly reached the corner and could see the tearoom up ahead. Lifting her hand slightly, she again pretended to look at the time.

Finding inspiration, she stopped and whirled around while at the same time craning her neck as if searching for someone.

The young woman was following her.

When she saw Evie had turned to look back, she dropped her newspaper and bent down to pick it up.

Evie saw Tom heading toward her, his pace steady.

Of course, she thought, he must have noticed the young woman was not following him.

Swinging back, Evie resumed walking toward the tearoom. When she reached it, she walked in and sat at a table that allowed her to look out the window at the passersby and see the door.

Two minutes later, the young woman walked by the tearoom. She appeared to be intent on continuing. However, stopping, she looked at her watch and, turning, she came inside the tearoom.

Without hesitating, she chose to sit at a table in the corner, diagonally opposite Evie.

A moment later, Evie saw Tom. He stood near the curb and was looking straight at her. Evie gave a small nod. She knew Tom had seen the young woman walk in, and he was probably waiting so he could make his entrance less conspicuous.

A waitress wearing a pristine white apron approached Evie to take her order. Rather than pretend to wait for someone, Evie went ahead and ordered some tea. "And some scones, please."

From the moment she'd sat down, the young woman had busied herself searching for something inside her handbag.

If she had only been intent on following them, she would not have come inside, Evie thought.

She had to be biding her time and waiting for the appropriate moment to make her move. Whatever that might be...

Tom walked in, his steps casual. When he reached Evie, he said, "He wasn't there, so I left a message."

Evie knew he'd just made up some fictional character he'd been to see.

There were two other people in the tearoom, and they were both busy enjoying their scones with jam and clotted cream.

All was quiet inside the tearoom and that meant the young woman must have heard Tom.

It didn't really matter if she'd fallen for the ruse. Evie assumed she must surely know that they knew that she was following them.

Leaning in, Evie whispered, "What do we do now? Wait for her to make a move?"

Nodding, Tom smiled. "It looks like we're having tea and scones."

The waitress set the teacup, teapot, and a platter of scones on the table.

"You should order something. These are for me," Evie said, her eyes bright with delight.

"Are you sure about that? Remember, you have new clothes to fit into, including a wedding dress."

"Fine, you can have one."

"Is she looking this way?" Tom whispered.

Evie gave the slightest shake of her head. The door to the tearoom opened and two women stepped inside, their chatter subdued as they gazed around and selected a place to sit. The door closed and the sounds of the street faded.

"She knows that we know," Evie murmured. And now it was up to either one of them to make the first move. "Now is as good a time as any." Before Tom could ask what brazen idea had cropped up in her mind, Evie looked directly at the young woman and smiled.

The young woman looked up and returned the smile.

When she did not follow up with a decisive action, Evie had to assume the exchange had been nothing more than two strangers making eye contact and acknowledging each other.

A waitress set a teapot and teacup down. She walked away and returned with a small plate. A moment later, the young woman picked up what looked to be a slice of lemon and dropped it into her teacup. Pouring the tea, she then sat back to enjoy it.

"I see a hint of disappointment in your face. I assume she didn't take the bait."

Evie was about to agree but she changed her mind. "Give her a moment. She's thinking."

Lifting the teacup to her lips, the young woman gazed out the window and then shifted her attention to Evie and Tom.

Evie imagined her playing with several scenarios and deciding which one would benefit her the most.

The young woman set her teacup down and searched through her handbag.

"She's going to approach us," Evie whispered.

"I'm sitting with my back to her," Tom complained. "What is she doing?"

"She's getting up. Now she's straightening her skirt and adjusting her hat. She's picked up her handbag... and, no, she hasn't left anything on the table."

"What do you mean?"

"Well, she might have decided to leave behind some sort of note for us to find, a piece of paper addressed to us."

"Saying what?" Tom smiled. "I'll be waiting outside. Follow at a discreet distance and I will lead you to a place where you will be assaulted by two ruffians, intent on stealing your possessions."

"Tom, you have a macabre imagination. How could you think ill of her? I'm sure she is a perfectly lovely person. After all, she smiled back at me."

Tom shook his head. "Women and their feminine wiles. You think you can lure someone in with a mere smile."

"But we can."

"With a smile?" He could not have sounded more incredulous.

"Oh dear…" Evie drew in a steadying breath. "It seems you require some enlightening. For your information, women have been employing the art of subtlety for eons. Once upon a time, not long ago, all one needed was a fan and one could convey any type of message across a room, tempting, taunting, and scintillating."

"You make it sound so intriguing." Tom laughed. "As if empires have crumbled at the sweep of a fan."

"I wouldn't disparage the art of the fan."

"Enlighten me."

Evie gave him a confident smile. "Drawing the fan across the cheek meant *I love you*. Twirling it in the left hand warned of being watched. It came in handy during a time when society imposed restrictions on couples or, rather, people wishing to become couples. Or people engaged in clandestine liaisons."

Tom looked bemused. "If I'd lived in those times, I'm sure I would have remained a bachelor because I would have misunderstood every single sign. As for a smile being enough to lure someone…" Tom chortled.

Evie looked up. "Hello."

A rosy tint bloomed on the young woman's cheeks. Looking uncertain, she held out a card. Evie noticed a slight trembling of her fingers, but her smile remained in place, although it mingled with a look of concern.

"This is awkward," she finally said, her voice almost a whisper.

Evie took the card and read, "Nell Joy."

"I'm a reporter. Although I prefer to think of myself as a writer." Her hesitation faded as she added, "Writing pieces for newspapers pays the bills. Of course, it's very competitive but I know I can always sell an article to the society pages. I saw the announcement for your upcoming nuptials. Congratulations..."

"Thank you." Evie looked at Tom who was studying Nell Joy with the intensity of someone determined to peel away a disguise. "Do please join us."

Nell Joy's eyes widened with surprise. "Yes, please."

Without any preamble, Tom said, "You've been following us."

"Yes, I'm sorry about that, but it was mostly by accident."

Tom's eyebrow quirked up. "How so?"

"When I saw you at the train station, I couldn't believe my luck. I was there doing my job. My next stop was *The Ritz* and there you were, headed in the same direction."

"Were you stalking other people there?" he asked.

"It's one of several places I frequent on the off chance that I might see someone interesting. The public loves to hear what glamorous people do."

"Did you hear that, Tom?" Evie grinned. "We're glamorous."

Nell Joy leaned forward and spoke with a sense of urgency, "I'll cut to the chase. As I said, I've read the announcement. You are getting married, and it would mean the world to me to have the scoop."

"You want to write about our wedding?" Tom held her gaze for a moment as if trying to determine the woman's sanity.

"Someone is going to do it."

"I can't believe there will be much interest in our wedding," Evie admitted. "It won't be a fashionable event. In fact, we're not even getting married in town. I doubt anyone will think it worth their while to travel to Berkshire just to see us getting married."

"You can have the final word on what I write. If you don't like something, I won't include it."

Nothing Evie said would dissuade the young woman. In her mind, this would give her a huge advantage over anyone else wishing to cover the event.

～

Later that day

The door to the first class compartment opened and Tom walked in, prompting Evie to look up from the book she'd been reading.

"Nothing. I've searched the length of this train and there is no sign of Nell Joy."

Evie set her book down. "Did she say she would be on this train? I don't think she did. In fact, I'm sure she mentioned catching a later one, or maybe waiting until tomorrow morning."

"And you believed her?" Tom sat opposite her. "She spent all this time following us. Do you really think she suddenly decided to lose sight of her prey? What do we really know about her?"

"Quite a lot by now. You said you checked all her references."

Tom gave a stiff nod.

"You telephoned the village where she was born." Evie smiled. "You spoke with the schoolteacher who took over from Nell Joy when she decided to pursue a career in writing. You then asked to speak with the vicar who had to run all the way from the vicarage to the post office because he doesn't have a telephone connected. The post mistress herself vouched for Nell Joy, saying she'd known her since she was born. Then you spoke with the editor at the newspaper and the lady's magazine who both assured you of her good character and reliability."

"They could all be her accomplices."

Evie laughed. "Tom, that would be a complicated web of deceit. Remember, she did not expect to cross paths with us."

"Another likely story. How do we know she didn't have someone from the village providing her with information about our travel plans?"

"We're the only ones who knew when we'd be traveling. Remember, we ended up leaving a day earlier. It was a spur of the moment decision." Wishing to change the subject, she said, "You never told me about the article you read. What did it say?"

"You're changing the subject?"

"I might be. Tom, I really don't see the harm in Nell Joy writing a few articles about our wedding."

"You're not worried about a complete stranger shadowing our every move? She followed us. How do we know she is really a reporter? I spoke with two people who claimed to be editors. For all we know, they were rewarded handsomely to pretend they knew her."

"When we first met Phillipa Brady we thought she was a suspicious character and now she is one of our best friends."

"Fine. But I'll reserve the right to say I told you so." Tom patted his pocket. "I don't have the newspaper with me. I must have packed it in the suitcase. Which reminds me, we arrived with two suitcases and we're returning with six suitcases and a trunk."

Evie's eyes danced around his face. "You're about to become a married man so it's time we have a talk."

"Let me guess, this is something I should turn a blind eye to."

Evie replied with a smile.

Standing up, Tom said, "I'm going to go see if I can find a copy of the newspaper. Someone must have one."

When Tom left, Evie picked up her book and settled back to read. Several minutes later, she looked up and saw a porter with a newspaper tucked in his pocket standing outside the compartment.

A smile was enough to prompt him to come in and ask, "Is there something you need, my lady?"

Recognizing him from the years of traveling on this line, she greeted him by name. "Mr. Rogers, might I borrow your newspaper, please?"

He obliged her, saying, "I've finished with it, my lady."

Thanking him, Evie skimmed through the first pages. Since Tom hadn't given her the slightest hint of what he'd read, she had no idea what she should look for.

And then she saw it…

Feeling more amused than concerned, Evie smiled.

"All eyes were on the Countess of Woodridge and her fiancé, Tom Winchester, as they took to the dancefloor."

Sir Tom Winchester, she silently corrected.

The brief article went on to describe their, at times, sultry moves, but not in great detail because the photograph captured them at a moment when they were both staring into each other's eyes. The picture said it all. Well, most of it, she thought, but not everything because they had followed the original steps, and that made the dance... sultry. In fact, she remembered walking back to their table and overhearing someone describing is as rather heated.

She looked for Nell Joy's name but didn't see it. As for Tom wanting to mention the article, well, she supposed it was interesting that someone should think their night out dancing was newsworthy.

Evie was about to set the newspaper aside when something caught her eye. She took a closer look at the photograph. "It can't be," she murmured. Narrowing her eyes, she tried to bring the background into better focus.

It was!

George Beecham?

Here, in England?

The door to the compartment opened and Tom walked in. "I found one, but I must return it within the next ten minutes. A lady wrestled it out of her husband's hands. He'd fallen asleep and will be waking up soon. And, when he does, he'll expect to find the newspaper in his hands. I believe her matrimonial harmony depends on me being punctual."

"No need to put her matrimonial harmony at risk." Evie folded the newspaper and waved it.

"Where did that come from?"

"The porter. I saw him walk by and smiled at him. He told me to keep it."

"You smiled? And he gave you the newspaper?"

"You should return that newspaper now." Sending him on his way, Evie had another look at the photograph. There was no mistaking the close set eyes and languid expression. After a quick calculation, she mused, "Fourteen years." In all that time, she hadn't once thought about him.

She followed the direction of his gaze and was not surprised to find it aimed straight at her.

Had the photograph captured the moment he'd recognized her? If it had, his blank expression failed to reveal his reaction to seeing her. Although, if he'd been happy to see her, he might have made an effort to approach her.

Perhaps she was wrong in thinking he had been looking at her.

Folding the newspaper, she set it aside and resumed reading her book. She managed to read one line before sliding her gaze over to the newspaper and the photograph staring up at her.

∼

The drawing room, Halton House

"It puzzles me, that is all I'm saying."

"My dear, Toodles, even in the midst of this organized chaos, we should be permitted to indulge in the sharing of a bit of news."

"It's gossip, and I don't understand why you trouble yourselves with such trifles."

Sara and Henrietta exchanged a look of surprise.

Recovering first, Sara said, "Trifles? They're our mainstay. How else are we supposed to entertain ourselves?"

Toodles helped herself to some tea. "Very well, you may continue."

Henrietta chortled. "We were going to with or without your approval. We only have a couple of days before the wedding guests descend upon us. This is our last opportunity to get this off our chests. After tomorrow, we'll have to be mindful of what we say." Henrietta skimmed through the letter she'd been holding. "Where was I? Oh, yes... *She* had been on the brink of ostracizing the lady in question."

Toodles interrupted, "*She?*"

"Yes, my dear. *She.*"

"Am I supposed to know this person. What have I missed?"

"There is only one *She.*"

"I see. This is actually a game."

"Yes, of course. Anyhow...*She* had issued an ultimatum."

Toodles murmured to herself, "Only one *She*. Let me see..."

"Oh, for heaven's sake. We're referring to her majesty."

"Ah, I see. Very well, continue."

"Never mind all that. You take all the fun out of it." Putting away her letter, Henrietta looked at the envelope Sara held. "I'd save that for another day."

"Just as well. My letter is replete with tragedies."

"Anyone we know?" Henrietta asked.

Sara shook her head. "Mr. Daniel Humes. He fell off his horse and broke his neck. He was the Earl of Cuthers' heir and is the third heir to have died well before his time. Mr. Humes was a cousin thrice removed. I suppose they'll have to search further afield."

Henrietta looked down into her teacup as if seeking solace. "There have been far too many tragedies and dreadful losses, but none so bizarre as King Alexander of Greece's calamitous end. He was bitten by a monkey and died of blood poisoning in 1920."

"I'm glad you got that off your chest," Toodles said. "We wouldn't want to cast a shadow over the wedding."

"There's no need to be sarcastic, my dear." Henrietta set her teacup down and gestured to the newspaper Toodles had picked up. "And what has you all intrigued?"

"Birdie and Tom."

"What about them?"

"They captivated the guests at *The Ritz* with a sultry Tango."

"What?"

Toodles handed her the newspaper.

Sara leaned in. "Oh, my. I don't need to read the article. The picture says it all."

Henrietta agreed with a nod. Her gaze shifted to the blurry background. "I don't recognize anyone but the photograph is focused on Evangeline and Tom. Although..." She frowned.

"What?" Sara asked.

"No, nothing." Henrietta handed the newspaper back to Toodles.

"Henrietta, I know that look. You saw something."

Henrietta tried to laugh it off. "Someone we know is bound to have been there. I'm sure we'll hear all about it soon enough." She looked away and worried her bottom lip. When she had a moment to herself, she would use her magnifying glass to get a closer look. At first sight, it had looked like...

No, it couldn't be him.

But it had to be. She would never mistake that languid look.

George Beecham.

What was he doing back in England?

Worse. What was he doing in that photograph, staring at Evangeline?

This did not bode well. Not at all.

CHAPTER 2

Home sweet home

Halton House

$\mathcal{E}$vie and Tom were met at the station by Edmonds and Millicent, who had been running errands in the village.

As Tom helped Evie off the train, his eyes scanned the length of the platform, his gaze narrowing as he scrutinized everyone coming and going.

Evie was equally engaged but, unlike Tom, she was not looking for Nell Joy.

"You can release my hand now, Tom."

Tom murmured under his breath, "Go ahead and say it. She's not on the train."

Evie grinned. "She might be waiting for the train to depart before jumping off it. We've already seen how daring she can be when she jumped inside the taxicab before it had even stopped."

Tom's eyebrows slammed together. "I hadn't thought of that."

"Milady," Millicent, having rushed off to organize the luggage, now hurried toward them. "Edmonds will have to come back for the luggage. It won't all fit in."

Unlike Tom, Millicent did not remark on the fact the luggage had multiplied. However, Evie felt compelled to explain, "The large trunk belongs to Toodles. I have no idea what's inside. Although I suspect it is full of magazines from back home, and, if you recall, I had placed a large order for new shoes and hats." She took a step and stopped to look back at Tom. "You're not seriously going to wait for the train to depart."

Shaking his head, Tom followed Evie to the motor, but not without expressing his objections about Nell Joy.

Evie turned to Millicent. "Did anything of interest happen while we were away?"

"There's been a frenzy of activity getting all the rooms ready for the guests and getting the house in order, milady. Toodles has been badgering Mrs. Horace to bake a chocolate wedding cake instead of the traditional one, and now Mrs. Horace has developed heart palpitations."

"Good heavens. Has she seen the doctor?"

"The heart palpitations come and go, milady. She's afflicted with them when Toodles goes down to the kitchen and always improves once Toodles leaves. It could be a coincidence, and I hope you don't think I'm suggesting Toodles is in any way responsible...I mean, I've always been several steps behind Toodles, so it's possible I might be responsible."

"I see." She wanted to ask how many times her granny had visited the kitchen and harassed Mrs. Horace about the chocolate cake but thought better of it. "Has Mrs. Horace considered baking a chocolate cake just to pacify Toodles?"

"No one dares to interfere, milady, so I doubt anyone has suggested it. It's almost become a battle of wills between Mrs. Horace and Toodles."

"I'll have a word with Toodles. It might be easier to stop her approaching Mrs. Horace than to ask Mrs. Horace to bake something outside of her schedule. She's going to be terribly busy over the next few days." They had some guests arriving well before the wedding day. And, Evie reminded herself, before long, she wouldn't have a moment to herself, not even to worry about George Beecham's unexpected appearance in that photograph. "Don't worry, Millicent. I'll do my best to keep Toodles away from Mrs. Horace."

"I'm sorry, milady. I didn't mean to burden you."

"And how is Edgar?"

"In his element, milady. He has a quiet confidence about him and knows he only needs to think of something that needs doing and someone will read his mind and do it."

"I'm not sure how to interpret that, Millicent." Was Edgar annoyed with people not preempting his needs and jumping into action? "Please let me know if there is anything I need to do. I'm afraid I'm not good at reading minds." Or people's intentions, she thought.

Evie's thoughts strayed back to George Beecham. The

last time she'd seen him, he had been about to board a ship headed for Hong Kong or some other exotic place.

Shaking her head, she looked up in time to see Edmonds mouthing, "Where's the luggage?"

"Never mind all that. Her ladyship is tired and wishes to go home."

Evie greeted the chauffeur, saying, "I'm afraid I got carried away in town. There are a few suitcases to collect."

When they were all settled in, Edmonds drove away from the train station, with Tom inevitably looking over his shoulder, prompting Evie to laugh.

"You still expect to see Nell Joy."

"She worked hard to get you to agree to this madness. Why wouldn't she hop on the first available train? She's trying to regain the upper hand, taking control of the situation by being unpredictable. That's why."

"In that case," Evie mused, "we'll be on our toes and ready to be ambushed." Ambushed by who knew what.

Or whom.

When they arrived, Evie stepped out of the motor and straightened her hat. "Millicent, is there anything else I should know about?"

Millicent looked askance and Evie was sure she nibbled on the edge of her lip as if trying to decide what to say or just how much she should divulge.

"The guest list, milady. It has undergone a thorough scrutiny."

Evie's eyebrows moved incrementally upward. Bit by bit, she formed a mental image of the dowagers and Toodles subjecting the guest list to a severe critique.

"I imagine I will hear all about it at dinner."

Millicent nodded. "I'll return to the train station with

Edmonds for the luggage. Your bath is being drawn as we speak. There are quite a few letters. You'll find them on your dresser."

Thanking Millicent, Evie squared her shoulders and headed toward the front entrance; her thoughts focused on the previous evening spent dancing.

Had George Beecham been staying at *The Ritz*?

She knew of only one person who could answer that. His cousin, Davina Beecham-Parks. Unfortunately, Evie had not heard from her in quite some time. Not through a lack of trying, she thought.

She had been one of her first acquaintances during those early days when she and her mother had navigated the waters of a foreign society. Davina had only just been presented and, soon after, had met Anthony Parks, the man she'd married only to lose him during the Great War.

Davina had spent the ensuing years traveling abroad, spending several years living in Paris. She had then returned to England, settling in a town house in Mayfair and avoiding the countryside. Her husband, Anthony Parks, had been a countryman through and through and Davina had embraced his way of life. Evie imagined it was simply too painful for her to spend any significant time in places that had meant so much to them both.

As she had not been able to contact her to issue an invitation to the wedding, Evie had assumed she had set off on her travels again. This was later confirmed by a mutual acquaintance.

"Oh, I've only just noticed there's no Edgar waiting for us."

Hearing her, Millicent rushed ahead, disappearing inside the house, and offering a reassuring smile when she emerged. "He is dealing with an emergency in the kitchen. Nothing to worry about, milady."

Evie exchanged a glance with Tom. She wanted to ask if the emergency had anything to do with Toodles and Mrs. Horace but decided to trust Edgar would deal with it all.

Walking inside, Tom helped her out of her coat as a footman hurried out of the drawing room and dealt with the front door.

"I've just realized something odd. Since coming to live here, I haven't opened or closed the front door once," Tom said, his tone bemused.

"And yet you still refuse to hire a valet."

"I'm a grown man. I can dress myself."

"But you're happy to have someone else open and close the door for you?"

He lowered his voice to say, "I wouldn't want to deprive anyone of their livelihood."

Evie looked toward the drawing room. "I'm going upstairs to freshen up. I think I'll need to have a clear head to deal with the next few days."

"I'll follow you up. I'm not ready to engage with the dowagers and Toodles."

Evie laughed. "You just want to go up and look out the window to see if you can spot Nell Joy hiding behind a tree."

"Yes, that too."

When she entered her room, she found Clare, one of the housemaids, coming out of the adjoining boudoir.

"Milady. Just in time. I've drawn the bath for you. You'll find everything you need all set up for you. I hope you don't mind me doing it. Only, Millicent said I should, and she's taken me under her wing and even calls me her protégé."

Evie assumed that meant Millicent had singled Clare out for a promotion and would eventually find a way to convince her Clare was the best person to take over her lady's maid duties.

Thanking her, Evie glanced at her dresser and saw a stack of envelopes, far more than she had expected to find. One caught her attention. It was much thicker than the others. Nothing that can't wait another half an hour, she thought.

While she had her bath, she replayed the entire previous evening in her mind and tried to think if she'd seen George Beecham. She knew there was a difference between seeing and looking at something. One could look at something without really seeing the details. Although, she knew the mind seemed to register far more than one usually acknowledged, and it was just a matter of prodding around it.

She told herself she must have caught a glimpse of him but had not made the connection. In the next breath, she argued with herself, thinking if she had seen George Beecham, even for the briefest moment, she would have known it straightaway.

Had he made a point of staying out of sight? It had been his habit to always hover around in corners where no one noticed him, always silently watching and waiting for heaven only knew what.

Reliving the previous evening several times, she eventually gave up.

Millicent entered just as Evie was adjusting her robe in place.

"I hope I haven't kept you waiting, milady. I was sorting through your luggage to see what needed to be pressed. I trust you found everything in order. Clare wanted to get everything just right, but I told her not to be so hard on herself if she didn't quite manage it."

Evie sat at her dresser and worked her way through the post while Millicent's chatter faded into the background.

While curious about the contents of the large envelope, it continued to sit at the bottom of the pile.

"Yes, she's efficient," Evie heard herself say even as her focus fixed on the letter she was reading.

"I will have all your luggage unpacked by tonight, milady. Clare will help me. That will give her the opportunity to see how I organize your garments."

Having reached the bottom of the stack, Evie studied the fat envelope. It had been sent from London but did not have a return address or sender's name.

Millicent mumbled something and Evie nodded absently. Turning to ask her to repeat what she'd said, Evie saw the door closing behind Millicent. She turned back to the envelope and slit it open.

It contained dozens of letters.

The first one was addressed to…

My dearest beloved…

Evie skimmed through the first of many letters. When she finished, she searched for the date. Frowning, she looked at the date on the rest of the letters. Some of the pages looked as if they had been folded several times, one even looked as if it had been crumpled. The earliest one was from ten years ago and they were all addressed to her.

My dearest beloved…

From George Beecham.

She read through several more letters and tried to make sense of them as they all included responses to supposed letters sent by…

Sent by someone else to George Beecham.

"Except that… his replies are all addressed to me."

Millicent walked in carrying an evening dress. "Clare did a wonderful job. The skirt needed pressing."

Puzzled over the letters, Evie went through the motions of dressing.

"Milady! It's on backwards."

"Oh!"

Those wretched letters.

Evie pushed out a breath and decided to put the matter aside until she could speak with Tom.

CHAPTER 3

Out of sight, out of mind

Woodridge family chapel

For two days, Evie didn't give any thought to George Beecham's letters; she'd been too busy with wedding decorations, menus, and rehearsals to give them a single moment of her time.

She had also decided to delay telling Tom. It seemed unfair to ruin these days leading up to the wedding. Although, she suspected he would find the letters amusing.

Or, perhaps not.

There was something odd about them.

Almost disturbingly so.

Evie dismissed the distracting thought.

Even if she'd wanted to fixate on the puzzling letters, life at Halton House had made it impossible to focus on anything other than the petty dramas erupting like spot fires.

Despite it being far too early, the dowagers and Toodles had thrown themselves into the task of decorating the hall. The day before, the theme had been blushing pink and light green. That combination had replaced the violets and blues of the previous day. That morning, Evie discovered everything had been taken down on a whim because the shade of pink in the roses had been too bright. The roses had been Henrietta's choice and she had been outvoted two to one. As a result, Evie's morning had been spent refereeing the trio as they waded through a massive selection of blooms.

Suddenly, Evie found herself thinking she should have taken firm action and destroyed the letters.

Her step faltered.

She looked around and tried to remember where she'd been headed.

"The bride is getting cold feet," Henrietta murmured.

Sara and Toodles turned toward Tom, who said, "Am I allowed to turn and look?"

"No," they both erupted. "And no cheating."

"It's a wedding rehearsal, for heaven's sake," Tom muttered. When the vicar's eyebrows hitched up in surprise, Tom gave him a reassuring smile.

"Birdie," Toodles called out. "Did you forget something?"

Evie gave a distracted shake of her head.

Why hadn't she disposed of the letters?

31

Why had she hidden them in the back of a drawer?

Straightening, Evie experienced a moment of clarity. She'd wanted to make sense of them and throwing them away would have made that impossible.

"Countess?" Tom called out and to the others, asked, "is she coming?"

"It's customary for the bride to be late," Henrietta declared.

Tom snorted. "To her wedding rehearsal?"

Evie looked up and saw Tom standing at the altar of the little Woodridge family chapel where they'd decided to hold the rehearsal.

Their new vicar smiled at her, his eyes crinkling with joyous amusement. By now, Evie recognized that as his resting face, a look that suggested he was always amused by something.

Edgar cleared his throat. In the absence of her father, who had yet to arrive, her butler had been only too happy to step in and walk her down the aisle.

She looked at the dowagers and Toodles standing at the front pews, each one signaling an encouragement.

"Oh, dear. Should we start again? No, we'll just pretend I did it right."

They resumed their entrance, their steps steady, with Edgar humming the wedding march tune under his breath.

The vicar gave a nod of approval. Then, for the first time since meeting him, Evie saw him frown.

She realized she'd slowed down and had nearly come to a stop again, stepping well out of tune of Edgar's humming.

For two days, she'd managed to remain focused in the

moment. It seemed her negligence was now costing her. Her mind flooded with thoughts of George Beecham and his curious letters.

He'd been at *The Ritz*. He'd seen her dancing. Yet he hadn't approached her. Had he been surprised to see her there? Had the fact he'd seen her prompted him to send the letters?

No. The letters had arrived before she'd returned to Halton House and definitely before the evening she'd spent at *The Ritz* dancing with Tom. She told herself to remember to ask Millicent for the precise date of their arrival so she could map out the sequence of events.

Intention, she thought.

George Beecham had written those letters over the years without posting them. Why had he sent them now? What did he hope to achieve?

"My lady?" Edgar whispered.

"Oh... Did I do it again?"

"I'm afraid so, my lady."

"I think I made the vicar frown." Nodding, Evie focused on Tom and hurried her step.

"Countess," Tom greeted her. "They wouldn't let me turn to look. Were you practicing leaving me at the altar?"

Evie leaned in and whispered, "Remind me to tell you about the letters."

"What letters?"

"I'll tell you later."

As they turned their attention to the vicar, Evie thought she heard Sara say, "The flower arrangements are lovely. I'm suddenly inspired. Do you think we could borrow the idea?"

"At this point," the vicar said, "I welcome the congregation and say we are gathered here and so on and so forth. Then you will say your vows and I will declare you husband and wife."

Tom looked at Evie. "We're already here. Why not do it right now?"

The vicar gasped in a breath, the reaction echoed by the dowagers and Toodles who surged forward.

Henrietta spoke first, "I think that's enough rehearsing for one day. Evangeline has done this before and Tom can just follow the prompts. Come along. You have guests arriving soon."

Evie thanked the vicar and as the others made their way out of the little chapel, she tugged Tom's sleeve. "I have to talk to you."

"You just used your serious tone. Is it something serious?"

"I don't know. I hope not. In fact, I doubt it is serious." She saw Henrietta looking over her shoulder at them. Hoping her voice wouldn't carry, she said, "I suppose it all began with me seeing the photograph of us dancing at *The Ritz*."

"Henrietta hasn't mentioned it and I'm sure she's seen it." Tom smiled. "Maybe she's reserving her opinions for a rainy day."

"That's odd. I hadn't thought about that and, you're right, she must have seen it. Maybe she's been too busy to say anything." And just as well, Evie thought. "There's something specific I wanted to say about it. I recognized someone in the photograph. Someone from my youth." Good heavens! If Henrietta had seen the photograph, she would have recognized George Beecham.

"Go on. You have my full attention."

She glanced back at the little stone chapel with vines covering the front and side walls and roses still in full bloom. "When I met Nicholas, he introduced me to all his friends and acquaintances. One of them was George Beecham. Nicholas joked about his friend being infatuated with me because he started spending more time at Halton House. He'd never had any interest in shooting or fishing. Suddenly, he developed a keen passion for it all."

"Because you were shooting and fishing with Nicholas?" Tom asked.

"Yes, quite possibly. It didn't occur to me at the time." At least, not until he'd made his feelings known to her. Not in words. He'd actually hinted at... at something. And that, Evie thought, was something she'd ease into. She couldn't just blurt it out to Tom. Although, she suspected Tom would have no trouble putting two and two together. "He'd come along and go through the paces, but he showed no real interest or enthusiasm."

"Not in the shooting and fishing," Tom said.

Evie looked down at the ground. "I wanted to wait until we returned to the house to tell you so I could show you the photograph. I'm sure I'm not imagining it. He appears to be looking straight at us and now..."

"What?"

"When we arrived, there was a stack of letters waiting for me. That's not unusual. However, one of the envelopes contained dozens of letters. Letters written but not sent. Not until now."

"I see. Would I be jumping to conclusions by saying they were love letters?"

Were they? Evie had read most of them, but she had

been absorbed by their mere existence. "They express a full range of emotions."

"Emotions? About what?"

Seeing her. Thinking about her. Recalling days and events.

In one letter, he'd described an overwhelming feeling of exultation as he'd recalled seeing the sun emerging from behind a cloud and lighting up her face.

"Is that what I have to compete with?"

"Tom, this is not the time to laugh at my expense."

He stifled his laughter and asked, "Out of curiosity, why did you wait so long to tell me?"

"I wanted to make sense of them. Instead, I put them out of my mind."

"And why did you choose to tell me now?"

Timing. Yes, the timing was essential. "At first, I couldn't believe he had sent them. Then, I felt confused. Why this and why now? What does he hope to achieve?"

"Do you think he poses a threat?" Tom asked.

"That's what I've been asking myself." Evie looked into the distance. "It makes no sense. He never expressed his feelings toward me."

"Not in words," Tom said.

"I can't think of a single moment when he betrayed the way he felt about me." Subtlety had never been her strength. To this day, she believed he had hinted at something, but she had dismissed it all as nonsense. "Except…"

"What?"

"After the wedding, we didn't see him again. I heard he'd gone traveling. If Nicholas knew something, he didn't tell me."

"Smart man. He didn't want to worry you." Tom fell

silent for a moment and then said, "You should have told me sooner."

Evie expected him to add something about sharing burdens and concerns, but he didn't. "If I remember correctly, you've been disappearing for hours on end, all in an effort to stay out of everyone's way, I'm sure."

Tom snorted. "I forgot to see what colored flowers they put up today."

Evie continued, "I didn't tell you straightaway because I wanted to diminish the significance of the letters." To her relief, he understood her reasoning.

"What changed your mind?"

"The last couple of days kept me busy but today it all came flooding in. I wanted to dismiss it all but now I wonder if I should take it seriously. I'm afraid it might be a case of waiting and seeing what happens next. For all I know, sending the letters might have been his catharsis. Now it's out of his system and he's closed the door on that chapter of his life and moved on."

But he's in England, she told herself.

In London!

Evie wished she hadn't felt compelled to tell Tom about the letters so close to the wedding. She feared it cast a veil of discordance, spoiling the days ahead.

Then again…

Keeping the information to herself would have been a contradiction. They worked as a team. Anything that affected her would also have an impact on Tom.

"You've suddenly fallen silent and that always worries me," he said.

"Right this minute I'm quite cross and full of resentment because the past is interfering with my life."

"Is he likely to do something unexpected?" he asked.

"Such as what? A sudden appearance at the church door when the vicar asks the congregation for just cause why we should not be joined together in holy matrimony?"

"Yes, precisely that."

She didn't think so. Despite being a close friend of the family, she'd never really known him. However, she didn't believe he could be capable of violence.

Would they need to take precautions? "I might need to carry a weapon to the church," she mused.

They walked on, the crunch of their footsteps on the gravel the only sound.

Reaching the house, Tom said, "The early arrivals are here."

"Oh, yes. Clyde Russell and quite possibly Augustus Warwick. They've always been as thick as thieves." Evie pushed out a breath and looked up. Her eyes narrowed incrementally as she focused on the sky blue roadster and the woman climbing out.

"Good heavens." Evie grabbed hold of Tom's hand and squeezed hard.

"What? What is it, Countess?"

"It's not Clyde Russell."

"Then who is it?"

"That's Davina Beecham."

CHAPTER 4

Surprise arrivals

"*D*avina Beecham-Parks, to be precise."

"Should I jump to conclusions and assume she is somehow related to George Beecham?" Tom asked.

"Yes. They are cousins."

Good heavens. What was she doing here?

The dowagers and Toodles had reached her and were engaged in a lively conversation. Instead of hurrying, Evie slowed down. If Tom found this curious, he did not mention it.

Evie had sent Davina an invitation. When she didn't receive a response, she'd reached out to a mutual friend and had been told Davina was traveling.

Evie broke the silence by telling Tom about her. "She knew practically everyone. When we first arrived in England, my mother and I were like fish out of water and

Davina made sure to introduce us to all her friends and acquaintances. I didn't think she'd come. Last I heard, she was traveling abroad." Explaining about her husband, Hugh Parks, she added, "When she lost him, she took up traveling. She's quite the social butterfly and spent a number of years in Paris and the Riviera. She's never been much of a correspondent, so I heard from her only occasionally. A brief note here and there."

"But you did issue an invitation."

"Yes. I suppose it must have reached her. Her people must have sent it on."

"And yet you're surprised to see her here."

"Yes, but that's because she must have interrupted her travels to come."

"Countess?" Tom stopped. "Is that, by any chance, George Beecham climbing out of the motor?"

Evie was looking at Henrietta who'd turned to look back at them.

Henrietta had most definitely seen the photograph, Evie thought. She could almost read Henrietta's expression. It was fixed on her and, Evie would bet anything Henrietta wasn't even blinking as she entertained a barrage of questions and tried to connect Davina's appearance to the photograph she had seen of George Beecham.

As they continued walking toward the group, Evie shifted her attention to the other person. Shaking her head, she said, "That's not a man."

"Are you sure? He looks like a man. He's dressed like a man."

"Tom, it's a woman. She's wearing trousers. They're quite fashionable."

"You're always dressed in the height of fashion. Yet I've never seen you wearing trousers."

"Not yet." Evie's step faltered. "Good heavens. That's Nell Joy."

"What? Are you sure?"

"Absolutely." What on earth was the reporter doing with Davina?

Evie saw Davina turn and, smiling, she stretched her arms out and called out, "There she is."

Reacting with a smile of her own, Evie hurried her step and hugged her old friend. "You came."

"Of course, I came. As soon as I heard. Do you remember Melanie? She's Lady Capell now." Davina didn't wait for Evie to respond. In her usual manner, she continued her tale. "I bumped into her in Cairo. She was about to set off on a cruise along the Nile and we dined with a group of people but managed to exchange a few tidbits from back home and she'd heard about your upcoming nuptials. Well, I don't need to tell you I was jumping for joy and eager to get confirmation. So I telegrammed the Mayfair house and they confirmed it all, saying the invitation had come in the mail but they hadn't known what to do with it. I rushed to my hotel and packed even before I'd made the travel arrangements, and here I am." Davina just barely stopped to catch her breath. "You wouldn't believe how hectic these past few years have been. Everyone I met was so busy doing something or other and it rubbed off on me. I've been desperately looking for something to do. Tried my hand at writing. You know, murder mysteries are becoming quite the rage. Then there were the artistic endeavors. Oh, but you'd know all about engaging in a worthwhile pursuit.

Look at you. You're a Lady Detective and you're getting married."

It took a moment for Evie to realize Davina had stopped talking. She turned to Nell Joy and smiled, but before she could say anything, Tom spoke up.

"And how did you happen to meet Nell Joy?"

"Oh... Oh, my goodness. And, of course, this is the man," Davina exclaimed.

Evie made the introductions and then glanced at Nell Joy.

Stepping forward, Nell Joy explained, "I'm afraid I will be throwing myself at your mercy. There was a mix up and my booking at the pub fell through."

Davina clapped her hands. "Of course, I forgot to mention. I found this young lady by the side of the road. She was sitting on her suitcase and looking rather glum. Imagine my surprise when she told me she'd met you both in London."

Evie gave Nell Joy a reassuring smile. "Say no more. Of course, you can stay with us." Two more people to accommodate, Evie thought and looked at Edgar who stood by the front door. Her butler, she knew, would take it all in his stride, while everyone else would be thrown into a hive of frenzied activity.

"Well," Sara said, "this has been rather exciting. Shall we go inside?"

As they walked in, Evie noticed Tom following at a distance. No doubt, she thought, fixating on Nell Joy's impromptu arrival, and imagining all sorts of scenarios. She'd soon hear about his suspicions and there were bound to be many.

Inside, Evie said, "I'm sure you're both desperate to

freshen up but we'll need a moment to organize the rooms. Meanwhile, would you like to come through to the drawing room? We were about to have some tea."

Davina exclaimed, "I am dying for a proper cup. Yes, please." She looked around the hall and added, "I could come back here in fifty years' time and the place would still look the same. Of course, we would be much altered, but... yes, everything would be instantly familiar. It's comforting, you know. Warms you with a feeling of belonging." She nodded. "Yes, it's good to be back."

Evie gestured toward the drawing room and was about to lead them in when she thought she heard the sound of a motor car approaching.

Turning, she looked toward the front entrance where Edgar stood overseeing the footmen who were bringing Davina's luggage inside.

"Edgar? Is that someone else coming?"

"Yes, my lady."

She searched her mind. They had been expecting a couple of early arrivals. It took her a moment to remember. "Augustus Warwick and Clyde Russell."

"Who are they?" Tom asked.

"Old friends. Augustus Warwick served and came back a changed man. Before the war, he'd excelled at leisure activities and nothing else. Now, he's taken charge of his family's estate. Does everything himself. Clyde Russell, I'm sure, is still the same old Clyde who enjoys lounging about, visiting one friend or another and doing lots of fishing and boating."

Tom snorted. "Admirers of yours?"

"Nonsense. They're like brothers to me. Surely you remember them from our early days in London. When I first returned to England, we had luncheon, and they visited a couple of times to make sure I'd settled in properly."

"Countess, you seem to forget something. When we first arrived, I was your chauffeur."

Evie sighed. Yes, sometimes, she did forget. "You were only pretending to be a chauffeur." Grinning, she added, "I wonder what other lies you've told me."

They moved toward the front entrance and looked out toward the drive. The motor approached at a sedate speed.

"A roadster."

"Yes, and I see two people." Heavens. "Oh, they've arrived together."

Tom hummed under his breath. "I take it this means Augustus and Clyde are both single men."

"Yes, although poor Augustus had planned on marrying a neighbor, Miriam Lennox. The war interrupted his plans and when he returned it was too late because she'd married someone else."

"And Clyde Russell?"

Evie smiled. "Dear Clyde. He's a bit of a layabout and the thought of finding a suitable wife has always struck him as being too much hard work."

They watched the motor come to a stop. Clyde Russell climbed out and waved. Tall and lanky, with honey blond hair swept back, he had an easy smile that always reached his bright blue eyes. He approached them in a lazy stride, removed his boating hat and bowed. "Lady Woodridge. Evie, my dear. So happy to be here. You'll have to excuse my attire."

Evie smiled at his striped burgundy and beige coat.

"Yes, what's that all about? Have you come straight from a regatta?"

"Almost." He signaled to Augustus who was dragging his feet and looking rather dejected. "I should apologize for my friend here. He's in a mood because he challenged me to a race, with me rowing and him driving along a stretch of road not far from here. You know the one I mean. Anyhow, I thought I should dress the part for the challenge to give me an edge."

"Yes, but what happened?"

"He forgot the road winds and the river is straight. Now he owes me."

Augustus reached them, saying, "I don't mind paying up. I just mind losing to you. Again." He smiled at Evie. "It's been too long."

Evie made the introductions.

"Aha! So this is the man who's taking you away from us," Clyde declared.

He and Augustus eyeballed Tom.

"We're both here to make sure you do right by this magnificent creature."

"Never mind all that, do come in," Evie invited.

As they took a step toward the entrance, the roar of a motor car had them all turning toward the drive.

"Ah, that'll be Gill Moore. He owes me money too. He heard we were coming today and decided to drop everything and come early."

All three men had been friends of her husband, Nicholas. Throughout the years, they had made a point of always keeping in touch.

She heard Tom push out a breath filled with resignation. She suspected there would be a lot of that over the next few days as more guests arrived and the house filled up.

"Come on in. The others are in the drawing room."

Evie showed them through and followed several steps behind with Tom saying, "Am I going to have to watch my back? I didn't care for the way they were eyeballing me."

As Clyde and Augustus headed for the drawing room, Evie and Tom returned to the front door.

"Tom, they are quite harmless. By the end of the week, you will all be the best of friends. I'm sure of it."

He rolled his eyes. "And what do you make of Miss Nell Joy's unexpected arrival?"

"As she said, there was a mistake with her booking at the pub. We had to give her shelter."

"You're too kind, Countess. Mark my word, she is up to no good."

"Tom, she's a guest."

"Yes, yes, I know. I'll be on my best behavior."

"Thank you."

Lowering his voice, he asked, "Are you going to ask Davina about George Beecham?"

Stopping at the front steps, she thought she would prefer to avoid the subject. It had already derailed her thoughts and disrupted her day. What good would come of raising the matter with Davina? How would she explain her concerns? "I'd rather leave it alone."

Turning, she waved at the approaching motor car.

The engine roared and then died down and Gill Moore climbed out. She hadn't seen him in a long while but he didn't seem to have changed that much.

"Lady Woodridge. Evie, my dear."

"Gill. Look at you. Still looking as though you've just heard a magnificent joke."

His eyes sparkled and he gave her a brisk smile. "It's my secret to getting through life. Hope you don't mind me dropping in early."

"Not at all. But you'll have to give Edgar some time to sort everything out." She introduced him to Tom.

Sizing him up, Gill extended his hand. "Look forward to getting to know you better."

As they turned to go inside, Evie thought she saw Tom grimace and rub his hand.

To her utter amazement, they were once more stopped by the sound of another motor car approaching.

"Good heavens. Who could it be this time?"

They both stepped out and saw a familiar motor car driving up.

Evie laughed. "It can't be. They're not expected until a day before the wedding."

Edgar cleared his throat. "We already have their rooms ready, my lady."

Tom's face brightened as he declared, "Perfect. At last, I'll have someone on my side."

Lord and Lady Evans alighted from their motor car, both looking excited.

"Caro," Evie exclaimed. "I can't think of a time when I've been happier to see you."

"Well, that's a proper welcome. I hope you don't mind. Henry just closed a case and, fearing he might be called away again, I insisted we come straightaway. I didn't even think to telephone."

Tom gave Henry Evans a hearty handshake. "You can't imagine how happy I am to see you."

"I'm sure there's a tale to tell. What's happened?"

"Nothing yet. But I suspect there are three fellows here plotting my demise."

"What nonsense," Evie said. "Tom is feeling outnumbered by a few of my old friends."

"Beaus?" Henry Evans asked.

"Not you too." She gestured toward the front door. "Come in and meet them."

For the briefest moment, Evie felt a sense of relief and comfort to have Caro and Henry Evans around.

If only she could make the feeling last.

The dining room, Halton House

The early arrivals and other guests all settled in and spent the rest of the afternoon recovering from their journey before joining everyone for drinks and then dinner.

Evie watched the dowagers and Toodles enjoying their conversations with Augustus, Clyde, and Gill, with Henrietta entertaining them with an exaggerated account of Evie's apparent cold feet.

Davina must have overheard the conversation because she leaned in and asked, "Did you really have cold feet?"

Laughing, Evie said, "I had a bout of disorganization. For a moment, I didn't know if I was coming or going."

"I love your little chapel. Are the roses still growing there?"

"Yes, our gardener does a fabulous job with them."

"I might visit the chapel tomorrow. I always found it to

be a great place for quiet contemplation. In your place, I would have held the ceremony there."

"Tom and I wanted to, but the villagers wouldn't hear of it. They want a wedding, which is rather odd because there have been quite a number of them recently."

"Will his relatives be attending?"

Evie hid her smile. "We invited them but, unfortunately, there was a slight delay in sending out the invitations, and we didn't give them enough time to make travel arrangements. I insisted they come when they could. That's when Tom misquoted Jane Austen."

"What did he say?"

"Invite my relatives? Are the halls of Halton House to be thus polluted?"

Evie glanced at Tom and was surprised to see him fully engaged in conversation with Nell Joy. He was even smiling. She hoped that meant he had found some sort of common ground with the reporter and wouldn't be pursuing any more suspicions about the enterprising young woman.

Although she had to admit Nell Joy's impromptu arrival piqued her curiosity. It seemed far too convenient for the booking at the pub to have fallen through. She had meant to get close to them and had achieved it by taking one step at a time, even if one of those steps had been left up to chance.

How had she known someone would drive along and rescue her?

Had she hoped to encounter them driving along?

She had no way of knowing if Nell Joy's ultimate aim had been to end up staying at the house. It definitely served her purpose far better. Now, she had a front row seat to the proceedings.

As Davina spoke about her time in Egypt, Evie found herself suddenly assailed with thoughts of George Beecham and his letters, possibly as a prompt to bring up the subject with Davina, something she had already decided would serve no purpose.

With Davina now engaged in conversation with Tom, Evie turned to Henry Evans, who said, "I feel I ought to apologize for our early arrival. As soon as I closed the case, Caro practically dragged me out of the house. She'd already organized the trunks and I was the last task on her list of things to do."

"Was it a difficult case?" she asked.

"At first, it appeared to be murder. The victim had changed his will and the previous beneficiary couldn't account for his whereabouts at the time of the victim's death."

"How did he die?"

"All signs pointed to him receiving a blow to the back of his head. But he was prone to falling and had a habit of hoarding things in his stables. The poor fellow just happened to fall at the wrong time, in the wrong place. One of the shelves, laden with too much junk, broke off and collapsed on top of him."

As Henry Evans told her about the case, Evie glanced at her guests sitting around the table and wondered what they would make of their bizarre conversation.

To her, it seemed almost natural to discuss murder cases and motives.

When they left the gentlemen to enjoy their cigars and brandy, Evie felt a growing need to leave the gathering and have a moment of quiet to collect her thoughts.

She accepted a drink from Edgar and sat listening to Caro's description of a luncheon she had hosted for a charity event. Despite following the thread of the conversation, every time she lifted the glass to her lips, a thought intruded, and she lowered her hand.

What if George Beecham turned up at the house?

The letters he'd sent her would make the meeting awkward. Would she pretend she hadn't received them?

A bark startled her. Holmes had woken up and found himself among the small gathering. After stretching and yawning, he strutted about the room, investigating the presence of the rowdy lot.

"He seems to like you, Davina," Henrietta said. "For some reason, he's never taken to me."

"There's a trick, Henrietta." Davina leaned in and whispered something which seemed to intrigue Henrietta.

Evie took advantage of the distraction and slipped out of the room, telling herself she only needed a moment to collect her thoughts and set herself back on track.

She found herself outside the house, walking along the path that led to the chapel. When she reached the edge of the house, she stopped. It was too dark to see the chapel clearly, but she didn't need to. Davina was right. It was the perfect place for contemplation and that was probably the reason why, after two days of not thinking about George Beecham, he had suddenly invaded her thoughts.

She would have to find an appropriate moment to question Davina about him.

Evie drew in a breath. Telling herself to put all that nonsense of the letters behind her, she returned to the drawing room where she found the gentlemen had joined a game of vying for Holmes' attention. If anyone had noticed her missing, they refrained from mentioning it.

When Evie retired for the evening, she found Millicent waiting for her and eager to convey the excitement everyone felt below stairs.

"Everyone is particularly intrigued by Miss Joy. You never mentioned hosting a newspaper reporter, milady. She doesn't have airs about her so that helps. Clare unpacked her suitcase and said she had one good dress. I don't know how she will make that last. We'll do our best, of course. Caro... I mean, Lady Evans, still doesn't have a lady's maid. I had to pull rank on everyone below stairs and tend to her myself. They were all scrambling to do it. Anyhow, I thought it was only right seeing as I had been her protégé and now I see where I get my chatty nature from. Although Lady Evans has far more interesting stories to tell."

Accustomed to listening to Millicent's lengthy stories, Evie smiled and nodded but her thoughts were already straying elsewhere.

Going against the decision she'd already made to ask Davina about her cousin, Evie decided she would simply wait and see what happened. "And if he comes, I'll deal with him myself."

"I'm sorry, milady. What was that?"

Startled, Evie looked up. "Oh, never mind me. Perhaps you could go through my wardrobe and find Miss Joy a spare dress for her to wear."

CHAPTER 5

Resolutions

The next morning

$\mathcal{I}$t was a bright new day and Evie resolved to make it so. She told herself that every time she tossed and turned.

"Milady, if you're not awake now, you soon will be when I stub my toe and yelp. I should have come in, drawn the curtains, and then brought the tray in. As it is, here I am unable to see beyond my nose and if I'm not careful the tray will land on your head. Now I'll have to back away, set the tray down, come back in, draw the curtains, fetch the tray…"

Evie had been asleep.

After a night of fretful tossing and turning, she had finally fallen into a deep slumber. Unfortunately, it had been riddled with nightmares of her wedding going all wrong with one person after the other jumping to their feet to state their objections. Even Henrietta had sprung to her feet. Although Evie couldn't remember if she had objected to the objections or objected to having her own objection drowned out by everyone else's.

Evie groaned and remembered something about Henrietta declaring she had the advantage of seniority, and it should be respected.

Flinging the bedcovers off, she sprung out of bed. "Stay where you are, Millicent. I'll draw the curtains."

Yawning, Evie drew the curtains and looked out at the clear blue sky. "It's a lovely day out there. I hope everyone will be keen to take long walks. To be perfectly honest, yesterday was almost too much for me. As much as I love the house being full of people, I was simply too distracted to enjoy their company."

Noticing Millicent standing by the bed still holding the tray, Evie mouthed an apology and returned to bed.

"Has Mr. Winchester gone down? I would hate to think the guests are having breakfast alone."

"Yes, he's keeping the gentlemen company. When I went down to the kitchen, I heard Mrs. Horace say she had all the trays to prepare because all the ladies were having breakfast in bed." She settled the tray down and went to look out the window. "I see one of the gentlemen has set out for a walk."

"I wonder who that might be. Not Clyde Russell, I'm sure. In fact, I'd be surprised if he's even down having breakfast. He's never been much of an early riser," Evie said as she buttered her toast.

"He has dark hair, milady."

"That could be Augustus or Gill."

Millicent swung away from the window. "I'll get your walking shoes out. You might want to join your guests."

Evie lifted the cup of coffee to her lips only to nearly drop it when she heard a shout. "What on earth was that? Did you hear that, Millicent?"

"I did, milady, and I think it came from outside." Rushing across the room, Millicent looked out the window. "Oh, there's a woman. She's running and her hands are flapping."

Hearing another shout, Evie set her tray aside, jumped out of bed and joined Millicent by the window. "Good heavens. That's Davina." She looked across the park and saw Augustus running toward her. "What on earth could have happened to her?"

She watched as Augustus reached Davina. He appeared to be asking her questions. Evie imagined him wanting to know what was wrong.

"Her mouth is gaping open, milady. I don't think she can speak."

"No. She looks utterly horrified. Good heavens." Evie swung away and reached for her robe.

"I'll get your slippers, milady," Millicent offered even as Evie was making her way to the door.

They both rushed out of the bedroom and flew down the stairs just as Tom ran out the front door.

"Thank goodness," was all she could say. Hugging the robe against her, Evie stepped out of the house and saw Tom reach Augustus and Davina.

Evie came to a stop at the front steps. She could see Tom trying to get Davina to talk but she was still gaping.

Evie took a couple of steps and was followed by Millicent. A part of her wanted to rush toward them to see if she could help, but she thought that would only add to the obvious confusion.

The sound of someone running out of the house had them both turning. Henry Evans appeared at the door and hurried toward Davina.

The three men took turns to encourage Davina, all to no avail, it seemed. They persevered, but it didn't take long to realize Tom and Henry were having no success.

"Milady, I think you should go to her."

"Yes, you might be right." As Evie took a step forward, she saw Davina thrust her arm out, her finger pointing in the direction of the chapel.

"It looks like something happened at the chapel, milady."

Someone else came out of the house. Evie looked over her shoulder and saw Clyde Russell and Gill Moore.

While Clyde stopped at the front steps, a napkin in his hand, Gill Moore walked at a brisk pace.

When he reached them, he asked, "Any idea what's happened?"

"None whatsoever." Evie watched him walk off toward the group. Tom and Henry appeared to be headed toward the chapel. While Davina had been left in Augustus' care.

"Should we follow, milady?"

Turning, she saw Clyde Russell had remained by the front door, his napkin still in his hand. While he kept his attention fixed on the unfolding situation, he did not move. She was about to look away when someone else emerged from the house.

Nell Joy.

"Good heavens." Whatever had happened, she didn't want the newspaper reporter to witness any of it.

"I guess that means not all the ladies had their breakfast in bed." Millicent sighed. "I'll stop her from following, milady."

Millicent sounded anything but enthusiastic. Thanking her, Evie hurried to catch up to Tom and Henry. They'd now reached the edge of the house where she'd stood the previous evening.

When she saw them continue past the house, she knew they were headed for the chapel.

Davina had mentioned going there.

What could she have seen there?

Despite wanting to catch up to Tom and Henry, Evie's steps slowed. Fear gripped her and tightened her chest. This did not look good.

She headed toward Augustus and Davina. Gill had reached them and, judging by the way his head moved from Davina to Augustus, Evie assumed he was trying to establish what had happened.

Whatever she had seen at the chapel had left her in a state of shock, only just barely able to function, but not well enough to communicate with the others.

Augustus was offering soothing words of support. Evie stood by, at first unable to say anything. Finally, she managed to utter her friend's name, "Davina." But there was no response. Her friend's eyes were wide open and unblinking and her mouth remained open but no words came out.

Augustus shook his head. "She hasn't said a word."

Evie saw Tom and Henry reach the chapel and go inside.

Feeling utterly helpless, she took Davina's hand. "Perhaps we should take her inside."

Gill offered his support. "Don't worry, we'll take her in."

Nodding, Evie turned and, squaring her shoulders, headed along the path, but her steps felt heavy and full of reluctance.

Everything had been going so well. Now, something had happened to disturb the joyful flow. Or rather, something else, Evie reminded herself, knowing those letters had already unsettled her, turning the last few days into a trial.

She came up to the entrance to the chapel just as Henry emerged.

"Not good, I'm afraid."

"What is it? What's happened?"

"Dead body."

"Who?"

He shook his head. "Don't know." He signaled toward the house. "I have to make a telephone call."

Evie remained by the entrance to the chapel, her shoulders knotted up with tension.

She was about to step inside when Tom came out.

"Henry just told me there's a body inside." Evie wanted Tom to deny it. Of course, he wouldn't. "Did you recognize him?"

"No."

She knew what would come next. The police would be

informed. The house would be swarming with police. Questions would be asked.

Evie frowned.

Heavens. Henry's first thought had been to make a telephone call. Obviously, to the police. When the police were involved, that meant someone had died under suspicious circumstances.

Yes, she knew what would come next.

She brushed her hands along her face and tried to clear the scrambled thoughts in her mind.

"I suppose I should see for myself..."

"You don't have to."

She took a moment to consider. "I must. It won't be my first dead body."

"If you're sure."

She wasn't. "Lead the way." She didn't know what to expect but she assumed the person would be somewhere inside the chapel, near the front pews or the altar. When Tom walked past it, she frowned but didn't say anything.

He led her through a side door. "Through here."

"The crypt?" There was an iron gate leading to the underground chamber. Tom walked ahead of her. Taking one step at a time, Evie focused on the back of his head.

Davina had been left unable to communicate. She'd probably never seen a dead person before.

What else could have elicited such a dramatic response?

What? Who?

Tom reached the bottom step and Evie followed. Closing her eyes briefly, she nodded. "It's George Beecham."

Tom must have turned to look at her and seen her eyes closed. Yet he didn't say anything.

Resigned to what she was about to see, she opened her eyes and stared at the body in front of her.

For the briefest moment she thought she was looking at a red rose, its petals scattered over George Beecham's chest. Then she realized she was looking at a blood stain.

"Are you sure?"

She confirmed it with a small nod.

Looking up, she saw the morning light filtering through from a narrow window high above. A small altar stood behind the body and one of the candles had been lit.

Stepping forward, Tom blocked the body from view.

Evie took that as a sign to return to the chapel. She shivered all the way. Then, they walked back to the house in silence.

Finally, she said, "I can now understand Davina's reaction. She should be seen by a doctor."

"I believe Henry was organizing that." Looking along the road leading to the house, he added, "As well as contacting the police. The local constabulary should be along soon."

Evie gasped.

There had been a murder at the Woodridge family chapel and the person just happened to be someone who'd been in Evie's thoughts for several days.

Augustus and Gill stepped out of the house and stood on the front steps looking out toward the park. Seeing them, they stepped aside to let them through.

"We were thinking of taking a walk," Augustus said.

"Henry Evans said there's a body in the chapel. Do you know who it is?" Gill asked.

When Evie told them, they both exchanged a look of surprise.

"How did he die?" Augustus asked.

Before Evie could tell them, Tom said, "We're not sure."

A motor car approached.

"It's the police," Tom said. "I should show them the way. They'll want to secure the scene."

Nodding, Evie went inside and met Henry as he came out of the drawing room.

"I gave her some brandy. The doctor should be along shortly."

"Has she said anything?"

"No."

"I'm not surprised. The man is... was her cousin. George Beecham."

"You knew him?"

Nodding, Evie gave him a brief murmured explanation. She knew Henry wanted to ask questions. It was in his nature to do so, but he held back.

"We should wait for the police."

Evie looked toward the drawing room door. "I should go change. This is going to be a long day. First, I'll go in and sit with her. She shouldn't be alone."

Henry shook his head. "I asked if she wanted me to get someone to sit with her and she managed to say she wanted to be alone for a moment."

Evie looked at the drawing room door again but didn't insist. Making her way upstairs, she tried to make sense of the morning by running the sequence of events in her mind.

She opened the door to her room and was greeted by Millicent.

"Milady. I've locked Nell Joy in the library, and I've drawn the bath for you."

Thanking her, Evie slipped the robe off.

"I'm sure you'll tell me what's happened in your own good time. There's no hurry."

"Davina found a body in the chapel." Evie turned and frowned. "Did you say you locked Nell Joy in the library?"

Millicent nibbled the edge of her lip. "Is that what came out of my mouth? Yes, I suppose it did. Well, she needed an incentive to stay in the library and that's the only one I could think of. She won't know I've locked the door unless she tries to leave the library." Millicent brightened. "She can always pull the bell cord for assistance. Anyway, the bath water is getting cold, and you were about to tell me about the dead man in the chapel."

"In the crypt, to be precise."

"How did he get there?"

"That's a very good question, Millicent. Could I bother you for a cup of tea, please, and I'm sure the others will want to hear the news. You should be the one to tell them."

Relieved of her duties, Millicent dashed off, leaving Evie to wonder what George Beecham had been doing in the Woodridge family crypt.

CHAPTER 6

A death at Halton House

*D*ressed and ready to face what she knew would be a difficult day, Evie made her way to Henrietta's room. While she was sure the dowager and the others had heard the news by now, she couldn't assume and had to make sure they'd been informed. Otherwise, they'd never forgive her.

She knocked on the door, walked in, and was not surprised to find Sara and Toodles there, although Henrietta felt compelled to explain their presence.

"The news is all over the house. The maid told us about the dead body in the chapel, and we decided there would be strength in numbers."

"I think you meant to say safety in numbers," Sara suggested.

"Oh, no, dear. There is strength in numbers. The three

of us together stand a better chance of..." Henrietta waved her hand, "whatever may come."

Sara shrugged. "I rather like the idea of safety in numbers."

"My dear, we have nothing to worry about. I have read enough mystery stories to know the elderly are the hardest to kill for some reason. Also, we are bound to remain untouched because someone must serve as witnesses. We do tell the best anecdotes."

Toodles sighed. "Henrietta doesn't want to say it, so I will. Either there was an intruder, who came here with the purpose of killing that man, or there is a murderer among us."

Shuddering, Henrietta spoke in a pensive tone, "I find it quite strange. When Connie brought in my breakfast tray, she delivered the day's forecast, something she always does before drawing the curtains. Then, she always steps back and signals toward the sky as if to confirm it. If the day is expected to be sunny and the sky is overcast, she then delivers a possible explanation, which always includes some sort of anecdote passed on from one family member or other. I enjoy the ones from her one eyed, lame, pipe smoking relative. They always include a scene from Shakespeare."

"Henrietta!" Sara snapped.

"Yes?"

"Do please get to the point."

"Oh, Connie was about to walk out when she stopped and informed me, ever so blithely, about a body having been found in the chapel. It was all the information she had, so I asked her to gather the troops."

"Henrietta means us," Sara explained. "She sent Connie to summon us to her chamber. I nearly choked on my tea."

Toodles straightened the teacup on the saucer as if about to say something, but she remained silent.

Henrietta, however, did not feel the need for restraint. "Someone..." her gaze slid to Toodles, "asked if the dead person was me. Connie refrained from answering because she felt it wasn't her place to say."

Toodles shrugged. "I merely wanted to find out if one of you had died. What is wrong with that?"

Henrietta sniffed. "You only asked about me and, I might add, you took your time getting here."

Shifting, Toodles turned her attention to Evie. "Birdie, do you know something about the man's identity? I've been told all the guests are accounted for."

Evie walked to the window and looked out. "Yes, I went to the chapel and identified him." Looking over her shoulder at Henrietta, she said, "It was George Beecham."

Henrietta's silent reaction was punctured by Sara's swift intake of breath.

"Well, you both seem to recognize the name. Was he, by any chance related to Davina?" Toodles asked.

When Evie nodded, Toodles rose to her feet and left the bedroom.

Shaking her head, Henrietta said, "I believe Toodles took exception to something I said."

"Sometimes, Henrietta, you can be awfully unkind," Sara chastised.

"Yes, well... Never mind all that. A man has died." Henrietta looked at Evie. "According to the rumors going around the house, he was killed."

"Yes, that appears to be the case." And, Evie thought,

such information could only have been obtained by eaves-dropping on conversations, working in tandem, snatching snippets of information and stitching it all together.

"Do you have any idea what George Beecham was doing here? I am quite familiar with the guest list, so I know his name was not on it."

Evie could only assume he had come to follow through on some sort of declaration. If she had to find a meaning in the letters he had sent her, she'd say they indicated some sort of intention; a desire or a need he hadn't been able to express before. But what had prompted it? Had he heard about her upcoming nuptials? Evie forced herself to consider the possibility he had then decided to seize a lost opportunity and turn it in his favor. Although, she had difficulty imagining someone entertaining the sort of affection for her they couldn't bring themselves to express.

She couldn't mention the letters because they would lead to hasty speculation, and this was something Evie wished to avoid until they knew more.

With any luck, Davina would be able to shed some light on George Beecham's presence here.

She tried to remember where she stood on the subject. She had changed her mind so many times, she couldn't recall.

"No, I don't know why he came here, Henrietta." She'd been about to say she hadn't seen him in years when she remembered the photograph in the newspaper. The one she knew Henrietta must have seen.

"I assume you were able to identify him because you saw the body."

Evie gave a pensive nod.

Sara shook her head. "Keep up, Henrietta. She told us she went to identify the body."

"Millicent should be here to take notes," Henrietta muttered. "My mornings are always hectic with thoughts of the previous day colliding with the new day's thoughts and now this. And you tell me to keep up?"

Evie remained standing by the window looking out across the park with its verdant lawns and wildlife going about its business. Soon, the police would arrive and there would be questions to answer.

The door to the bedroom opened and Toodles walked in. "This is why I took so long in answering Henrietta's summons." She waved a magazine. "When Connie came in with the breakfast tray, I'd been reading this. It's one of the magazines Birdie brought back for me."

Evie read the front cover page. "*Collier's*. Isn't that a gentlemen's magazine?"

"I like to be informed," Toodles declared. "Anyhow, the article which caught my interest is part of a series titled *Letters from India*. They were written by George Beecham. The name sounded familiar, and I wondered if he was related to Davina."

If it was the same George Beecham, it meant they could place him in India. All these years, she'd had no idea where he had disappeared to.

"In this letter, he talks about ending his travels and returning to England after a long absence. He must have been a man of leisure because he spent a great deal of time talking about the sights and how he enjoyed painting watercolors of the sceneries."

"How do we know it's the same George Beecham?"

Sara asked. "It's possible there are other people with the same name."

Henrietta glanced at Evie. "A number of years ago, he decided to go traveling."

Evie waited for Henrietta to say more, but she didn't. For reasons known only to her, she failed to mention the fact George Beecham had set off on his travels after Evie had married Nicholas.

"You're right," Sara said. "I remember he used to visit often and then he didn't. Life can become a whirlwind of activities and events and one loses track. Sometimes, we are so busy we barely notice someone's absence. And then, of course, there was the war. Those years dulled my memory."

"Who found him?" Toodles asked.

Evie told them what she knew.

"Davina? What was she doing in the chapel so early in the morning?" Sara asked. "It strikes me as odd. Is it just me?"

"She might have wanted a moment of quiet reflection," Evie suggested. "She mentioned it last night."

Toodles skimmed through the magazine and then set it down. "How did he die?"

Evie pictured the red stain and how it had bloomed on his shirt. "He was shot."

After a long silence, Henrietta said, "How bizarre. When Connie told me about the body, it did not occur to wonder how he had died and, unlike Toodles, I didn't give any thought to the identity of the deceased."

Toodles exchanged a glance with Sara. "I wonder what that says about you."

"I believe I was merely dwelling on the fact a man had

died here. I'm a creature of habit and, in the morning, I find my thoughts tend to contemplate at leisure."

"A moment ago," Sara said, "you complained about your thoughts from the previous day clashing with the new day's thoughts. That sounds rather turbulent, not contemplative."

"Are you really going to analyze every single word I say?"

"No, I suppose I shouldn't. Especially not when there is a killer among us," Sara murmured.

Evie stilled. The thought hadn't crossed her mind. She searched for other possibilities and could only think of one. Someone might have wandered into the estate. She glanced at Toodles and remembered her mentioning it. Of course, it didn't make sense. Unless, the killer had known George Beecham would be here.

"Evangeline, how are you feeling?" Henrietta asked. "This has happened so close to your wedding day. Do you think the police will find the culprit soon? I would hate to think of your wedding being postponed."

"Right now, that is the least of my concerns, Henrietta. There are the guests to consider, those already here and those about to arrive."

Henrietta gave a firm nod. "I suppose we must be philosophical and carry on, not as if nothing had happened, but rather, as usual."

"Isn't that the same thing?" Sara asked.

"I never claimed to be a philosopher. In any case, we still need to make a firm decision about the flowers. I refuse to be outnumbered, so we must adopt a different approach. I believe seniority will work for me. After all, my days are somewhat limited. Yes, I should be indulged."

Sara looked at Toodles and they both snorted.

Henrietta rolled her eyes. "Very well, then we will carry on as usual and bicker. That should take our minds off this unsavory business."

"And how long do you think we can keep that up before we start poking around and suspecting the guests of murder?" Toodles asked.

"My dear, George Beecham was not expected here. We were in the chapel yesterday. The guests arrived in the afternoon. George Beecham must have come during the night when the early arrivals were asleep. None of the guests could have known he was here. The killer must be an outsider. Any reasonable person would see that and agree with me."

"Thank you, Henrietta. Your reasoning has snapped me out of my stupor." Evie hadn't been able to think past the fact George Beecham had come to Halton House.

Davina's arrival had been a surprise.

She'd been expecting Gill Moore, but not yesterday. Although, his early arrival didn't surprise her, especially since Clyde had explained he'd decided to join them after hearing they were coming down.

As for Augustus and Clyde...

She looked up in thought. Yes, she had been expecting them and the fact they'd traveled together didn't surprise her since they were often seen together at social events, belonged to the same clubs, and often visited each other.

Then there was Nell Joy.

Evie stepped back from the window. She'd forgotten about the reporter. Evie remembered she had been the last person to rush out of the house and then she saw her standing with Clyde near the front door. Evie knew she would have to have a word with her and make sure she didn't intrude on Davina's moment of grieving.

Heavens, she hadn't thought about that.

Poor Davina.

George Beecham had been her closest relative. In her mind, her husband's death must still be fresh. Now she would have to contend with another loss.

Evie drew in a slow breath. She felt for her friend. It would take some time for her to come to terms with losing her cousin.

Evie didn't know how close Davina had been with her cousin or even if they had kept in touch all these years. What would she be able to tell them about George? And when? How long would it take for her to recover from the shock?

One could never tell how a person would react to the death of a relative. It all depended on the person's character. She'd seen people go about as if nothing had happened, either because they excelled at hiding their emotions or because they simply took things in their stride. After all, death was part of the deal - an inevitable cycle.

But this was different, she thought.

George Beecham had not died a natural death.

Someone had pulled the trigger, either by accident or deliberately.

Frowning, Evie wondered why she'd jumped to the conclusion George had been shot. She'd seen the blood stain, but the fatal wound could have been caused by something else. A knife, perhaps.

There was a light knock at the door and the lady's

maid, Connie, entered. Seeing them all still there, she said, "I can come back later to help you dress, milady."

Sara and Toodles stood up and Evie said, "I should go down and see how Davina is faring. When I came up, the doctor had just been summoned. She was quite shaken by her experience."

Sara murmured, "I might need to change. This outfit looks far too cheerful for today. Yes, something muted would be more suitable." She looked at Toodles.

"What?" Toodles asked.

Sara gave her orange and blue dress a pointed look.

"Oh, good heavens. You expect me to change? You know I only wear bright colors."

Hearing this, Henrietta snorted, "This might be a good time to consider a more suitable wardrobe."

"Suitable? For my age? Is that what you mean?"

Henrietta grinned. "Feel free to interpret my remarks however you wish. Only, do please cast a positive light on them as they are full of my best intentions."

Evie left them to their decision making and made her way down. When she heard hurried steps approaching, she looked up and saw Caro rushing down the stairs.

Sounding out of breath, Caro said, "I can't believe it. I forced Henry to tell me every single detail, and I still can't believe it. He says you know the dead man."

"I'm afraid so."

"When does Lotte Mannering arrive? We'll need all the help we can get to get to the bottom of this."

"She isn't due to arrive until the day before the wedding."

"You should send word to her. I'm sure she'll drop whatever she is doing and rush here."

"Dear Caro, the police will arrive soon and I'm sure they will sort everything out in no time."

"I've forbidden Henry from becoming involved," Caro declared. "Not that I think he'll listen to me, but it's worth a try. We're here to support you and celebrate your upcoming nuptials. Oh, my goodness. Please tell me it's all still going ahead."

"There's nothing I would like more than to reassure you but, for now, I think we'll need to focus on this business being dealt with."

"How well did you know the man?"

Drawing in a deep breath, Evie shrugged and told Caro the story of how George Beecham had come into her life. "I actually met his cousin, Davina, first."

"And the moment he saw you, he fell in love with you," Caro mused.

"That is precisely the sort of opinion I wish to avoid, Caro. I can't believe he had been infatuated and carried a torch for me all these years."

Lowering her voice, Caro said, "That newspaper reporter will have to be kept under close guard. At the risk of sounding like a seasoned dowager, think of the scandal. If she catches wind of the connection between you and that man, she will want to use it to her advantage. Not that I blame her. It's difficult enough to survive in a man's world. She is right in the thick of it, competing against male reporters." Caro placed her hand on Evie's shoulder. "I've said my piece, now I'll be quiet."

They found Tom and Henry Evans in the hall, outside the drawing room.

"The doctor is still with Davina," Henry said.

"What about the police?" Evie asked. Forgetting what

Caro had said, she continued, "I mean, of course, you are the police, but I assume you won't be investigating. Or will you?"

Caro looked at her husband, her eyes narrowing slightly.

Henry Evans averted his gaze. "No, I will not be investigating. However, I've been asked to assist. A couple of constables have arrived and they're making sure no one goes inside the chapel. There will be a detective arriving soon."

The drawing room door opened. Turning, Evie saw a young man looking pensive, his brow furrowed slightly.

"That's the doctor," Tom said.

Noticing them, he approached and introduced himself as Doctor Farley.

"Mrs. Beecham-Parks is asking for you," he told Evie. "She's still rather shaken by her experience. I've offered her a sedative, but she prefers to remain lucid. She shouldn't exert herself but if she wishes to talk about her experience, then she should."

Taking a moment to collect her thoughts, Evie entered the drawing room and found Davina standing by the window, one hand in her pocket and the other resting on the windowsill.

Reluctant to ask how she was feeling, Evie offered, "Would you like me to ring for some tea?"

Davina turned and looked surprised. "Tea?"

Evie wasn't sure if she should apologize or offer a platitude to explain her offer of tea.

Davina's shoulders lowered. Walking away from the window, she sat down on a chair in front of the fireplace.

"Tea would be perfect, of course. A soothing tonic for any occasion."

She sounded like her normal self, albeit a little weary. Evie rang for tea and sat opposite Davina.

Without being asked, Davina said, "I'm fine now. My reaction is difficult to explain."

"You don't have to."

Davina closed her eyes for a moment. "Oh, but I do. I've never experienced such shock and if I don't speak now, I'm afraid I never will." She made a gesture with her hand and then slipped it inside her pocket. "I've never seen a dead person. So many thoughts went through my mind. Recognizing him made it even worse. There he was, dead. Even as I looked at the wound, I asked myself how he'd died. I kept looking at his white shirt stained red. For the briefest moment, I thought he might have spilled something on himself. Then it occurred to me that he hadn't just died, he'd been killed. That's probably when I panicked and fled. Suddenly, I felt afraid for my own life. Is that usual? You've come across dead bodies. Is that how you feel?" Looking straight at Evie, Davina leaned forward.

"I've never thought about it."

Davina's look became intense as she asked, "When was the last time you saw him?"

Strictly speaking, Evie hadn't seen him at *The Ritz*. Once again, she thought she didn't wish to complicate matters. She couldn't explain this reasoning, but she remained reluctant to mention the newspaper photograph. She insisted she had no excuse for her reluctance, other than to avoid giving explanations.

"One summer, long ago. It's hard to say. For a long time, he was always here and then he wasn't."

Davina gave a pensive nod. "He decided to travel. It's strange, he never told me why. I always thought of him as someone content to remain in the one place. You know he loved his books and could spend an entire day in his library without feeling the need to socialize. Even when he was with a large party of people, he had this ability to fade into the background." Davina frowned. "Who would do that to him?"

"The police will look into possible motives and will most likely ask you about his friends and acquaintances." Evie looked down at her hands. "Did you know he was in London?"

Davina sprung to her feet. Pulling the cardigan around her, she hugged herself and walked to the window. "I hadn't spoken with him in months."

Months?

Evie knew Davina had been traveling in Egypt, while George Beecham had, presumably, been in India.

"Where did you last see him?"

"See him? No, I hadn't seen him in years, so I suppose I can't say we talked. He wrote to me and his letters were always conversational, sounding almost as if he'd just walked in and was picking up the thread from a previous conversation. Long before returning to England, I'd traveled to Tangiers and found a letter waiting for me at one of our mutual friend's house. When I traveled back to Cairo, there was another letter. He never knew where I'd be so George would often write and send letters all over the place, knowing that I would eventually land in one of those places."

"The police will most likely ask about those letters. Did you keep them?"

Davina gave her a brisk smile. "My dear, I travel light. Or, rather, I have enough luggage and don't need any excess. Besides, who keeps letters? It's not as if I go around noting down every conversation I have just in case the police decide to question me." She returned to her chair. "So, what happens now?"

"What do you mean?"

"George was killed. It's obvious someone killed him. I'm not familiar with the process. Do the police sweep in and investigate?"

"Yes, they're due to arrive soon. They'll interview everyone staying at the house and collect evidence."

"Interview us?" She curled her fingers around the armrest and leaned forward. "Do you think someone here killed him?"

The fact her friend was talking now didn't necessarily mean she was over the shock. Only a moment before she'd said her cousin had been killed. Now, her voice filled with disbelief.

This was a question that would be asked many times, Evie thought. Someone had killed him. Who? How? Why? When? "Right now, it's impossible to believe someone you know might be capable of murder."

"Murder?" Davina sounded shocked. Almost as if the idea hadn't occurred to her.

Was there a difference between killing and murdering?

She'd never thought about it. The result was the same, but the intention, she knew, was different.

Motive.

Evie wondered if Davina's reaction had something to

do with the shock she'd experienced or if she thought of murder as being a malicious act and impossible to associate with her cousin.

Then again, she might be in denial and not quite willing to accept George Beecham's death, by any means.

She'd found her cousin dead. She'd seen him with her own eyes, but how long would it take for reality to sink in and for her to accept the fact of his demise?

It would take time and then time would take care of smoothing out the edges of the initial shock until it faded or was completely erased from her memory.

"Isn't that jumping to conclusions?" Davina asked. "Why do you think someone murdered him?"

Evie didn't wish to spell out the obvious. The blood soaked shirt screamed murder. As for the reason for killing him...

She knew nothing about his life during all his years of traveling about. He might have become involved with the wrong person. He might have caused someone an injury. If she turned her focus to it, she could entertain endless scenarios.

Yes, but only one would fit this particular scene, she thought. Like a separate piece of a jigsaw puzzle, slotting into place to complete the entire picture.

Davina broke eye contact and looked about the room, her eyes frantic, her words sharp, "Someone thought he was an intruder and shot him. He was followed here. He sought refuge here. Yes, he might have been fleeing for his life only to have it extinguished here. Right here, Evie. In your house."

Davina pinned Evie with a fixed stare that turned into a fierce glare.

This was not the Davina she knew but her behavior was understandable. "We all want answers, and we will get them."

Davina responded with an abrupt shake of her head. "What now?"

Now came the hardest part. Now they waited.

Evie brushed her hands along her thighs and stood up. "A walk might do you good. Or a rest. We'll have luncheon and then find some way to distract ourselves. Life as we know it has been ruptured and we need to try to reestablish some sort of order or sense of normality. I'm sorry but that is all I have to offer. There's not going to be an easy solution."

The door opened, and Edgar walked in. Evie remembered she'd rang the bell cord. Turning, she asked Davina, "Would you like tea here or would you like to join us in the library?"

Davina stood up. "I'll join you there in a moment."

Nodding, Evie left, saying to Edgar, "We'll have tea in the library, please, Edgar." She then remembered Nell Joy. "Assuming we can access the library."

"Ah, yes. The reporter. She has been liberated from her unlawful imprisonment." Edgar closed his eyes for a moment. "If you'd like, I will have a word with Millicent."

"That won't be necessary, Edgar. She only did what she thought was right at the time."

"Very well, my lady." Closing the drawing room door, he added, "Mr. Winchester and Lord Evans have just made their way to the library. I'm not sure where the others are."

"They'll be along soon, I'm sure." Meanwhile, she could have a word with Tom and Henry. "Oh, where is Caro?"

"Lady Evans has stepped out for a walk, my lady."

Evie smiled at Edgar's insistence on adhering to a formal address when referring to Caro. Indeed, all the servants insisted on it as due reverence for one of their own being elevated to the nobility.

Before entering the library, Evie glanced over her shoulder and looked toward the drawing room. There had been something odd about Davina's tone. It had changed from lackluster to a hard tone filled with accusation.

She knew Davina was in shock, but where had her anger come from? And why did she feel it had been aimed directly at her?

CHAPTER 7

Gunshot in the night

The library

$\mathcal{E}$vie found Tom and Henry standing by the window, their attention fixed on the expanse of landscape beyond. They stood with their hands inside their pockets, their shoulders lowered.

Evie imagined them trying to find answers, giving up and turning their attention to the outside world where everything had a reason for being.

As she joined them, Tom asked, "How is she?"

"Traumatized. She's found her voice again and is eager for answers." More than eager, she thought, remembering Davina's change in tone, from distant to a sharpness that focused on accusations. Her thoughts had been muddled, but that was to be expected.

"We've been talking about the gunshot."

"The one we didn't hear?" Evie asked.

Henry nodded. "I'm prepared to hazard a guess and say he was shot shortly before dawn at close range."

Evie closed her eyes for a moment. Had she stirred in her sleep? Had her subconscious mind heard the shot? What had been her first thoughts upon waking? If she had been entertaining any thoughts, they would have dispersed when Millicent entered carrying the breakfast tray. "Close range. Does that suggest he knew the killer?" Evie asked.

"Either he knew the killer, or he was caught by surprise."

But what had he been doing in the chapel?

If George Beecham had come here on some sort of mission to dissuade her from going through with the wedding, why hadn't he come to the house? The question simply wouldn't leave her alone.

"Are you sure he was shot?" Evie asked.

Henry Evans nodded. "I took a closer look. Also, the bullet went right through him and lodged in the wall behind him. Had the killer been standing on the stairs looking down, the bullet would have lodged lower down on the wall." He shook his head. "It is more likely the killer stood right in front of him."

George Beecham knew his killer, and possibly trusted him enough to get close to him without fearing for his life.

Edgar walked in and set a tray on the table.

Thanking him, Evie helped herself to a cup of tea.

"The question remains," Henry said, "Why was he here? Tom tells me he was not an invited guest."

Evie knew it was time to share what she knew. She would need to mention the letters and let Henry make of them what he would.

They might explain George Beecham's reason for coming to Halton House. However, Evie didn't see how they would explain his presence at the chapel.

Then again, the letters themselves spoke of his strange state of mind.

Evie glanced at Tom. "We might have an idea about that. Tom can tell you. I'm going to try to enjoy a cup of tea." Sitting down, Evie listened as Tom gave Henry a succinct summary, mentioning the letters Evie had received as well as the newspaper photograph.

After a long silence, Henry asked, "Do you have a copy of the newspaper?"

Tom nodded. "I'll hunt it down for you." He walked over to a table where the newspapers were stacked and went through them.

"Do we know when the detective will arrive?" Evie asked, if only to interrupt the silence that had settled around them.

"Sometime today. I wasn't given a specific time."

Taking a sip of her tea, she lowered the cup. "Nell Joy. Has anyone seen her?"

Henry signaled toward the window. "We saw her going out for a walk. She was headed for the folly. Tom's been telling me about her."

Evie smiled. "He was already suspicious of her. This gives him a solid reason to suspect her. No doubt, the police will look into her background. Tom already did a thorough investigation, contacting everyone who knows her, including the vicar from the village where she lived before moving to London."

In the background, Tom snorted. "That just goes to show how she has spent her entire life creating a veil of deceit."

The edge of Evie's lip kicked up. "As you can see, he is determined to only see the worst in her."

"What about your other guests? Can you think of a reason why one of them might have wanted to kill George Beecham?"

Evie set her teacup down, stood up, and walked to the window. "George had been living abroad for years. I can't imagine any of them kept in contact with him, but you should make sure. Or, rather, the detective should ask them."

"Here it is," Tom said as he walked toward them, a newspaper in hand. "Evie says he's looking straight at her, and I agree." He held the page up and winced. "I can't make out his expression. It's hard to say if he's pleased to have seen her." He looked up and smiled at Evie. "I'm sure he was overjoyed and... positively too overwhelmed to even approach you."

Henry studied the photograph. "Yes, he is most definitely looking at Evie. Why do you think he didn't approach you? Tom tells me George Beecham was well known to you."

"It's been some years since we last saw each other and..." Evie shrugged. "He was my husband's friend. We were merely acquaintances."

"And this photograph was taken at *The Ritz*," Henry said.

"Yes." Evie studied the image. How could she not have sensed him? There was such an intensity to his gaze, she should have noticed him. "I supposed the police will contact the hotel to find out if he'd been staying there. In fact, it should be easy enough to establish a few solid facts, such as when he'd returned to England." After some thought, she added, "If he'd been staying at *The Ritz*, the police will also be able to find out if he left early."

"I assume he had an estate somewhere," Henry Evans said.

"Yes, in Yorkshire. Now that I think about it, if he'd only just returned after a long absence, it would have made more sense for him to go there."

"Maybe he was intent on renewing his acquaintance with you," Tom suggested, his tone hinting at sarcasm.

"Tom, do I need to remind you poor George is now dead?"

"My apologies."

"Do you still have the letters?" Henry asked.

"Yes, of course. They're rather odd."

"How so?"

"It's the way they're written. Almost as if I've actually replied to them." She looked toward the door and wondered if Davina had decided against joining them.

"Do the others know?" Tom asked.

"Henrietta, Sara and Toodles? Yes. And, for some reason known only to them, they are quite calm about it all. It might have been too much of a surprise and now they're nonplussed. I'm sure they'll eventually stir into action. Although Henrietta is determined to simply get on with her day as if nothing had happened. Which, in itself, is odd. Of course, she'd only just woken up so, by midday, she might change her mind."

Henry checked his watch. "It's a waiting game now. At least, the constables have arrived and secured the scene."

"Here's a strange thought. You asked about the possibility of my guests having motives." She shook her head. "Forget I said anything."

"Countess. Out with it. There's no point in suggesting you have an idea and then dismiss it without first telling us about it."

"Very well. Of course, everyone here will be a suspect."

Tom looked at Henry Evans.

"Everyone except Henry and Caro, of course. Anyhow, I wonder if we should also suspect the guests who have yet to arrive. It's rather a bizarre idea." She went to the table and poured herself another cup of tea. "Yes, do forget I mentioned it. I'm sure there is a simple explanation. I would like to think someone followed him here."

"Yes, that would be convenient," Tom agreed. "Especially as Nell Joy went to a lot of trouble to come here."

Evie tried to glare at Tom but, in the end, she laughed.

When she recovered, she told them how Millicent had followed her request to make sure Nell Joy didn't interfere by locking her in the library. "Edgar referred to it as false imprisonment."

"I would have given anything to see that," Tom said as he chortled. "And I'm glad Millicent is on our side."

Setting her empty teacup down, she looked at the time. "Henry, where would you start your investigation?"

"I'd hate to say it, but I would be inclined to clear your name first."

Good heavens.

"But only because I'd be forced to consider the case without bias."

"Meaning, I should rush upstairs and destroy the incriminating letters."

"Not at all. The fact you kept them suggests you have nothing to hide."

Evie smiled. "That could be a perfect ruse. I've never thought of myself as cunning."

He sat opposite her and studied her for a moment. "Those letters are key to the investigation. Once we establish why they were sent, we might be able to consider options that are not evident at the moment."

Evie stood up and paced around the library. She expected Tom to make a joke of Henry's suggestion that she would be a prime suspect, but he didn't and that worried her.

"You'll have to excuse me. I need to speak with Millicent."

Walking out of the library, she almost expected Henry to stop her. She knew she could have rung for Millicent, but she needed to move away from that moment when she'd had to ponder the possibility of being considered a suspect.

"Prepare to defend yourself," she murmured and headed for the stairs.

In her room, she dug out the fat envelope and set it down on the dresser. Instead of removing the letters and having a thorough read through them, she stood by the dresser looking out the window.

In the distance, she saw Nell Joy sitting at the folly looking back at the house. If news of the death had reached her, she had to be thinking how she could use it to her advantage.

At least she wasn't already writing her article or rushing to the village to send a telegram to her newspaper.

She definitely had an exclusive story.

The Countess of Woodridge caught in the middle of a murder investigation.

Is she a suspect?

What is the connection between the Countess of Woodridge and a dead man found in her chapel?

Evie groaned.

When she'd first become involved in murder investigations, her main concern had been to keep the Woodridge family name free of scandal and here she was, right in the thick of it.

The sound of someone running along the hallway had her swinging away from the window.

"What now?"

Millicent burst in. "Milady. Here you are."

"What is it, Millicent?"

Millicent stopped in the middle of the room. "Oh, nothing really. I'd just been waiting for you to come up. I knew you would eventually, so... I hope you don't mind, I mean... you most likely will mind. I had the footmen and the maids keep an eye out. You'd been in the library for a long while and I was beginning to worry."

"Nothing's happened yet, Millicent. The detective who is going to investigate the case hasn't arrived, and we were just trying to make sense of the few facts we have."

"So you are investigating."

"I can hardly stop myself from observing and forming opinions. That's usually all I do."

Millicent wrung her hands. Looking uncertain, she asked, "Do you think the killer is staying in the house?"

"I'd prefer not to suspect one of my guests." She'd known them for such a long time, if one of them turned out to be a killer, it would fracture her confidence. "Have you seen the dowagers and Toodles?"

"They've had their morning tea in the conservatory and were going to spend the rest of the morning there, out of everyone's way, or so I heard."

"That sounds sensible. Henrietta is determined to carry on as usual."

Hesitating, Millicent asked, "Would you like me to prepare a room for your investigation? The conservatory would be ideal. The windows face the lawn and the park beyond, and we can keep an eye on everyone's comings and goings."

It seemed too extreme, Evie thought. She trusted the police to solve the case with expediency. With any luck, Henry Evans would keep them abreast of the situation.

Yet she found herself saying, "I don't see any harm in it, Millicent."

Digging inside her ample pocket, Millicent produced a fountain pen and a small notebook. "Motive. Who stands to gain by George Beecham's death."

"Yes, that's the right place to start."

"That could take us in many directions, milady. Perhaps we need to focus on the obvious. Who stands to inherit?"

"I see. You want to start straightaway."

"Now is always the best time, milady."

Evie turned toward the window. To her surprise, she saw Davina headed for the folly where Nell Joy still sat.

Having suffered such an intense shock, Evie expected her friend to seek her own company and avoid people altogether.

"I'm sure George Beecham had a will. As it is, Davina is his only living relative."

"Didn't you say he had been living abroad for many years?" Millicent asked. "He might have met someone. We all have our scruples and try to abide by them, however, some men living abroad forget all about the normal rules of society and do things they wouldn't otherwise do, such as take up with a woman without the sanctity of marriage. And that, we all know, can result in surprises, wanted or otherwise."

Evie looked over her shoulder at Millicent, her eyebrows raised slightly.

"Oh, did I say too much?"

"Never, Millicent. You know I always wish you to speak your mind."

"Yes, thank you. Except, sometimes, I'm not entirely certain what my mind is trying to say."

Evie turned back to the scene in the folly. "There is one person I can think of who stands to inherit."

"Davina Beecham-Parks?"

"Yes. But as you pointed out, we don't know what George Beecham got up to during his travels. That could open an entire new avenue of possibilities." If he had established some sort of relationship, and then produced an offspring…

Evie tapped her chin and tried to follow the thread of her own thoughts.

She pictured George Beecham breaking all ties with

his paramour. Abandoning her without any thought of her future.

Shaking her head, she decided he would not... could not have done such a callous thing.

Regardless, if he had abandoned someone, they might have felt incensed enough to seek revenge.

Nodding, Evie said, "Davina is the most likely person to inherit. Add that to the notes. Also, a question mark, because, as you say, there might be someone else, someone left behind."

"Should we include all the other guests?" Millicent asked.

"Yes, of course. However, I don't know how much contact they've had with George Beecham over the years, and I can't say that I've ever heard about any trouble, such as a slight."

"People have killed for less, milady."

"Yes, and I shouldn't be too hasty in assuming there had never been any problems between them. An insult, a snub, something we think of as insignificant, might have festered over time."

Millicent agreed. "Yes. Until it reached boiling point and the person decided this would be the perfect opportunity." Holding her pen up, she said, "Clyde Russell?"

"He is always unfazed by events." Evie remembered him standing by the front door, his napkin in hand. He'd watched the others rush toward Davina and she imagined him thinking there was no need for him to join the fray. "He would simply be too lazy to commit murder."

Millicent smiled. "That would make him the perfect killer. Or he might consider engaging someone else to perform the murder for him."

Good heavens. "That would never have occurred to me." After a moment, she shook her head. "I simply cannot think of a single instance when Clyde might have taken offence or experienced something that would justify committing such a grievous act."

"So he's never been injured in any way, shape or form."

"If he has been, he would always choose to shrug it off and continue on his way."

"Too lazy to kill," Millicent wrote and added in a murmur, "But there's always a first time."

"Augustus Warwick." Evie shook her head. "His life revolves around his estate, and, like Clyde, he gives no thought to grievances of any measure." Evie glanced at the folly and saw Nell Joy and Davina still talking.

"Then again…"

"What?" Millicent prompted.

Evie shrugged. "I'm not sure. It's those things that happen without anyone noticing. When he returned from the war, he found his fiancée had married someone else. I still can't believe she did that. How did it happen? Did someone seed an idea in her mind?"

"You think something prompted her to break off the engagement and settle for the first man who made an offer and Augustus Warwick has spent all these years hunting down the person responsible?"

"Your astuteness never fails to impress me, Millicent."

"I hide it well, milady. That way, no one can ever suspect me."

Heavens, she'd thought of everything.

"Gill Moore," Evie murmured.

"He's obviously a man of means," Millicent offered.

"Yes, I believe his grandfather did quite well out of the

railways, both here and in America. He traveled there in search of a wife and found himself doing business. That's as much as Gill ever revealed about his family and situation."

"Situations," Millicent mused. "Those can change. Sometimes, they are visible through little things, such as not having a valet."

"None of the gentlemen here do."

"The poor upkeep of their clothes. I'll ask one of the footmen to poke around."

"Even if they don't travel with valets, they often have someone looking after their affairs, Millicent. Someone like a butler. These days, their tasks are broad and varied."

"Yes, Edgar thanks his lucky stars every day. These days, there are fewer butlers allowed to carry on that role without having to take on other duties. They call it economizing."

"Still, even if his circumstances have changed, I don't see a reason for him killing George Beecham."

"For the inheritance," Millicent offered.

Turning, Evie said, "That will most likely go to Davina."

Millicent blinked. "He is single."

"Oh. Oh, heavens. I see what you mean." Feeling a sudden chill, Evie brushed her hands along her arms.

"I think that's about everyone here." Millicent closed her notebook. "What happens now?"

"The police will want to speak with everyone in the house," Evie mused. "The cause of death is clear but how it happened needs to be explained. There was a gunshot and yet no one appears to have heard it. It's puzzling. Lord

Evans thinks George was killed in the early hours of the morning."

"It's always darkest before the dawn," Millicent offered. "That is usually the busiest time in the kitchen, indeed, in the house. Everyone is keen to start the day, doing as much as possible, in case they run out of time. We all rush about, and Mrs. Horace sometimes shouts out her orders because she can't hear herself think and she assumes no one else can, so she needs to raise her voice."

It took a moment for Evie to get her thoughts back on track. "They might not realize it, but someone must have seen or heard something."

Millicent gave a slow shake of her head. "They're simply too busy. Remember, they're below stairs. The maids who go up to ready the rooms, draw the curtains but don't have the time to look out the windows because they have to rush off to their next task. It's a never ending cycle, milady." Millicent looked up in thought. "Then again, I suppose where there is repetition, there is the possibility of noticing something unusual."

Evie smiled. "Right now, you are the brightest person in the room, Millicent."

"As I often say, there is always a first time."

"The stables," Evie continued. "I know the stable boys are alert to any sound that might disturb the horses. Then there's George Mills. He has a cottage just beyond the stables and that's closer to the chapel."

"Mr. Lawson," Millicent said. "He's the new groundskeeper and lives in the gatehouse. He's been with us for two months now. I suppose he falls into two categories. Possible witness or killer."

Evie chuckled. "Poor Mr. Lawson." Evie leaned forward until her head rested on the glass pane.

Why hadn't they heard the gunshot?

"I've been awakened in the early hours by a clap of thunder or a bird squawking or shrieking. This was a gunshot. A sharp report. Someone must have heard it."

Millicent pushed out a breath. "Everyone retired quite late, milady, and... the maids and footmen said there were a lot of empty glasses to clear away, and I heard Mrs. Horace hurrying the scullery maid, saying all the glasses needed to be washed so the merry making could begin all over." Millicent gave a slow shake of her head. "There have been so many changes in large houses such as this one, I wonder if the scullery maid will eventually disappear from existence. The other day, I noticed the milk being delivered in the village by a lorry driver instead of a horse and cart."

Evie spoke in a distracted tone, "Halton House will go on." Nicholas had made sure of that, securing the house and its holdings for future generations. "Where were we?"

Millicent sighed. "That brings us to Nell Joy."

The reporter.

Had she been too quick to trust her, falling for her story and doing all she could to assist her in her endeavors?

"How would she have ever met George Beecham?" Evie stilled. Nell Joy had told them she had been rushing from the train station to the hotels where the glamorous people stayed. All in an effort to see someone of interest and report on their activities.

What if...?

What if she had seen George Beecham and asked

about him?

Even after a lengthy absence, someone was bound to remember him or know something about his family.

Oh, yes. I knew his father.

I met his grandfather...

If one waited long enough, one always encountered someone who knew someone and has news about them.

"It all sounds convoluted," Evie said to herself. "But not beyond the realm of possibilities. However, why would Nell Joy then go on to kill him?"

Hearing her, Millicent suggested, "Because she wanted a brilliant headline. That would certainly make her career shine."

Evie turned to look at Millicent.

"You are a gold mine, Millicent. I don't say it often enough."

"So you agree it's possible."

"Perhaps. However, you excel at seeing beyond the obvious. You seem to have a talent for weaving a tale out of a single thread."

"Shall I write it down?"

Evie nodded. "We can't afford to dismiss any idea."

She turned back to the view beyond the window.

Davina and Nell Joy were still talking.

"I'll contact Lotte Mannering. She's still in London and might be able to scratch the surface and find something useful."

Another thought occurred to her.

The photograph used in the newspaper article couldn't be the only one in existence. There must be others taken on the night, and who knew what they might reveal.

"We seem to have our work cut out for us, Millicent.

Well done." She looked down at the envelope containing all the letters George Beecham had sent her. "Millicent."

"Yes, milady?"

"I have a task for you. Would you mind reading through these letters, please." Evie looked up. "That reminds me. I meant to ask you when this arrived. Do you remember?"

Millicent turned several pages of her notebook. "I have been noting down the names of the senders, just in case you forget to respond." She turned another page. "Here it is. Large envelope, no sender name or address. Arrived..." Millicent looked up. "Three days before you returned from London."

Three days!

Add one day for the letter to make its way to her.

Had George Beecham seen her several days before that night of dancing at *The Ritz*?

What had happened during the days in-between?

She imagined him seeing her and making discreet inquiries, asking how long she was staying at the hotel.

What if he had followed them around town? They had been so busy keeping track of Nell Joy, they might have missed being followed by someone else.

What if, on that last night, he had urged himself to approach her, only to lose his courage.

Had he then decided to follow her to Halton House?

Evie's gaze dropped to the floor.

She was missing something vital.

The trigger. The event. The moment when George had decided to return to England.

Something...

Someone had prompted him to do so.

CHAPTER 8

On the Case

*T*here was a knock at the door, but no one came in. Millicent set her notebook down and went to answer it. Lowering her voice, she said, "Clare, I've told you, once you knock, you can come in, but only after making sure no one has said you couldn't."

"That's precisely what I was doing. Waiting for a response and none came so I decided to count to ten before turning the doorknob."

"Very well. What is it?"

"I was sent up to search for her ladyship. Is she here?"

"Don't sound so impertinent."

"But that's the tone of voice you use?"

"Are you saying I sound impertinent? It's my voice. I can't alter it. And, yes, her ladyship is here."

"Well, they've told me to tell her, although, I'm telling

you first, but I'm sure I can trust you to pass on the information… They've said to tell her ladyship the police motor car is making its way here."

"Why didn't you say so instead of prattling on about knocking and whatnot. Thank you, Clare. We'll be down momentarily."

"Oh, my. You do have airs about you. Did you know? And don't take exception to me saying so because you told me to tell you if I ever heard you speaking as if you have airs. Well, you just did."

Evie heard a yelp and couldn't even begin to imagine what Millicent had done to make Clare yelp.

Closing the door, Millicent said, "The police are here, milady."

"Finally."

"Since they will likely wish to speak with the guests first, I'll stay here and get started on the letters."

Thanking her, Evie went down to join the others.

Tom and Henry were already in the hall, ready to greet the police.

Edgar stood at the open door.

"I'm feeling on edge," Henry Evans said. "Is this how it usually is?"

Tom and Evie nodded.

"We always wonder what sort of detective we'll get."

They heard a motor car come to a stop outside and a door opening and closing.

"There's only one of them."

"Are you complaining, Countess?"

The detective appeared at the door, removed his hat and coat and handed them to Edgar.

Evie was surprised by his youth. He couldn't be older than thirty, she thought.

Tall, with broad shoulders, his brown hair was slightly ruffled by his hat. He looked relaxed and almost eager, his dark eyes dancing around the hall, taking it all in before looking at Henry, Tom and finally at Evie.

Henry Evans stepped forward and introduced himself.

"Ah, yes. I was told there was a detective here and a titled one at that. I'm Detective Inspector"

A squeal was followed by a firm command, which clearly fell on deaf ears.

Henrietta!

The sound of her steps was punctuated by further commands and a harsh reprimand. "Holmes, you naughty boy. No, Holmes. Stop that, at once, you disobedient rascal."

The detective cleared his throat. "As I was saying, I'm Detective Inspector Holmes."

Unaware of the arrival of the detective, Henrietta burst into the hall, saying, "Evangeline! Call off your unruly dog. It's nipping at my heels, quite literally." She came to a stop and only then noticed the detective. "Oh, I didn't realize we had company."

"This is Lady Henrietta, the Dowager Countess of Woodridge," Henry Evans said.

"How do you do? I'm Detective Inspector Holmes."

"You're not. Really? Well... I suppose it's a family name. Not much you can do about that. I just hope there isn't a character trait attached to it."

The detective looked at Henrietta and then at Holmes. Without betraying his thoughts, he reached inside his coat and removed a small black notebook. Scribbling a note, he then looked up. "I will be interviewing everyone. But first, I should like to have a private word with Lord Evans. Is there a room we can use?"

"The library," Evie said.

Thanking her, the detective and Henry Evans withdrew into the library.

Evie glanced at Tom. "Well, that more or less puts Henry in his place. He's not Detective Evans. He's Lord Evans."

"That's giving him a taste of his own medicine. When we first met him, he warned us not to meddle in the investigation."

"Did he? I don't remember."

"You're too forgiving, Countess."

Evie turned to Henrietta and was about to say something when Sara and Toodles emerged from the drawing room.

"It's a simple chocolate cake recipe. I just don't understand why she can't whip it all together."

"Mrs. Horace already has the wedding cake prepared. It's a traditional fruit cake."

"And yet, I insist, there is room for more. Anyway, it's not as if I can press her to make it. I have been barred. Barred from the kitchen. Can she even do that?"

"She obviously can because you can't gain access to the kitchen."

They both stopped and stared at Evie and Tom.

"What's happened?" Toodles asked.

"Holmes has been playing up," Henrietta declared. "And the detective has finally arrived. He's having a private word with Henry Evans. And his name is Holmes too."

"Whose name?"

"The detective's name. It's Holmes." Henrietta shook her head. "That will make things awkward. At least, for me. Worse, he does not have a sense of humor. I do not trust a man who does not possess a humorous bone in his body. I can only jump to conclusions and say he leads a dull existence."

Sara laughed. "How can you know for sure, Henrietta? For all you know, he might belong to a theatrical society and enjoys spending his spare time strutting about the stage." She looked at Edgar. "And we have proof of that. Edgar is all proper and would never betray himself with an inappropriate expression. Yet we know he loves the theater."

Henrietta raised an eyebrow. "I'm sure you will soon form your own opinions about the detective. Now, where is that naughty Holmes? Oh, there you are, you rascal."

"Will he want to speak with us?" Sara asked.

"I'm sure he'll want to interrogate everyone," Henrietta declared."

Holmes sniffed Henrietta's shoes and barked.

"Stop that at once."

Toodles nudged Sara and whispered, "Henrietta followed Davina's advice and rubbed bacon on her shoes. She is determined to get Holmes to like her."

"It'll wear off in no time."

Henry Evans appeared at the library door. "He's ready now and he'd like to speak with everyone. In no particular order."

Only one person stepped forward with willingness and enthusiasm.

~

The library

"Lady Woodridge."

Henrietta looked around her. "Which one? Yes, I realize I am the only one here but there are three Lady Woodridges living in this house. Do you have the right one?"

If the detective felt any confusion, he did not express it. "We were introduced earlier. I believe you are the Dowager Countess of Woodridge."

"Ah, I see. Well, as a matter of fact there are two dowagers living in this house. At least, at the current moment. We used to live in the dower house, but the roof developed a leak. It's been fixed now, thank goodness. It's such a lovely house and I wouldn't want the treasures inside it ruined. We continue to live here because Evangeline insists upon it."

"Lady Henrietta."

"Yes, that's definitely me. Young man, you mustn't think you are indulging me and taking into consideration my advanced years. Life offers us very few chances to shine. That was your moment to show off your observation skills. You did splendidly."

"Thank you." He drew in a deep breath and looked down at the blank page on his notebook. "I understand the victim, George Beecham, was known to everyone here."

"That is almost correct. Toodles, that's Evangeline's grandmother who has been living here for longer than anyone cares to remember, didn't know him. Of course, she might have, if he'd lived long enough to make a proper visit and come through the front door instead of skulking about."

"Is that what you think he did? Come here by stealth?"

"In the cover of darkness," Henrietta confirmed. "He was up to no good. Why else would he be so secretive?"

"So, as far as you knew, he was not expected to be present here." He turned the page on his notebook. "And yet, his cousin, Davina Beecham-Parks, is a guest."

"There is history. Things that happened in the past. One day, George was here, and the next he wasn't. Just as yesterday he was alive, and today he is dead."

The detective glanced at Henry Evans who sat nodding his head in agreement.

That seemed to surprise the detective who found himself wondering if he had missed something significant.

"If you will indulge me, I would like to retrace some steps," he said.

Henrietta's eyes danced about the room. "At your peril. Remember, I am almost in my dotage. My declining years might have rendered me incapable of remembering the past in any great detail. You see, in order to retain memories, one must summarize them and leave out pieces that might not be of any use. Excess information can be a burden. Then again, I have heard say it is only a matter of making more room for storage in one's mind. Personally, I do try to retain as much as I can, and I have been giving serious thought to compiling a memoir."

"And what would you write about George Beecham?"

"I would feel compelled to say he was an odd fellow

but only because I find silence awkward. He used to visit a great deal but never said much. He was physically present but always gave the impression of being far away."

"Do you know why he visited?"

"For the company, of course. One must give him the benefit of the doubt and assume he simply did not have much to say. Or, he might have had too much to say but felt the people present might not understand his way of thinking. He loved his books and, for all we know, he might have been a serious philosopher of life. I've tried to immerse myself in the studies of the great thinkers, but I lack the patience and had to abandon the pursuit because I would argue with the great philosophers who never bothered to argue back. It simply left too many questions unanswered. I realize that might have been their joke on me and I refuse to be the source of someone's amusement."

The detective straightened. "Did something happen to prompt his departure? I understand he never returned to England. At least, not until now."

Henrietta looked away from the detective and at Henry Evans. "He left soon after Evangeline's marriage to my grandson, Nicholas. Should we jump to conclusions and say he had lost hope? I don't know. He has taken that secret to his grave."

"Hope of what?"

Henry Evans leaned in and whispered something to the detective who then nodded.

"Are you suggesting there might or might not have been something going on between Lady Woodridge and George Beecham?" the detective asked.

The question surprised Henry Evans who leaned in and had a hurried conversation.

Henrietta cleared her throat. "I suspect you are jumping to conclusions. Let me clarify. George Beecham was a quiet young man. You must surely have come to that conclusion. If you didn't, then I was not clear enough. If he harbored any feelings for Lady Woodridge, he did not act upon them. That is one way of seeing it. Some might argue that the fact he left England could be interpreted as a sign of him taking action and removing himself from the object of his obsession."

"By cutting his loses?"

Henrietta beamed. "Precisely."

The detective brushed a finger along his forehead.

"Time can alter a person and change the course of their destiny," Henrietta murmured. "He dashed back for reasons only known to him."

"Would you allow me to propose a scenario?" the detective asked.

"By all means, do."

"If someone posed a threat to this house, would it be reasonable to say you would do everything within your power to ensure no harm came to anyone living here?"

It took a moment for Henrietta to answer. Her words were measured and emphatic. "Are you accusing me of murder?"

"Lady Henrietta, you *insisted* on being interviewed. Indeed, you demanded to be interviewed first."

"Yes, anyone can see I am the one closest to the end. It could come at any time, and I wished to have my say, just in case."

"Is there anything you wish to add that might be of relevance to this investigation?"

Irritated, Henrietta declared, "Young man, everything I say is of relevance."

~

The hall

Evie paced around the hall. She couldn't think of anything that might throw light on the case. Stopping, she looked at Tom. "He should be trying to find out who had been in touch with him during his stay abroad."

"Meaning, he's wasting his time interviewing us?" Tom asked.

"Precisely." Turning, she paced to the end of the hall and swung back.

Gill Moore and Augustus Warwick walked in, followed by Clyde Russell, who said, "Your butler rounded us up."

Sara and Toodles sat near the fireplace and watched with a measure of impatience as they had both been on their way out for a walk and now had to sit and wait.

"I can't imagine what he hopes to learn from me," Sara said. "I hadn't seen George Beecham in so many years."

"And I never even met him," Toodles said.

Evie came to a stop in front of the fireplace and murmured to herself, "I knew he'd be trouble, the moment I saw him."

The door to the library opened and Henrietta stepped out, her chin raised, her manner imperial.

The detective followed and stood for a moment looking at the group before saying, "Tom Winchester, please."

~

The library

"Tell me what happened," the detective encouraged.

"We were having breakfast."

"Could you be more specific?"

"I had kippers." Tom stilled. He knew the detective wanted the names of everyone else who'd sat down to breakfast, but his mind zeroed in on something Evie had just said.

I knew he'd be trouble, the moment I saw him.

What had she meant?

Had she been referring to George Beecham's appearance at *The Ritz*?

"Gill Moore came down first," Tom continued. "He was followed by Augustus Warwick."

"Augustus was the first person to see Davina Beecham-Parks?" the detective asked.

"Yes."

"How did he seem to you. When he came to breakfast…"

"What do you mean?"

"Did he look agitated?"

"Not really. He didn't eat much. After a bite of toast and some coffee, he said he needed to walk off the previous night's excess."

"Food or drink?"

"Both."

"Who else was at breakfast?"

"Clyde Russell joined us last. Oh, and Henry, of course. Then we heard the shout."

"Not a scream?"

"No, it was a garbled shout, as if the person wanted to draw attention but couldn't quite get the words out or there were too many words and they all got mixed up. I immediately ran out and saw Augustus with Davina."

For the briefest moment, Tom remembered thinking a man had been assaulting her. But then he'd recognized Augustus.

"What happened next?"

"Then Henry joined us, and Davina managed to point toward the chapel. Or somewhere beyond the path. At first, we didn't know which. There's an open field beyond the chapel. As we couldn't see anything that might have caused her so much distress, we decided it had to be something inside the chapel."

"We?"

"Henry and I. We rushed in. We had no idea what we'd find. For a moment, I thought she might have seen a ghost. Her reaction just didn't make sense."

"Tell me what you saw."

Tom explained how they'd searched the chapel and had ended up in the crypt. Focusing on facts, he described the positioning of the body.

"And there was one candle lit?"

Tom nodded.

The detective made a note. "Did you find a weapon?"

"If I had, it would still be there."

"So nothing has been removed from the scene."

Tom nodded and realized the detective hadn't been to the chapel. Instead, he had chosen to interview everyone. He found that odd.

"Were you left alone with the body?"

"Briefly, when Henry went to telephone the police."

"What did you do?"

"I had another look around to see if there was anything out of place."

"So you're familiar with the crypt."

"No. I was looking for something that might have been dropped." He shrugged. "I thought I might see a sign of someone's presence, something like a footprint."

"And then?"

"I walked out. My intention was to stand by the door, but I found Lady Woodridge there. She offered to identify the body."

"Why?"

"Because this is her house and she thought it might be someone from the estate." Tom looked down at his hands. Evie had known who it was before he'd stepped aside.

"Tell me about Lady Woodbridge's reaction to the photograph."

Tom did not answer straightaway. He knew the detective had jumped from the scene at the chapel to another moment, one they hadn't talked about, which led him to assume Henry Evans had provided the information about the photograph. "She was puzzled."

"When did she alert you to its existence?"

Tom frowned. Had he mentioned the photograph first?

He couldn't remember.

If he admitted that, he knew he would cast doubt over Evie.

Tom shrugged. "We were on the train. I'd misplaced my copy of the newspaper, so I had to hunt one down." He looked up for a moment and realized it was all coming back to him. He'd told her about the photograph. Yes, he'd mentioned it first.

He was sure of it.

The detective referred to his notes and then said, "She identified him as George Beecham. What was her reaction?"

She hadn't told him straightaway. In fact, he remembered a porter had given her a copy of the newspaper. She'd seen the article and the accompanying photograph. They'd discussed it briefly and then she'd sent him away to return the copy of the newspaper he'd found.

He gave a small nod.

Yes, she'd told him about it at the rehearsal.

"Stunned."

No, he corrected himself, not at the rehearsal. Evie had told him about George Beecham after they'd left the chapel. They'd been heading back to the house…

She had waited several days before telling him about the man in the photograph. The man who had now been found dead in the chapel.

The detective looked at him for a moment and then said, "But, unlike Davina Beecham-Parks, Lady Woodridge was able to communicate."

Tom frowned. "Are you referring to the photograph?"

"No, I'm referring to the moment when Lady Woodridge identified the body. My apologies for the confusion."

Tom wondered if the confusion had been deliberate. "Lady Woodridge has seen quite a few bodies."

"Would you say she is *sangfroid?*"

"No. I would say she is capable of standing in front of a dead body and process the information without falling to pieces. Her reactions are different to those of other women. She has a reasonable mind. She does, however, become..." He searched for the right description. "I would say, her words are more measured. She doesn't say more than she has to. Although sometimes she apologizes for stating the obvious. That's usually a sign she is processing what she's seen and is, in fact, quite shocked."

"You've made a study of her."

"I spend a great deal of time with her."

"And how do you react when you see a dead body?"

"I say even less than she does."

"You also process what you see?"

Tom couldn't tell if the detective was mocking him or simply reinforcing what he'd said.

The detective closed his notebook. Looking up, he drew in a deep breath. "I understand you and Lady Woodridge have come across numerous dead bodies. Would you say her reaction has always been the same?"

Tom didn't need to think about his response. "She has always been succinct and never dramatic."

"Succinct? Would you give me an example."

"Good heavens. My goodness. Oh."

"And her expressions are never garbled?"

"Never."

"So Lady Woodridge is well versed in the art of reacting to disturbing scenes."

Tom gritted his teeth. "I did not say that. Nor did I imply it."

"But would you agree she is capable of always reacting in a controlled manner to such scenes?"

"I would never make such a claim."

"Because everyone is, at one time or other, capable of acting out of character?"

A storm brewed in Tom's head. The reaction caught him by surprise. At that moment, he wanted to throttle the detective. Given time, he knew he could come up with a better release. Putting him in a room with Henrietta and locking the door would do the trick.

He drew in a calming breath, but it failed to soothe him. "Are you mad? You can't possibly consider Lady Woodridge as a suspect."

The edge of the detective eye crinkled. "Lady Woodridge? Which one?"

CHAPTER 9

Tempers flare

The hall

"Waiting is such a burden." Looking at the library door, Henrietta shuddered. Then she looked at Evie and shook her head. "We should all withdraw to the drawing room. I feel like" she broke off and looked down at Holmes. A twinkle appeared in her eye as she pondered the possibility of doing something entirely out of character. "Never mind all that. Would anyone care for some tea?"

Everyone shifted. Sara and Toodles stood up.

Evie stopped her pacing. Looking toward the front door, she saw Nell Joy and Davina entering.

They'd been informed of the detective's presence but had chosen to take their time in returning to the house.

Anyone observing them would think they had been as thick as thieves, getting their version of events in order and making sure their stories did not clash.

Evie's thoughts were interrupted when the door to the library opened, and Tom stepped out.

He looked furious.

As he joined Evie, the detective appeared at the door. Seeing Nell Joy and Davina, he looked over his shoulder. Evie imagined he asked Henry Evans to identify them.

Nodding, the detective called out, "Miss Nell Joy. Would you please join me in the library?"

Nell Joy walked at a brisk pace and entered without hesitation.

The door to the library closed and everyone's shoulders lowered.

Henrietta cleared her throat. "Tea? In the drawing room."

One by one, they followed her, with the exception of Tom and Evie who remained in the hall standing by the fireplace.

Tom waited until they were alone to say, "He hasn't been to the chapel. What sort of detective is he? The first thing they always do is visit the scene of the crime. It doesn't make sense. He is supposed to be objective. Now he is going to be influenced by everything everyone's said."

Evie couldn't hold back a chuckle. "Think of it. Henrietta went in first. His head must be spinning."

"Yes, at one point, I wished him the torturous fate of being locked up in a room with Henrietta."

"Was he truly awful?"

"He's cunning. Don't let that youthful air about him fool you." Tom looked at his watch. Frowning, he glanced toward the drawing room.

"What is it?"

"Augustus Warwick. The detective wanted to know if he'd seemed agitated. I remember him having a bite of toast, a sip of his coffee and then..." he frowned again. "He looked at his watch."

"And you find that strange?"

"He'd just come down to breakfast. There's a clock on the mantle. He actually sat opposite it, so he only needed to look up. Who looks at their watch when they've just sat down to breakfast?"

Evie thought about it. "Someone who needs to be somewhere else. When Caro brought up my breakfast tray, she looked out the window and saw a man walking in the park. I didn't think anything of it at the time, at least, I don't think I did. She couldn't identify him and when I finally saw him, I realized, from a distance, he looked a lot like Gill Moore. I'm sure that's not relevant." She looked at Tom the way she often did when they exchanged ideas. Anyone watching them, might suspect them of being able to read each other's minds.

"Gill came down at the same time I did and did not move until we heard the shout. Even then, I think he took his time responding."

"Yes, but I can't remember if he came out before or after Clyde Russell. After, I think."

Tom shook his head. "It's the little things we see but don't really put any meaning to at the time. That's what you always say. Yes, Augustus might have been thinking about being or needing to be somewhere else at a specific time."

"To serve as witness?"

"To what?" Tom asked.

Evie knew Tom didn't require a response. This was merely their way of scratching around, thinking about what they'd seen but not really noticed, until now.

Finally, she said, "I'm not prepared to point the finger of suspicion his way."

"Not yet."

She agreed with a nod. "I suppose we could apply the same reasoning to Gill Moore. He wanted to put himself in a specific place at a specific time. He stayed in the dining room even after you and Henry had dashed out."

Glancing toward the library door, she thought about Nell Joy. "The reporter sat outside for a long while."

"I see. She's the reporter now. Are you distancing yourself from her?"

"You'd like that."

"I must admit, yes, I would. She is the odd one out," Tom mused.

"If you think about it, Tom, everyone's presence at Halton House is rather odd, with the exception of Clyde Russell. I expected him to come when he did. While I also knew Augustus would arrive, I should be surprised he came with Clyde, but I'm not. It was never a certainty, but they live near each other and spend a lot of time socializing with the same people and in the same places. Davina's appearance was a surprise. I'd issued the invitation but didn't think she'd hear about it in time. She must have arrived in England several days ago and yet she made no effort to contact me to say she'd be coming."

"You're forgetting one other person."

"Am I?" Evie smiled. "I'm sure I thought of everyone."

"I know you're teasing me," Tom warned.

She was, of course. "Nell Joy is far too obvious to be a suspect. Before you say it, yes, I realize that works in her favor."

Edgar and a footman carrying a tray walked by and headed toward the drawing room.

"Should we join the others?" Tom asked.

"Not yet."

"Admit it. You're fixating on Nell Joy."

"I'd hate to think she fooled me. But what motive could she possibly have for killing George Beecham?" Smiling, she told him about Millicent's suggestion.

"Millicent is worth her weight in gold."

"Yes. People have killed for less. Getting the story, being right here at the scene and capturing every moment of it would put her story on the front page of every newspaper. She could name her price."

"What do you think she's saying in there?" Tom asked.

"I noticed her talking with you during dinner. Apart from that, I can't say that I kept track of her. So I don't know what she's seen or heard."

"I saw her spending time with everyone in the drawing room," Tom offered. "She listened a great deal and I think it's because she knows which questions to ask."

"Leading questions?"

He nodded. "The type of questions that get the person talking about themselves. That's the key to a good conversationalist. They never talk about themselves and always get the other person talking."

"Which means they never reveal anything pertinent

about themselves."

"Yes, and when they are forced to say something, they might rely on an alternative *persona* invented for the purpose."

"Yes," Evie agreed, "or they are vague and quick to turn the conversation back to the other person."

Tom checked his watch. "She's been in there a while."

Evie couldn't imagine what she would have to say. "Oh."

Tom gave her his attention.

"We know George saw us at *The Ritz* but we were not aware of his presence there. She, on the other hand, might have noticed him because she'd been searching the hotels for someone of interest. Then, she might have noticed him watching us."

Tom brushed a finger along his chin. "We need to find out if George Beecham had been staying at the hotel." He looked toward the library. "I think Lotte Mannering might be our best option."

"Yes, she's still in London." Evie looked around. "There's another telephone in Edgar's office below stairs."

They both turned toward the library.

"Should we wait for her to come out?" Evie asked.

Tom nodded. "I wouldn't mind seeing her. A lot can be revealed by a person's expression, especially if they know they are not being watched."

They waited a few moments in silence.

Noticing Tom studying her, she asked, "What?"

"When did you first see the photograph?"

Evie knew immediately which photograph he was referring to. "On the train. Remember, you mentioned it."

"Yes, I mentioned us, but not George Beecham."

"That's right. Because you didn't know about him."

Tom looked away and murmured, "You didn't say anything about recognizing him."

Evie stared into space. "You're right. I didn't. I wonder why?" She tried to think back but her mind was engaged in the moment and everything that had happened since she'd woken up.

"Can you remember what you thought when you saw him?" Tom prompted.

"Or felt?" Evie suggested. "I couldn't say with any certainty. Do you think the detective will ask me?" She answered her own question. "Yes, I suppose he will."

Tom nodded. "He wanted to know if I thought you were cold-blooded."

Evie gaped at him. Lowering her voice, she asked, "Do you think he suspects me?"

"He probably suspects everyone. Including Henry."

After a moment of silence, she asked, "What was your response?"

"To what?"

"To the detective's question about me being cold-blooded."

"Oh." He grinned. "I defended you to the end."

"That doesn't answer the question."

"Fine, I went into great detail, explaining about your reasoning mind. Then, I think I lost track of what I was saying."

Sounding aghast, Evie demanded, "You couldn't focus?"

"He has a way about him. Also…"

"What?"

"When he asked questions, I had to think hard because

I couldn't just blurt out an answer."

"Why not?"

"Because I didn't want to say something that might be misinterpreted. Anyhow, I found myself derailed more than once. My thoughts strayed."

Understanding, Evie said, "That happens to me all the time. It can be a curse or a blessing. Sometimes, it can be useful because I've come up with ideas I hadn't considered before." She looked at him. "Did you, by any chance, come up with something useful?"

"I can't remember. Now I'm thinking I should start carrying around a notebook." He looked toward the drawing room. "Where's Caro?"

"I don't remember seeing her here. She must have gone out for a walk." Biting the edge of her lip, she said, "Nell Joy really must have a lot to say. Either that, or the detective has a lot of questions for her. I hope Henry hasn't been asked to keep us in the dark. I should hate to think he's been forced to choose sides. Not that there are sides." She sighed. "This puts us in a difficult position. Perhaps we shouldn't expect Henry to help us."

"I think she's coming out."

The door to the library opened and Nell Joy stepped out. She had her hands inside her pockets and her head lowered. Looking up, her eyes widened, almost as if she'd suddenly thought of something significant.

Evie thought she looked surprised. Then she remembered everyone else had been here when she'd been asked to step inside.

Nell Joy pressed her hand to her chest and looked over her shoulder, almost as if to see if someone was watching her.

As she walked toward them, the detective stepped out. Seeing them, he asked, "Where is everyone?"

"In the drawing room," Tom said.

The detective frowned.

Evie imagined him thinking he would now have to cross the hall to call in the next person.

Henry emerged and, glancing at them, he walked across and entered the drawing room. A moment later, he came out with Augustus Warwick.

Nell Joy waited until the library door closed again, to say, "That was unexpected and interesting. I've never been interrogated by the police. This is what it must feel like to be blooded."

"Blooded?" Tom asked.

"Like in a fox hunt. When it's your first time, the master of the hunt smears the blood of the fox…"

"Never mind," Tom said. "You were in there a long time."

"I had trouble explaining my presence here. So I had tell him about our first encounter and even admit to having followed you. At first, that set off alarm bells. I could tell he was suspicious of me."

"And how did you dissuade him of that notion?" Tom asked.

"Mr. Winchester, I deal with facts. If I had an active imagination, I would become a writer of fictitious stories and quite possibly make my fortune. I gave him the facts. That is my forte. He took many notes, and I took great delight in seeing him do so."

"He must have had a lot of questions for you," Evie remarked.

"Yes." She gave her a tight smile. "He repeated himself.

I thought he might be trying to catch me out on a lie. Then, I had to explain my presence here again. That was something he found extremely difficult to accept. He also wanted to know about my impressions. I couldn't really help him because I've only spent an evening here and that hasn't been long enough to form any opinions."

Was that the truth, or was she merely trying to remain on her good side?

"I'm just glad it's over now," Nell Joy said.

"It's not," Tom declared. "It's only ever over when the killer is apprehended. Right now, there is a person who thinks they are getting away with murder, but they are wrong."

Nell Joy's cheeks colored.

Tom crossed his arms. "Are you going to write about all this?"

Nell Joy looked at Evie. "As soon as I was liberated from my false imprisonment, I decided I needed time to think." She looked down at the floor. "You were extremely generous in allowing me to witness the days before your wedding and, suddenly, here I was with a story worthy of the front page. You might not realize this, but such a story would make my career and cement my future."

"And?" Tom asked. "What did you decide to do?"

"It was a difficult decision to make, and it probably tells me a great deal about myself. I can't imagine you would be happy about me taking advantage of this situation or even abusing of your hospitality. A part of me wishes I could be that type of person. However..." she shrugged. "I'm here to report on your wedding. I won't be selling the story about the death to the newspapers. Although..."

"Yes?" Tom's voice filled with impatience.

"When all this is resolved, I will still be in possessing of a newsworthy item. The inside story, so to speak. With your permission, I would like to be able to write a piece."

Evie had some understanding of the newspaper business. She had a relative who owned a newspaper in New York and she and Tom had a friend who owned a newspaper in London. "We'll talk afterwards."

Nell Joy nodded. "Well, that's something. At least you're not showing me the door."

Smiling, Evie gestured across the hall. "The others are in the drawing room. I believe tea has been served."

"I think I would like to take another walk."

They watched her head out. Tom waited until he could be sure she wouldn't hear him to say, "A likely story."

"She's actually very smart."

"Yes, she's woven a credible tale."

"Tom!"

"Fine, how is she smart?"

"She must know we have contacts. Staying on our good side will benefit her more than having a story that might or might not make her career."

"Are you saying you are willing to help her?"

"She said she's only just discovered something about herself. She wants to write the wedding piece. That tells me she is not a sensationalist news reporter. She is more interested in the sort of stories that might appear in ladies' magazines."

"I can't decide if you are generous or gullible."

"Well, don't ask me for an opinion because I wouldn't know what to say." Evie straightened. "I think it's time to contact Lotte Mannering."

They headed down to Edgar's office with Tom saying, "The stairs here are narrower. Have you ever noticed?"

"No, I can't say that I have."

As they came closer to the kitchen, they heard the hive of activity, with Mrs. Horace issuing orders and her assistants rushing about.

A woman emerged from a room and appeared to be headed to the kitchen. Seeing them, she stopped and hurried toward them, a series of keys on chains swinging from her waist. "My lady."

"Mrs. Arnold." The fact she rarely spoke with the housekeeper was a testament to the woman's ability to run the household like a well-oiled machine. "I suppose you've heard about the commotion."

"Yes, we've been eager for information."

"I'm afraid there's not much of it. There is a detective here and he will want to speak with everyone. I can only assume he'll want to know if anyone saw or heard something. There's no need to feel apprehensive." She looked at Tom. "Meanwhile, Mr. Winchester and I would like to use the telephone in Edgar's office."

"Of course. Although... Lady Evans is using it at this very moment."

"Caro?"

"She said you wouldn't mind."

"Of course, not. I hope nothing is wrong."

"I couldn't really say, my lady."

"Thank you, Mrs. Arnold. We'll... we'll wait for her to finish."

Nodding, Mrs. Arnold withdrew into the kitchen.

Evie signaled to a room. "That's Edgar's office."

"Are we going to eavesdrop?"

"Certainly not."

They didn't have long to wait. The door opened and Caro stepped out. "Oh." Her cheeks colored.

"Caro. We were wondering where you were."

"I was just headed upstairs. A maid told me the police had arrived." She gestured to the office. "I should tell you because you're bound to find out soon enough. I took it upon myself to telephone Lotte Mannering."

"Heavens. Tom and I were just about to contact her."

Nodding, Caro said, "I hope you don't mind. She is still in London, and I thought she might be able to find something of interest about George Beecham."

"Great minds think alike," Tom said.

"Since I'd only had a hurried conversation with you, I spoke to the dowagers and Toodles and they told me what they knew. It was enough to form a fuller picture. There's the question of whether George Beecham had travelled to India and when he'd come to England. Lotte will find out when he arrived at The Ritz. I assume you'd also want to know when he left."

Evie gave a vigorous nod. "That's really all I'd thought of asking Lotte. If she can find out about his travels to India, we'll be in a better position."

"I also mentioned Nell Joy."

"That shows supreme thinking," Tom said. "It's good to know I have an ally. Evie has been too accepting and trusting of that young woman."

Caro tilted her head in thought.

"What is it?" Evie asked.

"I'm not sure. When I spoke with Henrietta, I had the feeling she knew something about George Beecham she wasn't sharing with me. I'm intrigued because Henrietta knows a great deal about many people. Someone her age has had years to hear rumors and stories about people. I find it odd. I never imagined Henrietta would keep secrets, but that's how it feels to me."

Evie thought back to Davina's arrival and how Henrietta had turned to look at her. At the time, she'd thought Henrietta had been thinking about seeing George Beecham in the photograph, but perhaps there had been something else. Something she'd never spoken of.

"Here comes Edgar." Caro smiled at him.

"My lady," he inclined his head. Turning to Evie, he said, "My lady, the detective is now interviewing Mr. Russell. I saw Mr. Warwick come out of the library and he looked rather pale, my lady. When he saw me, he asked for a *stiff drink*. He drank it in one gulp and went out for a walk. The way he looked at the empty glass makes me think he would have preferred to sit in a corner with a glass and a bottle for comfort."

Caro looked at Tom. "Have you been interviewed?"

Tom nodded.

"How was it. Did you find it dreadful?"

"It was awkward and not something I wish to repeat any time soon." Tom looked at his watch. "If Augustus Warwick has only now come out, it means he was in there for a while. Quite possibly as long as Nell Joy. The detective must be gathering momentum."

"I doubt he'll get anything out of Clyde," Evie mused. "When Tom and Henry rushed toward the chapel, he remained by the front door. I didn't see him when we returned but I assume he went to the dining room to finish his breakfast." Evie had never known him to worry about anything. She'd sometimes heard him say the less he knew, the better because people who knew things were always in high demand and that seemed too much of a bother.

A couple of footmen rushed by, prompting Evie to say, "We should get out of everyone's way."

Edgar patted his pocket. "How remiss of me. I almost forgot. Millicent gave me a note to pass to you if I happened to see you."

"What does it say?"

"It's folded, my lady, and Millicent did not reveal the contents to me."

Evie took the note and read it. "She has secured the conservatory for us and will be there, ready to employ her excellent shorthand skills to keep track of our ideas." She folded the piece of paper and slipped it inside her pocket. "Millicent thinks we should put our heads together and investigate."

Her mind had been churning the pitiful amount of information they had and, so far, it had failed to produce any new insights.

"I don't really know what she hopes we'll achieve. It's not as if we can go around the detective's back and inter-view everyone. That would be bad form. After all, I am their hostess. I can't have them thinking I'm suspicious of them."

"Offending your guests should be the least of your concerns, Countess. Remember, one of them could well turn out to be a killer."

Evie led them up, her thoughts on how they would manage to poke their noses around without being noticed.

CHAPTER 10

Framed

The conservatory

hey crossed the hall and, as they turned toward the conservatory, Tom said, "I'm going outside for a walk. I wouldn't mind catching up with Augustus. He might be willing to share his experience with the detective. Then again, he might want to put it all behind him."

"Good luck. Caro and I will be in the conservatory."

They found Millicent busy writing in her notebook. She looked up. "You got my note."

Millicent had organized some wicker chairs near one of the windows. Settling down, Evie took a moment to look around the pretty room with its glass ceiling and tall windows. As always, the indoor plants were thriving.

"Yes, I got your note. Did you read the letters?"

Millicent nodded. "They are odd. I could almost believe you had been carrying on a lengthy correspondence over the years."

"What do you make of that?" Evie asked Caro.

Without giving it much thought, Caro said, "They did not arrive here by accident. Someone wanted you to be in possession of them."

"But that would suggest there is a complicated plan to..." Evie shrugged. "I honestly can't even begin to imagine what could be at stake or what the killer hopes to achieve."

Caro exchanged a look with Millicent before saying, "Isn't it obvious?"

"Not to me."

Caro nodded. "Someone wants to frame you for the death of George Beecham."

"To what end? Wait... You're right. We might be looking at this all wrong. Yes, what if I'm the target and George Beecham a victim, sacrificed in order to point the finger of suspicion my way?"

Caro and Millicent both nodded.

"That's insane. Why would anyone wish to do that?"

"The usual reasons. Revenge," Caro said.

"Or..." Millicent surged to her feet and paced about. "What if one of the men had been in love with you all these years. They missed their opportunity once and they know they are about to do so again because you're about to marry Mr. Winchester. Anger has festered inside them. Raw and unforgiving." Millicent's voice became fierce.

"They love you and yet they detest the very sight of you. So they have set their sights on Davina. Not just her. They also want the fortune she stands to inherit but first they must get George Beecham out of the way. They do it and they point the finger of suspicion at you by planting those letters."

Evie and Caro stared at Millicent, their eyes wide with a mixture of intrigue and surprise.

Millicent shrugged. "It's just a thought."

Caro recovered first. "Millicent, would you care to explain how they managed to convince George Beecham to return to England? And... and if the killer is or was in love with Evie, why would he now transfer his love to Davina? Does the killer wish to get his hands on any inheritance?"

"It's possible he fell for her ladyship thinking he could also have her fortune. Now, he'll settle for someone else with a fortune. This act of revenge has been a long time in the making," Millicent explained. "And during all that festering of emotions, the killer lost sight of his initial anger. You know the type. They always blame someone else for their woes. Now their anger is all twisted and fouled by the misunderstanding..." Millicent searched for the right word, "*festering* inside them." She nodded. "First, they cultivated their friendship with George Beecham. They saw him as a gullible, lonely young man who was secretly in love with her ladyship. They then proceeded to exploit this." Millicent looked up. Nodding, she continued, "The killer fed him lies full of hope, suggesting that if he wrote to her ladyship, it would encourage her to express her secret love for him. And so he did and the letters flew back and forth. Only, it wasn't her ladyship responding but rather the killer pretending to be her ladyship."

"The killer pretended…" Caro looked confused.

"Yes, the killer convinced George Beecham that it would be best if he sent the letters to him and then he would personally hand them over to her ladyship. That way, Edgar wouldn't suspect and then be called upon to provide proof that her ladyship had been receiving clandestine letters."

Caro gaped. "Oh, I see."

"Anyhow, when the time was ripe, the killer lured George Beecham back to England and that's when he planted the evidence by sending all the letters to her ladyship."

"The letters he had been hoarding."

Millicent nodded.

Caro looked at Evie. "I can almost believe it."

"Yes," Evie agreed. "But who could have gone to so much trouble?"

Augustus?

Clyde… Gill?

Shrugging, Millicent sat down and said, "Or, maybe the killer just wanted the money, and he knew he could get it by marrying Davina. But that puts the existence of the letters back into question."

"Not necessarily," Evie said. "If the killer's ultimate plan was to gain access to the inheritance through Davina, then he would want George here." She nodded. "George knew his killer. We've been asking ourselves why George came here, and we were curious why he went to the chapel."

Millicent piped in, "He was lured here with instructions to wait in the chapel because you were going to meet him there."

Good heavens.

Anyone might have seen her walking out of the house late at night. She'd wanted to clear her head, but her presence outside could easily be misconstrued.

Caro nudged Millicent. "You've upset her. Come up with another theory."

"Oh, dear. No, there's no need. I mean, if you have another theory, by all means, do share it with us. I'm simply astonished by the idea of someone going to so much trouble."

"They've had years, milady. Remember the festering."

"What about Davina?" Caro asked. "I assume she is the sole heiress."

"Yes, I imagine she is. They didn't have any other family, not that I know of."

"Could she have wanted to get her hands on the money now rather than later? She might not have meant to involve you. I'm thinking that if I wanted to kill someone for personal gain, I would set the scene somewhere with a lot of possible suspects."

Millicent nodded in agreement. "All these years, Davina Beecham-Parks must have known something about her cousin's unrequited love for her ladyship.

Caro frowned. "Yes, about that…"

"It's a long story, Caro." Evie turned away. If she delved into her memory, she knew she would find traces of moments when George tried to express his feelings for her—moments she dismissed him with the indifference of youth. She hadn't exactly been unfeeling. She had simply not known how to deal with the awkward situation.

"Does Henrietta know about George Beecham carrying a torch for you?" Caro asked.

"Yes, I'm sure she does. You said it yourself. She knows a lot about many people."

~

The library

The detective looked at his watch. "I suppose we should stop for a break."

Henry Evans stood up. "Luncheon will be served soon."

Straightening his tie, the detective mused, "I should make my way to the village. I take it there is a pub there."

Henry Evans took the liberty to say, "Nonsense. You'll be expected to eat here."

"Right... Well, I won't argue with that. Now, shall we visit the chapel?"

"The body will have been removed by now."

"Yes, I know. It should be on a slab being prodded for further evidence," the detective said, his tone matter of fact. "I would still like to see the chapel." As they walked out, he asked, "Which one of those three men would you likely suspect? Gill Moore, Augustus Warwick, or Clyde Russell?"

"I don't see how any of them would have a reason for killing someone right here, at the house of one of their oldest friends."

Outside, Henry Evans looked toward the park and saw Tom walking with Augustus Warwick.

"What do you think those two are talking about?" the detective asked.

"They're probably wondering why you haven't visited the chapel until now."

"True, most detectives would head to the scene of the crime first. It hasn't been disturbed. There are constables making sure of that. The dead body is hardly going to talk to me."

Henry Evans found that curious. In all his years working as a detective, he'd never met anyone so reluctant to see the scene of the crime. It made no sense. And, in his opinion, dead people did talk. In fact, they had a great deal to say.

"I suppose the chapel is far enough away from the house to have muffled the sound of a gunshot," the detective observed.

A second later, a gunshot was heard in the distance and birds scattered in every direction.

"I heard that loud and clear," Henry Evans said. "And I imagine it would be even louder in the dead of night when all else is quiet."

~

The conservatory

Looking out the window, Evie watched Henry Evans and the detective head toward the chapel. "About time," she said.

"They're not going to spend much time there," Millicent said. "I'm sure luncheon will be ready soon and the

135

body has already been taken away. What are they going to look at?"

Evie turned to Millicent and apologized. "I hope I didn't keep you from your meal."

"Not at all, milady. I've been snatching bits and pieces here and there all day long. It's amazing how it all accumulates. Every time I happen to be in the kitchen, Mrs. Horace encouraged me to try one of her delectable cakes or sandwiches. Now that I think about it, she was probably rewarding me in the hope that I might give her news of everything happening upstairs. I should let everyone know I'm open to bribes. This could turn into a lucrative business." Millicent looked up and out the window. "There's Mr. Winchester. He found Augustus Warwick and they're deep in conversation. Oh dear, Mr. Warwick is flapping his arms about. That can't be a good sign." She huffed out a breath. "All that talk of food has made me hungry." She set her fountain pen down. "Unless you need me for anything else…"

"Feel free to stop now, Millicent. We'll return here after luncheon. Although, I might be delayed because I suspect the detective might be ready to speak with me by then."

～

The dining room

"I'm surprised they haven't all asked for trays to be taken up to their rooms," Caro whispered. "I've never seen such a morose group of people in my life."

Henry Evans entered the dining room, followed by the detective who said, "Lady Woodridge, I hope I'm not imposing."

"Not at all, detective. A place has been set for you."

Everyone busied themselves with napkins and the tableware designs. Anything to distract themselves from the day's events.

Davina was the first to speak. "I'm dying to see your wedding gown."

"My dressmaker has done a wonderful job, although she wasn't entirely sure about my choice of colors."

"So you won't be wearing white."

"I felt the occasion called for something different."

Henrietta lifted her glass in a silent toast.

"You seem cheerful about something," Sara remarked.

"My dear, it is my perpetual state of being. I find it energizing."

"To be cheerful?"

"Yes. Don't you feel uplifted by happiness?"

"I do, but not every moment of the day gives me reason to be happy."

"Ah, but it's a state of mind. One must merely choose to be happy."

Surprised, Toodles asked, "Where has this philosophizing come from?"

"I was suddenly reminded of it today. I can't remember exactly where it happened." Narrowing her eyes, Henrietta gave the detective a pointed look.

Toodles turned to the detective. "Have you made any progress?"

"I'm afraid not, Mrs... or is it Lady? I'm sorry, it's slipped my mind."

"Oh, I'm not a Mrs. or a Lady. I'm Toodles."

"Toodles?"

"Yes, that is my name."

"Of course. Oh, yes. I remember now. You're Lady Woodridge's grandmother."

Henrietta laughed and whispered, "It's too tempting, but I won't succumb. On second thought, yes, I will." Speaking up, she said, "Toodles is most definitely not my grandmother." She turned to Sara. "Is she yours?"

Sara replied with a disapproving frown prompting Henrietta to say, "You haven't been interviewed by him. Wait until you are, and then we'll see."

Clyde Russell walked in and apologized for his tardiness. "I fell asleep under a book. Or, rather, the book fell on my face when I dozed off. That reminds me of a time I fell asleep under a tree and was woken up by something falling on my head. I thought it might have been a walnut. It was, but it didn't fall on me by itself. A squirrel threw it at me. Since I didn't feel I had done anything to deserve it, I threw the walnut back. To this day, I believe the squirrel caught it." He looked about the table and smiled. "Have we found the killer among us?"

"Not yet," Davina offered. "Then again, the detective hasn't spoken with everyone. I suppose the interviews will resume after luncheon."

Nodding, the detective confirmed it, "Yes, I'm afraid so."

"We saw you going to the chapel," Caro said. "Did you find anything of interest there?"

"I can't say that I did. But, at least, I am now familiar with it."

"You didn't want to see the body?"

"It was enough for Lord Evans to have seen it. I trust his judgment and opinion."

Davina leaned in and whispered, "Anyone would think he's squeamish."

It seemed highly unlikely, Evie thought. Although, not impossible.

"Detective, do you think this is the killer's first offence or has he left a trail of bodies in his wake?" Henrietta asked.

"While it is too early to say, in my opinion, the killer has not done this before, but they are adept at killing."

Henrietta looked around the table. "What does that mean?"

"It simply means that the killer is familiar with death, the way a countryperson is accepting of the cycle of life."

"That's inconvenient because we were rather hoping the killer would turn out to be an intruder."

"Henrietta, you can't expect everyone, including killers, to be obliging just so you can have a good night's rest."

"Why not? It's not too much to ask."

Toodles set her wine glass down and looked at Evie. "Birdie, I hope you don't have any activities planned that involve guns."

"As a matter of fact, I did. Shooting around the clock is becoming quite popular. Remember, you brought it to our attention when you read an article about it in one of your magazines. It's been around since 1920."

"If you ask me, they need to come up with a better name."

"What does it involve?" Sara asked.

"A clay disc is thrown in the air, and you try to shoot it."

When Evie saw Henrietta eye the detective, she just knew she was about to launch another line of prodding.

"Detective, do you think your business here will be concluded today?"

"I doubt it, my lady."

"And where will you be staying? There is no room at the pub." Henrietta shrugged. "I supposed we could put you up for the night."

The detective looked at Evie. "That would be very kind, indeed. If it wouldn't be too much of an imposition."

"You have already imposed, detective," Henrietta said. "Meaning, you are already here and there are many rooms at Halton House. That's settled. By the way, where would you have returned to?"

"London."

"You're from the Yard?" Henrietta chortled. "Once, I heard a detective say he was from the yard, and it brought images of mucking stalls and shoveling horse manure."

"Henrietta! We are eating," Sara complained.

"Yes, we are." Henrietta made a point of looking at Sara's plate. "That bird on your plate had a heartbeat and, not long ago, it had been enjoying a day in the sunshine. Look at it now."

"Regardless, we don't wish to think of such things." Sara took a sip of wine.

Henrietta's eyes beamed with amusement. "Do you happen to know how wine is made?"

"I imagine there is some sort of pressing machinery used."

Henrietta shook her head. "It's more likely to be made

by men and women crushing the grapes with their bare feet. Think about it."

Sara set her wine glass down and muttered under her breath, "Is nothing sacred?"

Luncheon progressed with everyone engaged in murmured conversations. Compared to the previous evening, the mood became quite subdued, with occasional efforts made at lightheartedness.

The detective was the first to finish his meal and excuse himself, saying he needed to prepare for the interviews.

Everyone immediately relaxed and, as they finished their meals, engaged in animated conversations.

Evie noticed one person who hadn't spoken a single word.

Nell Joy.

She had watched and listened but had not contributed any ideas or opinions.

Augustus Warwick had been quiet at first but after the entrée and a glass of wine, he had relaxed, sharing a few remarks with Tom and Caro, who sat at either side of him.

"Is anyone up for a spot of fishing?" Augustus asked.

Clyde and Gill offered to go along with him but didn't promise to participate.

"I might take some paper along with me and see if I can entice Gill into racing me. We can make paper boats."

"Are you by any chance short of funds?" Gill asked. "You've been doing well out of me. Or are you intent on bleeding me dry for the simple pleasure of doing so?"

Clyde grinned. "I know you have deep pockets.

Besides, it's not about the money. It's about winning. And I do enjoy coming first. Or so I'm told."

"Why say it if you're not sure?" Augustus asked.

Clyde gave it some thought. "I suppose I'm a victim of my own success. I've been labeled a ruthless competitor, so I'm stuck with it."

"You could try letting us win," Augustus suggested.

With the meal over, everyone dispersed, heading off in pursuit of a distraction.

Evie walked several steps behind Henrietta and saw her draw the attention of a footman. She had a quick word with him and then seemed satisfied with the exchange.

Walking beside her, Tom said, "I wonder what that was about?"

"We will soon find out, I'm sure," Evie mused. "I suppose those of us who have as yet to be interviewed need to linger near the library."

"I'll keep you company, Countess."

When they reached the hall, she asked, "Did you manage to get any information out of Augustus?"

"Only after I offered him a swig from my flask."

"I didn't realize you carried one."

"In the absence of a pipe, I thought I might try it out. Although, I do still wish to acquire a pipe." He looked at the fireplace. "See, I could be tapping it right now and using it to emphasize a point or earn myself some thinking time."

"You haven't made any points."

"But I might. Anyhow, Augustus revealed something we were not aware of. A few months ago, he travelled to India and met up with George Beecham."

"You don't say. He never mentioned it. How did the detective get the information out of him?"

"Everyone who travels now must have a passport. It seems the detective's late arrival had something to do with him doing some research. I've spoken with Henry, and he confirmed that when he contacted the Yard, he was asked for specific information about the people staying here."

"The detective came prepared. I wonder what he found out about us."

Henry came out of the library. Seeing them, he said, "He wants to interview all the servants now."

"Really?" Evie looked confused. "What about me and Davina. I'm sure she hasn't been interviewed."

"He's being considerate. Davina suffered a tremendous shock and you, as hostess, are under a great deal of pressure. He'll most likely speak with you both tomorrow."

"Countess, surely that's a relief."

Indeed, it was. She hadn't been looking forward to being questioned.

"Come to think of it, Sara and Toodles haven't been interviewed either."

Henry smiled. "The detective didn't feel it necessary. Not after his experience questioning Henrietta."

Tom laughed. "She is our secret weapon."

"Henry, you might want to talk to Edgar," she suggested. "He's the best person to liaise with and organize the servants."

Nodding, Henry returned to the library, presumably to pull the bell cord and summon Edgar.

"He can't be entirely happy playing the role of second fiddle," Evie observed.

Moments later, Evie looked up and saw Davina walking out of the drawing room. She looked toward the front door and possibly considered going out for a walk when she noticed them and crossed the hall.

When she reached them, Evie said, "I'm sure you'll be relieved to hear the detective has postponed speaking with us until tomorrow."

"I wondered if he'd forgotten about me." Davina gave Evie a tight smile. "I suppose this frees me up to go for a walk. I'm still feeling on edge and rather restless."

As she headed outside, Evie picked up the thread of the conversation she'd been having with Tom. "Augustus went to India?"

"He says he went there to close some business accounts and deal with a house that had belonged to his great uncle. He hadn't expected to encounter anyone he knew, because, as far as he was concerned, he didn't know anyone living there. Those are his words. Anyhow, Augustus was invited to dine at a big wig's house and that's where he found George Beecham. Following that encounter, he saw him every other day until he concluded his business and returned to England. In his opinion, it was only a chance encounter, but the detective believes he withheld information. He then proceeded to prod Augustus about George's state of mind."

"And?"

"He was the same old George, and he hadn't given any indication he planned on returning to England. Augustus fears the detective doesn't believe him and suspects he is somehow involved in luring George Beecham to England."

"How long ago was his visit to India?"

"Three months ago."

"Maybe Augustus was the trigger."

"Trigger?"

"I've been thinking something or someone prompted George to return to England." Evie remembered the article Toodles had shown them. "Give me a moment. I need to fetch something."

She rushed upstairs and headed for Toodle's room. After a quick search, she found the magazine.

As she headed for the stairs, she decided to get a shawl from her room. The weather was too fine for fires to be lit but all that standing about and waiting... just the thought was enough to make her shiver.

She entered her room and searched for the shawl she wanted. When she found it, she thought she should take the letters down with her. Tom hadn't seen them yet and he might be able to provide his impressions of them.

With the shawl on her arm, she looked around the room and decided to also take a handkerchief. She found that in a drawer next to the dresser. As she turned to reach for the letters, her fingers met with empty space.

The envelope was not where she'd left it.

Looking around, she searched her room.

Millicent had sat here reading the letters.

Had she taken them with her? Walking around the bed, she pulled the bell cord. Millicent was most likely waiting in the conservatory. If another maid came, she would have to simply go searching for Millicent herself.

Turning, she looked at her bedside drawer and smiled. "Millicent must have put them away. I should have thought of that."

However, they were not in the drawer.

Thinking Millicent might have found a new hiding place, she went through the wardrobe and even looked inside her hat boxes.

Millicent walked in just as Evie emitted a frustrated growl.

"Milady?"

"The letters, Millicent. Do you have them?"

"No, milady. I put them back on the dresser."

Thinking they might have fallen off, Evie looked around the dresser. "They're not here."

They stood in the middle of the room, their eyes darting around in a frantic effort to locate the letters.

"Milady, do you think someone took them?"

"If someone took them, that means the killer is actually one of the guests."

Determined to find them, Millicent said she would organize a search of everyone's room. "They have to be in the house."

That set Evie's mind at ease. Nodding, she made her way down.

"What's wrong?" Tom asked.

"The letters are not where they're supposed to be. Before you suggest it, Millicent did not take them."

"Someone else?"

Nodding, she looked around the hall. "Someone who wanted to read them or simply take them." Pushing out a hard breath, she waved the magazine. "At least I found this." She pointed to the cover. "Two months old. Toodles thinks the article was written by George Beecham. They're called Letters from India."

"So George decided to return shortly after his encounter with Augustus."

"Yes, but what does it mean?"

"As you said, it might have been a trigger. Maybe it was enough to have seen Augustus."

Or maybe Augustus had set something in motion.

A plan. A master plan, which involved manipulating a man into returning to England.

And then what?

Evie tried to see Augustus Warwick as the man responsible for killing George and simply couldn't manage it.

"I can see that you can't come up with a motive," Tom said. "What about the fiancée? The woman who abandoned him for another man. Did someone seed the idea or was she the type of woman to transfer her affections without a second thought?"

The war had changed people. Who knew why she had broken off the engagement with Augustus. "I've already considered that scenario." Smiling, she told him about Millicent's theory.

"Millicent should turn her ideas into a book." Tom laughed. "Instead of worrying about Nell Joy, we should be focused on Millicent. She could easily write an *exposé* about life at Halton House."

"Could we please focus on the current crisis? If you're suggesting George had something to do with it, I just can't see it. What would he gain by convincing Augustus' fiancée to break off the engagement?"

"Misery loves company," Tom suggested. "We assume George was in love with you and he couldn't abide seeing anyone else happy, so he ruined Augustus' prospects of happiness."

"That's Millicent's theory in a nutshell. But, by the

time Augustus' fiancée took up with someone else, George had already left the country. So he can't have been responsible."

"You're right. Pity, it would have been a solid reason. Augustus then finds out the truth and decides to seek his revenge. As interesting as the theory is, I don't understand why he would then set the murder scene at your house. Does Augustus have a bone to pick with you?"

The edge of Tom's eyes crinkled so Evie knew he wanted to lighten the mood.

Evie pushed out a breath. "Anyhow, no, I can't see Augustus as the killer."

"You're right. The killer wouldn't be shaken the way he was. I wouldn't be surprised to find him at the pub right now, considering his fate behind bars or, worse, the gallows. It wouldn't be the first time a man was wrongfully accused, and he knows it."

"I'm glad he was outside. That gives him an alibi," Evie said.

"For what?"

"He can't possibly be responsible for taking the letters."

CHAPTER 11

Yes and no

*E*vie felt it her duty to remain in the hall and offer support to the servants going in to be interviewed. The process was swift. No one had seen or heard anything.

Millicent walked toward them; her manner composed. When she reached them, however, Evie saw her cheeks were flushed and her breath was coming hard and fast.

"Millicent!"

"Should I offer her my flask?" Tom asked.

"Milady, what if I say the wrong thing?"

"What do you mean?"

"I might blurt out something I shouldn't. You know what I'm like, one moment I sound like a sage, all knowing and wise, and the next moment, I'm... I'm like a cartwheel, wobbling and about to come unhinged. I can

149

see it about to happen, I know I should stop and fix it. Instead, I persevere and push on and, before I know it, the wheel comes off and... Well, I'm the wheel, in case you were wondering, and I start to spill things, meaning, I blurt out the first thing that comes to my mind and it doesn't always make sense."

Tom suggested keeping her answers short, preferably to yes and no.

"Yes and no?"

"Yes," Tom confirmed.

"Yes?"

Evie elbowed Tom. "She's practicing."

"Did I sound convincing?"

"Of course. You'll do very well, Millicent," Evie assured her.

The door to the library opened and Clare hurried out, her knuckles pressed to her mouth, her eyes shimmering with unshed tears.

"Clare!" Millicent exclaimed.

"It was dreadful. I felt so guilty. I'm sure he now thinks I'm the killer."

Henry Evans peered out. Seeing Millicent, he beckoned her over.

Evie put her arm around Clare's shoulder and tried to comfort her, while at the same time giving Millicent a nod of encouragement.

"I imagine the detective will need a comforting arm around his shoulder after he interviews Millicent." He tapped his coat pocket. "Or he might prefer a shot of brandy."

Ignoring him, Evie said, "Clare, go down to the

kitchen and have a strong cup of tea. I'm sure that will help."

Nodding, Clare scurried away.

The library

"Millicent."

"That's right. That's my name. I mean… Yes."

"What do you know about this unfortunate incident?"

"No."

"No?"

"No, nothing."

"Have you seen or heard anything unusual?" the detective asked.

"N-no." She looked up in thought.

"Has something come to mind?"

"Y-yes."

The detective leaned forward and gave her an encouraging nod. "What's on your mind?"

"My mind?"

He nodded.

"Holmes," Millicent blurted out.

"Yes?"

"Holmes has been unusually naughty, and dogs have a way of sensing things. He's been nipping at Lady Henrietta's heels but I'm sure she's not guilty of anything, well, not anything truly evil, but then why would Holmes do that? It's occurred to me that he might be distressed by the presence of a killer in the house. A killer intent on framing an innocent person."

"An innocent person?"

Millicent nodded.

"And who might this innocent person be?"

"Millicent shrugged. "No."

"No?"

"No, I don't know, not really."

The detective pushed out a breath, sat back, and thanked her for her time.

Henry Evans smiled. "You're free to go, Millicent."

Pressing her hand to her mouth, Millicent rushed out of the library.

"Millicent?" Did he upset you too?" Evie asked.

Letting her hand drop, Millicent shook her head. "I almost blurted out something I shouldn't. I'm so glad he said I could go when he did because everything nearly spilled out of me. Just like a wobbly cartwheel..."

"I'm sure you did very well," Evie assured her.

"I'll be in the conservatory if you need me, milady. It might be best if I stay well out of sight for a while."

Evie looked at Tom. "A breath of fresh air, please."

"Lead the way."

They were met by sunshine and the slightest hint of a breeze.

Standing in the middle of the park, Evie looked back at the house. "I've just realized we'll be spending the night under the same roof as the killer. Reason tells me we'll be in no danger, but I can't help feeling jittery."

"I don't blame you. At least, the detective will be on hand."

They walked on until they reached the lake where they

saw Augustus casting a line, Clyde Russell standing beside him waving his arms about.

"I guess Gill decided not to join them," she said. Looking across the park, she added, "I spoke too soon. There he is, heading toward them."

He stopped near a copse of trees. Several minutes later, he was still standing there.

"He must find those trees captivating," Tom said.

For a moment, Gill disappeared out of sight.

"Where did he go?" Tom asked.

"There he is. He just stepped back. Now he's headed to the lake." She followed his progress and saw Clyde wave to him.

"That's interesting." Tom signaled to the copse of trees. "Davina just emerged from the shadows of the trees."

"I hope she doesn't see us."

"Us? Why not?"

Evie shrugged. "Because then she'll know we've seen her and Gill together."

"And she might think we know something we shouldn't? What's his money situation like?"

"I heard Clyde say he has deep pockets." Evie looked toward the house. Narrowing her gaze, she noticed someone looking out toward the park.

"I'm feeling thirsty. I think I'll go back inside for a drink."

Tom tapped his pocket.

Evie laughed. "It's not that kind of thirst."

"The flask doesn't seem to be working for me. I'll have to do something about getting a pipe."

As Evie drew closer to the house, she was able to identify the person she'd seen at the window.

Henrietta.

She remembered something Caro had said earlier about Henrietta knowing a great deal about many people.

Evie reached the house and headed straight upstairs, making her way to Henrietta's room.

Knocking on the door, she entered and found Henrietta still standing by the window.

"Evangeline. Why aren't you outside enjoying the lovely sunshine?"

"I might ask the same question."

"Oh, I was feeling a little fatigued."

"Shouldn't you lie down?"

"Oh, no. I might fall asleep and miss something."

Evie joined her by the window. "Tom was just wondering about Gill's state of affairs."

"His finances?" Henrietta laughed. "It'll be several generations before anyone has to worry. Then again, there might not be anyone to worry because he's not married. I hope he's made a will."

"We know George Beecham was well off, but we don't know if he'd been able to sustain it all."

Henrietta appeared to want to say something but then pursed her lips.

A rare sight, Evie thought.

"You know something."

"I rather like to think I know a great deal about many things and then I snap out of my delusion."

"Henrietta. If you know something that might help us understand what's happened, please share it."

"It's common knowledge, my dear."

"Not common enough for me to know about it."

Henrietta smiled. "That's because you don't concern

yourself with trivial matters." She drew away from the window and sat down on a chair. "Davina is not his only relative."

That was news to Evie.

"There are others. There have always been others. Others no one talks about. The forgotten ones."

Henrietta's voice appeared to drift off into the distance.

"Did you know a twisted ankle caused his mother's death?"

"George Beecham's mother?"

Henrietta nodded.

"Heavens, no, I didn't know."

Henrietta nodded. "She was full of life. *Joie de vivre.* Always fleeting from place to place. One day, she rushed down the stairs in a new pair of shoes and that's when she twisted her ankle. Then, her toe became infected, and the infection got into her blood-stream. She lost a leg but not her love of life. She was wheeled about all over the place and even hosted a ball within a week of losing her leg. Then, a moment of carelessness ended it all. I believe a main artery opened and they couldn't stop the bleeding. In the end, she bled to death. Gone. In the prime of her life. George must have been eight years old. Everyone thought his father would remarry in no time. He was a handsome man. Instead, he climbed the turret to release his despair to the heavens, lost his footing and fell to his death."

Evie thought Henrietta would say grief had been his undoing.

"He was mad. A lunatic. He probably imagined seeing

her spirit wafting away and tried to catch it only to fall to his death."

"I'm sure he was sick with grief. Surely, we can't judge someone for loving too much."

"His mother spent the last years of her life in a lunatic asylum. She wasn't alone. Her sister was already there. Not a single generation has been spared. They all end the same way. Quite mad."

"Including George?"

"Did you ever think of him as normal?" Henrietta shook her head. "Everyone welcomed him into their homes. But the moment he set his sights on one of their daughters, measures were taken. The daughters were usually sent away, just long enough for George to move on." Shrugging, Henrietta murmured, "Perhaps it all happened for the best." Henrietta looked out the window in silence. After a long moment, she said, "All that talking has made me thirsty." She stood up and headed for the door. "Coming?"

Evie gave a slow nod and followed her out.

"Is the detective still trying to claw his way to the truth?"

"I think he's nearly finished interviewing the servants. At least, he's being thorough and appearing to leave no stone unturned."

"And yet he did not visit the chapel when he first arrived. That strikes me as odd. Do you think he's squeamish? Yes, he must be."

They met Toodles rushing out of her room.

"Someone is on a mission." Henrietta chortled. "I know that look. I believe she is about to storm the kitchen. She is determined to have a chocolate cake for your wedding."

"Grans?"

"Not now, Birdie. I'm focused."

"See?" Henrietta whispered. "She will not be deterred."

Toodles hurried past them and down the stairs.

"You know there is only one way to stop her, but we can't possibly trip her up. We'd be up on a charge of murder."

"I suppose I should go after her and make sure she doesn't give Mrs. Horace heart palpitations."

"I'd go with you, but I've already come down one set of stairs."

Henrietta made her way to the drawing room while Evie followed Toodles.

Halfway down the stairs leading to the kitchen, she saw Edgar about to make his way up. He waited for them to reach the bottom, before saying, "My lady. Lotte Mannering has just telephoned. She said she will telephone again in ten minutes." He gestured toward his office.

"Don't mind me, Birdie. You go ahead and wait for the telephone call, and I will attend to my business."

Evie thought she heard Mrs. Horace groan. "She must have heard Toodles." Hurrying after her, she reached the door to the kitchen just as Mrs. Horace was clutching her heart.

"I'm not falling for that trick again, Mrs. Horace. It's a simple cake recipe and I fail to see why you are being so stubborn. And don't tell me you don't have all the ingredients. This kitchen is a veritable cornucopia. Where's the store cupboard? Would someone please point me in the direction of the store cupboard. I will bake the cake myself."

Mrs. Horace tipped her head back and groaned. "This is it. I'm about to draw my last breath. Someone please fetch the vicar. I wish to make my peace."

Evie gave Mrs. Horace an apologetic smile. Turning, she saw Toodles standing by an open door, her hands on her hips.

"See? It's overflowing with ingredients."

Before anyone could stop her, Toodles had loaded her arms with all the ingredients she needed.

"There's even brandied cherries." Toodles looked about her and found a young girl staring at her. "You look like a kitchen maid. Help me with these and get some mixing bowls and spoons and... anything you think I might need to whip this cake into shape."

The young kitchen maid bobbed a curtsy and hurried to assist Toodles.

"Grans."

"Not now, Birdie. We're baking a cake."

"Grans. The kitchen is about to become busy with the evening meal. And... and afternoon tea. See, they have the cakes out and the kettle is about to boil."

"This is a big kitchen, Birdie. There is room for everyone."

Evie sidled up to her and lowered her voice to a hard whisper. "Granny! Stop this right this instant. You are interfering with the schedule. Anyway, if you bake a chocolate cake now, it won't be any good for the wedding. It's too early. That's why they bake the fruitcake."

Toodles growled. "I taught you to be reasonable and now you're using it against me. How could you?"

"You know I'm right."

Toodles glowered at Mrs. Horace. "Why won't she bake me the cake?"

"Did you ask nicely?"

"Of course, I did. I mean... I'm sure I did."

"Toodles. Put down the flour."

Evie gave the young kitchen maid an encouraging nod. She took the container of flour and sugar from Toodles and backed away.

"Now, Toodles. Come along."

Mrs. Horace fanned herself with one hand and with the other hand continued to clutch her chest.

"You know she's faking it," Toodles muttered.

Edgar cleared his throat. "Lotte Mannering is on the telephone, my lady."

Thanking him, Evie guided Toodles away from the kitchen with a promise that they would come back when the time was right.

"I hope you realize you are treating me like a child."

"Yes, and I'm afraid it's a sign of worse things to come."

Toodles shook her head. "I refuse to allow a simple request to be turned into an act of petulance."

"I think you are both being quite stubborn. We shall have to find a middle ground, but not today."

Toodles made her way up the stairs with Edgar following, possibly to make sure she didn't sneak back downstairs. While Evie hurried to take the telephone call.

"Lotte! Have you found something?" Evie listened with interest and tried to remember everything Lotte revealed to her.

They had confirmation. George Beecham had been staying at *The Ritz* and he had left the very day they had left.

"We knew he had been living in India," Evie said. "One of the guests, Augustus Warwick confirmed it." When Evie asked if she would try to come to Halton House earlier than planned, Lotte suggested she might be of more value if she stayed in London a while longer.

Lotte asked her about the guests and Evie provided her with the names of the three men. Brushing a finger along her brow, she added, "Nell Joy. She's a reporter. And Davina Beecham-Parks. She's been traveling in Egypt."

Lotte promised to telephone as soon as she found anything of interest. Disconnecting the call, Evie took a moment to process the information.

She was about to turn away when she noticed a row of keys hanging on hooks. Halton House was large, and she imagined there were dozens of keys, as well as duplicates.

She had no idea why she'd noticed them.

Turning toward the door, she headed for the stairs and then it came to her.

"Heavens. Why didn't I think of it before?"

Had anyone noticed?

She hurried up the stairs and rushed through the hall looking for Tom. Remembering she'd left him outside, she walked out into the sunshine and searched for him.

The conservatory

Millicent pointed toward the folly. "Mr. Winchester, I think her ladyship might be looking for you."

Caro went to stand at the window. "Yes, she's definitely looking about her. You should go to her."

"Or," Millicent said, "we could all wave our arms, jump up and down and call out to her. She's bound to notice the way one notices things out of the corner of one's eye."

"There's madness in Millicent's reasoning or reasoning in her madness." Caro shrugged. "I can't decide which."

Tom watched as Millicent and Caro coordinated themselves into jumping, waving their arms whilst calling out to Evie.

To his utter astonishment, Evie turned toward the house and looked directly at the conservatory. She gave a firm nod and headed toward them.

"See, it worked," Millicent declared. "She's coming."

Tom had no words.

He simply stood watching Evie hurrying toward them, her face bright with excitement.

"Her ladyship must have thought of something and now she's eager to tell us and we're all going to feel like dullards for not noticing."

"Not noticing what?" Caro asked.

"Whatever she's about to reveal to us. She's always saying that we look but don't always see. Although Edgar excels at doing both. He always notices when someone has swept the dust under the carpet instead of into a dustpan. Nothing ever escapes him."

Tom saw Evie stop at the French door leading to the conservatory, almost as if she wanted to get her thoughts in order.

"She might want you to open the door for her, Mr. Winchester."

Tom hurried forward just as Evie drew in a breath, nodded, and opened the door.

"Here you all are."

"Milady, I'm sure Mr. Winchester meant to open the door for you, but you were too quick."

Evie nodded and gave them a brilliant smile. "The iron gate to the crypt."

They all looked at each other. Millicent shrugged. "It's well-oiled. I know that because one of the stable boys goes around oiling all the doors."

"Yes, but that's not what I'm thinking, Millicent. The gate was open."

Again, they all nodded.

"Open," Evie exclaimed. "Unlocked. It's always kept locked, and that means there is a key somewhere. Or maybe two keys." She looked away. "Oh, I should have asked Edgar but I'm sure he would have confirmed it. He must have a key for the gate and there's probably another one in the chapel somewhere and maybe Mrs. Arnold has one too. She has lots of keys."

They all nodded.

"So why was the gate unlocked? Who unlocked it? Did the killer unlock it? How did the killer get the keys?"

Tom brushed his hand across his chin. "We've already decided the killer is right here. This confirms it."

"George must have made his way inside the house and retrieved the key."

Millicent looked confused. "In the dead of night? How did he gain access to the house?"

"He knew the house inside and out," Evie said. Looking at Tom, she frowned. "You don't look convinced."

"We've been assuming George Beecham was lured here, presumably by you. It would make sense for you to have unlocked the gate. Or, rather, the person pretending to be you. The one who'd been sending all those letters to George, pretending to be you."

Evie gaped. "You're right."

Davina Beecham-Parks.

Gill Moore.

Augustus Warwick.

Clyde Russell.

Tom's jaw clenched. "Darn it! That means it couldn't be Nell Joy. She's never set foot inside this house."

"Miss Joy will be relieved to hear that," Millicent said. "She's no longer a suspect."

Evie swung away from them and faced the park. Clyde Russell was the least likely suspect. They knew Augustus had met George in India. He claimed it had been by accident. Then there was Gill Moore. What had he been saying to Davina when he'd met her in the park earlier? Had they been having clandestine meetings all along?

"Are you going to let the detective know?" Caro asked.

"Yes, of course."

Millicent whispered, "Her ladyship is not rushing off to tell him."

Hearing her, Evie said, "I'll mention it during dinner."

Tom nodded.

Caro beamed. "Splendid idea. That way, we get to watch people's reactions."

Turning, Evie saw Millicent's downcast expression. "I believe my cousin, twice removed, has just arrived and will be joining us for dinner."

Millicent's eyes rose incrementally. She mouthed, "Me?"

Caro wove her arm through Millicent's. "Come along, I'll talk you through it. You know I played the role. We'll have to find you something suitable to wear."

"Me?" Millicent repeated.

"Yes, you. Now, stop being a dullard. You'll need your wits about you and, take my advice, the less you say the better. Just smile and nod. We could explain your silence by saying you've lost your voice. Yes, you're suffering from a bout of laryngitis. Yes, that's a perfect plan. You'll be Evie's cousin, twice removed. That's rather a privilege. I was thrice removed. We'll need to come up with a name for you." Caro turned to Evie. "Is she an English cousin or an American cousin?"

Millicent found her voice and piped in, "Oh, may I be American? Someone transplanted from England. Perhaps I could be a relative from an Irish arm of the family."

"We'll work out the details," Caro said. "Just don't bring in any pirates. We can't have you swept off by a pirate and shipwrecked off the coast of Maine. That would sound too ludicrous."

Left alone with Tom, Evie sighed.

"By now, the killer will be thinking they got away with it. What are the chances they'll react to me saying the killer is someone familiar with the house?"

"Someone is bound to show more interest or an unusual reaction." Tom pushed out a breath.

"What? Oh, are you about to tell me this proves nothing? Because, of course, you'd be right. However, I believe there is a strong argument in favor of one of the guests being responsible for unlocking the iron gate. Remember, they were all here. In fact, we can now dismiss the idea of an intruder. They wouldn't know where to look for the key." Evie's cheeks flooded with heat.

Tom grinned. "You've just thought of something. And you probably don't want to say what it is."

Looking askance, she murmured, "The vicar. He's the only other person who would have known where to find the key. Tom, we can't possibly suspect our new vicar. We only just got him. At this rate, we will be banned from ever having another vicar."

CHAPTER 12

Unlocked secrets

Later that evening

At the sound of a knock at her door, Evie turned.

"Should I answer it, milady?" Clare asked.

The door opened.

"No need, Clare."

Caro walked in. Smiling, she made a sweeping gesture with her hand and Millicent followed her inside. "Ta-da." Caro closed the door and laughed. "May I present to you Millicent, your cousin twice removed. We decided she should remain Millicent to avoid confusion. That decision was reached after we realized it wouldn't be as confusing to refer to her as Millicent, even when she was… is Millicent."

"Yes, of course. It makes perfect sense, but why are you dressed in black, Millicent? Couldn't you find something more cheerful to wear?"

Millicent looked at Caro who answered on her behalf. "Millicent is in mourning. She wanted to wear a veil, but I managed to talk her out of it. Anyhow, she thought being in mourning would justify her silence."

"And is she practicing now?" Evie asked.

Millicent spoke in a harsh whisper, "Laryngitis."

"Yes, of course."

"We've consulted with the dowagers and Toodles, who suggested Millicent had been staying in her apartment at the *Dakota*. At first, Millicent thought she would need to make up stories about the wilderness and riding horses but then Toodles explained it was only the name of the building and not the location."

"So, Cousin Millicent has been living in New York and originally hails from…"

"Ireland," Caro said.

"Is Millicent not going to talk at all?" Evie asked.

"We thought it best to keep it to a minimum, starting now."

Frowning, Evie asked, "And whom is she in mourning for?"

Millicent grinned. "My aunt Eugenia. We were very close. But you don't need to worry, she was not related to you."

Caro nudged her. "Laryngitis, Millicent. No talking."

"Well," Evie sighed.

"Oh, dear. I know that sigh," Caro said. "You're having second thoughts."

"Yes, unfortunately. I'm just not sure where it will all lead to. I don't mean you, Millicent. Perhaps we should just sit down to dinner and not even think of the lasts twenty-four hours. This could all backfire on me."

"But it's the whole purpose of the evening." Caro insisted she had to make the best of the information she had and see who reacted to the news of the unlocked gate.

Although still reluctant, Evie agreed to go through with it.

Checking her reflection to make sure everything was in order, she gestured to the door. "Shall we?"

They made their way down to the drawing room. The dowagers and Toodles were chatting with Gill and Clyde, while Augustus and Tom sat with Nell Joy and Davina.

"Everyone, I'd like you all to meet my cousin who's just arrived from America. This is Millicent. As excited as she is to be here, she is recovering from a bout of laryngitis."

If anyone recognized the real Millicent, they did not say.

Tom excused himself from the group and approached them. "Millicent, what a pleasure it is to finally meet you. Evie has told me so much about you." Lowering his voice, he looked at Evie and asked, "Are you going to wait for the right time?"

"Is there such a thing?" Evie wondered. Once she mentioned the unlocked gate and the fact the keys could only be procured from inside the house, everyone would finally realize there was a killer among them.

The detective entered.

"He came prepared," Tom murmured.

Evie glanced at him and saw that, like all the gentlemen, he was dressed in tails.

Tom added, "I'm guessing he knew he'd be invited to stay here for the duration." He looked at the detective for a moment. "He's clean-shaven and quite proper. A perfect disguise, don't you think?"

"Heavens, are you about to point the finger of suspicion his way?"

"It would make his career. Think about it. He sets you up as the killer, comes here to investigate the case, solves it by unmasking you. You're sentenced to hang, and he becomes an overnight sensation."

Evie's fingers pressed against her throat. "Is that your way of saying ambition can lead to a life of crime? If he has framed me, then it means he killed George Beecham."

Millicent's eyes brightened and she whispered, "We have a new motive. Ambition."

Caro murmured, "Imagine killing people just so you can get a promotion and have a bigger office space."

Tom cocked an eyebrow. "Nothing is beyond the realm of possibilities."

"Heavens, I'm glad there's a lock on my door. The most expedient way to success would be to kill me and make it look like suicide."

They all focused on the detective and followed his progress around the room.

"Drink?" Tom offered. "I'll pour it myself so you can be sure it won't be poisoned."

Evie gave him a nervous smile. "How very reassuring."

Millicent cleared her throat. "I believe I am recovering and might be able to speak, after all. It seems sensible to prepare for any and all outcomes. I wish to be able to scream without drawing attention to the fact that I'd lost my voice."

Edgar walked in and gave Evie a nod. Seeing Millicent, he stilled for a fraction of a second, and then appeared to sigh with resignation.

"Everyone, shall we go through to the dining room?"

Evie led them through with Tom following by her side, saying, "I know it's not fashionable, but I am not leaving your side tonight."

"Because the moment I mention the unlocked gate, the killer will assume they are cornered and do something extraordinarily silly?"

"Too late to remove the knives from the table," he said. "In your place, I'd sit as far away as possible from the carving knife."

Murmured conversations rose and fell. Unlike other dinners, no one felt compelled to draw attention to themselves or bring up a particular subject of conversation. The tone would remain subdued until someone forgot the circumstances surrounding them. Or until Evie decided to make her revelation.

Without realizing it, Evie sat surrounded by those she knew she could trust.

Davina surprised everyone present by asking, "Does anyone get away with murder these days?"

The detective studied her for a moment. "Not for very long. The advances in criminology these days means we are better equipped than we have ever been. Detection has become a science and those of us in the profession make a study of it, becoming more proficient with each case we solve."

"And less proficient with those cases you don't solve?" Henrietta asked.

"All cases are inevitably solved, my lady. Crime does not pay."

"And yet there is a constant demand for an increase in police presence." Henrietta chortled. "Isn't there a risk of the police stimulating the increase of crime in order to gain job security?"

"Heavens, Henrietta, you've come down with a bad case of cynicism."

"It's merely an observation. I'm more interested to know what happens when the detective fails to find a single reliable witness, one with good hearing."

"I suppose you are referring to the gunshot no one heard."

"Yes. What is your explanation for that?"

"From what I understand, you all enjoyed the evening."

"Are you suggesting we all fell into our beds in a drunken stupor?"

"We did have a late night," Sara reminded her. "The house is massively large, and the walls are thick and paneled, and some of us sleep with pillows over our heads."

The murmured conversations resumed, the main course was served, and Millicent chose that moment to find her voice and say, "Cousin Evie made an interesting observation. She was telling me about the case and remarked on the fact the iron gate leading to the crypt was always kept locked."

Everyone fell silent.

The detective stilled.

Millicent reached for her glass and took a quick sip of

wine. Followed by another, before saying, "I thought it was an interesting observation." She looked around the table. "It suggests the killer knew how to open the iron gate."

"The killer or George Beecham," Clyde said.

Gill nodded. "He was certainly familiar with the layout of the house."

Evie reached for her glass. Before taking a drink, she said, "The house is locked up at night." That's when she realized the key must have been removed before everyone had retired for the evening.

George Beecham had not broken into the house to get the keys.

The killer had simply availed himself of the keys sometime during the day or even the evening.

Lifting the glass to her lips, she realized she hadn't taken the time to observe her guests' reactions.

Davina set her fork down and tilted her head in thought. "So someone intent on killing George came into the house, removed the key to the gate, made their way to the chapel, unlocked the gate and, presumably, returned the key."

Evie looked up and searched for Edgar. He must have read her mind because he shook his head as if to indicate all keys were accounted for.

Davina looked around the table. "I suppose in a large house such as this one, it's possible to miss someone walking in. Most times, we're all together in one room or another."

Evie had been convinced they had already dismissed the idea of an intruder. An outsider had always been preferable to the killer being someone she knew, but it hadn't made sense. Now, she wasn't so sure.

The detective cleared his throat. "Be that as it may, the fact remains, the iron gate had been unlocked when it should have been locked. This is something that escaped my notice."

Henrietta smiled at him. "Heavens, that's an embarrassing admission to make. Your honesty does you credit."

The subject of the unlocked gate remained the topic of conversation throughout the evening.

When Evie retired to her room, Millicent rushed in to help her prepare for bed. "I'm sorry I'm late, milady. I had to step out of my alter ego and into my regular self."

"Millicent, you are to be commended. If you hadn't brought up the subject of the keys, I doubt I would have had the courage. I'd been tossing it about in my mind, waiting for the right moment. I should have realized there was never going to be a right moment. It had to be created. You obviously saw the opportunity and you grabbed it."

Millicent's cheeks colored. "I simply blurted it out, milady. And, if you recall, I wasn't supposed to talk. I wonder if anyone noticed my swift recovery? There was no mention of it."

"That's because you created the perfect diversion, Millicent. Everyone focused on the unlocked iron gate."

"Yes. Unfortunately, I was so carried away with my performance, I forgot to observe people's reactions."

"Me too."

CHAPTER 13

The next day

The detective adjusted his tie, inspected the splendid shine on his freshly polished shoes, and made his way out of his room. Nearing the staircase, he heard a scratching sound approaching at rapid speed.

He looked over his shoulder and saw the wretched dog hurtling toward him. The detective stepped to one side and looked toward the other end of the hallway. He thought he saw someone duck inside a room, but he couldn't be sure.

Swinging away, he hurried along the hallway, but the dog caught up with him and lunged for his foot with a surprisingly ferocious growl.

"Stop that. Stop that. Get away." The detective tried to remember the commands the dowager had employed. "Holmes, you naughty boy."

The dining room

Making her way down to breakfast, Evie entered the dining room and found the detective and Tom deep in conversation.

At the sound of her entrance, the detective sprung back and appeared to brace himself.

"Good morning." She went to the sideboard to make her selection and greeted Edgar. Smiling at him, she whispered, "Are we all accounted for?"

"I believe so, my lady."

Evie selected some scrambled eggs and, as she turned, was astonished to find Henrietta entering the morning room, her face brimming with joy.

"Henrietta! What are you doing up and about so early?"

"Today promised to be an entertaining day and, so far, it has paid dividends."

As soon as the door closed behind Henrietta, it opened again, and a footman entered carrying a tray. He was followed by the sound of scuttling, little feet.

"Holmes!" Evie exclaimed. "What are you doing here?"

The detective shot to his feet and, shielding himself with his napkin, jumped back.

When Evie saw Holmes make a mad dash for the detective, she tried to stop him, "Holmes. What's come over you?"

Smiling, Henrietta said, "He seems to have transferred his affections to the detective."

Evie hurried to set her plate down and grab Holmes before he could do some serious damage to the detective's shoe. He had already latched on to the laces and it took some effort to separate him from his bounty. "I do apologize. I have no idea what's come over him. He's usually so well behaved."

"No need to apologize, my lady." He gave a nervous chuckle. "Dogs will be dogs."

Evie took him out to the hall and, wagging her finger at him, sent him on his way.

When she returned to the dining room, she found Gill and Augustus seated at the table. "Where did you two come from?"

"We were outside, taking in the fresh air, then came in through the French doors."

She noticed they were both hiding their smiles. No doubt they had witnessed the scene between the detective and Holmes.

"Glad to see we survived the night," Gill remarked, only to say, "I hope that's not in bad taste. Or, heaven forbid, tempting fate."

Evie glanced up at the clock. She assumed the detective would sit down with Davina. Then, it would be her turn.

She ate her breakfast without paying much attention to it. Halfway through her scrambled eggs, Clyde walked in.

"Who here is willing to admit to locking their doors last night?" he asked as he helped himself to a full breakfast.

"Certainly not me," Henrietta declared. "In fact, I was

almost tempted to leave the door ajar as an open invitation."

Clyde set his plate down next to her and said, "I imagine you didn't get any sleep last night, Lady Henrietta."

"On the contrary." Henrietta grinned and looked straight at the detective. "I slept the sleep of the innocent."

∾

The library

"Is there anything else you wish to add, Mrs. Beecham-Parks?"

Davina looked down at her hands. Shrugging, she dug inside her pocket and produced a piece of paper. "Yes, there is something I wish to show you. I wasn't sure about it, because… Well, as you know, I suffered a severe shock, and I didn't know whom I could trust."

"What is it?"

"I found this is my cousin's hand. He was clutching it. When I removed it, a piece tore off." She searched inside her pocket and produced a small piece of paper.

The detective took both pieces and examined them. "I'll meet you," he read and turned the larger piece of paper over.

Davina gave a stiff nod. "There's only bit of writing and the rest has been torn off. I assume the killer tried to take it and encountered the same problem I did. The page tore off. They'd just killed someone so they must have been in a hurry to escape."

The shrill sound of the telephone ringing startled them.

Henry Evans stood up and hurried toward the desk.

As he took the call, the detective said, "You should have handed this to us earlier. I won't press the issue because I understand you've been in a state of shock, but this is vital information." He thanked her and concluded the interview.

Davina stood up and left.

Shaking his head, the detective studied the piece of paper. When Henry Evans ended the call, the detective said, "We should be able to match the handwriting."

Nodding, Henry said, "The forensics results have come in. The bullet did not go through him. It was still inside him." Henry slipped his hands inside his pockets and looked down at his shoes.

"What's the explanation?" the detective asked.

"The bullet lodged in the wall matches the bullet in the body."

"The killer missed the shot?"

Henry nodded. "Not only that. As it is, there were two shots. It was bad enough when we didn't hear one shot."

Nodding, the detective handed him the piece of paper. "What do you make of this?"

Henry read it. "'I'll meet you. He'd been expecting someone. But where's the rest?"

"Davina suggested the killer might have snatched it and that's when the paper tore."

"And the killer would have been in a hurry to flee so they left this behind?" Henry Evans frowned. He recognized the paper.

"What is it?"

"This paper looks familiar. The color, the texture… It's from *The Ritz*." And he knew of two other people who'd recently stayed there.

"What about the handwriting? Does that look familiar?"

It didn't. "No, but handwriting can be altered."

The detective leaned back and closed his eyes. "I understand she might still be in shock but it's no excuse. She should have handed that over as soon as she found it." He shook his head. "Then there's the unlocked iron gate leading to the crypt. That kept me awake half the night."

"I've spoken with the butler. He says there are several sets of keys," Henry said. "One of them is kept in the vestry. That door is locked and the only person who has the key is the vicar."

"Are we going to suspect the vicar?"

"No. He's a recent arrival and can account for all his movements."

"So you've spoken with him."

"I spoke with the verger. He keeps track of the vicar's every move. As I said, he's new here and, since his arrival, he's been kept very busy." Henry set the piece of paper down on the table. "There's one more person to interview." Henry stepped out of the library and went in search of Lady Woodridge.

He found her in the conservatory, sitting with Caro, Millicent, and Tom. Before escorting her to the library, he told them about the bullets.

"There were two shots," Evie said. "But how can that be? It was bad enough when we didn't hear one shot."

The library

"Lady Woodridge. When was the last time you were in London?"

"Just recently. Tom and I stayed at *The Ritz*. When Tom showed me the photograph of us dancing and I noticed George Beecham looking straight at me, I couldn't stop thinking about all those days we stayed there and how I didn't notice his presence." When she finished her explanation, she realized she'd probably said too much.

Yes and no answers, Evie told herself.

"And before that?"

"What do you mean?"

"Did you go to town by yourself?"

Evie searched her mind. "Oh, yes, I did. I had to tie some loose ends."

"What sort of *loose ends.*"

Evie didn't care for the emphasis he placed on those two words. "The last few months had been rather busy, and I'd had to cancel several appointments. They needed to be rescheduled." She stopped and thought she could have phrased her response better.

"You went alone."

"Yes."

"Is that usual?"

"No."

"Why did you go alone?"

"Because I had appointments to keep, and they were rather tedious. I felt it would be more expedient if I went alone."

"Expedient. You didn't wish to waste time?"

"I didn't wish to subject Tom to a dull time waiting for me."

"Did you meet anyone?"

"My dentist. I was not happy to see him. The sound of his drill gives me nightmares."

"So your appointments were of a professional nature."

"Yes."

"On these occasions that you traveled to town by yourself, did you stay at The Ritz?"

"I did."

"But you own a house in town."

"I do."

"Why didn't you stay there?"

"It was easier to stay in a hotel."

"Easier? In what way?"

"These were overnight stays, and I didn't want to bother the servants. They have to make the bed and rush about opening rooms that are not in use while we're in the country." Evie looked down at her hands. She only now realized George Beecham had been staying at The Ritz during those two trips to town.

"Lady Woodridge, do you own a revolver?"

"Yes."

"And when was the last time you fired it?"

"Several months ago. I couldn't really say exactly when. I was practicing."

"Target practice?"

"Yes."

"Lady Woodridge, would you kindly surrender your weapon."

"Certainly." She turned to Henry Evans. "Would you please pull the bell cord?"

Henry Evans blinked and looked at the detective, his eyes slightly wide.

He stood up and walked to the fireplace, pulled the bell cord, and turned to face Evie.

Evie suspected he wanted to say something, but no words came out. Returning to his chair, he sat down. After a moment of reflection, he turned to the detective. "I really fail to see what possible reason you might have for thinking Lady Woodridge is in any way responsible for the death of George Beecham."

Edgar walked in.

"Ah, Edgar. Would you ask Millicent to fetch my revolver, please. It's on the bedside table, inside the Japanese lacquered box. She knows where to find it."

"Certainly, my lady." He turned and stopped to ask, "Would anyone care for some tea."

No one did. Although, Evie thought Henry Evans could do with a brandy.

Moments later, Edgar returned. At a signal from Evie, he handed the revolver to the detective.

He lifted it to his nose and sniffed it.

Looking up, he stared at Evie. "You said you'd fired this several months ago."

"Yes."

The detective handed the revolver to Henry. He hesitated and then lifted the revolver and sniffed it.

"Lady Woodridge. This revolver has recently been fired."

CHAPTER 14

Moment of truth

The library

*E*vie heard the thump of her heart punching against her chest.

"Lady Woodridge, you mentioned receiving an envelope packed full of letters."

Evie nodded.

"Would you kindly hand them over?"

Evie managed to shake her head.

"No?"

"No?"

She was staring straight ahead and saw the detective exchange a look with Henry that spoke of confusion.

"Why not?"

She pushed out the words. "I don't have them."

"Evie?" Henry's voice sounded incredulous.

"Someone took them," she said. "One moment they were in my room and then they weren't."

She heard a commotion outside the library. The hurried steps seemed to be going around in circles.

Suddenly, the door to the library opened and Tom walked in, followed by Edgar.

Out of the corner of her eye, she saw Tom glaring at the detective, then his gaze dropped to the revolver.

Evie closed her eyes and drew in a deep breath. A part of her wanted to picture what would happen next. But she refused to allow images of her being arrested to take shape in her mind. It simply couldn't happen.

Instead, she tried to focus on something amusing.

Evie thought of Henrietta and Sara, dressed in their elegant gowns, and bantering like children.

That put a smile on her face. She tried harder and focused on remembering a witty exchange. Instead, she recalled something Sara had said. Something about Halton House being massive and the walls thick and paneled.

"Tom?"

"Yes, I'm right here."

"Do you have your revolver?"

Tom cleared his throat. "Yes."

"Tom, would you be a dear and go down to the crypt?"

"You want me to—"

"Go to the crypt and fire a bullet straight at the wall."

Evie opened her eyes. When she saw Tom walk out of the library, she closed her eyes again and pictured him walking to the chapel. She imagined his pace would be steady and determined.

Along the way, she thought he might slow down as he suddenly understood what she wanted him to do.

Then his pace would pick up again.

Evie smiled.

She saw him entering the chapel and making his way to the crypt.

And, she thought, right about now he would fire his weapon.

The clock on the mantle struck the hour then the room fell silent.

Evie listened. Then she strained to hear.

The silence remained undisturbed.

A moment passed and was followed by another moment.

She pictured Tom returning. A few seconds later, she heard his footsteps and then he was standing beside her again.

For the longest moment, no one spoke. Then Tom said, "Henry. If you go to the chapel, you'll find a bullet lodged in the wall, right next to the one you saw."

The detective surged to his feet. "I'll go."

Evie had never been good at waiting. But she had no option.

Finally, the detective returned. She saw him nod.

"We didn't hear it," Henry said.

"The walls in the chapel are as thick as the walls at Halton House," Evie said. "Of course, that doesn't really prove my innocence."

The telephone rang.

"But that might. I'm guessing that's Lotte Mannering with vital information."

"It had better be," Tom growled.

~

The drawing room

Evie reminded herself to thank her lucky stars. If Lotte Mannering hadn't telephoned... Well, she might have come up with another idea.

"Millicent, would you please read the first note you made?" No one mentioned the fact Millicent bore a striking resemblance to her cousin, Millicent.

Digging inside her pocket, Millicent produced her little notebook and read, "Motive. Who stands to gain by George Beecham's death." She read the following lines to herself and smiled. "You thought it was the right place to start."

"Did you make a note of what you then said?" Evie asked.

"Of course. Considering how much I can prattle on, sometimes, it's useful to jot things down because I might discover some sense amongst all the twaddle. Let me see... Here it is, I then said, that could take us in many directions."

Evie nodded. "I think that was the killer's intention. Because the obvious suspect would be the person who stood to inherit. Isn't that right, Millicent?"

Referring to her notes, Millicent nodded. "Yes, that's exactly what I said."

Evie looked at Henry Evans. "Lord Evans investigated such a case recently. All eyes had been on the person who stood to inherit." She looked at Davina. She sat staring at her glass of brandy. The Egyptian motifs on her dress were repeated on the scarf she wore wrapped decorously around her neck and shoulders. She had recovered from her initial shock and now sat, much as one would in a smart gathering, looking both intrigued and utterly bored.

Detective Inspector Holmes stood to one side observing everyone present. To Evie's surprise, he had not interrupted, nor had he objected to her speaking.

"There were a couple of people who stood to gain by George Beecham's death, myself included. There were also a few people we imagined might benefit but we dissuaded ourselves from believing it." That piqued everyone's interest. She saw several people shift and exchange glances. "I've always claimed I'd been introduced to him by my husband, Nicholas. In fact, I had met George during my first few days in London. Davina introduced him to me. It had been a chance encounter, which then kept recurring."

Henrietta's lips pursed and her gaze sharpened.

"It seemed easier to dismiss those early encounters because I didn't wish to explain how my natural instinct urged me to turn away from him."

Henrietta's lips now moved. Caro sat next to her and leaned in as if to hear what she was saying. But Henrietta shook her head, dismissing the need to speak up.

"It should have been obvious from the start. The killer would be the person who stood to inherit. For various reasons, far too many to name, we focused on other possibilities. In the end, we agreed that George Beecham had been lured here, but the trap was set a long time ago." Evie turned and looked at Henrietta. For once, the dowager sat in silence, her expression suggesting she was lost in thought. Evie was not fooled. Henrietta had been following the conversation, even as she entertained her own reminiscences.

Evie continued, "Lotte Mannering has been instrumental in sourcing some valuable information, but more on that later." She looked around the room before saying, "If you return to Halton House sometime in the distant future, the house will still be here with all its fine furnishings and paintings, but you will be much altered." Evie looked at Davina. "Is that how you put it?"

To her surprise, Davina nodded.

Madness ran in George Beecham's family. He had been a strange man, much like his father and others in his family. Including his father's sister.

Davina's mother.

"You travelled extensively over the years. Not just to France and Egypt."

Davina smiled. "India in the monsoon season can be magical. Here we have rain and cold. There, it's rain and heat. I could have sat on the veranda listening to the rain falling all day long." Davina spoke in a dreamy tone. "Every time I left, George wanted to return with me, but I would tell him you weren't ready for him yet. That's how I kept him away. And then he wouldn't stay away. When he came, he found the letters I'd promised to forward to you. That made him angry." Davina looked at Evie. "He should not have sent them to you. I had to come and retrieve them. I knew it would be risky and it was because George followed me."

Evie found it difficult to hear the rest.

Davina knew she was slipping away, the same way her mother had slipped away into a state of madness. She had been seeing it in her cousin. All these years, she had struggled with keeping him at a distance while being unable to leave him entirely alone.

Turning, Evie walked to the window and gazed out, while Davina continued to recite the many reasons why her hand had been forced.

Evie closed her eyes and saw herself denying the possibility of Davina taking such extreme measures. She had no trouble seeing herself insisting the killer had to be someone else because it couldn't possibly be Davina.

But it was.

She took comfort in knowing that soon Davina might not even remember what she had done. She hoped that day of blissful ignorance came quickly for her.

The Wedding Day

"Stand still, milady. There are a million and one buttons on this gown."

"Yes, I'm sorry about that, Millicent. I don't know what Madam Courbet was thinking, but I'll tell you what I'm thinking and what Tom will think. She is a wicked woman, putting so many buttons in my gown."

"This color is making me crave a sweet."

"It's pale sage."

"Oh, I'm thinking it looks more like mint and I do enjoy a mint sweet, especially when the sun shines. Don't ask me why because I wouldn't know what to say."

There was a knock at the door, prompting Millicent to yelp and call out, "In a minute."

She took two minutes before answering. She had a murmured conversation and returned, saying, "It was

Connie. Lady Henrietta sent her to assure you the day had dawned bright and beautiful and would remain so, according to her one-legged, one-eyed, pipe smoking, uncle... or was it lame, cross-eyed... Never mind. It's a clear blue sky, just as I told you it was when I drew the curtains."

Another knock at the door made Millicent growl. Before she could rush to answer it, the door opened and the dowagers and Toodles walked in.

"Here she is. Glad to see you getting ready to go through with the wedding," Henrietta said.

"What a strange thing to say, Henrietta." Sara shook her head.

"I'm trying to stave off the threat of turning into a dull old woman. Best to be remembered for saying the oddest things than to be forgotten."

"Birdie, you look beautiful."

Henrietta snorted. "Is that the best you can do? She looks radiant. And that's saying a lot, considering what she has recently gone through."

"I hope you're all going to behave during the ceremony."

"We wouldn't dare spoil it for you. The same can't be said for... Well, enough said on the matter. If your parents ate bad oysters, then we shall blame the oysters. Although, why they had to eat oysters when they should have been thinking of making their way to you is beyond comprehension. What were they thinking?" Henrietta looked at Toodles. "Your daughter should have known better than to go around eating oysters that made her sick."

"What can I say? I gave her all the advantages my position could afford, I made sure she was well educated, I brought her up to have her own mind. Eating oysters before her daughter's wedding was always going to be her decision to make."

"I'm only glad they are recovering. Those illnesses can be quite draining." Evie dabbed on some fragrance.

A knock at the door was followed by Clare calling out, "It's me, I'm coming in."

Millicent shook her head. "She might take longer to train, but we'll get there in the end."

Clare walked in and held out an envelope. "It's a letter."

Everyone stilled.

Grumbling, Millicent said, "Don't just say it's a letter. We can see it's a letter. Who sent it?"

"Oh." Clare turned the envelope and read out, "Mr. Winchester."

Henrietta's legs gave way from under her. "He is leaving Evangeline at the altar even before she gets to the church."

Sara and Toodles rushed to assist her with Sara saying, "Smelling salts. We need smelling salts. She's fading fast."

Henrietta peeled an eye open. "No need for smelling salts. One whiff of Toodles' fragrance is enough to revive me or give me a final push to the great beyond. Give me a moment." She drew in a deep breath. "Dear heavens. What is in that fragrance. Sulfur?"

"I do not smell like rotten eggs."

"I think she's recovered," Sara claimed.

"Yes, and I think we might need to arm ourselves with shotguns."

Henrietta blinked. "And round up a posse to hunt down that rascal, Winchester, who has abandoned our dear Evangeline at the last moment?"

Evie took the envelope and walked to the window. Outside, the world looked normal. Despite the histrionics, she knew the letter would only contain an amusing stray thought.

She smiled at the thought of him accepting his wedding gift with good grace. But that wasn't the Tom she knew. Oh, no. He would grumble about the gift, and she'd never hear the end of it.

A valet, Countess?

A valet?

I'm a grown man.

She removed the single sheet of paper and read it.

"Well? What does it say?" Henrietta demanded. "Is he boarding a boat as we speak?"

"He wishes me a good morning." Reading the rest, Evie sighed. Her shoulders lowered and she looked up.

"Toodles, stand closer to me. I believe I will need reviving again."

Evie cleared her throat. "This is certainly unexpected."

"She's going to draw this out. Just give us the blow now, Evangeline. We'll worry about the consequences to my health afterward."

Evie turned to face them. "Tom says I should retain the title of Lady Woodridge."

"Good heavens," they all exclaimed, with Toodles adding, "He's gone and done a runner."

Evie waited for them to settle down. "He says that as chatelaine of this house, I should remain Lady Woodridge, at least until Seth comes of age." Shrugging, she added, "He wants to avoid confusion. Later, if I wish it, I can become Lady Winchester."

Henrietta pressed her hand to her chest. "You may step

away Toodles. We should have known better than to lose our trust in Tom."

Clare sniffed and murmured, "That is so romantic." In the next breath, she yelped. "Oh, there is something else."

Evie turned the page.

Yes, there was something else. But not in the letter.

Clare dug inside her pocket and produced a small velvet box. She handed it to Evie and stepped back.

Opening it, Evie said, "This arrived yesterday. It's from his mother who apologizes for not being able to be here."

She removed a pendant.

"He says I must surely have something old, and something new, something borrowed, but if I don't have something blue, it would give him great pleasure if I wore this sapphire pendant."

"The man has hidden talents," Henrietta mused. "Not least of which is the ability to nearly send me to an early grave."

"Early?" Toodles chortled.

"Does he actually say he will see you soon?" Sara asked.

An alarming knock sounded at the door. It opened and Caro rushed in. "Henry…" She struggled to catch her breath. "Henry says"

Henrietta groaned. "Toodles. Your sulfuric scent is needed."

Looking confused, Caro said, "Henry says to tell you they are on their way to the church. And that Tom wishes you to break tradition and arrive on time."

Fanning herself, Henrietta said, "A short while ago, when we walked in, everything looked to be proceeding as normal. Now, I'm not so sure."

Toodles reached inside her beaded handbag and withdrew a flask. "Here, keep this handy."

"That's just what we don't need," Sara warned. "Two sips of brandy and Henrietta is likely to become rowdy."

Taking the pendant, Millicent put it on and stepped back. "It's perfect." Millicent turned to the others.

That seemed to be enough for everyone to shift and move toward the door.

"I'll be along shortly," Evie called out.

"Fine, but don't keep Edgar waiting too long," Millicent warned. "He still can't believe he gets to walk you down the aisle."

Evie took a moment to thank her lucky stars. In a moment, she would be driven to the village church. After the ceremony, she and Tom would ride in an open carriage along the cobbled street and the villagers would cheer and wish them well. She hadn't seen the decorations, but she knew they would be splendid. Then everyone would enjoy a breakfast, including two types of wedding cake. There would be the traditional fare and Toodles' favorite chocolate cake. Then, she and Tom would set off into the sunset in search of more adventures.

Before anyone could sigh and reminisce, they would do it all over again. A repeat performance for his relatives who would be visiting at the same time as Seth, the young Earl of Woodridge, and of course, her parents, who would have recovered by then.

One wedding at a time, she thought and made her way down and onward to her bright new future.

***

Printed in Great Britain
by Amazon

37494282R00116

BRITISH ENGLISH

ENGLISH LATVIAN

THEME-BASED DICTIONARY

Contains over 3000 commonly used words

Theme-based dictionary British English-Latvian - 3000 words
British English collection

By Andrey Taranov

T&P Books vocabularies are intended for helping you learn, memorize and review foreign words. The dictionary is divided into themes, covering all major spheres of everyday activities, business, science, culture, etc.

The process of learning words using T&P Books' theme-based dictionaries gives you the following advantages:

- Correctly grouped source information predetermines success at subsequent stages of word memorization
- Availability of words derived from the same root allowing memorization of word units (rather than separate words)
- Small units of words facilitate the process of establishing associative links needed for consolidation of vocabulary
- Level of language knowledge can be estimated by the number of learned words

T&P Books Publishing
www.tpbooks.com

ISBN: 978-1-78400-205-3

This book is also available in E-book formats.
Please visit www.tpbooks.com or the major online bookstores.

LATVIAN THEME-BASED DICTIONARY
British English collection

T&P Books vocabularies are intended to help you learn, memorize, and review foreign words. The vocabulary contains over 3000 commonly used words arranged thematically.

- Vocabulary contains the most commonly used words
- Recommended as an addition to any language course
- Meets the needs of beginners and advanced learners of foreign languages
- Convenient for daily use, revision sessions, and self-testing activities
- Allows you to assess your vocabulary

Special features of the vocabulary

- Words are organized according to their meaning, not alphabetically
- Words are presented in three columns to facilitate the reviewing and self-testing processes
- Words in groups are divided into small blocks to facilitate the learning process
- The vocabulary offers a convenient and simple transcription of each foreign word

The vocabulary has 101 topics including:

Basic Concepts, Numbers, Colors, Months, Seasons, Units of Measurement, Clothing & Accessories, Food & Nutrition, Restaurant, Family Members, Relatives, Character, Feelings, Emotions, Diseases, City, Town, Sightseeing, Shopping, Money, House, Home, Office, Working in the Office, Import & Export, Marketing, Job Search, Sports, Education, Computer, Internet, Tools, Nature, Countries, Nationalities and more ...

TABLE OF CONTENTS

PRONUNCIATION GUIDE

Letter	Latvian example	T&P phonetic alphabet	English example

Vowels

A a	adata	[ɑ]	shorter than in park, card
Ā ā	ābols	[ɑ:]	father, answer
E e	egle	[e], [æ]	pet, absent
Ē ē	ērglis	[e:], [æ:]	longer than in bell
I i	izcelsme	[i]	shorter than in feet
Ī ī	īpašums	[i:]	feet, meter
O o	okeāns	[o], [o:]	floor, doctor
U u	ubags	[u]	book
Ū ū	ūdens	[u:]	pool, room

Consonants

B b	bads	[b]	baby, book
C c	cālis	[ts]	cats, tsetse fly
Č č	čaumala	[tʃ]	church, French
D d	dambis	[d]	day, doctor
F f	flauta	[f]	face, food
G g	gads	[g]	game, gold
Ģ ģ	ģitāra	[dʲ]	median, radio
H h	haizivs	[h]	home, have
J j	janvāris	[j]	yes, New York
K k	kabata	[k]	clock, kiss
Ķ ķ	ķilava	[tʲ/tʲʲ]	between soft [t] and [k], like tune
L l	labība	[l]	lace, people
Ļ ļ	ļaudis	[ʎ]	daily, million
M m	magone	[m]	magic, milk
N n	nauda	[n]	name, normal
Ņ ņ	ņaudēt	[ɲ]	canyon, new
P p	pakavs	[p]	pencil, private
R r	ragana	[r]	rice, radio
S s	sadarbība	[s]	city, boss
Š š	šausmas	[ʃ]	machine, shark
T t	tabula	[t]	tourist, trip

Letter	Latvian example	T&P phonetic alphabet	English example
V v	vabole	[v]	very, river
Z z	zaglis	[z]	zebra, please
Ž ž	žagata	[ʒ]	forge, pleasure

Comments

* Letters **Qq, Ww, Xx, Yy** used in foreign loanwords only
** Standard Latvian and all of the Latvian dialects have fixed initial stress (with a few minor exceptions).

ABBREVIATIONS
used in the dictionary

English abbreviations

ab.	-	about
adj	-	adjective
adv	-	adverb
anim.	-	animate
as adj	-	attributive noun used as adjective
e.g.	-	for example
etc.	-	et cetera
fam.	-	familiar
fem.	-	feminine
form.	-	formal
inanim.	-	inanimate
masc.	-	masculine
math	-	mathematics
mil.	-	military
n	-	noun
pl	-	plural
pron.	-	pronoun
sb	-	somebody
sing.	-	singular
sth	-	something
v aux	-	auxiliary verb
vi	-	intransitive verb
vi, vt	-	intransitive, transitive verb
vt	-	transitive verb

Latvian abbreviations

s	-	feminine noun
s dsk	-	feminine plural
v, s	-	masculine, feminine
v	-	masculine noun
v dsk	-	masculine plural

BASIC CONCEPTS

1. Pronouns

I, me	es	[es]
you	tu	[tu]
he	viņš	[viɲʃ]
she	viņa	[viɲa]
it	tas	[tas]
we	mēs	[meːs]
you (to a group)	jūs	[juːs]
they	viņi	[viɲi]

2. Greetings. Salutations

Hello! (fam.)	Sveiki!	[svɛiki!]
Hello! (form.)	Esiet sveicināts!	[ɛsiɛt svɛitsinaːts!]
Good morning!	Labrīt!	[labriːt!]
Good afternoon!	Labdien!	[labdiɛn!]
Good evening!	Labvakar!	[labvakar!]
to say hello	sveicināt	[svɛitsinaːt]
Hi! (hello)	Čau!	[tʃau!]
greeting (n)	sveiciens (v)	[svɛitsiɛns]
to greet (vt)	pasveicināt	[pasvɛitsinaːt]
How are you?	Kā iet?	[kaː iɛt?]
What's new?	Kas jauns?	[kas jauns?]
Goodbye! (form.)	Uz redzēšanos!	[uz redzeːʃanɔs!]
Bye! (fam.)	Atā!	[ataː!]
See you soon!	Uz tikšanos!	[uz tikʃanɔs!]
Farewell!	Ardievu!	[ardiɛvu!]
to say goodbye	atvadīties	[atvadiːtiɛs]
Cheers!	Nu tad pagaidām!	[nu tad pagaidaːm!]
Thank you! Cheers!	Paldies!	[paldiɛs!]
Thank you very much!	Liels paldies!	[liɛls paldiɛs!]
My pleasure!	Lūdzu	[luːdzu]
Don't mention it!	Nav par ko	[nav par kɔ]
It was nothing	Nav par ko	[nav par kɔ]
Excuse me! (fam.)	Atvaino!	[atvainɔ!]
Excuse me! (form.)	Atvainojiet!	[atvainɔjiɛt!]
to excuse (forgive)	piedot	[piɛdɔt]
to apologize (vi)	atvainoties	[atvainɔtiɛs]
My apologies	Es atvainojos	[es atvainɔjɔs]

I'm sorry!	Piedodiet!	[piɛdɔdiɛt!]
to forgive (vt)	piedot	[piɛdɔt]
It's okay! (that's all right)	Tas nekas	[tas nɛkas]
please (adv)	lūdzu	[lu:dzu]

Don't forget!	Neaizmirstiet!	[neaizmirstiɛt!]
Certainly!	Protams!	[prɔtams!]
Of course not!	Protams, ka nē!	[prɔtams, ka ne:!]
Okay! (I agree)	Piekrītu!	[piɛkri:tu!]
That's enough!	Pietiek!	[piɛtiɛk!]

3. Questions

Who?	Kas?	[kas?]
What?	Kas?	[kas?]
Where? (at, in)	Kur?	[kur?]
Where (to)?	Uz kurieni?	[uz kuriɛni?]
From where?	No kurienes?	[nɔ kuriɛnes?]
When?	Kad?	[kad?]
Why? (What for?)	Kādēļ?	[ka:de:lʲ?]
Why? (~ are you crying?)	Kāpēc?	[ka:pe:ts?]

What for?	Kam?	[kam?]
How? (in what way)	Kā?	[ka:?]
What? (What kind of ...?)	Kāds?	[ka:ds?]
Which?	Kurš?	[kurʃ?]

To whom?	Kam?	[kam?]
About whom?	Par kuru?	[par kuru?]
About what?	Par ko?	[par kɔ?]
With whom?	Ar ko?	[ar kɔ?]

How many?	Cik daudz?	[tsik daudz?]
How much?	Cik?	[tsik?]
Whose?	Kura? Kuras? Kuru?	[kura?], [kuras?], [kuru?]

4. Prepositions

with (accompanied by)	ar	[ar]
without	bez	[bez]
to (indicating direction)	uz	[uz]
about (talking ~ ...)	par	[par]
before (in time)	pirms	[pirms]
in front of ...	priekšā	[priɛkʃa:]

under (beneath, below)	zem	[zem]
above (over)	virs	[virs]
on (atop)	uz	[uz]
from (off, out of)	no	[nɔ]
of (made from)	no	[nɔ]
in (e.g. ~ ten minutes)	pēc	[pe:ts]
over (across the top of)	caur	[tsaur]

5. Function words. Adverbs. Part 1

Where? (at, in)	Kur?	[kur?]
here (adv)	šeit	[ʃɛit]
there (adv)	tur	[tur]

somewhere (to be)	kaut kur	[kaut kur]
nowhere (not anywhere)	nekur	[nɛkur]

by (near, beside)	pie ...	[piɛ ...]
by the window	pie loga	[piɛ lɔga]

Where (to)?	Uz kurieni?	[uz kuriɛni?]
here (e.g. come ~!)	šurp	[ʃurp]
there (e.g. to go ~)	turp	[turp]
from here (adv)	no šejienes	[nɔ ʃejiɛnes]
from there (adv)	no turienes	[nɔ turiɛnes]

close (adv)	tuvu	[tuvu]
far (adv)	tālu	[taːlu]

near (e.g. ~ Paris)	pie	[piɛ]
nearby (adv)	blakus	[blakus]
not far (adv)	netālu	[nɛtaːlu]

left (adj)	kreisais	[krɛisais]
on the left	pa kreisi	[pa krɛisi]
to the left	pa kreisi	[pa krɛisi]

right (adj)	labais	[labais]
on the right	pa labi	[pa labi]
to the right	pa labi	[pa labi]

in front (adv)	priekšā	[priɛkʃaː]
front (as adj)	priekšējs	[priɛkʃeːjs]
ahead (the kids ran ~)	uz priekšu	[uz priɛkʃu]

behind (adv)	mugurpusē	[mugurpuseː]
from behind	no mugurpuses	[nɔ mugurpuses]
back (towards the rear)	atpakaļ	[atpakalʲ]

middle	vidus (v)	[vidus]
in the middle	vidū	[viduː]

at the side	sānis	[saːnis]
everywhere (adv)	visur	[visur]
around (in all directions)	apkārt	[apkaːrt]

from inside	no iekšpuses	[nɔ iɛkʃpuses]
somewhere (to go)	kaut kur	[kaut kur]
straight (directly)	taisni	[taisni]
back (e.g. come ~)	atpakaļ	[atpakalʲ]

from anywhere	no kaut kurienes	[nɔ kaut kuriɛnes]
from somewhere	nez no kurienes	[nez nɔ kuriɛnes]

firstly (adv)	pirmkārt	[pirmka:rt]
secondly (adv)	otrkārt	[ɔtrka:rt]
thirdly (adv)	treškārt	[treʃka:rt]

suddenly (adv)	pēkšņi	[pe:kʃɲi]
at first (in the beginning)	sākumā	[sa:kuma:]
for the first time	pirmo reizi	[pirmɔ rɛizi]
long before ...	ilgu laiku pirms ...	[ilgu laiku pirms ...]
anew (over again)	no jauna	[nɔ jauna]
for good (adv)	uz visiem laikiem	[uz visiɛm laikiɛm]

never (adv)	nekad	[nɛkad]
again (adv)	atkal	[atkal]
now (adv)	tagad	[tagad]
often (adv)	bieži	[biɛʒi]
then (adv)	tad	[tad]
urgently (quickly)	steidzami	[stɛidzami]
usually (adv)	parasti	[parasti]

by the way, ...	starp citu ...	[starp tsitu ...]
possible (that is ~)	iespējams	[iɛspe:jams]
probably (adv)	ticams	[titsams]
maybe (adv)	varbūt	[varbu:t]
besides ...	turklāt, ...	[turkla:t, ...]
that's why ...	tādēļ ...	[ta:de:lʲ ...]
in spite of ...	neskatoties uz ...	[neskatɔties uz ...]
thanks to ...	pateicoties ...	[patɛitsɔties ...]

what (pron.)	kas	[kas]
that (conj.)	kas	[kas]
something	kaut kas	[kaut kas]
anything (something)	kaut kas	[kaut kas]
nothing	nekas	[nɛkas]

who (pron.)	kas	[kas]
someone	kāds	[ka:ds]
somebody	kāds	[ka:ds]

nobody	neviens	[neviɛns]
nowhere (a voyage to ~)	nekur	[nɛkur]
nobody's	neviena	[neviɛna]
somebody's	kāda	[ka:da]

so (I'm ~ glad)	tā	[ta:]
also (as well)	tāpat	[ta:pat]
too (as well)	arī	[ari:]

6. Function words. Adverbs. Part 2

Why?	Kāpēc?	[ka:pe:ts?]
for some reason	nez kāpēc	[nez ka:pe:ts]
because ...	tāpēc ka ...	[ta:pe:ts ka ...]
for some purpose	nez kādēļ	[nez ka:de:lʲ]
and	un	[un]

or	vai	[vai]
but	bet	[bet]
for (e.g. ~ me)	priekš	[priɛkʃ]

too (excessively)	pārāk	[paːraːk]
only (exclusively)	tikai	[tikai]
exactly (adv)	tieši	[tiɛʃi]
about (more or less)	apmēram	[apmɛːram]

approximately (adv)	aptuveni	[aptuveni]
approximate (adj)	aptuvens	[aptuvens]
almost (adv)	gandrīz	[gandriːz]
the rest	pārējais	[paːreːjais]

the other (second)	cits	[tsits]
other (different)	cits	[tsits]
each (adj)	katrs	[katrs]
any (no matter which)	jebkurš	[jebkurʃ]
many, much (a lot of)	daudz	[daudz]
many people	daudzi	[daudzi]
all (everyone)	visi	[visi]

in return for ...	apmaiņā pret ...	[apmaiɲaː pret ...]
in exchange (adv)	pretī	[preti:]
by hand (made)	ar rokām	[ar rɔkaːm]
hardly (negative opinion)	diez vai	[diɛz vai]

probably (adv)	laikam	[laikam]
on purpose (intentionally)	tīšām	[tiːʃaːm]
by accident (adv)	nejauši	[nejauʃi]

very (adv)	ļoti	[lʲoti]
for example (adv)	piemēram	[piɛmɛːram]
between	starp	[starp]
among	vidū	[vidu:]
so much (such a lot)	tik daudz	[tik daudz]
especially (adv)	īpaši	[iːpaʃi]

NUMBERS. MISCELLANEOUS

7. Cardinal numbers. Part 1

0 zero	nulle	[nulle]
1 one	viens	[viɛns]
2 two	divi	[divi]
3 three	trīs	[tri:s]
4 four	četri	[tʃetri]
5 five	pieci	[piɛtsi]
6 six	seši	[seʃi]
7 seven	septiņi	[septiɲi]
8 eight	astoņi	[astɔɲi]
9 nine	deviņi	[deviɲi]
10 ten	desmit	[desmit]
11 eleven	vienpadsmit	[viɛnpadsmit]
12 twelve	divpadsmit	[divpadsmit]
13 thirteen	trīspadsmit	[tri:spadsmit]
14 fourteen	četrpadsmit	[tʃetrpadsmit]
15 fifteen	piecpadsmit	[piɛtspadsmit]
16 sixteen	sešpadsmit	[seʃpadsmit]
17 seventeen	septiņpadsmit	[septiɲpadsmit]
18 eighteen	astoņpadsmit	[astɔɲpadsmit]
19 nineteen	deviņpadsmit	[deviɲpadsmit]
20 twenty	divdesmit	[divdesmit]
21 twenty-one	divdesmit viens	[divdesmit viɛns]
22 twenty-two	divdesmit divi	[divdesmit divi]
23 twenty-three	divdesmit trīs	[divdesmit tri:s]
30 thirty	trīsdesmit	[tri:sdesmit]
31 thirty-one	trīsdesmit viens	[tri:sdesmit viɛns]
32 thirty-two	trīsdesmit divi	[tri:sdesmit divi]
33 thirty-three	trīsdesmit trīs	[tri:sdesmit tri:s]
40 forty	četrdesmit	[tʃetrdesmit]
41 forty-one	četrdesmit viens	[tʃetrdesmit viɛns]
42 forty-two	četrdesmit divi	[tʃetrdesmit divi]
43 forty-three	četrdesmit trīs	[tʃetrdesmit tri:s]
50 fifty	piecdesmit	[piɛtsdesmit]
51 fifty-one	piecdesmit viens	[piɛtsdesmit viɛns]
52 fifty-two	piecdesmit divi	[piɛtsdesmit divi]
53 fifty-three	piecdesmit trīs	[piɛtsdesmit tri:s]
60 sixty	sešdesmit	[seʃdesmit]
61 sixty-one	sešdesmit viens	[seʃdesmit viɛns]

| 62 sixty-two | sešdesmit divi | [seʃdesmit divi] |
| 63 sixty-three | sešdesmit trīs | [seʃdesmit tri:s] |

70 seventy	septiŋdesmit	[septiŋdesmit]
71 seventy-one	septiŋdesmit viens	[septiŋdesmit viɛns]
72 seventy-two	septiŋdesmit divi	[septiŋdesmit divi]
73 seventy-three	septiŋdesmit trīs	[septiŋdesmit tri:s]

80 eighty	astoŋdesmit	[astoŋdesmit]
81 eighty-one	astoŋdesmit viens	[astoŋdesmit viɛns]
82 eighty-two	astoŋdesmit divi	[astoŋdesmit divi]
83 eighty-three	astoŋdesmit trīs	[astoŋdesmit tri:s]

90 ninety	deviŋdesmit	[deviŋdesmit]
91 ninety-one	deviŋdesmit viens	[deviŋdesmit viɛns]
92 ninety-two	deviŋdesmit divi	[deviŋdesmit divi]
93 ninety-three	deviŋdesmit trīs	[deviŋdesmit tri:s]

8. Cardinal numbers. Part 2

100 one hundred	simts	[simts]
200 two hundred	divsimt	[divsimt]
300 three hundred	trīssimt	[tri:simt]
400 four hundred	četrsimt	[tʃetrsimt]
500 five hundred	piecsimt	[piɛtsimt]

600 six hundred	sešsimt	[seʃsimt]
700 seven hundred	septiŋsimt	[septiŋsimt]
800 eight hundred	astoŋsimt	[astoŋsimt]
900 nine hundred	deviŋsimt	[deviŋsimt]

1000 one thousand	tūkstotis	[tu:kstotis]
2000 two thousand	divi tūkstoši	[divi tu:kstoʃi]
3000 three thousand	trīs tūkstoši	[tri:s tu:kstoʃi]
10000 ten thousand	desmit tūkstoši	[desmit tu:kstoʃi]
one hundred thousand	simt tūkstoši	[simt tu:kstoʃi]
million	miljons (v)	[miljons]
billion	miljards (v)	[miljards]

9. Ordinal numbers

first (adj)	pirmais	[pirmais]
second (adj)	otrais	[otrais]
third (adj)	trešais	[treʃais]
fourth (adj)	ceturtais	[tsɛturtais]
fifth (adj)	piektais	[piɛktais]

sixth (adj)	sestais	[sestais]
seventh (adj)	septītais	[septi:tais]
eighth (adj)	astotais	[astotais]
ninth (adj)	devītais	[devi:tais]
tenth (adj)	desmitais	[desmitais]

COLORS. UNITS OF MEASUREMENT

10. Colours

colour	krāsa (s)	[kra:sa]
shade (tint)	nokrāsa (s)	[nɔkra:sa]
hue	tonis (v)	[tɔnis]
rainbow	varavīksne (s)	[varavi:ksne]

white (adj)	balts	[balts]
black (adj)	melns	[melns]
grey (adj)	pelēks	[pɛle:ks]

green (adj)	zaļš	[zalʲʃ]
yellow (adj)	dzeltens	[dzeltens]
red (adj)	sarkans	[sarkans]

blue (adj)	zils	[zils]
light blue (adj)	gaiši zils	[gaiʃi zils]
pink (adj)	rozā	[rɔza:]
orange (adj)	oranžs	[ɔranʒs]
violet (adj)	violets	[viɔlets]
brown (adj)	brūns	[bru:ns]

golden (adj)	zelta	[zelta]
silvery (adj)	sudrabains	[sudrabains]

beige (adj)	bēšs	[be:ʃs]
cream (adj)	krēmkrāsas	[kre:mkra:sas]
turquoise (adj)	zilganzaļš	[zilganzalʲʃ]
cherry red (adj)	ķiršu brīns	[tʲirʃu bri:ns]
lilac (adj)	lillā	[lilla:]
crimson (adj)	aveņkrāsas	[aveɲkra:sas]

light (adj)	gaišs	[gaiʃs]
dark (adj)	tumšs	[tumʃs]
bright, vivid (adj)	spilgts	[spilgts]

coloured (pencils)	krāsains	[kra:sains]
colour (e.g. ~ film)	krāsains	[kra:sains]
black-and-white (adj)	melnbalts	[melnbalts]
plain (one-coloured)	vienkrāsains	[viɛnkra:sains]
multicoloured (adj)	daudzkrāsains	[daudzkra:sains]

11. Units of measurement

weight	svars (v)	[svars]
length	garums (v)	[garums]

width	platums (v)	[platums]
height	augstums (v)	[augstums]
depth	dziļums (v)	[dziľums]
volume	apjoms (v)	[apjɔms]
area	laukums (v)	[laukums]

gram	grams (v)	[grams]
milligram	miligrams (v)	[miligrams]
kilogram	kilograms (v)	[kilɔgrams]
ton	tonna (s)	[tɔnna]
pound	mārciņa (s)	[maːrtsiɲa]
ounce	unce (s)	[untse]

metre	metrs (v)	[metrs]
millimetre	milimetrs (v)	[milimetrs]
centimetre	centimetrs (v)	[tsentimetrs]
kilometre	kilometrs (v)	[kilɔmetrs]
mile	jūdze (s)	[juːdze]

inch	colla (s)	[tsɔlla]
foot	pēda (s)	[pɛːda]
yard	jards (v)	[jards]

| square metre | kvadrātmetrs (v) | [kvadraːtmetrs] |
| hectare | hektārs (v) | [xektaːrs] |

litre	litrs (v)	[litrs]
degree	grāds (v)	[graːds]
volt	volts (v)	[vɔlts]
ampere	ampērs (v)	[ampɛːrs]
horsepower	zirgspēks (v)	[zirgspeːks]

quantity	daudzums (v)	[daudzums]
a little bit of ...	nedaudz ...	[nɛdaudz ...]
half	puse (s)	[puse]
dozen	ducis (v)	[dutsis]
piece (item)	gabals (v)	[gabals]

| size | izmērs (v) | [izmɛːrs] |
| scale (map ~) | mērogs (v) | [meːrɔgs] |

minimal (adj)	minimāls	[minimaːls]
the smallest (adj)	vismazākais	[vismazaːkais]
medium (adj)	vidējs	[videːjs]
maximal (adj)	maksimāls	[maksimaːls]
the largest (adj)	vislielākais	[vislɛlaːkais]

12. Containers

canning jar (glass ~)	burka (s)	[burka]
tin, can	bundža (s)	[bundʒa]
bucket	spainis (v)	[spainis]
barrel	muca (s)	[mutsa]
wash basin (e.g., plastic ~)	bļoda (s)	[bľɔda]

19

tank (100L water ~)	tvertne (s)	[tvertne]
hip flask	blāšķe (s)	[blaʃťe]
jerrycan	kanna (s)	[kanna]
tank (e.g., tank car)	cisterna (s)	[tsisterna]

mug	krūze (s)	[kru:ze]
cup (of coffee, etc.)	tase (s)	[tase]
saucer	apakštase (s)	[apakʃtase]
glass (tumbler)	glāze (s)	[gla:ze]
wine glass	pokāls (v)	[pɔka:ls]
stock pot (soup pot)	kastrolis (v)	[kastrɔlis]

| bottle (~ of wine) | pudele (s) | [pudɛle] |
| neck (of the bottle, etc.) | kakliņš (v) | [kakliɲʃ] |

carafe (decanter)	karafe (s)	[karafe]
pitcher	krūka (s)	[kru:ka]
vessel (container)	trauks (v)	[trauks]
pot (crock, stoneware ~)	pods (v)	[pɔds]
vase	vāze (s)	[va:ze]

bottle (perfume ~)	flakons (v)	[flakɔns]
vial, small bottle	pudelīte (s)	[pudeli:te]
tube (of toothpaste)	tūbiņa (s)	[tu:biɲa]

sack (bag)	maiss (v)	[mais]
bag (paper ~, plastic ~)	maisiņš (v)	[maisiɲʃ]
packet (of cigarettes, etc.)	paciņa (s)	[patsiɲa]

box (e.g. shoebox)	kārba (s)	[ka:rba]
crate	kastīte (s)	[kasti:te]
basket	grozs (v)	[grɔzs]

MAIN VERBS

13. The most important verbs. Part 1

to advise (vt)	dot padomu	[dɔt padɔmu]
to agree (say yes)	piekrist	[piɛkrist]
to answer (vi, vt)	atbildēt	[atbilde:t]
to apologize (vi)	atvainoties	[atvainɔtiɛs]
to arrive (vi)	atbraukt	[atbraukt]
to ask (~ oneself)	jautāt	[jauta:t]
to ask (~ sb to do sth)	lūgt	[lu:gt]
to be (vi)	būt	[bu:t]
to be afraid	baidīties	[baidi:tiɛs]
to be hungry	gribēt ēst	[gribe:t e:st]
to be interested in ...	interesēties	[intɛrɛse:tiɛs]
to be needed	būt vajadzīgam	[bu:t vajadzi:gam]
to be surprised	brīnīties	[bri:ni:tiɛs]
to be thirsty	gribēt dzert	[gribe:t dzert]
to begin (vt)	sākt	[sa:kt]
to belong to ...	piederēt	[piɛdɛre:t]
to boast (vi)	lielīties	[liɛli:tiɛs]
to break (split into pieces)	lauzt	[lauzt]
to call (~ for help)	saukt	[saukt]
can (v aux)	spēt	[spe:t]
to catch (vt)	ķert	[tʲert]
to change (vt)	mainīt	[maini:t]
to choose (select)	izvēlēties	[izvɛ:le:tiɛs]
to come down (the stairs)	nokāpt	[nɔka:pt]
to compare (vt)	salīdzināt	[sali:dzina:t]
to complain (vi, vt)	sūdzēties	[su:dze:tiɛs]
to confuse (mix up)	sajaukt	[sajaukt]
to continue (vt)	turpināt	[turpina:t]
to control (vt)	kontrolēt	[kɔntrɔle:t]
to cook (dinner)	gatavot	[gatavɔt]
to cost (vt)	maksāt	[maksa:t]
to count (add up)	sarēķināt	[sare:tʲina:t]
to count on ...	paļauties uz ...	[palʲauties uz ...]
to create (vt)	izveidot	[izvɛidɔt]
to cry (weep)	raudāt	[rauda:t]

14. The most important verbs. Part 2

to deceive (vi, vt)	krāpt	[kra:pt]
to decorate (tree, street)	izrotāt	[izrɔta:t]

to defend (a country, etc.)	aizstāvēt	[aizsta:ve:t]
to demand (request firmly)	prasīt	[prasi:t]
to dig (vt)	rakt	[rakt]

to discuss (vt)	apspriest	[apspriɛst]
to do (vt)	darīt	[dari:t]
to doubt (have doubts)	šaubīties	[ʃaubi:tiɛs]
to drop (let fall)	nomest	[nɔmest]
to enter (room, house, etc.)	ieiet	[iɛiɛt]

to excuse (forgive)	piedot	[piɛdɔt]
to exist (vi)	eksistēt	[eksiste:t]
to expect (foresee)	paredzēt	[paredze:t]
to explain (vt)	paskaidrot	[paskaidrɔt]
to fall (vi)	krist	[krist]

to fancy (vt)	patikt	[patikt]
to find (vt)	atrast	[atrast]
to finish (vt)	beigt	[bɛigt]
to fly (vi)	lidot	[lidɔt]
to follow ... (come after)	sekot ...	[sekɔt ...]

to forget (vi, vt)	aizmirst	[aizmirst]
to forgive (vt)	piedot	[piɛdɔt]
to give (vt)	dot	[dɔt]
to give a hint	dot mājienu	[dɔt ma:jiɛnu]
to go (on foot)	iet	[iɛt]

to go for a swim	peldēties	[pelde:tiɛs]
to go out (for dinner, etc.)	iziet	[iziɛt]
to guess (the answer)	uzminēt	[uzmine:t]

to have (vt)	būt	[bu:t]
to have breakfast	brokastot	[brɔkastɔt]
to have dinner	vakariņot	[vakariŋɔt]
to have lunch	pusdienot	[pusdiɛnɔt]
to hear (vt)	dzirdēt	[dzirde:t]

to help (vt)	palīdzēt	[pali:dze:t]
to hide (vt)	slēpt	[sle:pt]
to hope (vi, vt)	cerēt	[tsɛre:t]
to hunt (vi, vt)	medīt	[medi:t]
to hurry (vi)	steigties	[stɛigtiɛs]

15. The most important verbs. Part 3

to inform (vt)	informēt	[infɔrme:t]
to insist (vi, vt)	uzstāt	[uzsta:t]
to insult (vt)	aizvainot	[aizvainɔt]
to invite (vt)	ielūgt	[iɛlu:gt]
to joke (vi)	jokot	[jɔkɔt]

| to keep (vt) | uzglabāt | [uzglaba:t] |
| to keep silent | klusēt | [kluse:t] |

to kill (vt)	nogalināt	[nɔgalina:t]
to know (sb)	pazīt	[pazi:t]
to know (sth)	zināt	[zina:t]
to laugh (vi)	smieties	[smiɛtiɛs]

to liberate (city, etc.)	atbrīvot	[atbri:vɔt]
to look for ... (search)	meklēt ...	[mekle:t ...]
to love (sb)	mīlēt	[mi:le:t]
to make a mistake	kļūdīties	[klʲu:di:tiɛs]
to manage, to run	vadīt	[vadi:t]

to mean (signify)	nozīmēt	[nɔzi:me:t]
to mention (talk about)	pieminēt	[piɛmine:t]
to miss (school, etc.)	kavēt	[kave:t]
to notice (see)	pamanīt	[pamani:t]
to object (vi, vt)	iebilst	[iɛbilst]

to observe (see)	novērot	[nɔve:rɔt]
to open (vt)	atvērt	[atve:rt]
to order (meal, etc.)	pasūtīt	[pasu:ti:t]
to order (mil.)	pavēlēt	[pavɛ:le:t]
to own (possess)	pārvaldīt	[pa:rvaldi:t]

to participate (vi)	piedalīties	[piɛdali:tiɛs]
to pay (vi, vt)	maksāt	[maksa:t]
to permit (vt)	atļaut	[atlʲaut]
to plan (vt)	plānot	[pla:nɔt]
to play (children)	spēlēt	[spɛ:le:t]

to pray (vi, vt)	lūgties	[lu:gtiɛs]
to prefer (vt)	dot priekšroku	[dɔt priɛkʃrɔku]
to promise (vt)	solīt	[sɔli:t]
to pronounce (vt)	izrunāt	[izruna:t]
to propose (vt)	piedāvāt	[piɛda:va:t]
to punish (vt)	sodīt	[sɔdi:t]

16. The most important verbs. Part 4

to read (vi, vt)	lasīt	[lasi:t]
to recommend (vt)	ieteikt	[iɛtɛikt]
to refuse (vi, vt)	atteikties	[attɛiktiɛs]
to regret (be sorry)	nožēlot	[nɔʒe:lɔt]
to rent (sth from sb)	īrēt	[i:re:t]

to repeat (say again)	atkārtot	[atka:rtɔt]
to reserve, to book	rezervēt	[rɛzerve:t]
to run (vi)	skriet	[skriɛt]
to save (rescue)	glābt	[gla:bt]

to say (~ thank you)	teikt	[tɛikt]
to scold (vt)	lamāt	[lama:t]
to see (vt)	redzēt	[redze:t]
to sell (vt)	pārdot	[pa:rdɔt]
to send (vt)	sūtīt	[su:ti:t]

to shoot (vi)	šaut	[ʃaut]
to shout (vi)	kliegt	[kliɛgt]
to show (vt)	parādīt	[para:di:t]
to sign (document)	parakstīt	[paraksti:t]

to sit down (vi)	sēsties	[se:stiɛs]
to smile (vi)	smaidīt	[smaidi:t]
to speak (vi, vt)	runāt	[runa:t]
to steal (money, etc.)	zagt	[zagt]
to stop (for pause, etc.)	apstāties	[apsta:tiɛs]

to stop (please ~ calling me)	pārtraukt	[pa:rtraukt]
to study (vt)	pētīt	[pe:ti:t]
to swim (vi)	peldēt	[pelde:t]
to take (vt)	ņemt	[ɲemt]
to think (vi, vt)	domāt	[dɔma:t]

to threaten (vt)	draudēt	[draude:t]
to touch (with hands)	pieskarties	[piɛskartiɛs]
to translate (vt)	tulkot	[tulkɔt]
to trust (vt)	uzticēt	[uztitse:t]
to try (attempt)	mēģināt	[me:dʲina:t]

to turn (e.g., ~ left)	pagriezties	[pagriɛztiɛs]
to underestimate (vt)	par zemu vērtēt	[par zɛmu ve:rte:t]
to understand (vt)	saprast	[saprast]
to unite (vt)	apvienot	[apviɛnɔt]
to wait (vt)	gaidīt	[gaidi:t]

to want (wish, desire)	gribēt	[gribe:t]
to warn (vt)	brīdināt	[bri:dina:t]
to work (vi)	strādāt	[stra:da:t]
to write (vt)	rakstīt	[raksti:t]
to write down	pierakstīt	[piɛraksti:t]

TIME. CALENDAR

17. Weekdays

Monday	pirmdiena (s)	[pirmdiɛna]
Tuesday	otrdiena (s)	[ɔtrdiɛna]
Wednesday	trešdiena (s)	[treʃdiɛna]
Thursday	ceturtdiena (s)	[tsɛturtdiɛna]
Friday	piektdiena (s)	[piɛktdiɛna]
Saturday	sestdiena (s)	[sestdiɛna]
Sunday	svētdiena (s)	[sve:tdiɛna]

today (adv)	šodien	[ʃɔdiɛn]
tomorrow (adv)	rīt	[ri:t]
the day after tomorrow	parīt	[pari:t]
yesterday (adv)	vakar	[vakar]
the day before yesterday	aizvakar	[aizvakar]

day	diena (s)	[diɛna]
working day	darba diena (s)	[darba diɛna]
public holiday	svētku diena (s)	[sve:tku diɛna]
day off	brīvdiena (s)	[bri:vdiɛna]
weekend	brīvdienas (s dsk)	[bri:vdiɛnas]

all day long	visa diena	[visa diɛna]
the next day (adv)	nākamajā dienā	[na:kamaja: diɛna:]
two days ago	pirms divām dienām	[pirms diva:m diɛna:m]
the day before	dienu iepriekš	[diɛnu iɛpriɛkʃ]
daily (adj)	ikdienas	[igdiɛnas]
every day (adv)	katru dienu	[katru diɛnu]

week	nedēļa (s)	[nɛdɛ:lʲa]
last week (adv)	pagājušajā nedēļā	[paga:juʃaja: nɛdɛ:lʲa:]
next week (adv)	nākamajā nedēļā	[na:kamaja: nɛdɛ:lʲa:]
weekly (adj)	iknedēļas	[iknɛdɛ:lʲas]
every week (adv)	katru nedēļu	[katru nɛdɛ:lʲu]
twice a week	divas reizes nedēļā	[divas rɛizes nɛdɛ:lʲa:]
every Tuesday	katru otrdienu	[katru ɔtrdiɛnu]

18. Hours. Day and night

morning	rīts (v)	[ri:ts]
in the morning	no rīta	[nɔ ri:ta]
noon, midday	pusdiena (s)	[pusdiɛna]
in the afternoon	pēcpusdienā	[pe:tspusdiɛna:]

evening	vakars (v)	[vakars]
in the evening	vakarā	[vakara:]

night	nakts (s)	[nakts]
at night	naktī	[nakti:]
midnight	pusnakts (s)	[pusnakts]

second	sekunde (s)	[sɛkunde]
minute	minūte (s)	[minu:te]
hour	stunda (s)	[stunda]
half an hour	pusstunda	[pustunda]
a quarter-hour	stundas ceturksnis (v)	[stundas tsɛturksnis]
fifteen minutes	piecpadsmit minūtes	[piɛtspadsmit minu:tes]
24 hours	diennakts (s)	[diɛnnakts]

sunrise	saullēkts (v)	[saulle:kts]
dawn	rītausma (s)	[ri:tausma]
early morning	agrs rīts (v)	[agrs ri:ts]
sunset	saulriets (v)	[saulriɛts]

early in the morning	agri no rīta	[agri nɔ ri:ta]
this morning	šorīt	[ʃɔri:t]
tomorrow morning	rīt no rīta	[ri:t nɔ ri:ta]

this afternoon	šodien	[ʃɔdiɛn]
in the afternoon	pēcpusdienā	[pe:tspusdiɛna:]
tomorrow afternoon	rīt pēcpusdienā	[ri:t pe:tspusdiɛna:]

| tonight (this evening) | šovakar | [ʃɔvakar] |
| tomorrow night | rītvakar | [ri:tvakar] |

at 3 o'clock sharp	tieši trijos	[tiɛʃi trijɔs]
about 4 o'clock	ap četriem	[ap tʃetriɛm]
by 12 o'clock	ap divpadsmitiem	[ap divpadsmitiɛm]

in 20 minutes	pēc divdesmit minūtēm	[pe:ts divdesmit minu:te:m]
in an hour	pēc stundas	[pe:ts stundas]
on time (adv)	laikā	[laika:]

a quarter to ...	bez ceturkšņa ...	[bez tsɛturkʃɲa ...]
within an hour	stundas laikā	[stundas laika:]
every 15 minutes	katras piecpadsmit minūtes	[katras piɛtspadsmit minu:tes]
round the clock	caurām dienām	[tsaura:m diɛna:m]

19. Months. Seasons

January	janvāris (v)	[janva:ris]
February	februāris (v)	[februa:ris]
March	marts (v)	[marts]
April	aprīlis (v)	[apri:lis]
May	maijs (v)	[maijs]
June	jūnijs (v)	[ju:nijs]

| July | jūlijs (v) | [ju:lijs] |
| August | augusts (v) | [augusts] |

September	septembris (v)	[septembris]
October	oktobris (v)	[ɔktobris]
November	novembris (v)	[nɔvembris]
December	decembris (v)	[detsembris]

spring	pavasaris (v)	[pavasaris]
in spring	pavasarī	[pavasari:]
spring (as adj)	pavasara	[pavasara]

summer	vasara (s)	[vasara]
in summer	vasarā	[vasara:]
summer (as adj)	vasaras	[vasaras]

autumn	rudens (v)	[rudens]
in autumn	rudenī	[rudeni:]
autumn (as adj)	rudens	[rudens]

winter	ziema (s)	[ziɛma]
in winter	ziemā	[ziɛma:]
winter (as adj)	ziemas	[ziɛmas]

month	mēnesis (v)	[mɛ:nesis]
this month	šomēnes	[ʃomɛ:nes]
next month	nākamajā mēnesī	[na:kamaja: mɛ:nesi:]
last month	pagājušajā mēnesī	[paga:juʃaja: mɛ:nesi:]

a month ago	pirms mēneša	[pirms mɛ:neʃa]
in a month (a month later)	pēc mēneša	[pe:ts mɛ:neʃa]
in 2 months (2 months later)	pēc diviem mēnešiem	[pe:ts diviɛm mɛ:neʃiɛm]
the whole month	visu mēnesi	[visu mɛ:nesi]
all month long	veselu mēnesi	[vesɛlu mɛ:nesi]

monthly (~ magazine)	ikmēneša	[ikmɛ:neʃa]
monthly (adv)	ik mēnesi	[ik mɛ:nesi]
every month	katru mēnesi	[katru mɛ:nesi]
twice a month	divas reizes mēnesī	[divas rɛizes mɛ:nesi:]

year	gads (v)	[gads]
this year	šogad	[ʃɔgad]
next year	nākamajā gadā	[na:kamaja: gada:]
last year	pagājušajā gadā	[paga:juʃaja: gada:]

a year ago	pirms gada	[pirms gada]
in a year	pēc gada	[pe:ts gada]
in two years	pēc diviem gadiem	[pe:ts diviɛm gadiɛm]
the whole year	visu gadu	[visu gadu]
all year long	veselu gadu	[vesɛlu gadu]

every year	katru gadu	[katru gadu]
annual (adj)	ikgadējs	[ikgade:js]
annually (adv)	ik gadu	[ik gadu]
4 times a year	četras reizes gadā	[tʃetras rɛizes gada:]

date (e.g. today's ~)	datums (v)	[datums]
date (e.g. ~ of birth)	datums (v)	[datums]
calendar	kalendārs (v)	[kalenda:rs]

half a year	**pusgads**	[pusgads]
six months	**pusgads** (v)	[pusgads]
season (summer, etc.)	**gadalaiks** (v)	[gadalaiks]
century	**gadsimts** (v)	[gadsimts]

TRAVEL. HOTEL

20. Trip. Travel

tourism, travel	tūrisms (v)	[tuːrisms]
tourist	tūrists (v)	[tuːrists]
trip, voyage	ceļojums (v)	[tselʲɔjums]
adventure	piedzīvojums (v)	[piɛdziːvɔjums]
trip, journey	brauciens (v)	[brautsiɛns]
holiday	atvaļinājums (v)	[atvalʲinaːjums]
to be on holiday	būt atvaļinājumā	[buːt atvalʲinaːjumaː]
rest	atpūta (s)	[atpuːta]
train	vilciens (v)	[viltsiɛns]
by train	ar vilcienu	[ar viltsiɛnu]
aeroplane	lidmašīna (s)	[lidmaʃiːna]
by aeroplane	ar lidmašīnu	[ar lidmaʃiːnu]
by car	ar automobili	[ar autɔmɔbili]
by ship	ar kuģi	[ar kudʲi]
luggage	bagāža (s)	[bagaːʒa]
suitcase	čemodāns (v)	[tʃemɔdaːns]
luggage trolley	bagāžas ratiņi (v dsk)	[bagaːʒas ratiɲi]
passport	pase (s)	[pase]
visa	vīza (s)	[viːza]
ticket	biļete (s)	[bilʲɛte]
air ticket	aviobiļete (s)	[aviɔbilʲɛte]
guidebook	ceļvedis (v)	[tselʲvedis]
map (tourist ~)	karte (s)	[karte]
area (rural ~)	apvidus (v)	[apvidus]
place, site	vieta (s)	[viɛta]
exotica (n)	eksotika (s)	[eksɔtika]
exotic (adj)	eksotisks	[eksɔtisks]
amazing (adj)	apbrīnojams	[apbriːnɔjams]
group	grupa (s)	[grupa]
excursion, sightseeing tour	ekskursija (s)	[ekskursija]
guide (person)	gids (v)	[gids]

21. Hotel

hotel	viesnīca (s)	[viɛsniːtsa]
motel	motelis (v)	[mɔtelis]
three-star (~ hotel)	trīszvaigžņu	[triːszvaigʒɲu]

29

five-star	pieczvaigžņu	[piɛtszvaigʒŋu]
to stay (in a hotel, etc.)	apmesties	[apmestiɛs]

room	numurs (v)	[numurs]
single room	vienvietīgs numurs (v)	[viɛnviɛti:gs numurs]
double room	divvietīgs numurs (v)	[divviɛti:gs numurs]
to book a room	rezervēt numuru	[rɛzerve:t numuru]

half board	pus pansija (s)	[pus pansija]
full board	pilna pansija (s)	[pilna pansija]

with bath	ar vannu	[ar vannu]
with shower	ar dušu	[ar duʃu]
satellite television	satelīta televīzija (s)	[sateli:ta tɛlevi:zija]
air-conditioner	kondicionētājs (v)	[kɔnditsionɛ:ta:js]
towel	dvielis (v)	[dviɛlis]
key	atslēga (s)	[atslɛ:ga]

administrator	administrators (v)	[administratɔrs]
chambermaid	istabene (s)	[istabɛne]
porter	nesējs (v)	[nɛse:js]
doorman	portjē (v)	[pɔrtje:]

restaurant	restorāns (v)	[restɔra:ns]
pub, bar	bārs (v)	[ba:rs]
breakfast	brokastis (s dsk)	[brɔkastis]
dinner	vakariņas (s dsk)	[vakariŋas]
buffet	zviedru galds (v)	[zviɛdru galds]

lobby	vestibils (v)	[vestibils]
lift	lifts (v)	[lifts]

DO NOT DISTURB	NETRAUCĒT	[netrautse:t]
NO SMOKING	SMĒĶĒT AIZLIEGTS!	[smɛ:tʲe:t aizliɛgts!]

22. Sightseeing

monument	piemineklis (v)	[piɛmineklis]
fortress	cietoksnis (v)	[tsiɛtɔksnis]
palace	pils (s)	[pils]
castle	pils (s)	[pils]
tower	tornis (v)	[tɔrnis]
mausoleum	mauzolejs (v)	[mauzɔlejs]

architecture	arhitektūra (s)	[arxitektu:ra]
medieval (adj)	viduslaiku	[viduslaiku]
ancient (adj)	senlaiku	[senlaiku]
national (adj)	nacionāls	[natsiɔna:ls]
famous (monument, etc.)	slavens	[slavens]

tourist	tūrists (v)	[tu:rists]
guide (person)	gids (v)	[gids]
excursion, sightseeing tour	ekskursija (s)	[ekskursija]
to show (vt)	parādīt	[para:di:t]

to tell (vt)	stāstīt	[staːstiːt]
to find (vt)	atrast	[atrast]
to get lost (lose one's way)	nomaldīties	[nɔmaldiːtiɛs]
map (e.g. underground ~)	shēma (s)	[sxɛːma]
map (e.g. city ~)	plāns (v)	[plaːns]

souvenir, gift	suvenīrs (v)	[suveniːrs]
gift shop	suvenīru veikals (v)	[suveniːru vɛikals]
to take pictures	fotografēt	[fotɔgrafeːt]
to have one's picture taken	fotografēties	[fotɔgrafeːtiɛs]

TRANSPORT

23. Airport

airport	lidosta (s)	[lidɔsta]
aeroplane	lidmašīna (s)	[lidmaʃiːna]
airline	aviokompānija (s)	[aviokɔmpaːnija]
air traffic controller	dispečers (v)	[dispetʃɛrs]
departure	izlidojums (v)	[izlidɔjums]
arrival	atlidošana (s)	[atlidɔʃana]
to arrive (by plane)	atlidot	[atlidɔt]
departure time	izlidojuma laiks (v)	[izlidɔjuma laiks]
arrival time	atlidošanās laiks (v)	[atlidɔʃanaːs laiks]
to be delayed	kavēties	[kaveːtiɛs]
flight delay	izlidojuma aizkavēšanās (s dsk)	[izlidɔjuma aizkave:ʃanaːs]
information board	informācijas tablo (v)	[infɔrmaːtsijas tablɔ]
information	informācija (s)	[infɔrmaːtsija]
to announce (vt)	paziņot	[paziɲɔt]
flight (e.g. next ~)	reiss (v)	[rɛis]
customs	muita (s)	[muita]
customs officer	muitas ierēdnis (v)	[muitas iɛreːdnis]
customs declaration	muitas deklerācija (s)	[muitas deklɛraːtsija]
to fill in (vt)	aizpildīt	[aizpildiːt]
to fill in the declaration	aizpildīt deklarāciju	[aizpildiːt deklaraːtsiju]
passport control	pasu kontrole (s)	[pasu kɔntrɔle]
luggage	bagāža (s)	[bagaːʒa]
hand luggage	rokas bagāža (s)	[rɔkas bagaːʒa]
luggage trolley	bagāžas ratiņi (v dsk)	[bagaːʒas ratiɲi]
landing	nolaišanās (s dsk)	[nɔlaiʃanaːs]
landing strip	nosēšanās josla (s)	[nɔseːʃanaːs jɔsla]
to land (vi)	nosēsties	[nɔseːstiɛs]
airstairs	traps (v)	[traps]
check-in	reģistrācija (s)	[redʲistraːtsija]
check-in counter	reģistrācijas galdiņš (v)	[redʲistraːtsijas galdiɲʃ]
to check-in (vi)	p011piereģistrēties	[piɛredʲistre:tiɛs]
boarding card	iekāpšanas talons (v)	[iɛkaːpʃanas talɔns]
departure gate	izeja (s)	[izeja]
transit	tranzīts (v)	[tranziːts]
to wait (vt)	gaidīt	[gaidiːt]

departure lounge	uzgaidāmā telpa (s)	[uzgaida:ma: telpa]
to see off	aizvadīt	[aizvadi:t]
to say goodbye	atvadīties	[atvadi:tiɛs]

24. Aeroplane

aeroplane	lidmašīna (s)	[lidmaʃi:na]
air ticket	aviobiļete (s)	[aviobilʲɛte]
airline	aviokompānija (s)	[aviokompa:nija]
airport	lidosta (s)	[lidosta]
supersonic (adj)	virsskaņas	[virskaɲas]

captain	kuģa komandieris (v)	[kudʲa komandiɛris]
crew	apkalpe (s)	[apkalpe]
pilot	pilots (v)	[pilots]
stewardess	stjuarte (s)	[stjuarte]
navigator	stūrmanis (v)	[stu:rmanis]

wings	spārni (v dsk)	[spa:rni]
tail	aste (s)	[aste]
cockpit	kabīne (s)	[kabi:ne]
engine	dzinējs (v)	[dzine:js]

| undercarriage (landing gear) | šasija (s) | [ʃasija] |
| turbine | turbīna (s) | [turbi:na] |

| propeller | propelleris (v) | [propelleris] |
| black box | melnā kaste (s) | [melna: kaste] |

| yoke (control column) | stūres rats (v) | [stu:res rats] |
| fuel | degviela (s) | [degviɛla] |

safety card	instrukcija (s)	[instruktsija]
oxygen mask	skābekļa maska (s)	[ska:beklʲa maska]
uniform	uniforma (s)	[uniforma]

| lifejacket | glābšanas veste (s) | [gla:bʃanas veste] |
| parachute | izpletnis (v) | [izpletnis] |

takeoff	pacelšanās (s dsk)	[patselʃana:s]
to take off (vi)	pacelties	[patseltiɛs]
runway	skrejceļš (v)	[skrejtselʲʃ]

| visibility | redzamība (s) | [redzami:ba] |
| flight (act of flying) | lidojums (v) | [lidojums] |

| altitude | augstums (v) | [augstums] |
| air pocket | gaisa bedre (s) | [gaisa bedre] |

seat	sēdeklis (v)	[sɛ:deklis]
headphones	austiņas (s dsk)	[austiɲas]
folding tray (tray table)	galdiņš (v)	[galdiɲʃ]
airplane window	iluminators (v)	[iluminators]
aisle	eja (s)	[eja]

25. Train

train	vilciens (v)	[viltsiɛns]
commuter train	elektrovilciens (v)	[ɛlektroviltsiɛns]
express train	ātrvilciens (v)	[a:trviltsiɛns]
diesel locomotive	dīzeļlokomotīve (s)	[di:zelʲlokɔmɔti:ve]
steam locomotive	lokomotīve (s)	[lɔkɔmɔti:ve]
coach, carriage	vagons (v)	[vagɔns]
buffet car	restorānvagons (v)	[restɔra:nvagɔns]
rails	sliedes (s dsk)	[sliɛdes]
railway	dzelzceļš (v)	[dzelztselʲʃ]
sleeper (track support)	gulsnis (v)	[gulsnis]
platform (railway ~)	platforma (s)	[platfɔrma]
platform (~ 1, 2, etc.)	ceļš (v)	[tselʲʃ]
semaphore	semafors (v)	[sɛmafɔrs]
station	stacija (s)	[statsija]
train driver	mašīnists (v)	[maʃi:nists]
porter (of luggage)	nesējs (v)	[nɛse:js]
carriage attendant	pavadonis (v)	[pavadɔnis]
passenger	pasažieris (v)	[pasaʒiɛris]
ticket inspector	kontrolieris (v)	[kɔntroliɛris]
corridor (in train)	koridors (v)	[kɔridɔrs]
emergency brake	stop-krāns (v)	[stɔp-kra:ns]
compartment	kupeja (s)	[kupeja]
berth	plaukts (v)	[plaukts]
upper berth	augšējais plaukts (v)	[augʃe:jais plaukts]
lower berth	apakšējais plaukts (v)	[apakʃe:jais plaukts]
bed linen, bedding	gultas veļa (s)	[gultas vɛlʲa]
ticket	biļete (s)	[bilʲɛte]
timetable	saraksts (v)	[saraksts]
information display	tablo (v)	[tablɔ]
to leave, to depart	atiet	[atiɛt]
departure (of train)	atiešana (s)	[atiɛʃana]
to arrive (ab. train)	ierasties	[iɛrastiɛs]
arrival	pienākšana (s)	[piɛna:kʃana]
to arrive by train	atbraukt ar vilcienu	[atbraukt ar viltsiɛnu]
to get on the train	iekāpt vilcienā	[iɛka:pt viltsiɛna:]
to get off the train	izkāpt no vilciena	[izka:pt nɔ viltsiɛna]
train crash	katastrofa (s)	[katastrofa]
to derail (vi)	noskriet no sliedēm	[nɔskriɛt nɔ sliɛde:m]
steam locomotive	lokomotīve (s)	[lɔkɔmɔti:ve]
stoker, fireman	kurinātājs (v)	[kurina:ta:js]
firebox	kurtuve (s)	[kurtuve]
coal	ogles (s dsk)	[ɔgles]

26. Ship

ship	kuģis (v)	[kudʲis]
vessel	kuģis (v)	[kudʲis]
steamship	tvaikonis (v)	[tvaikɔnis]
riverboat	motorkuģis (v)	[mɔtɔrkudʲis]
cruise ship	laineris (v)	[laineris]
cruiser	kreiseris (v)	[krɛiseris]
yacht	jahta (s)	[jaxta]
tugboat	velkonis (v)	[velkɔnis]
barge	barža (s)	[barʒa]
ferry	prāmis (v)	[pra:mis]
sailing ship	burinieks (v)	[buriniɛks]
brigantine	brigantīna (s)	[briganti:na]
ice breaker	ledlauzis (v)	[ledlauzis]
submarine	zemūdene (s)	[zɛmu:dɛne]
boat (flat-bottomed ~)	laiva (s)	[laiva]
dinghy	laiva (s)	[laiva]
lifeboat	glābšanas laiva (s)	[gla:bʃanas laiva]
motorboat	kuteris (v)	[kuteris]
captain	kapteinis (v)	[kaptɛinis]
seaman	matrozis (v)	[matrɔzis]
sailor	jūrnieks (v)	[ju:rniɛks]
crew	apkalpe (s)	[apkalpe]
boatswain	bocmanis (v)	[bɔtsmanis]
ship's boy	junga (v)	[juŋga]
cook	kuģa pavārs (v)	[kudʲa pava:rs]
ship's doctor	kuģa ārsts (v)	[kudʲa a:rsts]
deck	klājs (v)	[kla:js]
mast	masts (v)	[masts]
sail	bura (s)	[bura]
hold	tilpne (s)	[tilpne]
bow (prow)	priekšgals (v)	[priɛkʃgals]
stern	pakaļgals (v)	[pakalʲgals]
oar	airis (v)	[airis]
screw propeller	dzenskrūve (s)	[dzenskru:ve]
cabin	kajīte (s)	[kaji:te]
wardroom	kopkajīte (s)	[kɔpkaji:te]
engine room	mašīnu nodaļa (s)	[maʃi:nu nodalʲa]
bridge	komandtiltiņš (v)	[kɔmandtiltiɲʃ]
radio room	radio telpa (s)	[radiɔ telpa]
wave (radio)	vilnis (v)	[vilnis]
logbook	kuģa žurnāls (v)	[kudʲa ʒurna:ls]
spyglass	tālskatis (v)	[ta:lskatis]
bell	zvans (v)	[zvans]

flag	karogs (v)	[karɔgs]
hawser (mooring ~)	tauva (s)	[tauva]
knot (bowline, etc.)	mezgls (v)	[mezgls]

| deckrails | rokturis (v) | [rɔkturis] |
| gangway | traps (v) | [traps] |

anchor	enkurs (v)	[enkurs]
to weigh anchor	pacelt enkuru	[patselt enkuru]
to drop anchor	izmest enkuru	[izmest enkuru]
anchor chain	enkurķēde (s)	[enkurtʲɛːde]

port (harbour)	osta (s)	[ɔsta]
quay, wharf	piestātne (s)	[piɛstaːtne]
to berth (moor)	pietauvot	[piɛtauvɔt]
to cast off	atiet no krasta	[atiɛt nɔ krasta]

trip, voyage	ceļojums (v)	[tselʲɔjums]
cruise (sea trip)	kruīzs (v)	[kruiːzs]
course (route)	kurss (v)	[kurs]
route (itinerary)	maršruts (v)	[marʃruts]

fairway (safe water channel)	kuģu ceļš (v)	[kudʲu tselʲʃ]
shallows	sēklis (v)	[seːklis]
to run aground	uzsēsties uz sēkļa	[uzseːsties uz seːklʲa]

storm	vētra (s)	[veːtra]
signal	signāls (v)	[signaːls]
to sink (vi)	grimt	[grimt]
Man overboard!	Cilvēks aiz borta!	[tsilveːks aiz bɔrta!]
SOS (distress signal)	SOS	[sɔs]
ring buoy	glābšanas riņķis (v)	[glaːbʃanas riɲtʲʲis]

CITY

27. Urban transport

bus, coach	autobuss (v)	[autobus]
tram	tramvajs (v)	[tramvajs]
trolleybus	trolejbuss (v)	[trolejbus]
route (of bus, etc.)	maršruts (v)	[marʃruts]
number (e.g. bus ~)	numurs (v)	[numurs]
to go by ...	braukt ar ...	[braukt ar ...]
to get on (~ the bus)	iekāpt	[iɛka:pt]
to get off ...	izkāpt	[izka:pt]
stop (e.g. bus ~)	pietura (s)	[piɛtura]
next stop	nākamā pietura (s)	[na:kama: piɛtura]
terminus	galapunkts (v)	[galapunkts]
timetable	saraksts (v)	[saraksts]
to wait (vt)	gaidīt	[gaidi:t]
ticket	biļete (s)	[biḷɛte]
fare	biļetes maksa (s)	[biḷɛtes maksa]
cashier (ticket seller)	kasieris (v)	[kasiɛris]
ticket inspection	kontrole (s)	[kɔntrɔle]
ticket inspector	kontrolieris (v)	[kɔntrɔliɛris]
to be late (for ...)	nokavēties	[nɔkave:tiɛs]
to miss (~ the train, etc.)	nokavēt ...	[nɔkave:t ...]
to be in a hurry	steigties	[stɛigtiɛs]
taxi, cab	taksometrs (v)	[taksɔmetrs]
taxi driver	taksists (v)	[taksists]
by taxi	ar taksometru	[ar taksɔmetru]
taxi rank	taksometru stāvvieta (s)	[taksɔmetru sta:vviɛta]
to call a taxi	izsaukt taksometru	[izsaukt taksɔmetru]
to take a taxi	nolīgt taksometru	[nɔli:gt taksɔmetru]
traffic	satiksme (s)	[satiksme]
traffic jam	sastrēgums (v)	[sastrɛ:gums]
rush hour	maksimālās slodzes laiks (v)	[maksima:la:s slɔdzes laiks]
to park (vi)	novietot auto	[nɔviɛtɔt autɔ]
to park (vt)	novietot auto	[nɔviɛtɔt autɔ]
car park	autostāvvieta (s)	[autɔsta:vviɛta]
underground, tube	metro (v)	[metrɔ]
station	stacija (s)	[statsija]
to take the tube	braukt ar metro	[braukt ar metrɔ]
train	vilciens (v)	[viltsiɛns]
train station	dzelzceļa stacija (s)	[dzelztsɛḷa statsija]

28. City. Life in the city

city, town	pilsēta (s)	[pilsε:ta]
capital city	galvaspilsēta (s)	[galvaspilsε:ta]
village	ciems (v)	[tsiεms]
city map	pilsētas plāns (v)	[pilsε:tas pla:ns]
city centre	pilsētas centrs (v)	[pilsε:tas tsentrs]
suburb	piepilsēta (s)	[piεpilsε:ta]
suburban (adj)	piepilsētas	[piεpilsε:tas]
outskirts	nomale (s)	[nɔmale]
environs (suburbs)	apkārtnes (s dsk)	[apka:rtnes]
city block	kvartāls (v)	[kvarta:ls]
residential block (area)	dzīvojamais kvartāls (v)	[dzi:vɔjamais kvarta:ls]
traffic	satiksme (s)	[satiksme]
traffic lights	luksofors (v)	[luksɔfɔrs]
public transport	sabiedriskais transports (v)	[sabiεdriskais transpɔrts]
crossroads	krustojums (v)	[krustɔjums]
zebra crossing	gājēju pāreja (s)	[ga:je:ju pa:reja]
pedestrian subway	pazemes pāreja (s)	[pazεmes pa:reja]
to cross (~ the street)	pāriet	[pa:riεt]
pedestrian	kājāmgājējs (v)	[ka:ja:mga:je:js]
pavement	trotuārs (v)	[trɔtua:rs]
bridge	tilts (v)	[tilts]
embankment (river walk)	krastmala (s)	[krastmala]
fountain	strūklaka (s)	[stru:klaka]
allée (garden walkway)	gatve (s)	[gatve]
park	parks (v)	[parks]
boulevard	bulvāris (v)	[bulva:ris]
square	laukums (v)	[laukums]
avenue (wide street)	prospekts (v)	[prɔspekts]
street	iela (s)	[iεla]
side street	šķērsiela (s)	[ʃťε:rsiεla]
dead end	strupceļš (v)	[struptselʲʃ]
house	māja (s)	[ma:ja]
building	ēka (s)	[ε:ka]
skyscraper	augstceltne (s)	[augsttseltne]
facade	fasāde (s)	[fasa:de]
roof	jumts (v)	[jumts]
window	logs (v)	[lɔgs]
arch	loks (v)	[lɔks]
column	kolona (s)	[kɔlɔna]
corner	stūris (v)	[stu:ris]
shop window	skatlogs (v)	[skatlɔgs]
signboard (store sign, etc.)	izkārtne (s)	[izka:rtne]
poster	afiša (s)	[afiʃa]
advertising poster	reklāmu plakāts (v)	[rekla:mu plaka:ts]

hoarding	reklāmu dēlis (v)	[rekla:mu de:lis]
rubbish	atkritumi (v dsk)	[atkritumi]
rubbish bin	atkritumu tvertne (s)	[atkritumu tvertne]
to litter (vi)	piegružot	[piɛgruʒɔt]
rubbish dump	izgāztuve (s)	[izga:ztuve]

telephone box	telefona būda (s)	[tɛlefɔna bu:da]
lamppost	laterna (s)	[laterna]
bench (park ~)	sols (v)	[sɔls]

police officer	policists (v)	[politsists]
police	policija (s)	[politsija]
beggar	nabags (v)	[nabags]
homeless (n)	bezpajumtnieks (v)	[bezpajumtniɛks]

29. Urban institutions

shop	veikals (v)	[vɛikals]
chemist, pharmacy	aptieka (s)	[aptiɛka]
optician (spectacles shop)	optika (s)	[ɔptika]
shopping centre	tirdzniecības centrs (v)	[tirdzniɛtsi:bas tsentrs]
supermarket	lielveikals (v)	[liɛlvɛikals]

bakery	maiznīca (s)	[maizni:tsa]
baker	maiznieks (v)	[maizniɛks]
cake shop	konditoreja (s)	[kɔnditɔreja]
grocery shop	pārtikas preču veikals (v)	[pa:rtikas pretʃu vɛikals]
butcher shop	gaļas veikals (v)	[gaļʲas vɛikals]

greengrocer	sakņu veikals (v)	[sakņu vɛikals]
market	tirgus (v)	[tirgus]

coffee bar	kafejnīca (s)	[kafejni:tsa]
restaurant	restorāns (v)	[restora:ns]
pub, bar	alus krogs (v)	[alus krɔgs]
pizzeria	picērija (s)	[pitse:rija]

hairdresser	frizētava (s)	[frizɛ:tava]
post office	pasts (v)	[pasts]
dry cleaners	ķīmiskā tīrītava (s)	[tʲi:miska: ti:ri:tava]
photo studio	fotostudija (s)	[fɔtostudija]

shoe shop	apavu veikals (v)	[apavu vɛikals]
bookshop	grāmatnīca (s)	[gra:matni:tsa]
sports shop	sporta preču veikals (v)	[spɔrta pretʃu vɛikals]

clothes repair shop	apģērbu labošana (s)	[apdʲe:rbu labɔʃana]
formal wear hire	apģērbu noma (s)	[apdʲe:rbu nɔma]
video rental shop	filmu noma (s)	[filmu nɔma]

circus	cirks (v)	[tsirks]
zoo	zoodārzs (v)	[zɔɔda:rzs]
cinema	kinoteātris (v)	[kinɔtea:tris]
museum	muzejs (v)	[muzejs]

library	bibliotēka (s)	[bibliotɛ:ka]
theatre	teātris (v)	[tea:tris]
opera (opera house)	opera (s)	[ɔpɛra]
nightclub	naktsklubs (v)	[naktsklubs]
casino	kazino (v)	[kazinɔ]

mosque	mošeja (s)	[mɔʃeja]
synagogue	sinagoga (s)	[sinagɔga]
cathedral	katedrāle (s)	[katedra:le]
temple	dievnams (v)	[diɛvnams]
church	baznīca (s)	[bazni:tsa]

college	institūts (v)	[institu:ts]
university	universitāte (s)	[univɛrsita:te]
school	skola (s)	[skɔla]

prefecture	prefektūra (s)	[prefektu:ra]
town hall	mērija (s)	[me:rija]
hotel	viesnīca (s)	[viɛsni:tsa]
bank	banka (s)	[banka]

embassy	vēstniecība (s)	[ve:stniɛtsi:ba]
travel agency	tūrisma aģentūra (s)	[tu:risma adˈentu:ra]
information office	izziņu birojs (v)	[izziņu birojs]
currency exchange	apmaiņas punkts (v)	[apmaiņas punkts]

| underground, tube | metro (v) | [metrɔ] |
| hospital | slimnīca (s) | [slimni:tsa] |

| petrol station | degvielas uzpildes stacija (s) | [degviɛlas uzpildes statsija] |
| car park | autostāvvieta (s) | [autɔsta:vviɛta] |

30. Signs

signboard (store sign, etc.)	izkārtne (s)	[izka:rtne]
notice (door sign, etc.)	uzraksts (v)	[uzraksts]
poster	plakāts (v)	[plaka:ts]
direction sign	ceļrādis (v)	[tselˈra:dis]
arrow (sign)	bultiņa (s)	[bultiņa]

caution	brīdinājums (v)	[bri:dina:jums]
warning sign	brīdinājums (v)	[bri:dina:jums]
to warn (vt)	brīdināt	[bri:dina:t]

rest day (weekly ~)	brīvdiena (s)	[bri:vdiɛna]
timetable (schedule)	saraksts (v)	[saraksts]
opening hours	darba laiks (v)	[darba laiks]

WELCOME!	LAIPNI LŪDZAM!	[laipni lu:dzam!]
ENTRANCE	IEEJA	[iɛeja]
WAY OUT	IZEJA	[izeja]
PUSH	GRŪST	[gru:st]
PULL	VILKT	[vilkt]

| OPEN | ATVĒRTS | [atve:rts] |
| CLOSED | SLĒGTS | [sle:gts] |

| WOMEN | SIEVIEŠU | [siɛviɛʃu] |
| MEN | VĪRIEŠU | [vi:riɛʃu] |

DISCOUNTS	ATLAIDES	[atlaides]
SALE	IZPĀRDOŠANA	[izpa:rdɔʃana]
NEW!	JAUNUMS!	[jaunums!]
FREE	BEZMAKSAS	[bezmaksas]

ATTENTION!	UZMANĪBU!	[uzmani:bu!]
NO VACANCIES	BRĪVU VIETU NAV	[bri:vu viɛtu nav]
RESERVED	REZERVĒTS	[rɛzerve:ts]

| ADMINISTRATION | ADMINISTRĀCIJA | [administra:tsija] |
| STAFF ONLY | TIKAI PERSONĀLAM | [tikai pɛrsɔna:lam] |

BEWARE OF THE DOG!	NIKNS SUNS	[nikns suns]
NO SMOKING	SMĒĶĒT AIZLIEGTS!	[smɛ:tɬe:t aizliɛgts!]
DO NOT TOUCH!	AR ROKĀM NEAIZTIKT	[ar rɔka:m neaiztikt]

DANGEROUS	BĪSTAMI	[bi:stami]
DANGER	BĪSTAMS	[bi:stams]
HIGH VOLTAGE	AUGSTSPRIEGUMS	[augstspriɛgums]
NO SWIMMING!	PELDĒT AIZLIEGTS!	[pelde:t aizliɛgts!]
OUT OF ORDER	NESTRĀDĀ	[nestra:da:]

FLAMMABLE	UGUNSNEDROŠS	[ugunsnedrɔʃs]
FORBIDDEN	AIZLIEGTS	[aizliɛgts]
NO TRESPASSING!	IEIEJA AIZLIEGTA	[iɛiɛja aizliɛgta]
WET PAINT	SVAIGI KRĀSOTS	[svaigi kra:sɔts]

31. Shopping

to buy (purchase)	pirkt	[pirkt]
shopping	pirkums (v)	[pirkums]
to go shopping	iepirkties	[iɛpirktiɛs]
shopping	iepirkšanās (s)	[iɛpirkʃana:s]

| to be open (ab. shop) | strādāt | [stra:da:t] |
| to be closed | slēgties | [sle:gtiɛs] |

footwear, shoes	apavi (v dsk)	[apavi]
clothes, clothing	apģērbs (v)	[apdʲe:rbs]
cosmetics	kosmētika (s)	[kɔsme:tika]
food products	pārtikas produkti (v dsk)	[pa:rtikas prɔdukti]
gift, present	dāvana (s)	[da:vana]

| shop assistant (masc.) | pārdevējs (v) | [pa:rdɛve:js] |
| shop assistant (fem.) | pārdevēja (s) | [pa:rdɛve:ja] |

| cash desk | kase (s) | [kase] |
| mirror | spogulis (v) | [spɔgulis] |

| counter (shop ~) | lete (s) | [lɛte] |
| fitting room | pielaikošanas kabīne (s) | [piɛlaikɔʃanas kabiːne] |

to try on	pielaikot	[piɛlaikɔt]
to fit (ab. dress, etc.)	derēt	[dɛreːt]
to fancy (vt)	patikt	[patikt]

price	cena (s)	[tsɛna]
price tag	cenas zīme (s)	[tsɛnas ziːme]
to cost (vt)	maksāt	[maksaːt]
How much?	Cik?	[tsik?]
discount	atlaide (s)	[atlaide]

inexpensive (adj)	ne visai dārgs	[ne visai daːrgs]
cheap (adj)	lēts	[leːts]
expensive (adj)	dārgs	[daːrgs]
It's expensive	Tas ir dārgi	[tas ir daːrgi]

hire (n)	noma (s)	[nɔma]
to hire (~ a dinner jacket)	paņemt nomā	[paɲemt nɔmaː]
credit (trade credit)	kredīts (v)	[krediːts]
on credit (adv)	uz kredīta	[uz krediːta]

CLOTHING & ACCESSORIES

32. Outerwear. Coats

clothes	apģērbs (v)	[apdʲeːrbs]
outerwear	virsdrēbes (s dsk)	[virsdrɛːbes]
winter clothing	ziemas drēbes (s dsk)	[ziɛmas drɛːbes]
coat (overcoat)	mētelis (v)	[mɛːtelis]
fur coat	kažoks (v)	[kaʒɔks]
fur jacket	puskažoks (v)	[puskaʒɔks]
down coat	dūnu mētelis (v)	[duːnu mɛːtelis]
jacket (e.g. leather ~)	jaka (s)	[jaka]
raincoat (trenchcoat, etc.)	apmetnis (v)	[apmetnis]
waterproof (adj)	ūdensnecaurlaidīgs	[uːdensnetsaurlaidiːgs]

33. Men's & women's clothing

shirt (button shirt)	krekls (v)	[krekls]
trousers	bikses (s dsk)	[bikses]
jeans	džinsi (v dsk)	[dʒinsi]
suit jacket	žakete (s)	[ʒakɛte]
suit	uzvalks (v)	[uzvalks]
dress (frock)	kleita (s)	[klɛita]
skirt	svārki (v dsk)	[svaːrki]
blouse	blūze (s)	[bluːze]
knitted jacket (cardigan, etc.)	vilnaina jaka (s)	[vilnaina jaka]
jacket (of woman's suit)	žakete (s)	[ʒakɛte]
T-shirt	sporta krekls (v)	[sporta krekls]
shorts (short trousers)	šorti (v dsk)	[ʃorti]
tracksuit	sporta tērps (v)	[sporta teːrps]
bathrobe	halāts (v)	[xalaːts]
pyjamas	pidžama (s)	[pidʒama]
jumper (sweater)	svīteris (v)	[sviːteris]
pullover	pulovers (v)	[pulovɛrs]
waistcoat	veste (s)	[veste]
tailcoat	fraka (s)	[fraka]
dinner suit	smokings (v)	[smɔkiŋgs]
uniform	uniforma (s)	[uniforma]
workwear	darba apģērbs (v)	[darba apdʲeːrbs]
boiler suit	kombinezons (v)	[kɔmbinezons]
coat (e.g. doctor's smock)	halāts (v)	[xalaːts]

34. Clothing. Underwear

underwear	veļa (s)	[vɛlʲa]
pants	bokseršorti (v dsk)	[bɔksɛrʃɔrti]
panties	biksītes (s dsk)	[biksi:tes]
vest (singlet)	apakškrekls (v)	[apakʃkrekls]
socks	zeķes (s dsk)	[zɛtʲes]

nightgown	naktskrekls (v)	[naktskrekls]
bra	krūšturis (v)	[kru:ʃturis]
knee highs (knee-high socks)	pusgarās zeķes (s dsk)	[pusgara:s zɛtʲes]
tights	zeķubikses (s dsk)	[zɛtʲubikses]
stockings (hold ups)	sieviešu zeķes (s dsk)	[siɛviɛʃu zɛtʲes]
swimsuit, bikini	peldkostīms (v)	[peldkɔsti:ms]

35. Headwear

hat	cepure (s)	[tsɛpure]
trilby hat	platmale (s)	[platmale]
baseball cap	beisbola cepure (s)	[bɛisbɔla tsɛpure]
flatcap	žokejcepure (s)	[ʒɔkejtsɛpure]

beret	berete (s)	[bɛrɛte]
hood	kapuce (s)	[kaputse]
panama hat	panama (s)	[panama]
knit cap (knitted hat)	adīta cepurīte (s)	[adi:ta tsɛpuri:te]

headscarf	lakats (v)	[lakats]
women's hat	cepurīte (s)	[tsɛpuri:te]

hard hat	ķivere (s)	[tʲivɛre]
forage cap	laiviņa (s)	[laiviɲa]
helmet	bruņu cepure (s)	[bruɲu tsɛpure]

bowler	katliņš (v)	[katliɲʃ]
top hat	cilindrs (v)	[tsilindrs]

36. Footwear

footwear	apavi (v dsk)	[apavi]
shoes (men's shoes)	puszābaki (v dsk)	[pusza:baki]
shoes (women's shoes)	kurpes (s dsk)	[kurpes]
boots (e.g., cowboy ~)	zābaki (v dsk)	[za:baki]
carpet slippers	čības (s dsk)	[tʃi:bas]

trainers	sporta kurpes (s dsk)	[spɔrta kurpes]
trainers	kedas (s dsk)	[kɛdas]
sandals	sandales (s dsk)	[sandales]

cobbler (shoe repairer)	kurpnieks (v)	[kurpniɛks]
heel	papēdis (v)	[pape:dis]

pair (of shoes)	pāris (v)	[pa:ris]
lace (shoelace)	aukla (s)	[aukla]
to lace up (vt)	saitēt	[saite:t]
shoehorn	kurpju velkamais (v)	[kurpju velkamais]
shoe polish	apavu krēms (v)	[apavu kre:ms]

37. Personal accessories

gloves	cimdi (v dsk)	[tsimdi]
mittens	dūraiņi (v dsk)	[du:raiɲi]
scarf (muffler)	šalle (s)	[ʃalle]

glasses	brilles (s dsk)	[brilles]
frame (eyeglass ~)	ietvars (v)	[iɛtvars]
umbrella	lietussargs (v)	[liɛtusargs]
walking stick	spieķis (v)	[spiɛtʲis]
hairbrush	matu suka (s)	[matu suka]
fan	vēdeklis (v)	[vɛ:deklis]

tie (necktie)	kaklasaite (s)	[kaklasaite]
bow tie	tauriņš (v)	[tauriɲʃ]
braces	bikšturi (v dsk)	[bikʃturi]
handkerchief	kabatlakatiņš (v)	[kabatlakatiɲʃ]

comb	ķemme (s)	[tʲemme]
hair slide	matu sprādze (s)	[matu spra:dze]
hairpin	matadata (s)	[matadata]
buckle	sprādze (s)	[spra:dze]

| belt | josta (s) | [jɔsta] |
| shoulder strap | siksna (s) | [siksna] |

bag (handbag)	soma (s)	[sɔma]
handbag	somiņa (s)	[sɔmiɲa]
rucksack	mugursoma (s)	[mugursɔma]

38. Clothing. Miscellaneous

fashion	mode (s)	[mɔde]
in vogue (adj)	moderns	[mɔderns]
fashion designer	modelētājs (v)	[mɔdɛlɛ:ta:js]

collar	apkakle (s)	[apkakle]
pocket	kabata (s)	[kabata]
pocket (as adj)	kabatas	[kabatas]
sleeve	piedurkne (s)	[piɛdurkne]
hanging loop	pakaramais (v)	[pakaramais]
flies (on trousers)	bikšu priekša	[bikʃu priɛkʃa]

zip (fastener)	rāvējslēdzējs (v)	[ra:ve:jsle:dze:js]
fastener	aizdare (s)	[aizdare]
button	poga (s)	[pɔga]

| buttonhole | pogcaurums (v) | [pɔgtsaurums] |
| to come off (ab. button) | atrauties | [atrautiɛs] |

to sew (vi, vt)	šūt	[ʃuːt]
to embroider (vi, vt)	izšūt	[izʃuːt]
embroidery	izšūšana (s)	[izʃuːʃana]
sewing needle	adata (s)	[adata]
thread	diegs (v)	[diɛgs]
seam	šuve (s)	[ʃuve]

to get dirty (vi)	notraipīties	[nɔtraipiːtiɛs]
stain (mark, spot)	traips (v)	[traips]
to crease, crumple (vi)	saburzīties	[saburziːtiɛs]
to tear, to rip (vt)	saplēst	[sapleːst]
clothes moth	kode (s)	[kɔde]

39. Personal care. Cosmetics

toothpaste	zobu pasta (s)	[zɔbu pasta]
toothbrush	zobu suka (s)	[zɔbu suka]
to clean one's teeth	tīrīt zobus	[tiːriːt zɔbus]

razor	skuveklis (v)	[skuveklis]
shaving cream	skūšanas krēms (v)	[skuːʃanas kreːms]
to shave (vi)	skūties	[skuːtiɛs]

| soap | ziepes (s dsk) | [ziɛpes] |
| shampoo | šampūns (v) | [ʃampuːns] |

scissors	šķēres (s dsk)	[ʃcɛːres]
nail file	nagu vīlīte (s)	[nagu viːliːte]
nail clippers	knaiblītes (s dsk)	[knaibliːtes]
tweezers	pincete (s)	[pintsɛte]

cosmetics	kosmētika (s)	[kɔsmeːtika]
face mask	maska (s)	[maska]
manicure	manikīrs (v)	[manikiːrs]
to have a manicure	taisīt manikīru	[taisiːt manikiːru]
pedicure	pedikīrs (v)	[pedikiːrs]

make-up bag	kosmētikas somiņa (s)	[kɔsmeːtikas sɔmiɲa]
face powder	pūderis (v)	[puːderis]
powder compact	pūdernīca (s)	[puːderniːtsa]
blusher	vaigu sārtums (v)	[vaigu saːrtums]

perfume (bottled)	smaržas (s dsk)	[smarʒas]
toilet water (lotion)	tualetes ūdens (v)	[tualɛtes uːdens]
lotion	losjons (v)	[lɔsjɔns]
cologne	odekolons (v)	[ɔdekɔlɔns]

eyeshadow	acu ēnas (s dsk)	[atsu ɛːnas]
eyeliner	acu zīmulis (v)	[atsu ziːmulis]
mascara	skropstu tuša (s)	[skrɔpstu tuʃa]
lipstick	lūpu krāsa (s)	[luːpu kraːsa]

nail polish	nagu laka (s)	[nagu laka]
hair spray	matu laka (s)	[matu laka]
deodorant	dezodorants (v)	[dezɔdɔrants]

cream	krēms (v)	[kre:ms]
face cream	sejas krēms (v)	[sejas kre:ms]
hand cream	rokas krēms (v)	[rɔkas kre:ms]
anti-wrinkle cream	pretgrumbu krēms (v)	[pretgrumbu kre:ms]
day cream	dienas krēms (v)	[diɛnas kre:ms]
night cream	nakts krēms (v)	[nakts kre:ms]
day (as adj)	dienas	[diɛnas]
night (as adj)	nakts	[nakts]

tampon	tampons (v)	[tampɔns]
toilet paper (toilet roll)	tualetes papīrs (v)	[tualɛtes papi:rs]
hair dryer	fēns (v)	[fe:ns]

40. Watches. Clocks

watch (wristwatch)	rokas pulkstenis (v)	[rɔkas pulkstenis]
dial	ciparnīca (s)	[tsiparni:tsa]
hand (of clock, watch)	bultiņa (s)	[bultiɲa]
metal bracelet	metāla siksniņa (s)	[mɛta:la siksniɲa]
watch strap	siksniņa (s)	[siksniɲa]

battery	baterija (s)	[baterija]
to be flat (battery)	izlādēties	[izla:de:tiɛs]
to change a battery	nomainīt bateriju	[nɔmaini:t bateriju]
to run fast	steigties	[stɛigtiɛs]
to run slow	atpalikt	[atpalikt]

wall clock	sienas pulkstenis (v)	[siɛnas pulkstenis]
hourglass	smilšu pulkstenis (v)	[smilʃu pulkstenis]
sundial	saules pulkstenis (v)	[saules pulkstenis]
alarm clock	modinātājs (v)	[mɔdina:ta:js]
watchmaker	pulksteņmeistars (v)	[pulksteɲmɛistars]
to repair (vt)	remontēt	[remɔnte:t]

EVERYDAY EXPERIENCE

41. Money

money	nauda (s)	[nauda]
currency exchange	maiņa (s)	[maiɲa]
exchange rate	kurss (v)	[kurs]
cashpoint	bankomāts (v)	[bankɔma:ts]
coin	monēta (s)	[mɔnɛ:ta]
dollar	dolārs (v)	[dɔla:rs]
euro	eiro (v)	[ɛirɔ]
lira	lira (s)	[lira]
Deutschmark	marka (s)	[marka]
franc	franks (v)	[franks]
pound sterling	sterliņu mārciņa (s)	[sterliɲu ma:rtsiɲa]
yen	jena (s)	[jena]
debt	parāds (v)	[para:ds]
debtor	parādnieks (v)	[para:dniɛks]
to lend (money)	aizdot	[aizdɔt]
to borrow (vi, vt)	aizņemties	[aizɲemtiɛs]
bank	banka (s)	[banka]
account	konts (v)	[kɔnts]
to deposit (vt)	noguldīt	[nɔguldi:t]
to deposit into the account	noguldīt kontā	[nɔguldi:t kɔnta:]
to withdraw (vt)	izņemt no konta	[izɲemt nɔ kɔnta]
credit card	kredītkarte (s)	[kredi:tkarte]
cash	skaidra nauda (v)	[skaidra nauda]
cheque	čeks (v)	[tʃeks]
to write a cheque	izrakstīt čeku	[izraksti:t tʃɛku]
chequebook	čeku grāmatiņa (s)	[tʃɛku gra:matiɲa]
wallet	maks (v)	[maks]
purse	maks (v)	[maks]
safe	seifs (v)	[sɛifs]
heir	mantinieks (v)	[mantiniɛks]
inheritance	mantojums (v)	[mantɔjums]
fortune (wealth)	mantība (s)	[manti:ba]
lease	rentēšana (s)	[rente:ʃana]
rent (money)	īres maksa (s)	[i:res maksa]
to rent (sth from sb)	īrēt	[i:re:t]
price	cena (s)	[tsɛna]
cost	vērtība (s)	[ve:rti:ba]

sum	summa (s)	[summa]
to spend (vt)	tērēt	[tɛ:re:t]
expenses	izdevumi (v dsk)	[izdɛvumi]
to economize (vi, vt)	taupīt	[taupi:t]
economical	taupīgs	[taupi:gs]

to pay (vi, vt)	maksāt	[maksa:t]
payment	samaksa (s)	[samaksa]
change (give the ~)	atlikums (v)	[atlikums]

tax	nodoklis (v)	[nɔdɔklis]
fine	sods (v)	[sɔds]
to fine (vt)	uzlikt naudas sodu	[uzlikt naudas sɔdu]

42. Post. Postal service

post office	pasts (v)	[pasts]
post (letters, etc.)	pasts (v)	[pasts]
postman	pastnieks (v)	[pastniɛks]
opening hours	darba laiks (v)	[darba laiks]

letter	vēstule (s)	[ve:stule]
registered letter	ierakstīta vēstule (s)	[iɛraksti:ta ve:stule]
postcard	pastkarte (s)	[pastkarte]
telegram	telegramma (s)	[tɛlegramma]
parcel	sūtījums (v)	[su:ti:jums]
money transfer	naudas pārvedums (v)	[naudas pa:rvɛdums]

to receive (vt)	saņemt	[saɲemt]
to send (vt)	nosūtīt	[nɔsu:ti:t]
sending	aizsūtīšana (s)	[aizsu:ti:ʃana]
address	adrese (s)	[adrɛse]
postcode	indekss (v)	[indeks]
sender	sūtītājs (v)	[su:ti:ta:js]
receiver	saņēmējs (v)	[saɲɛ:me:js]

name (first name)	vārds (v)	[va:rds]
surname (last name)	uzvārds (v)	[uzva:rds]
postage rate	tarifs (v)	[tarifs]
standard (adj)	parasts	[parasts]
economical (adj)	ekonomisks	[ekɔnɔmisks]

weight	svars (v)	[svars]
to weigh (~ letters)	svērt	[sve:rt]
envelope	aploksne (s)	[aplɔksne]
postage stamp	marka (s)	[marka]
to stamp an envelope	uzlīmēt marku	[uzli:me:t marku]

43. Banking

bank	banka (s)	[banka]
branch (of bank, etc.)	nodaļa (s)	[nɔdalʲa]

| consultant | konsultants (v) | [kɔnsultants] |
| manager (director) | pārvaldnieks (v) | [paːrvaldniɛks] |

bank account	konts (v)	[kɔnts]
account number	konta numurs (v)	[kɔnta numurs]
current account	tekošais konts (v)	[tekɔʃais kɔnts]
deposit account	iekrājumu konts (v)	[iɛkraːjumu kɔnts]

to open an account	atvērt kontu	[atveːrt kɔntu]
to close the account	aizvērt kontu	[aizveːrt kɔntu]
to deposit into the account	nolikt kontā	[nɔlikt kɔntaː]
to withdraw (vt)	izņemt no konta	[izɲemt nɔ kɔnta]

deposit	ieguldījums (v)	[iɛguldiːjums]
to make a deposit	veikt ieguldījumu	[vɛikt iɛguldiːjumu]
wire transfer	pārskaitījums (v)	[paːrskaiti:jums]
to wire, to transfer	pārskaitīt	[paːrskaiti:t]

| sum | summa (s) | [summa] |
| How much? | Cik? | [tsik?] |

| signature | paraksts (v) | [paraksts] |
| to sign (vt) | parakstīt | [paraksti:t] |

credit card	kredītkarte (s)	[kredi:tkarte]
code (PIN code)	kods (v)	[kɔds]
credit card number	kredītkartes numurs (v)	[kredi:tkartes numurs]
cashpoint	bankomāts (v)	[bankɔma:ts]

cheque	čeks (v)	[tʃeks]
to write a cheque	izrakstīt čeku	[izraksti:t tʃɛku]
chequebook	čeku grāmatiņa (s)	[tʃɛku gra:matiɲa]

loan (bank ~)	kredīts (v)	[kredi:ts]
to apply for a loan	griezties pēc kredīta	[griɛzties pe:ts kredi:ta]
to get a loan	ņemt kredītu	[ɲemt kredi:tu]
to give a loan	dot kredītu	[dɔt kredi:tu]
guarantee	garantija (s)	[garantija]

44. Telephone. Phone conversation

telephone	tālrunis (v)	[ta:lrunis]
mobile phone	mobilais tālrunis (v)	[mɔbilais ta:lrunis]
answerphone	autoatbildētājs (v)	[autɔatbildɛ:ta:js]

| to call (by phone) | zvanīt | [zvani:t] |
| call, ring | zvans (v) | [zvans] |

to dial a number	uzgriezt telefona numuru	[uzgriɛzt tɛlefɔna numuru]
Hello!	Hallo!	[xallɔ!]
to ask (vt)	pajautāt	[pajauta:t]
to answer (vi, vt)	atbildēt	[atbilde:t]
to hear (vt)	dzirdēt	[dzirde:t]
well (adv)	labi	[labi]

not well (adv)	slikti	[slikti]
noises (interference)	traucējumi (v dsk)	[trautse:jumi]
receiver	klausule (s)	[klausule]
to pick up (~ the phone)	noņemt klausuli	[noɲemt klausuli]
to hang up (~ the phone)	nolikt klausuli	[nolikt klausuli]
busy (engaged)	aizņemts	[aizɲemts]
to ring (ab. phone)	zvanīt	[zvani:t]
telephone book	telefona grāmata (s)	[tɛlefona gra:mata]
local (adj)	vietējais	[viɛte:jais]
local call	vietējais zvans (v)	[viɛte:jais zvans]
trunk (e.g. ~ call)	starppilsētu	[starppilsɛ:tu]
trunk call	starppilsētu zvans (v)	[starppilsɛ:tu zvans]
international (adj)	starptautiskais	[starptautiskais]
international call	starptautiskais zvans (v)	[starptautiskais zvans]

45. Mobile telephone

mobile phone	mobilais tālrunis (v)	[mobilais ta:lrunis]
display	displejs (v)	[displejs]
button	poga (s)	[poga]
SIM card	SIM-karte (s)	[sim-karte]
battery	baterija (s)	[baterija]
to be flat (battery)	izlādēties	[izla:de:tiɛs]
charger	uzlādes ierīce (s)	[uzla:des iɛri:tse]
menu	izvēlne (s)	[izve:lne]
settings	uzstādījumi (v dsk)	[uzsta:di:jumi]
tune (melody)	melodija (s)	[melodija]
to select (vt)	izvēlēties	[izvɛ:le:tiɛs]
calculator	kalkulators (v)	[kalkulators]
voice mail	autoatbildētājs (v)	[autoatbildɛ:ta:js]
alarm clock	modinātājs (v)	[modina:ta:js]
contacts	telefona grāmata (s)	[tɛlefona gra:mata]
SMS (text message)	SMS-ziņa (s)	[sms-ziɲa]
subscriber	abonents (v)	[abonents]

46. Stationery

ballpoint pen	lodīšu pildspalva (s)	[lodi:ʃu pildspalva]
fountain pen	spalvaskāts (v)	[spalvaska:ts]
pencil	zīmulis (v)	[zi:mulis]
highlighter	marķieris (v)	[martˡiɛris]
felt-tip pen	flomasteris (v)	[flomasteris]
notepad	bloknots (v)	[bloknots]
diary	dienasgrāmata (s)	[diɛnasgra:mata]

ruler	lineāls (v)	[linea:ls]
calculator	kalkulators (v)	[kalkulatɔrs]
rubber	dzēšgumija (s)	[dze:ʃgumija]
drawing pin	piespraude (s)	[piɛspraude]
paper clip	saspraude (s)	[saspraude]

glue	līme (s)	[li:me]
stapler	skavotājs (v)	[skavɔta:js]
hole punch	caurumotājs (v)	[tsaurumɔta:js]
pencil sharpener	zīmuļu asināmais (v)	[zi:mulʲu asina:mais]

47. Foreign languages

language	valoda (s)	[valɔda]
foreign (adj)	svešs	[sveʃs]
foreign language	svešvaloda (s)	[sveʃvalɔda]
to study (vt)	pētīt	[pe:ti:t]
to learn (language, etc.)	mācīties	[ma:tsi:tiɛs]

to read (vi, vt)	lasīt	[lasi:t]
to speak (vi, vt)	runāt	[runa:t]
to understand (vt)	saprast	[saprast]
to write (vt)	rakstīt	[raksti:t]

fast (adv)	ātri	[a:tri]
slowly (adv)	lēni	[le:ni]
fluently (adv)	brīvi	[bri:vi]

rules	noteikumi (v dsk)	[nɔtɛikumi]
grammar	gramatika (s)	[gramatika]
vocabulary	leksika (s)	[leksika]
phonetics	fonētika (s)	[fɔne:tika]

textbook	mācību grāmata (s)	[ma:tsi:bu gra:mata]
dictionary	vārdnīca (s)	[va:rdni:tsa]
teach-yourself book	pašmācības grāmata (s)	[paʃma:tsi:bas gra:mata]
phrasebook	sarunvārdnīca (s)	[sarunva:rdni:tsa]

cassette, tape	kasete (s)	[kasɛte]
videotape	videokasete (s)	[videɔkasɛte]
CD, compact disc	kompaktdisks (v)	[kɔmpaktdisks]
DVD	DVD (v)	[dvd]

alphabet	alfabēts (v)	[alfabe:ts]
to spell (vt)	izrunāt pa burtiem	[izruna:t pa burtiɛm]
pronunciation	izruna (s)	[izruna]

accent	akcents (v)	[aktsents]
with an accent	ar akcentu	[ar aktsentu]
without an accent	bez akcenta	[bez aktsenta]

word	vārds (v)	[va:rds]
meaning	nozīme (s)	[nɔzi:me]
course (e.g. a French ~)	kursi (v dsk)	[kursi]

| to sign up | pierakstīties | [piɛraksti:tiɛs] |
| teacher | pasniedzējs (v) | [pasniɛdze:js] |

translation (process)	tulkošana (s)	[tulkoʃana]
translation (text, etc.)	tulkojums (v)	[tulkojums]
translator	tulks (v)	[tulks]
interpreter	tulks (v)	[tulks]

| polyglot | poliglots (v) | [poliglots] |
| memory | atmiņa (s) | [atmiɲa] |

MEALS. RESTAURANT

48. Table setting

spoon	karote (s)	[karɔte]
knife	nazis (v)	[nazis]
fork	dakša (s)	[dakʃa]

cup (e.g., coffee ~)	tase (s)	[tase]
plate (dinner ~)	šķīvis (v)	[ʃcʲiːvis]
saucer	apakštase (s)	[apakʃtase]
serviette	salvete (s)	[salvɛte]
toothpick	zobu bakstāmais (v)	[zɔbu baksta:mais]

49. Restaurant

restaurant	restorāns (v)	[restɔraːns]
coffee bar	kafejnīca (s)	[kafejni:tsa]
pub, bar	bārs (v)	[ba:rs]
tearoom	tēju nams (v)	[te:ju nams]

waiter	oficiants (v)	[ɔfitsiants]
waitress	oficiante (s)	[ɔfitsiante]
barman	bārmenis (v)	[ba:rmenis]

menu	ēdienkarte (s)	[e:diɛnkarte]
wine list	vīnu karte (s)	[vi:nu karte]
to book a table	rezervēt galdiņu	[rɛzerve:t galdiɲu]

course, dish	ēdiens (v)	[e:diɛns]
to order (meal)	pasūtīt	[pasu:ti:t]
to make an order	pasūtīt	[pasu:ti:t]

aperitif	aperitīvs (v)	[aperiti:vs]
starter	uzkožamais (v)	[uzkɔʒamais]
dessert, pudding	deserts (v)	[dɛserts]

bill	rēķins (v)	[re:tʲins]
to pay the bill	samaksāt rēķinu	[samaksa:t re:tʲinu]
to give change	iedot atlikumu	[iɛdɔt atlikumu]
tip	dzeramnauda (s)	[dzɛramnauda]

50. Meals

food	ēdiens (v)	[e:diɛns]
to eat (vi, vt)	ēst	[ɛ:st]

breakfast	brokastis (s dsk)	[brɔkastis]
to have breakfast	brokastot	[brɔkastɔt]
lunch	pusdienas (s dsk)	[pusdiɛnas]
to have lunch	pusdienot	[pusdiɛnɔt]
dinner	vakariņas (s dsk)	[vakariɲas]
to have dinner	vakariņot	[vakariɲɔt]

appetite	apetīte (s)	[apeti:te]
Enjoy your meal!	Labu apetīti!	[labu apeti:ti!]

to open (~ a bottle)	atvērt	[atve:rt]
to spill (liquid)	izliet	[izliɛt]
to spill out (vi)	izlieties	[izliɛtiɛs]

to boil (vi)	vārīties	[va:ri:tiɛs]
to boil (vt)	vārīt	[va:ri:t]
boiled (~ water)	vārīts	[va:ri:ts]
to chill, cool down (vt)	atdzesēt	[atdzɛse:t]
to chill (vi)	atdzesēties	[atdzɛse:tiɛs]

taste, flavour	garša (s)	[garʃa]
aftertaste	piegarša (s)	[piɛgarʃa]

to slim down (lose weight)	tievēt	[tiɛve:t]
diet	diēta (s)	[diɛ:ta]
vitamin	vitamīns (v)	[vitami:ns]
calorie	kalorija (s)	[kalɔrija]
vegetarian (n)	veģetārietis (v)	[vɛdʲɛta:riɛtis]
vegetarian (adj)	veģetāriešu	[vɛdʲɛta:riɛʃu]

fats (nutrient)	tauki (v dsk)	[tauki]
proteins	olbaltumvielas (s dsk)	[ɔlbaltumviɛlas]
carbohydrates	ogļhidrāti (v dsk)	[ɔglʲxidra:ti]
slice (of lemon, ham)	šķēlīte (s)	[ʃtʲe:li:te]
piece (of cake, pie)	gabals (v)	[gabals]
crumb (of bread, cake, etc.)	gabaliņš (v)	[gabaliɲʃ]

51. Cooked dishes

course, dish	ēdiens (v)	[e:diɛns]
cuisine	virtuve (s)	[virtuve]
recipe	recepte (s)	[retsepte]
portion	porcija (s)	[pɔrtsija]

salad	salāti (v dsk)	[sala:ti]
soup	zupa (s)	[zupa]

clear soup (broth)	buljons (v)	[buljɔns]
sandwich (bread)	sviestmaize (s)	[sviɛstmaize]
fried eggs	ceptas olas (s dsk)	[tseptas ɔlas]

hamburger (beefburger)	hamburgers (v)	[xamburgɛrs]
beefsteak	bifšteks (v)	[bifʃteks]
side dish	piedeva (s)	[piɛdɛva]

spaghetti	spageti (v dsk)	[spageti]
mash	kartupeļu biezenis (v)	[kartupɛlʲu biɛzenis]
pizza	pica (s)	[pitsa]
porridge (oatmeal, etc.)	biezputra (s)	[biɛzputra]
omelette	omlete (s)	[ɔmlɛte]

boiled (e.g. ~ beef)	vārīts	[va:ri:ts]
smoked (adj)	kūpināts	[ku:pina:ts]
fried (adj)	cepts	[tsepts]
dried (adj)	žāvēts	[ʒa:ve:ts]
frozen (adj)	sasaldēts	[sasalde:ts]
pickled (adj)	marinēts	[marine:ts]

sweet (sugary)	salds	[salds]
salty (adj)	sāļš	[sa:lʲʃ]
cold (adj)	auksts	[auksts]
hot (adj)	karsts	[karsts]
bitter (adj)	rūgts	[ru:gts]
tasty (adj)	garšīgs	[garʃi:gs]

to cook in boiling water	vārīt	[va:ri:t]
to cook (dinner)	gatavot	[gatavɔt]
to fry (vt)	cept	[tsept]
to heat up (food)	uzsildīt	[uzsildi:t]

to salt (vt)	piebērt sāli	[piɛbe:rt sa:li]
to pepper (vt)	piparot	[piparɔt]
to grate (vt)	rīvēt	[ri:ve:t]
peel (n)	miza (s)	[miza]
to peel (vt)	mizot	[mizɔt]

52. Food

meat	gaļa (s)	[galʲa]
chicken	vista (s)	[vista]
poussin	cālis (v)	[tsa:lis]
duck	pīle (s)	[pi:le]
goose	zoss (s)	[zɔs]
game	medījums (v)	[medi:jums]
turkey	tītars (v)	[ti:tars]

pork	cūkgaļa (s)	[tsu:kgalʲa]
veal	teļa gaļa (s)	[tɛlʲa galʲa]
lamb	jēra gaļa (s)	[je:ra galʲa]
beef	liellopu gaļa (s)	[liɛllopu galʲa]
rabbit	trusis (v)	[trusis]

sausage (bologna, pepperoni, etc.)	desa (s)	[dɛsa]
vienna sausage (frankfurter)	cīsiņš (v)	[tsi:siɲʃ]
bacon	bekons (v)	[bekɔns]
ham	šķiņķis (v)	[ʃtʲiɲtʲis]
gammon	šķiņķis (v)	[ʃtʲiɲtʲis]
pâté	pastēte (s)	[pastɛ:te]

liver	aknas (s dsk)	[aknas]
mince (minced meat)	malta gaļa (s)	[malta gaļa]
tongue	mēle (s)	[mɛ:le]

egg	ola (s)	[ɔla]
eggs	olas (s dsk)	[ɔlas]
egg white	baltums (v)	[baltums]
egg yolk	dzeltenums (v)	[dzeltenums]

fish	zivs (s)	[zivs]
seafood	jūras produkti (v dsk)	[ju:ras produkti]
crustaceans	vēžveidīgie (v dsk)	[ve:ʒvɛidi:giɛ]
caviar	ikri (v dsk)	[ikri]

crab	krabis (v)	[krabis]
prawn	garnele (s)	[garnɛle]
oyster	austere (s)	[austɛre]
spiny lobster	langusts (v)	[laŋgusts]
octopus	astoņkājis (v)	[astoŋka:jis]
squid	kalmārs (v)	[kalma:rs]

sturgeon	store (s)	[stɔre]
salmon	lasis (v)	[lasis]
halibut	āte (s)	[a:te]

cod	menca (s)	[mentsa]
mackerel	skumbrija (s)	[skumbrija]
tuna	tuncis (v)	[tuntsis]
eel	zutis (v)	[zutis]

trout	forele (s)	[fɔrɛle]
sardine	sardīne (s)	[sardi:ne]
pike	līdaka (s)	[li:daka]
herring	siļķe (s)	[siļʲtʲe]

bread	maize (s)	[maize]
cheese	siers (v)	[siɛrs]
sugar	cukurs (v)	[tsukurs]
salt	sāls (v)	[sa:ls]

rice	rīsi (v dsk)	[ri:si]
pasta (macaroni)	makaroni (v dsk)	[makarɔni]
noodles	nūdeles (s dsk)	[nu:dɛles]

butter	sviests (v)	[sviɛsts]
vegetable oil	augu eļļa (s)	[augu elʲa]
sunflower oil	saulespuķu eļļa (s)	[saulespuʲu elʲa]
margarine	margarīns (v)	[margari:ns]

| olives | olīvas (s dsk) | [ɔli:vas] |
| olive oil | olīveļļa (s) | [ɔli:velʲa] |

milk	piens (v)	[piɛns]
condensed milk	kondensētais piens (v)	[kɔndensɛ:tais piɛns]
yogurt	jogurts (v)	[jɔgurts]
soured cream	krējums (v)	[kre:jums]

cream (of milk)	salds krējums (v)	[salds kre:jums]
mayonnaise	majonēze (s)	[majɔnɛ:ze]
buttercream	krēms (v)	[kre:ms]

cereal grains (wheat, etc.)	putraimi (v dsk)	[putraimi]
flour	milti (v dsk)	[milti]
tinned food	konservi (v dsk)	[kɔnservi]

cornflakes	kukurūzas pārslas (s dsk)	[kukuru:zas pa:rslas]
honey	medus (v)	[mɛdus]
jam	džems, ievārījums (v)	[dʒems], [iɛva:ri:jums]
chewing gum	košļājamā gumija (s)	[kɔʃlʲa:jama: gumija]

53. Drinks

water	ūdens (v)	[u:dens]
drinking water	dzeramais ūdens (v)	[dzɛramais u:dens]
mineral water	minerālūdens (v)	[minɛra:lu:dens]

still (adj)	negāzēts	[nɛga:ze:ts]
carbonated (adj)	gāzēts	[ga:ze:ts]
sparkling (adj)	dzirkstošs	[dzirkstɔʃs]
ice	ledus (v)	[lɛdus]
with ice	ar ledu	[ar lɛdu]

non-alcoholic (adj)	bezalkoholisks	[bɛzalkɔxɔlisks]
soft drink	bezalkoholiskais dzēriens (v)	[bɛzalkɔxɔliskais dze:riɛns]
refreshing drink	atspirdzinošs dzēriens (v)	[atspirdzinɔʃs dze:riɛns]
lemonade	limonāde (s)	[limɔna:de]

spirits	alkoholiskie dzērieni (v dsk)	[alkɔxɔliskiɛ dze:riɛni]
wine	vīns (v)	[vi:ns]
white wine	baltvīns (v)	[baltvi:ns]
red wine	sarkanvīns (v)	[sarkanvi:ns]

liqueur	liķieris (v)	[litʲiɛris]
champagne	šampanietis (v)	[ʃampaniɛtis]
vermouth	vermuts (v)	[vermuts]

whisky	viskijs (v)	[viskijs]
vodka	degvīns (v)	[degvi:ns]
gin	džins (v)	[dʒins]
cognac	konjaks (v)	[kɔnjaks]
rum	rums (v)	[rums]

coffee	kafija (s)	[kafija]
black coffee	melnā kafija (s)	[melna: kafija]
white coffee	kafija (s) ar pienu	[kafija ar piɛnu]
cappuccino	kapučīno (v)	[kaputʃi:nɔ]
instant coffee	šķīstošā kafija (s)	[ʃtʲi:stɔʃa: kafija]

| milk | piens (v) | [piɛns] |
| cocktail | kokteilis (v) | [kɔktɛilis] |

milkshake	piena kokteilis (v)	[piɛna kɔktɛilis]
juice	sula (s)	[sula]
tomato juice	tomātu sula (s)	[tɔmaːtu sula]
orange juice	apelsīnu sula (s)	[apɛlsiːnu sula]
freshly squeezed juice	svaigi spiesta sula (s)	[svaigi spiɛsta sula]

beer	alus (v)	[alus]
lager	gaišais alus (v)	[gaiʃais alus]
bitter	tumšais alus (v)	[tumʃais alus]

tea	tēja (s)	[teːja]
black tea	melnā tēja (s)	[melna: te:ja]
green tea	zaļā tēja (s)	[zalʲa: te:ja]

54. Vegetables

| vegetables | dārzeņi (v dsk) | [da:rzeɲi] |
| greens | zaļumi (v dsk) | [zalʲumi] |

tomato	tomāts (v)	[tɔma:ts]
cucumber	gurķis (v)	[gurtʲis]
carrot	burkāns (v)	[burka:ns]
potato	kartupelis (v)	[kartupelis]
onion	sīpols (v)	[si:pɔls]
garlic	ķiploks (v)	[tʲiplɔks]

cabbage	kāposti (v dsk)	[ka:pɔsti]
cauliflower	puķkāposti (v dsk)	[putʲka:pɔsti]
Brussels sprouts	Briseles kāposti (v dsk)	[brisɛles ka:pɔsti]
broccoli	brokolis (v)	[brɔkɔlis]

beetroot	biete (s)	[biɛte]
aubergine	baklažāns (v)	[baklaʒa:ns]
courgette	kabacis (v)	[kabatsis]
pumpkin	ķirbis (v)	[tʲirbis]
turnip	rācenis (v)	[ra:tsenis]

parsley	pētersīlis (v)	[pɛ:tɛrsi:lis]
dill	dilles (s dsk)	[dilles]
lettuce	dārza salāti (v dsk)	[da:rza sala:ti]
celery	selerija (s)	[sɛlerija]

| asparagus | sparģelis (v) | [spardʲelis] |
| spinach | spināti (v dsk) | [spina:ti] |

| pea | zirnis (v) | [zirnis] |
| beans | pupas (s dsk) | [pupas] |

| maize | kukurūza (s) | [kukuru:za] |
| kidney bean | pupiņas (s dsk) | [pupiɲas] |

sweet paper	graudu pipars (v)	[graudu pipars]
radish	redīss (v)	[redi:s]
artichoke	artišoks (v)	[artiʃoks]

55. Fruits. Nuts

fruit	auglis (v)	[auglis]
apple	ābols (v)	[a:bɔls]
pear	bumbieris (v)	[bumbiɛris]
lemon	citrons (v)	[tsitrɔns]
orange	apelsīns (v)	[apɛlsi:ns]
strawberry (garden ~)	zemene (s)	[zɛmɛne]

tangerine	mandarīns (v)	[mandari:ns]
plum	plūme (s)	[plu:me]
peach	persiks (v)	[pɛrsiks]
apricot	aprikoze (s)	[aprikɔze]
raspberry	avene (s)	[avɛne]
pineapple	ananāss (v)	[anana:s]

banana	banāns (v)	[bana:ns]
watermelon	arbūzs (v)	[arbu:zs]
grape	vīnoga (s)	[vi:nɔga]
sour cherry	skābais ķirsis (v)	[ska:bais tʲirsis]
sweet cherry	saldais ķirsis (v)	[saldais tʲirsis]
melon	melone (s)	[melɔne]

grapefruit	greipfrūts (v)	[grɛipfru:ts]
avocado	avokado (v)	[avɔkadɔ]
papaya	papaija (s)	[papaija]
mango	mango (v)	[maŋgɔ]
pomegranate	granātābols (v)	[grana:ta:bɔls]

redcurrant	sarkanā jāņoga (s)	[sarkana: ja:ɲɔga]
blackcurrant	upene (s)	[upɛne]
gooseberry	ērkšķoga (s)	[e:rkʃtʲɔga]
bilberry	mellene (s)	[mellɛne]
blackberry	kazene (s)	[kazɛne]

raisin	rozīne (s)	[rɔzi:ne]
fig	vīģe (s)	[vi:dʲe]
date	datele (s)	[datɛle]

peanut	zemesrieksts (v)	[zɛmesriɛksts]
almond	mandeles (s dsk)	[mandɛles]
walnut	valrieksts (v)	[valriɛksts]
hazelnut	lazdu rieksts (v)	[lazdu riɛksts]
coconut	kokosrieksts (v)	[kɔkɔsriɛksts]
pistachios	pistācijas (s dsk)	[pista:tsijas]

56. Bread. Sweets

bakers' confectionery (pastry)	konditorejas izstrādājumi (v dsk)	[kɔnditorejas izstra:da:jumi]
bread	maize (s)	[maize]
biscuits	cepumi (v dsk)	[tsɛpumi]
chocolate (n)	šokolāde (s)	[ʃɔkɔla:de]

chocolate (as adj)	šokolādes	[ʃɔkɔlaːdes]
candy (wrapped)	konfekte (s)	[kɔnfekte]
cake (e.g. cupcake)	kūka (s)	[kuːka]
cake (e.g. birthday ~)	torte (s)	[tɔrte]

| pie (e.g. apple ~) | pīrāgs (v) | [piːraːgs] |
| filling (for cake, pie) | pildījums (v) | [pildiːjums] |

jam (whole fruit jam)	ievārījums (v)	[iɛvaːriːjums]
marmalade	marmelāde (s)	[marmɛlaːde]
waffles	vafeles (s dsk)	[vafɛles]
ice-cream	saldējums (v)	[saldeːjums]
pudding (Christmas ~)	pudiņš (v)	[pudiɲʃ]

57. Spices

salt	sāls (v)	[saːls]
salty (adj)	sāļš	[saːlʲʃ]
to salt (vt)	piebērt sāli	[piɛbeːrt saːli]

black pepper	melnie pipari (v dsk)	[melniɛ pipari]
red pepper (milled ~)	paprika (s)	[paprika]
mustard	sinepes (s dsk)	[sinɛpes]
horseradish	mārrutki (v dsk)	[maːrrutki]

condiment	piedeva (s)	[piɛdɛva]
spice	garšviela (s)	[garʃviɛla]
sauce	mērce (s)	[meːrtse]
vinegar	etiķis (v)	[ɛtitʲis]

anise	anīss (v)	[aniːs]
basil	baziliks (v)	[baziliks]
cloves	krustnagliņas (s dsk)	[krustnagliɲas]
ginger	ingvers (v)	[iŋgvɛrs]
coriander	koriandrs (v)	[kɔriandrs]
cinnamon	kanēlis (v)	[kaneːlis]

sesame	sezams (v)	[sɛzams]
bay leaf	lauru lapa (s)	[lauru lapa]
paprika	paprika (s)	[paprika]
caraway	ķimenes (s dsk)	[tʲimɛnes]
saffron	safrāns (v)	[safraːns]

PERSONAL INFORMATION. FAMILY

58. Personal information. Forms

name (first name)	**vārds** (v)	[va:rds]
surname (last name)	**uzvārds** (v)	[uzva:rds]
date of birth	**dzimšanas datums** (v)	[dzimʃanas datums]
place of birth	**dzimšanas vieta** (s)	[dzimʃanas viɛta]
nationality	**tautība** (s)	[tauti:ba]
place of residence	**dzīves vieta** (s)	[dzi:ves viɛta]
country	**valsts** (s)	[valsts]
profession (occupation)	**profesija** (s)	[prɔfesija]
gender, sex	**dzimums** (v)	[dzimums]
height	**augums** (v)	[augums]
weight	**svars** (v)	[svars]

59. Family members. Relatives

mother	**māte** (s)	[ma:te]
father	**tēvs** (v)	[te:vs]
son	**dēls** (v)	[dɛ:ls]
daughter	**meita** (s)	[mɛita]
younger daughter	**jaunākā meita** (s)	[jauna:ka: mɛita]
younger son	**jaunākais dēls** (v)	[jauna:kais dɛ:ls]
eldest daughter	**vecākā meita** (s)	[vetsa:ka: mɛita]
eldest son	**vecākais dēls** (v)	[vetsa:kais dɛ:ls]
brother	**brālis** (v)	[bra:lis]
elder brother	**vecākais brālis** (v)	[vetsa:kais bra:lis]
younger brother	**jaunākais brālis** (v)	[jauna:kais bra:lis]
sister	**māsa** (s)	[ma:sa]
elder sister	**vecākā māsa** (s)	[vetsa:ka: ma:sa]
younger sister	**jaunākā māsa** (s)	[jauna:ka: ma:sa]
cousin (masc.)	**brālēns** (v)	[bra:lɛ:ns]
cousin (fem.)	**māsīca** (s)	[ma:si:tsa]
mummy	**māmiņa** (s)	[ma:miɲa]
dad, daddy	**tētis** (v)	[te:tis]
parents	**vecāki** (v dsk)	[vetsa:ki]
child	**bērns** (v)	[be:rns]
children	**bērni** (v dsk)	[be:rni]
grandmother	**vecmāmiņa** (s)	[vetsma:miɲa]
grandfather	**vectēvs** (v)	[vetste:vs]
grandson	**mazdēls** (v)	[mazdɛ:ls]

| granddaughter | mazmeita (s) | [mazmɛita] |
| grandchildren | mazbērni (v dsk) | [mazbe:rni] |

uncle	onkulis (v)	[ɔnkulis]
aunt	tante (s)	[tante]
nephew	brāļadēls, māsasdēls (v)	[bra:lʲadɛ:ls], [ma:sasdɛ:ls]
niece	brāļameita, māsasmeita (s)	[bra:lʲamɛita], [ma:sasmɛita]

mother-in-law (wife's mother)	sievasmāte, vīramāte (s)	[siɛvasma:te], [vi:rama:te]
father-in-law (husband's father)	sievastēvs, vīratēvs (v)	[siɛvaste:vs], [vi:rate:vs]
son-in-law (daughter's husband)	znots (v)	[znɔts]
stepmother	pamāte (s)	[pama:te]
stepfather	patēvs (v)	[pate:vs]

infant	krūts bērns (v)	[kru:ts be:rns]
baby (infant)	zīdainis (v)	[zi:dainis]
little boy, kid	mazulis (v)	[mazulis]

wife	sieva (s)	[siɛva]
husband	vīrs (v)	[vi:rs]
spouse (husband)	dzīvesbiedrs (v)	[dzi:vesbiɛdrs]
spouse (wife)	dzīvesbiedre (s)	[dzi:vesbiɛdre]

married (masc.)	precējies	[pretse:jiɛs]
married (fem.)	precējusies	[pretse:jusiɛs]
single (unmarried)	neprecējies	[nepretse:jiɛs]
bachelor	vecpuisis (v)	[vetspuisis]
divorced (masc.)	šķīries	[ʃtʲi:riɛs]
widow	atraitne (s)	[atraitne]
widower	atraitnis (v)	[atraitnis]

relative	radinieks (v)	[radiniɛks]
close relative	tuvs radinieks (v)	[tuvs radiniɛks]
distant relative	tāls radinieks (v)	[ta:ls radiniɛks]
relatives	radi (v dsk)	[radi]

orphan (boy)	bārenis (v)	[ba:renis]
orphan (girl)	bārene (s)	[ba:rɛne]
guardian (of a minor)	aizbildnis (v)	[aizbildnis]
to adopt (a boy)	adoptēt zēnu	[adɔpte:t zɛ:nu]
to adopt (a girl)	adoptēt meiteni	[adɔpte:t mɛiteni]

60. Friends. Colleagues

friend (masc.)	draugs (v)	[draugs]
friend (fem.)	draudzene (s)	[draudzɛne]
friendship	draudzība (s)	[draudzi:ba]
to be friends	draudzēties	[draudze:tiɛs]

| pal (masc.) | draugs (v) | [draugs] |
| pal (fem.) | draudzene (s) | [draudzɛne] |

partner	partneris (v)	[partneris]
chief (boss)	šefs (v)	[ʃefs]
superior (n)	priekšnieks (v)	[priɛkʃniɛks]
owner, proprietor	īpašnieks (v)	[iːpaʃniɛks]
subordinate (n)	padotais (v)	[padotais]
colleague	kolēģis (v)	[kɔleːdʲis]

acquaintance (person)	paziņa (v, s)	[paziɲa]
fellow traveller	ceļabiedrs (v)	[tsɛlʲabiɛdrs]
classmate	klases biedrs (v)	[klases biɛdrs]

neighbour (masc.)	kaimiņš (v)	[kaimiɲʃ]
neighbour (fem.)	kaimiņiene (s)	[kaimiɲiɛne]
neighbours	kaimiņi (v dsk)	[kaimiɲi]

HUMAN BODY. MEDICINE

61. Head

head	galva (s)	[galva]
face	seja (s)	[seja]
nose	deguns (v)	[dɛguns]
mouth	mute (s)	[mute]

eye	acs (s)	[ats]
eyes	acis (s dsk)	[atsis]
pupil	acs zīlīte (s)	[ats ziːliːte]
eyebrow	uzacs (s)	[uzats]
eyelash	skropsta (s)	[skrɔpsta]
eyelid	plakstiņš (v)	[plakstiɲʃ]

tongue	mēle (s)	[mɛːle]
tooth	zobs (v)	[zɔbs]
lips	lūpas (s dsk)	[luːpas]
cheekbones	vaigu kauli (v dsk)	[vaigu kauli]
gum	smaganas (s dsk)	[smaganas]
palate	aukslējas (s dsk)	[auksleːjas]

nostril	nāsis (s dsk)	[naːsis]
chin	zods (v)	[zɔds]
jaw	žoklis (v)	[ʒɔklis]
cheek	vaigs (v)	[vaigs]

forehead	piere (s)	[piɛre]
temple	deniņi (v dsk)	[deniɲi]
ear	auss (s)	[aus]
back of the head	pakausis (v)	[pakausis]
neck	kakls (v)	[kakls]
throat	rīkle (s)	[riːkle]

hair	mati (v dsk)	[mati]
hairstyle	frizūra (s)	[frizuːra]
haircut	matu griezums (v)	[matu griɛzums]
wig	parūka (s)	[paruːka]

moustache	ūsas (s dsk)	[uːsas]
beard	bārda (s)	[baːrda]
to have (a beard, etc.)	ir	[ir]
plait	bize (s)	[bize]
sideboards	vaigubārda (s)	[vaigubaːrda]

red-haired (adj)	ruds	[ruds]
grey (hair)	sirms	[sirms]
bald (adj)	plikgalvains	[plikgalvains]
bald patch	plika galva (s)	[plika galva]

ponytail	zirgaste (s)	[zirgaste]
fringe	mati uz pieres (v)	[mati uz pjɛres]

62. Human body

hand	delna (s)	[delna]
arm	roka (s)	[rɔka]

finger	pirksts (v)	[pirksts]
toe	kājas īkšķis (v)	[ka:jas i:kʃtʲis]
thumb	īkšķis (v)	[i:kʃtʲis]
little finger	mazais pirkstiņš (v)	[mazais pirkstiɲʃ]
nail	nags (v)	[nags]

fist	dūre (s)	[du:re]
palm	plauksta (s)	[plauksta]
wrist	plaukstas locītava (s)	[plaukstas lɔtsi:tava]
forearm	apakšdelms (v)	[apakʃdelms]
elbow	elkonis (v)	[elkɔnis]
shoulder	augšdelms (v)	[augʃdelms]

leg	kāja (s)	[ka:ja]
foot	pēda (s)	[pɛ:da]
knee	celis (v)	[tselis]
calf (part of leg)	apakšstilbs (v)	[apakʃstilbs]
hip	gurns (v)	[gurns]
heel	papēdis (v)	[pape:dis]

body	ķermenis (v)	[tʲermenis]
stomach	vēders (v)	[vɛ:dɛrs]
chest	krūškurvis (v)	[kru:ʃkurvis]
breast	krūts (s)	[kru:ts]
flank	sāns (v)	[sa:ns]
back	mugura (s)	[mugura]
lower back	krusti (v dsk)	[krusti]
waist	viduklis (v)	[viduklis]

navel (belly button)	naba (s)	[naba]
buttocks	gūžas (s dsk)	[gu:ʒas]
bottom	dibens (v)	[dibens]

beauty spot	dzimumzīme (s)	[dzimumzi:me]
birthmark (café au lait spot)	dzimumzīme (s)	[dzimumzi:me]
tattoo	tetovējums (v)	[tetɔve:jums]
scar	rēta (s)	[rɛ:ta]

63. Diseases

illness	slimība (s)	[slimi:ba]
to be ill	slimot	[slimɔt]
health	veselība (s)	[vɛseli:ba]
runny nose (coryza)	iesnas (s dsk)	[iɛsnas]

tonsillitis	angīna (s)	[aŋgi:na]
cold (illness)	saaukstēšanās (s)	[saaukste:ʃana:s]
to catch a cold	saaukstēties	[saaukste:tiɛs]

bronchitis	bronhīts (v)	[brɔnxi:ts]
pneumonia	plaušu karsonis (v)	[plauʃu karsɔnis]
flu, influenza	gripa (s)	[gripa]

shortsighted (adj)	tuvredzīgs	[tuvredzi:gs]
longsighted (adj)	tālredzīgs	[ta:lredzi:gs]
strabismus (crossed eyes)	šķielēšana (s)	[ʃtʲiɛle:ʃana]
squint-eyed (adj)	šķielējošs	[ʃtʲiɛle:jɔʃs]
cataract	katarakta (s)	[katarakta]
glaucoma	glaukoma (s)	[glaukɔma]

stroke	insults (v)	[insults]
heart attack	infarkts (v)	[infarkts]
myocardial infarction	miokarda infarkts (v)	[miɔkarda infarkts]
paralysis	paralīze (s)	[parali:ze]
to paralyse (vt)	paralizēt	[paralize:t]

allergy	alerģija (s)	[alerdʲija]
asthma	astma (s)	[astma]
diabetes	diabēts (v)	[diabe:ts]

| toothache | zobu sāpes (s dsk) | [zɔbu sa:pes] |
| caries | kariess (v) | [kariɛs] |

diarrhoea	caureja (s)	[tsaureja]
constipation	aizcietējums (v)	[aiztsiɛte:jums]
stomach upset	gremošanas traucējumi (v dsk)	[gremɔʃanas trautse:jumi]
food poisoning	saindēšanās (s)	[sainde:ʃana:s]
to get food poisoning	saindēties	[sainde:tiɛs]

arthritis	artrīts (v)	[artri:ts]
rickets	rahīts (v)	[raxi:ts]
rheumatism	reimatisms (v)	[rɛimatisms]
atherosclerosis	ateroskleroze (s)	[aterɔsklerɔze]

gastritis	gastrīts (v)	[gastri:ts]
appendicitis	apendicīts (v)	[apenditsi:ts]
cholecystitis	holecistīts (v)	[xɔletsisti:ts]
ulcer	čūla (s)	[tʃu:la]

measles	masalas (s dsk)	[masalas]
rubella (German measles)	masaliņas (s dsk)	[masaliņas]
jaundice	dzeltenā kaite (s)	[dzeltɛna: kaite]
hepatitis	hepatīts (v)	[xɛpati:ts]

schizophrenia	šizofrēnija (s)	[ʃizɔfre:nija]
rabies (hydrophobia)	trakumsērga (s)	[trakumse:rga]
neurosis	neiroze (s)	[nɛirɔze]
concussion	smadzeņu satricinājums (v)	[smadzɛņu satritsina:jums]
cancer	vēzis (v)	[ve:zis]
sclerosis	skleroze (s)	[sklerɔze]

multiple sclerosis	multiplā skleroze (s)	[multipla: skleroze]
alcoholism	alkoholisms (v)	[alkɔxɔlisms]
alcoholic (n)	alkoholiķis (v)	[alkɔxɔlitʲis]
syphilis	sifiliss (v)	[sifilis]
AIDS	AIDS (v)	[aids]
tumour	audzējs (v)	[audze:js]
malignant (adj)	ļaundabīgs	[lʲaundabi:gs]
benign (adj)	labdabīgs	[labdabi:gs]
fever	drudzis (v)	[drudzis]
malaria	malārija (s)	[mala:rija]
gangrene	gangrēna (s)	[gaŋgrɛ:na]
seasickness	jūras slimība (s)	[ju:ras slimi:ba]
epilepsy	epilepsija (s)	[epilepsija]
epidemic	epidēmija (s)	[epide:mija]
typhus	tīfs (v)	[ti:fs]
tuberculosis	tuberkuloze (s)	[tuberkulɔze]
cholera	holēra (s)	[xɔlɛ:ra]
plague (bubonic ~)	mēris (v)	[me:ris]

64. Symptoms. Treatments. Part 1

symptom	simptoms (v)	[simptɔms]
temperature	temperatūra (s)	[tempɛratu:ra]
high temperature (fever)	augsta temperatūra (s)	[augsta tempɛratu:ra]
pulse	pulss (v)	[puls]
dizziness (vertigo)	galvas reibšana (s)	[galvas rɛibʃana]
hot (adj)	karsts	[karsts]
shivering	drebuļi (v dsk)	[drɛbulʲi]
pale (e.g. ~ face)	bāls	[ba:ls]
cough	klepus (v)	[klɛpus]
to cough (vi)	klepot	[klepɔt]
to sneeze (vi)	šķaudīt	[ʃtʲʲaudi:t]
faint	ģībonis (v)	[dʲi:bɔnis]
to faint (vi)	paģībt	[padʲi:bt]
bruise (hématome)	zilums (v)	[zilums]
bump (lump)	puns (v)	[puns]
to bang (bump)	atsisties	[atsistiɛs]
contusion (bruise)	sasitums (v)	[sasitums]
to get a bruise	sasisties	[sasistiɛs]
to limp (vi)	klibot	[klibɔt]
dislocation	izmežģījums (v)	[izmeʒdʲi:jums]
to dislocate (vt)	izmežģīt	[izmeʒdʲi:t]
fracture	lūzums (v)	[lu:zums]
to have a fracture	dabūt lūzumu	[dabu:t lu:zumu]
cut (e.g. paper ~)	iegriezums (v)	[iɛgriɛzums]
to cut oneself	sagriezties	[sagriɛztiɛs]
bleeding	asiņošana (s)	[asiɲoʃana]

| burn (injury) | apdegums (v) | [apdɛgums] |
| to get burned | apdedzināties | [apdedzina:tiɛs] |

to prick (vt)	sadurt	[sadurt]
to prick oneself	sadurties	[sadurtiɛs]
to injure (vt)	sabojāt	[saboja:t]
injury	traumēšana (s)	[traume:ʃana]
wound	ievainojums (v)	[iɛvainojums]
trauma	trauma (s)	[trauma]

to be delirious	murgot	[murgot]
to stutter (vi)	stostīties	[stosti:tiɛs]
sunstroke	saules dūriens (v)	[saules du:riɛns]

65. Symptoms. Treatments. Part 2

| pain, ache | sāpes (s dsk) | [sa:pes] |
| splinter (in foot, etc.) | skabarga (s) | [skabarga] |

sweat (perspiration)	sviedri (v dsk)	[sviɛdri]
to sweat (perspire)	svīst	[svi:st]
vomiting	vemšana (s)	[vemʃana]
convulsions	krampji (v dsk)	[krampji]

pregnant (adj)	grūta	[gru:ta]
to be born	piedzimt	[piɛdzimt]
delivery, labour	dzemdības (s dsk)	[dzemdi:bas]
to deliver (~ a baby)	dzemdēt	[dzemde:t]
abortion	aborts (v)	[aborts]

breathing, respiration	elpošana (s)	[elpoʃana]
in-breath (inhalation)	ieelpa (s)	[iɛelpa]
out-breath (exhalation)	izelpa (s)	[izelpa]
to exhale (breathe out)	izelpot	[izelpot]
to inhale (vi)	ieelpot	[iɛelpot]

disabled person	invalīds (v)	[invali:ds]
cripple	kroplis (v)	[kroplis]
drug addict	narkomāns (v)	[narkoma:ns]

deaf (adj)	kurls	[kurls]
mute (adj)	mēms	[me:ms]
deaf mute (adj)	kurlmēms	[kurlme:ms]

mad, insane (adj)	traks	[traks]
madman	trakais (v)	[trakais]
(demented person)		
madwoman	traka (s)	[traka]
to go insane	zaudēt prātu	[zaude:t pra:tu]

gene	gēns (v)	[ge:ns]
immunity	imunitāte (s)	[imunita:te]
hereditary (adj)	mantojams	[mantojams]
congenital (adj)	iedzimts	[iɛdzimts]

69

virus	vīruss (v)	[vi:rus]
microbe	mikrobs (v)	[mikrɔbs]
bacterium	baktērija (s)	[bakte:rija]
infection	infekcija (s)	[infektsija]

66. Symptoms. Treatments. Part 3

| hospital | slimnīca (s) | [slimni:tsa] |
| patient | pacients (v) | [patsiɛnts] |

diagnosis	diagnoze (s)	[diagnɔze]
cure	ārstēšana (s)	[a:rste:ʃana]
medical treatment	ārstēšana (s)	[a:rste:ʃana]
to get treatment	ārstēties	[a:rste:tiɛs]
to treat (~ a patient)	ārstēt	[a:rste:t]
to nurse (look after)	apkopt	[apkɔpt]
care (nursing ~)	apkope (s)	[apkope]
operation, surgery	operācija (s)	[ɔpɛra:tsija]
to bandage (head, limb)	pārsiet	[pa:rsiɛt]
bandaging	pārsiešana (s)	[pa:rsiɛʃana]

vaccination	potēšana (s)	[pote:ʃana]
to vaccinate (vt)	potēt	[pote:t]
injection	injekcija (s)	[injektsija]
to give an injection	injicēt	[injitse:t]

attack	lēkme (s)	[le:kme]
amputation	amputācija (s)	[amputa:tsija]
to amputate (vt)	amputēt	[ampute:t]
coma	koma (s)	[kɔma]
to be in a coma	būt komā	[bu:t kɔma:]
intensive care	reanimācija (s)	[reanima:tsija]

to recover (~ from flu)	atveseļoties	[atvɛseļɔtiɛs]
condition (patient's ~)	stāvoklis (v)	[sta:vɔklis]
consciousness	apziņa (s)	[apziņa]
memory (faculty)	atmiņa (s)	[atmiņa]

to pull out (tooth)	izraut	[izraut]
filling	plomba (s)	[plɔmba]
to fill (a tooth)	plombēt	[plɔmbe:t]

| hypnosis | hipnoze (s) | [xipnɔze] |
| to hypnotize (vt) | hipnotizēt | [xipnɔtize:t] |

67. Medicine. Drugs. Accessories

medicine, drug	zāles (s dsk)	[za:les]
remedy	līdzeklis (v)	[li:dzeklis]
to prescribe (vt)	izrakstīt	[izraksti:t]
prescription	recepte (s)	[retsepte]

tablet, pill	tablete (s)	[tablɛte]
ointment	ziede (s)	[ziɛde]
ampoule	ampula (s)	[ampula]
mixture	mikstūra (s)	[mikstu:ra]
syrup	sīrups (v)	[si:rups]
pill	zāļu kapsula (s)	[za:lʲu kapsula]
powder	pulveris (v)	[pulveris]

gauze bandage	saite (s)	[saite]
cotton wool	vate (s)	[vate]
iodine	jods (v)	[jods]

plaster	plāksteris (v)	[pla:ksteris]
eyedropper	pipete (s)	[pipɛte]
thermometer	termometrs (v)	[termɔmetrs]
syringe	šļirce (s)	[ʃlʲirtse]

| wheelchair | ratiņkrēsls (v) | [ratiŋkre:sls] |
| crutches | kruķi (v dsk) | [krutʲi] |

painkiller	pretsāpju līdzeklis (v)	[pretsa:pju li:dzeklis]
laxative	caurejas līdzeklis (v)	[tsaurejas li:dzeklis]
spirits (ethanol)	spirts (v)	[spirts]
medicinal herbs	zāle (s)	[za:le]
herbal (~ tea)	zāļu	[za:lʲu]

[handwritten annotations, partially legible]

darass ... uzmāntieс
subject to intimidation ... vai baidīšana
harrasing men
torment

abuse
abused   treat a person with cruelty or violence
regulary repeatedly
prosecuted
spean in an insulting
offensive way
a ntely remces

FLAT

68. Flat

flat	dzīvoklis (v)	[dziːvɔklis]
room	istaba (s)	[istaba]
bedroom	guļamistaba (s)	[guļamistaba]
dining room	ēdamistaba (s)	[ɛːdamistaba]
living room	viesistaba (s)	[viɛsistaba]
study (home office)	kabinets (v)	[kabinets]
entry room	priekštelpa (s)	[priɛkʃtelpa]
bathroom	vannas istaba (s)	[vannas istaba]
water closet	tualete (s)	[tualɛte]
ceiling	griesti (v dsk)	[griɛsti]
floor	grīda (s)	[griːda]
corner	kakts (v)	[kakts]

69. Furniture. Interior

furniture	mēbeles (s dsk)	[meːbɛles]
table	galds (v)	[galds]
chair	krēsls (v)	[kreːsls]
bed	gulta (s)	[gulta]
sofa, settee	dīvāns (v)	[diːvaːns]
armchair	atpūtas krēsls (v)	[atpuːtas kreːsls]
bookcase	grāmatplaukts (v)	[graːmatplaukts]
shelf	plaukts (v)	[plaukts]
wardrobe	drēbju skapis (v)	[dreːbju skapis]
coat rack (wall-mounted ~)	pakaramais (v)	[pakaramais]
coat stand	stāvpakaramais (v)	[staːvpakaramais]
chest of drawers	kumode (s)	[kumɔde]
coffee table	žurnālu galdiņš (v)	[ʒurnaːlu galdiɲʃ]
mirror	spogulis (v)	[spɔgulis]
carpet	paklājs (v)	[paklaːjs]
small carpet	paklājiņš (v)	[paklaːjiɲʃ]
fireplace	kamīns (v)	[kamiːns]
candle	svece (s)	[svetse]
candlestick	svečturis (v)	[svetʃturis]
drapes	aizkari (v dsk)	[aizkari]
wallpaper	tapetes (s dsk)	[tapɛtes]

blinds (jalousie)	žalūzijas (s dsk)	[ʒaluːzijas]
table lamp	galda lampa (s)	[galda lampa]
wall lamp (sconce)	gaismeklis (v)	[gaismeklis]
standard lamp	stāvlampa (s)	[staːvlampa]
chandelier	lustra (s)	[lustra]

leg (of chair, table)	kāja (s)	[kaːja]
armrest	elkoņa balsts (v)	[elkoɲa balsts]
back (backrest)	atzveltne (s)	[atzveltne]
drawer	atvilktne (s)	[atvilktne]

70. Bedding

bedclothes	gultas veļa (s)	[gultas vɛlʲa]
pillow	spilvens (v)	[spilvens]
pillowslip	spilvendrāna (s)	[spilvendraːna]
duvet	sega (s)	[sɛga]
sheet	palags (v)	[palags]
bedspread	pārsegs (v)	[paːrsegs]

71. Kitchen

kitchen	virtuve (s)	[virtuve]
gas	gāze (s)	[gaːze]
gas cooker	gāzes plīts (v)	[gaːzes pliːts]
electric cooker	elektriskā plīts (v)	[ɛlektriska: pliːts]
oven	cepeškrāsns (v)	[tsɛpeʃkraːsns]
microwave oven	mikroviļņu krāsns (v)	[mikrovilʲɲu kraːsns]

refrigerator	ledusskapis (v)	[lɛduskapis]
freezer	saldētava (s)	[saldɛːtava]
dishwasher	trauku mazgājamā mašīna (s)	[trauku mazgaːjama: maʃiːna]

mincer	gaļas mašīna (s)	[galʲas maʃiːna]
juicer	sulu spiede (s)	[sulu spiɛde]
toaster	tosters (v)	[tɔstɛrs]
mixer	mikseris (v)	[mikseris]

coffee machine	kafijas aparāts (v)	[kafijas apara:ts]
coffee pot	kafijas kanna (s)	[kafijas kanna]
coffee grinder	kafijas dzirnaviņas (s)	[kafijas dzirnaviɲas]

kettle	tējkanna (s)	[teːjkanna]
teapot	tējkanna (s)	[teːjkanna]
lid	vāciņš (v)	[vaːtsiɲʃ]
tea strainer	sietiņš (v)	[siɛtiɲʃ]

spoon	karote (s)	[karɔte]
teaspoon	tējkarote (s)	[teːjkarɔte]
soup spoon	ēdamkarote (s)	[ɛːdamkarɔte]
fork	dakša (s)	[dakʃa]

knife	nazis (v)	[nazis]
tableware (dishes)	galda piederumi (v dsk)	[galda piedɛrumi]
plate (dinner ~)	šķīvis (v)	[ʃḱiːvis]
saucer	apakštase (s)	[apakʃtase]

shot glass	glāzīte (s)	[glaːziːte]
glass (tumbler)	glāze (s)	[glaːze]
cup	tase (s)	[tase]

sugar bowl	cukurtrauks (v)	[tsukurtrauks]
salt cellar	sālstrauks (v)	[saːlstrauks]
pepper pot	piparu trauciņš (v)	[piparu trautsiɲʃ]
butter dish	sviesta trauks (v)	[sviɛsta trauks]

stock pot (soup pot)	kastrolis (v)	[kastrɔlis]
frying pan (skillet)	panna (s)	[panna]
ladle	smeļamkarote (s)	[smɛlʲamkarɔte]
colander	caurduris (v)	[tsaurduris]
tray (serving ~)	paplāte (s)	[paplaːte]

bottle	pudele (s)	[pudɛle]
jar (glass)	burka (s)	[burka]
tin (can)	bundža (s)	[bundʒa]

bottle opener	atvere (s)	[atvɛre]
tin opener	atvere (s)	[atvɛre]
corkscrew	korķviļķis (v)	[kortʲvilʲtʲis]
filter	filtrs (v)	[filtrs]
to filter (vt)	filtrēt	[filtreːt]

| waste (food ~, etc.) | atkritumi (v dsk) | [atkritumi] |
| waste bin (kitchen ~) | atkritumu tvertne (s) | [atkritumu tvertne] |

72. Bathroom

bathroom	vannas istaba (s)	[vannas istaba]
water	ūdens (v)	[uːdens]
tap	krāns (v)	[kraːns]
hot water	karsts ūdens (v)	[karsts uːdens]
cold water	auksts ūdens (v)	[auksts uːdens]

toothpaste	zobu pasta (s)	[zɔbu pasta]
to clean one's teeth	tīrīt zobus	[tiːriːt zɔbus]
toothbrush	zobu birste (s)	[zɔbu birste]

to shave (vi)	skūties	[skuːtiɛs]
shaving foam	skūšanās putas (s)	[skuːʃanaːs putas]
razor	skuveklis (v)	[skuveklis]

to wash (one's hands, etc.)	mazgāt	[mazgaːt]
to have a bath	mazgāties	[mazgaːtiɛs]
shower	duša (s)	[duʃa]
to have a shower	iet dušā	[iɛt duʃaː]
bath	vanna (s)	[vanna]

| toilet (toilet bowl) | klozetpods (v) | [klɔzetpɔds] |
| sink (washbasin) | izlietne (s) | [izliɛtne] |

| soap | ziepes (s dsk) | [ziɛpes] |
| soap dish | ziepju trauks (v) | [ziɛpju trauks] |

sponge	sūklis (v)	[suːklis]
shampoo	šampūns (v)	[ʃampuːns]
towel	dvielis (v)	[dviɛlis]
bathrobe	halāts (v)	[xalaːts]

laundry (process)	veļas mazgāšana (s)	[vɛlʲas mazgaːʃana]
washing machine	veļas mazgājamā mašīna (s)	[vɛlʲas mazga:jama: maʃiːna]
to do the laundry	mazgāt veļu	[mazga:t vɛlʲu]
washing powder	veļas pulveris (v)	[vɛlʲas pulveris]

73. Household appliances

TV, telly	televizors (v)	[tɛlevizɔrs]
tape recorder	magnetofons (v)	[magnetɔfɔns]
video	videomagnetofons (v)	[videɔmagnetɔfɔns]
radio	radio uztvērējs (v)	[radiɔ uztvɛːreːjs]
player (CD, MP3, etc.)	atskaņotājs (v)	[atskaɲotaːjs]

video projector	video projektors (v)	[videɔ prɔjektɔrs]
home cinema	mājas kinoteātris (v)	[maːjas kinɔtea:tris]
DVD player	DVD atskaņotājs (v)	[dvd atskaɲota:js]
amplifier	pastiprinātājs (v)	[pastiprina:ta:js]
video game console	spēļu konsole (s)	[spɛːlʲu kɔnsɔle]

video camera	videokamera (s)	[videɔkamɛra]
camera (photo)	fotoaparāts (v)	[fɔtɔapara:ts]
digital camera	digitālais fotoaparāts (v)	[digita:lais fɔtɔapara:ts]

vacuum cleaner	putekļu sūcējs (v)	[puteklʲu su:tse:js]
iron (e.g. steam ~)	gludeklis (v)	[gludeklis]
ironing board	gludināmais dēlis (v)	[gludina:mais de:lis]

telephone	tālrunis (v)	[ta:lrunis]
mobile phone	mobilais tālrunis (v)	[mɔbilais ta:lrunis]
typewriter	rakstāmmašīna (s)	[raksta:mmaʃi:na]
sewing machine	šujmašīna (s)	[ʃujmaʃi:na]

microphone	mikrofons (v)	[mikrɔfɔns]
headphones	austiņas (s dsk)	[austiɲas]
remote control (TV)	pults (v)	[pults]

CD, compact disc	kompaktdisks (v)	[kɔmpaktdisks]
cassette, tape	kasete (s)	[kasɛte]
vinyl record	plate (s)	[plate]

THE EARTH. WEATHER

74. Outer space

space	kosmoss (v)	[kɔsmɔs]
space (as adj)	kosmiskais	[kɔsmiskais]
outer space	kosmiskā telpa (s)	[kɔsmiska: telpa]
world	visums (v)	[visums]
universe	pasaule (s)	[pasaule]
galaxy	galaktika (s)	[galaktika]
star	zvaigzne (s)	[zvaigzne]
constellation	zvaigznājs (v)	[zvaigzna:js]
planet	planēta (s)	[planɛ:ta]
satellite	pavadonis (v)	[pavadɔnis]
meteorite	meteorīts (v)	[mɛteɔri:ts]
comet	komēta (s)	[kɔmɛ:ta]
asteroid	asteroīds (v)	[asterɔi:ds]
orbit	orbīta (s)	[ɔrbi:ta]
to revolve	griezties ap	[griɛzties ap]
(~ around the Earth)		
atmosphere	atmosfēra (s)	[atmɔsfɛ:ra]
the Sun	Saule (s)	[saule]
solar system	Saules sistēma (s)	[saules sistɛ:ma]
solar eclipse	Saules aptumsums (v)	[saules aptumsums]
the Earth	Zeme (s)	[zɛme]
the Moon	Mēness (v)	[mɛ:nes]
Mars	Marss (v)	[mars]
Venus	Venēra (s)	[vɛnɛ:ra]
Jupiter	Jupiters (v)	[jupitɛrs]
Saturn	Saturns (v)	[saturns]
Mercury	Merkus (v)	[merkus]
Uranus	Urāns (v)	[ura:ns]
Neptune	Neptūns (v)	[neptu:ns]
Pluto	Plutons (v)	[plutɔns]
Milky Way	Piena ceļš (v)	[piɛna tseḷʃ]
Great Bear (Ursa Major)	Lielais Lācis (v)	[liɛlais la:tsis]
North Star	Polārzvaigzne (s)	[pɔla:rzvaigzne]
Martian	marsietis (v)	[marsiɛtis]
extraterrestrial (n)	citplanētietis (v)	[tsitplanе:tiɛtis]

alien	atnācējs (v)	[atna:tse:js]
flying saucer	lidojošais šķīvis (v)	[lidɔjɔʃais ʃtʲi:vis]
spaceship	kosmiskais kuģis (v)	[kɔsmiskais kudʲis]
space station	orbitālā stacija (s)	[ɔrbita:la: statsija]
blast-off	starts (v)	[starts]

engine	dzinējs (v)	[dzine:js]
nozzle	sprausla (s)	[sprausla]
fuel	degviela (s)	[degviɛla]

| cockpit, flight deck | kabīne (s) | [kabi:ne] |
| aerial | antena (s) | [antɛna] |

porthole	iluminators (v)	[iluminatɔrs]
solar panel	saules baterija (s)	[saules baterija]
spacesuit	skafandrs (v)	[skafandrs]

| weightlessness | bezsvara stāvoklis (v) | [bezsvara sta:vɔklis] |
| oxygen | skābeklis (v) | [ska:beklis] |

| docking (in space) | savienošanās (s) | [saviɛnɔʃana:s] |
| to dock (vi, vt) | savienoties | [saviɛnɔtiɛs] |

observatory	observatorija (s)	[ɔbservatɔrija]
telescope	teleskops (v)	[tɛleskɔps]
to observe (vt)	novērot	[nɔve:rɔt]
to explore (vt)	pētīt	[pe:ti:t]

75. The Earth

the Earth	Zeme (s)	[zɛme]
the globe (the Earth)	zemeslode (s)	[zɛmeslɔde]
planet	planēta (s)	[planɛ:ta]

atmosphere	atmosfēra (s)	[atmɔsfɛ:ra]
geography	ģeogrāfija (s)	[dʲeɔgra:fija]
nature	daba (s)	[daba]

globe (table ~)	globuss (v)	[glɔbus]
map	karte (s)	[karte]
atlas	atlants (v)	[atlants]

| Europe | Eiropa (s) | [ɛirɔpa] |
| Asia | Āzija (s) | [a:zija] |

| Africa | Āfrika (s) | [a:frika] |
| Australia | Austrālija (s) | [austra:lija] |

America	Amerika (s)	[amerika]
North America	Ziemeļamerika (s)	[ziɛmɛlʲamerika]
South America	Dienvidamerika (s)	[diɛnvidamerika]

| Antarctica | Antarktīda (s) | [antarkti:da] |
| the Arctic | Arktika (s) | [arktika] |

76. Cardinal directions

north	ziemeļi (v dsk)	[ziɛmeļi]
to the north	uz ziemeļiem	[uz ziɛmeļiɛm]
in the north	ziemeļos	[ziɛmeļɔs]
northern (adj)	ziemeļu	[ziɛmeļu]

south	dienvidi (v dsk)	[diɛnvidi]
to the south	uz dienvidiem	[uz diɛnvidiɛm]
in the south	dienvidos	[diɛnvidɔs]
southern (adj)	dienvidu	[diɛnvidu]

west	rietumi (v dsk)	[riɛtumi]
to the west	uz rietumiem	[uz riɛtumiɛm]
in the west	rietumos	[riɛtumɔs]
western (adj)	rietumu	[riɛtumu]

east	austrumi (v dsk)	[austrumi]
to the east	uz austrumiem	[uz austrumiɛm]
in the east	austrumos	[austrumɔs]
eastern (adj)	austrumu	[austrumu]

77. Sea. Ocean

sea	jūra (s)	[juːra]
ocean	okeāns (v)	[ɔkeaːns]
gulf (bay)	jūras līcis (v)	[juːras liːtsis]
straits	jūras šaurums (v)	[juːras ʃaurums]

land (solid ground)	sauszeme (s)	[sauszɛme]
continent (mainland)	kontinents (v)	[kɔntinents]
island	sala (s)	[sala]
peninsula	pussala (s)	[pusala]
archipelago	arhipelāgs (v)	[arxipɛlaːgs]

bay, cove	līcis (v)	[liːtsis]
harbour	osta (s)	[ɔsta]
lagoon	lagūna (s)	[laguːna]
cape	zemesrags (v)	[zɛmesrags]

atoll	atols (v)	[atɔls]
reef	rifs (v)	[rifs]
coral	korallis (v)	[kɔrallis]
coral reef	koraļļu rifs (v)	[kɔraļļu rifs]

deep (adj)	dziļš	[dziļʃ]
depth (deep water)	dziļums (v)	[dziļums]
abyss	dzelme (s)	[dzelme]
trench (e.g. Mariana ~)	ieplaka (s)	[iɛplaka]

current (Ocean ~)	straume (s)	[straume]
to surround (bathe)	apskalot	[apskalɔt]
shore	krasts (v)	[krasts]

coast	piekraste (s)	[piɛkraste]
flow (flood tide)	paisums (v)	[paisums]
ebb (ebb tide)	bēgums (v)	[bɛːgums]
shoal	sēklis (v)	[seːklis]
bottom (~ of the sea)	gultne (s)	[gultne]

wave	vilnis (v)	[vilnis]
crest (~ of a wave)	viļņa mugura (s)	[viļɲa mugura]
spume (sea foam)	putas (s)	[putas]

storm (sea storm)	vētra (s)	[veːtra]
hurricane	viesulis (v)	[viɛsulis]
tsunami	cunami (v)	[tsunami]
calm (dead ~)	bezvējš (v)	[bezveːjʃ]
quiet, calm (adj)	mierīgs	[miɛriːgs]

| pole | pols (v) | [pɔls] |
| polar (adj) | polārais | [pɔlaːrais] |

latitude	platums (v)	[platums]
longitude	garums (v)	[garums]
parallel	paralēle (s)	[paralɛːle]
equator	ekvators (v)	[ekvatɔrs]

sky	debess (s)	[dɛbes]
horizon	horizonts (v)	[xɔrizɔnts]
air	gaiss (v)	[gais]

lighthouse	bāka (s)	[baːka]
to dive (vi)	nirt	[nirt]
to sink (ab. boat)	nogrimt	[nɔgrimt]
treasures	dārgumi (v dsk)	[daːrgumi]

78. Seas & Oceans names

Atlantic Ocean	Atlantijas okeāns (v)	[atlantijas ɔkeaːns]
Indian Ocean	Indijas okeāns (v)	[indijas ɔkeaːns]
Pacific Ocean	Klusais okeāns (v)	[klusais ɔkeaːns]
Arctic Ocean	Ziemeļu Ledus okeāns (v)	[ziɛmɛlʲu lɛdus ɔkeaːns]

Black Sea	Melnā jūra (s)	[melna: juːra]
Red Sea	Sarkanā jūra (s)	[sarkana: juːra]
Yellow Sea	Dzeltenā jūra (s)	[dzeltɛna: juːra]
White Sea	Baltā jūra (s)	[balta: juːra]

Caspian Sea	Kaspijas jūra (s)	[kaspijas juːra]
Dead Sea	Nāves jūra (s)	[naːves juːra]
Mediterranean Sea	Vidusjūra (s)	[vidusjuːra]

| Aegean Sea | Egejas jūra (s) | [ɛgejas juːra] |
| Adriatic Sea | Adrijas jūra (s) | [adrijas juːra] |

| Arabian Sea | Arābijas jūra (s) | [ara:bijas juːra] |
| Sea of Japan | Japāņu jūra (s) | [japa:ɲu juːra] |

79

| Bering Sea | Beringa jūra (s) | [beriŋga ju:ra] |
| South China Sea | Dienvidķīnas jūra (s) | [diɛnvidtʲi:nas ju:ra] |

Coral Sea	Koraļļu jūra (s)	[kɔralʲʲu ju:ra]
Tasman Sea	Tasmāna jūra (s)	[tasma:na ju:ra]
Caribbean Sea	Karību jūra (s)	[kari:bu ju:ra]

| Barents Sea | Barenca jūra (s) | [barentsa ju:ra] |
| Kara Sea | Karas jūra (s) | [karas ju:ra] |

North Sea	Ziemeļjūra (s)	[ziɛmelʲju:ra]
Baltic Sea	Baltijas jūra (s)	[baltijas ju:ra]
Norwegian Sea	Norvēģu jūra (s)	[nɔrvɛ:dʲu ju:ra]

79. Mountains

mountain	kalns (v)	[kalns]
mountain range	kalnu virkne (s)	[kalnu virkne]
mountain ridge	kalnu grēda (s)	[kalnu grɛ:da]

summit, top	virsotne (s)	[virsɔtne]
peak	smaile (s)	[smaile]
foot (~ of the mountain)	pakāje (s)	[paka:je]
slope (mountainside)	nogāze (s)	[nɔga:ze]

volcano	vulkāns (v)	[vulka:ns]
active volcano	darvojošais vulkāns (v)	[darvɔjɔʃais vulka:ns]
dormant volcano	nodzisušais vulkāns (v)	[nɔdzisuʃais vulka:ns]

eruption	izvirdums (v)	[izvirdums]
crater	krāteris (v)	[kra:teris]
magma	magma (s)	[magma]
lava	lava (s)	[lava]
molten (~ lava)	karstais	[karstais]

canyon	kanjons (v)	[kanjɔns]
gorge	aiza (s)	[aiza]
crevice	plaisa (s)	[plaisa]
abyss (chasm)	bezdibenis (v)	[bezdibenis]

pass, col	pāreja (s)	[pa:reja]
plateau	plato (v)	[platɔ]
cliff	klints (s)	[klints]
hill	pakalns (v)	[pakalns]

glacier	ledājs (v)	[lɛda:js]
waterfall	ūdenskritums (v)	[u:denskritums]
geyser	geizers (v)	[gɛizɛrs]
lake	ezers (v)	[ɛzɛrs]

plain	līdzenums (v)	[li:dzenums]
landscape	ainava (s)	[ainava]
echo	atbalss (s)	[atbals]
alpinist	alpīnists (v)	[alpi:nists]

rock climber	klinšu kāpējs (v)	[klinʃu kaːpeːjs]
to conquer (in climbing)	iekarot	[iɛkarɔt]
climb (an easy ~)	uzkāpšana (s)	[uzkaːpʃana]

80. Mountains names

The Alps	Alpi (v dsk)	[alpi]
Mont Blanc	Monblāns (v)	[mɔnblaːns]
The Pyrenees	Pireneji (v dsk)	[pirɛneji]

The Carpathians	Karpati (v dsk)	[karpati]
The Ural Mountains	Urālu kalni (v dsk)	[uraːlu kalni]
The Caucasus Mountains	Kaukāzs (v)	[kaukaːzs]
Mount Elbrus	Elbruss (v)	[elbrus]

The Altai Mountains	Altaja kalni (v)	[altaja kalni]
The Tian Shan	Tjanšana kalni (v)	[tjanʃana kalni]
The Pamir Mountains	Pamirs (v)	[pamirs]
The Himalayas	Himalaji (v dsk)	[ximalaji]
Mount Everest	Everests (v)	[ɛvɛrests]

| The Andes | Andu kalni (v dsk) | [andu kalni] |
| Mount Kilimanjaro | Kilimandžaro (v) | [kilimandʒarɔ] |

81. Rivers

river	upe (s)	[upe]
spring (natural source)	ūdens avots (v)	[uːdens avɔts]
riverbed (river channel)	gultne (s)	[gultne]
basin (river valley)	upes baseins (v)	[upes basɛins]
to flow into ...	ieplūst ...	[iɛpluːst ...]

| tributary | pieteka (s) | [piɛtɛka] |
| bank (of river) | krasts (v) | [krasts] |

current (stream)	straume (s)	[straume]
downstream (adv)	plūsmas lejtecē	[pluːsmas lejtetseː]
upstream (adv)	plūsmas augštecē	[pluːsmas augʃtetseː]

inundation	plūdi (v dsk)	[pluːdi]
flooding	pali (v dsk)	[pali]
to overflow (vi)	pārplūst	[paːrpluːst]
to flood (vt)	appludināt	[appludinaːt]

| shallow (shoal) | sēklis (v) | [seːklis] |
| rapids | krāce (s) | [kraːtse] |

dam	dambis (v)	[dambis]
canal	kanāls (v)	[kanaːls]
reservoir (artificial lake)	ūdenskrātuve (s)	[uːdenskraːtuve]
sluice, lock	slūžas (s)	[sluːʒas]
water body (pond, etc.)	ūdenstilpe (s)	[uːdenstilpe]

swamp (marshland)	purvs (v)	[purvs]
bog, marsh	staignājs (v)	[staigna:js]
whirlpool	virpulis (v)	[virpulis]

stream (brook)	strauts (v)	[strauts]
drinking (ab. water)	dzeramais	[dzɛramais]
fresh (~ water)	sājš	[sa:jʃ]

| ice | ledus (v) | [lɛdus] |
| to freeze over (ab. river, etc.) | aizsalt | [aizsalt] |

82. Rivers names

| Seine | Sēna (s) | [sɛ:na] |
| Loire | Luāra (s) | [lua:ra] |

Thames	Temza (s)	[temza]
Rhine	Reina (s)	[rɛina]
Danube	Donava (s)	[dɔnava]

Volga	Volga (s)	[vɔlga]
Don	Dona (s)	[dɔna]
Lena	Ļena (s)	[lʲɛna]

Yellow River	Huanhe (s)	[xuanxe]
Yangtze	Jandzi (s)	[jandzi]
Mekong	Mekonga (s)	[mekɔnga]
Ganges	Ganga (s)	[gaŋga]

Nile River	Nīla (s)	[ni:la]
Congo River	Kongo (s)	[kɔŋgɔ]
Okavango River	Okavango (s)	[ɔkavaŋgɔ]
Zambezi River	Zambezi (s)	[zambezi]
Limpopo River	Limpopo (s)	[limpɔpɔ]
Mississippi River	Misisipi (s)	[misisipi]

83. Forest

| forest, wood | mežs (v) | [meʒs] |
| forest (as adj) | meža | [meʒa] |

thick forest	meža biezoknis (v)	[meʒa biɛzɔknis]
grove	birze (s)	[birze]
forest clearing	nora (s)	[nɔra]

| thicket | krūmājs (v) | [kru:ma:js] |
| scrubland | krūmi (v dsk) | [kru:mi] |

footpath (troddenpath)	taciņa (s)	[tatsiɲa]
gully	grava (s)	[grava]
tree	koks (v)	[kɔks]
leaf	lapa (s)	[lapa]

leaves (foliage)	lapas (s dsk)	[lapas]
fall of leaves	lapkritis (v)	[lapkritis]
to fall (ab. leaves)	lapas krīt	[lapas kri:t]
top (of the tree)	virsotne (s)	[virsɔtne]

branch	zariņš (v)	[zariɲʃ]
bough	zars (v)	[zars]
bud (on shrub, tree)	pumpurs (v)	[pumpurs]
needle (of pine tree)	skuja (s)	[skuja]
fir cone	čiekurs (v)	[tʃiɛkurs]

hollow (in a tree)	dobums (v)	[dɔbums]
nest	ligzda (s)	[ligzda]
burrow (animal hole)	ala (s)	[ala]

trunk	stumbrs (v)	[stumbrs]
root	sakne (s)	[sakne]
bark	miza (s)	[miza]
moss	sūna (s)	[su:na]

to uproot (remove trees or tree stumps)	atcelmot	[attselmɔt]
to chop down	cirst	[tsirst]
to deforest (vt)	izcirst	[iztsirst]
tree stump	celms (v)	[tselms]

campfire	ugunskurs (v)	[ugunskurs]
forest fire	ugunsgrēks (v)	[ugunsgre:ks]
to extinguish (vt)	dzēst	[dze:st]

forest ranger	mežinieks (v)	[meʒiniɛks]
protection	augu aizsargāšana (s)	[augu aizsarga:ʃana]
to protect (~ nature)	dabas aizsardzība	[dabas aizsardzi:ba]
poacher	malumednieks (v)	[malumedniɛks]
steel trap	lamatas (s dsk)	[lamatas]

to pick (mushrooms)	sēņot	[se:ɲot]
to pick (berries)	ogot	[ɔgɔt]
to lose one's way	apmaldīties	[apmaldi:tiɛs]

84. Natural resources

natural resources	dabas resursi (v dsk)	[dabas rɛsursi]
minerals	derīgie izrakteņi (v dsk)	[deri:giɛ izrakteɲi]
deposits	iegulumi (v dsk)	[iɛgulumi]
field (e.g. oilfield)	atradne (s)	[atradne]

to mine (extract)	iegūt rūdu	[iɛgu:t ru:du]
mining (extraction)	ieguve (s)	[iɛguve]
ore	rūda (s)	[ru:da]
mine (e.g. for coal)	raktuve (s)	[raktuve]
shaft (mine ~)	šahta (s)	[ʃaxta]
miner	oglracis (v)	[ɔglʲratsis]
gas (natural ~)	gāze (s)	[ga:ze]

gas pipeline	gāzes vads (v)	[ga:zes vads]
oil (petroleum)	nafta (s)	[nafta]
oil pipeline	naftas vads (v)	[naftas vads]
oil well	naftas tornis (v)	[naftas tornis]
derrick (tower)	urbjtornis (v)	[urbjtornis]
tanker	tankkuģis (v)	[tankkudʲis]

sand	smiltis (s dsk)	[smiltis]
limestone	kaļķakmens (v)	[kalʲtʲakmens]
gravel	grants (s)	[grants]
peat	kūdra (s)	[ku:dra]
clay	māls (v)	[ma:ls]
coal	ogles (s dsk)	[ɔgles]

iron (ore)	dzelzs (s)	[dzelzs]
gold	zelts (v)	[zelts]
silver	sudrabs (v)	[sudrabs]
nickel	niķelis (v)	[nitʲelis]
copper	varš (v)	[varʃ]

zinc	cinks (v)	[tsinks]
manganese	mangāns (v)	[maŋga:ns]
mercury	dzīvsudrabs (v)	[dzi:vsudrabs]
lead	svins (v)	[svins]

mineral	minerāls (v)	[minɛra:ls]
crystal	kristāls (v)	[krista:ls]
marble	marmors (v)	[marmɔrs]
uranium	urāns (v)	[ura:ns]

85. Weather

weather	laiks (v)	[laiks]
weather forecast	laika prognoze (s)	[laika prɔgnɔze]
temperature	temperatūra (s)	[tempɛratu:ra]
thermometer	termometrs (v)	[termɔmetrs]
barometer	barometrs (v)	[barɔmetrs]

humid (adj)	mitrs	[mitrs]
humidity	mitrums (v)	[mitrums]
heat (extreme ~)	tveice (s)	[tvɛitse]
hot (torrid)	karsts	[karsts]
it's hot	karsts laiks	[karsts laiks]

it's warm	silts laiks	[silts laiks]
warm (moderately hot)	silts	[silts]

it's cold	auksts laiks	[auksts laiks]
cold (adj)	auksts	[auksts]

sun	saule (s)	[saule]
to shine (vi)	spīd saule	[spi:d saule]
sunny (day)	saulains	[saulains]
to come up (vi)	uzlēkt	[uzle:kt]

to set (vi)	rietēt	[riɛte:t]
cloud	mākonis (v)	[ma:kɔnis]
cloudy (adj)	mākoņains	[ma:koɲains]
rain cloud	melns mākonis (v)	[melns ma:kɔnis]
somber (gloomy)	apmācies	[apma:tsiɛs]

rain	lietus (v)	[liɛtus]
it's raining	līst lietus	[li:st liɛtus]
rainy (~ day, weather)	lietains	[liɛtains]
to drizzle (vi)	smidzina	[smidzina]

pouring rain	stiprs lietus (v)	[stiprs liɛtus]
downpour	lietusgāze (s)	[liɛtusga:ze]
heavy (e.g. ~ rain)	stiprs	[stiprs]
puddle	peļķe (s)	[pelʲtʲe]
to get wet (in rain)	samirkt	[samirkt]

fog (mist)	migla (s)	[migla]
foggy	miglains	[miglains]
snow	sniegs (v)	[sniɛgs]
it's snowing	krīt sniegs	[kri:t sniɛgs]

86. Severe weather. Natural disasters

thunderstorm	pērkona negaiss (v)	[pe:rkɔna nɛgais]
lightning (~ strike)	zibens (v)	[zibens]
to flash (vi)	zibēt	[zibe:t]

thunder	pērkons (v)	[pe:rkɔns]
to thunder (vi)	dārdēt	[da:rde:t]
it's thundering	dārd pērkons	[da:rd pe:rkɔns]

hail	krusa (s)	[krusa]
it's hailing	krīt krusa	[kri:t krusa]

to flood (vt)	appludināt	[appludina:t]
flood, inundation	ūdens plūdi (v dsk)	[u:dens plu:di]

earthquake	zemestrīce (s)	[zɛmestri:tse]
tremor, quake	trieciens (v)	[triɛtsiɛns]
epicentre	epicentrs (v)	[epitsentrs]

eruption	izvirdums (v)	[izvirdums]
lava	lava (s)	[lava]

twister	virpuļvētra (s)	[virpulʲve:tra]
tornado	tornado (v)	[tɔrnadɔ]
typhoon	taifūns (v)	[taifu:ns]

hurricane	viesulis (v)	[viɛsulis]
storm	vētra (s)	[ve:tra]
tsunami	cunami (v)	[tsunami]
cyclone	ciklons (v)	[tsiklɔns]
bad weather	slikts laiks (v)	[slikts laiks]

fire (accident)	**ugunsgrēks** (v)	[ugunsgre:ks]
disaster	**katastrofa** (s)	[katastrofa]
meteorite	**meteorīts** (v)	[mɛteɔri:ts]

avalanche	**lavīna** (s)	[lavi:na]
snowslide	**sniega gāze** (s)	[sniɛga ga:ze]
blizzard	**sniegputenis** (v)	[sniɛgputenis]
snowstorm	**sniega vētra** (s)	[sniɛga ve:tra]

FAUNA

87. Mammals. Predators

predator	plēsoņa (s)	[ple:soŋa]
tiger	tīģeris (v)	[ti:dʲeris]
lion	lauva (s)	[lauva]
wolf	vilks (v)	[vilks]
fox	lapsa (s)	[lapsa]
jaguar	jaguārs (v)	[jagua:rs]
leopard	leopards (v)	[leɔpards]
cheetah	gepards (v)	[gɛpards]
black panther	pantera (s)	[pantɛra]
puma	puma (s)	[puma]
snow leopard	sniega leopards (v)	[sniɛga leɔpards]
lynx	lūsis (v)	[lu:sis]
coyote	koijots (v)	[kɔijɔts]
jackal	šakālis (v)	[ʃaka:lis]
hyena	hiēna (s)	[xiɛ:na]

88. Wild animals

animal	dzīvnieks (v)	[dzi:vniɛks]
beast (animal)	zvērs (v)	[zvɛ:rs]
squirrel	vāvere (s)	[va:vɛre]
hedgehog	ezis (v)	[ɛzis]
hare	zaķis (v)	[zatʲis]
rabbit	trusis (v)	[trusis]
badger	āpsis (v)	[a:psis]
raccoon	jenots (v)	[jenɔts]
hamster	kāmis (v)	[ka:mis]
marmot	murkšķis (v)	[murkʃtʲis]
mole	kurmis (v)	[kurmis]
mouse	pele (s)	[pɛle]
rat	žurka (s)	[ʒurka]
bat	sikspārnis (v)	[sikspa:rnis]
ermine	sermulis (v)	[sermulis]
sable	sabulis (v)	[sabulis]
marten	cauna (s)	[tsauna]
weasel	zebiekste (s)	[zebiɛkste]
mink	ūdele (s)	[u:dɛle]

| beaver | bebrs (v) | [bebrs] |
| otter | ūdrs (v) | [u:drs] |

horse	zirgs (v)	[zirgs]
moose	alnis (v)	[alnis]
deer	briedis (v)	[briɛdis]
camel	kamielis (v)	[kamiɛlis]

bison	bizons (v)	[bizɔns]
aurochs	sumbrs (v)	[sumbrs]
buffalo	bifelis (v)	[bifelis]

zebra	zebra (s)	[zebra]
antelope	antilope (s)	[antilɔpe]
roe deer	stirna (s)	[stirna]
fallow deer	dambriedis (v)	[dambriɛdis]
chamois	kalnu kaza (s)	[kalnu kaza]
wild boar	mežacūka (s)	[meʒatsu:ka]

whale	valis (v)	[valis]
seal	ronis (v)	[rɔnis]
walrus	valzirgs (v)	[valzirgs]
fur seal	kotiks (v)	[kɔtiks]
dolphin	delfīns (v)	[delfi:ns]

bear	lācis (v)	[la:tsis]
polar bear	baltais lācis (v)	[baltais la:tsis]
panda	panda (s)	[panda]

monkey	pērtiķis (v)	[pe:rtitʲis]
chimpanzee	šimpanze (s)	[ʃimpanze]
orangutan	orangutāns (v)	[ɔraŋguta:ns]
gorilla	gorilla (s)	[gɔrilla]
macaque	makaks (v)	[makaks]
gibbon	gibons (v)	[gibɔns]

elephant	zilonis (v)	[zilɔnis]
rhinoceros	degunradzis (v)	[dɛgunradzis]
giraffe	žirafe (s)	[ʒirafe]
hippopotamus	nīlzirgs (v)	[ni:lzirgs]

| kangaroo | ķengurs (v) | [tʲeŋgurs] |
| koala (bear) | koala (s) | [kɔala] |

mongoose	mangusts (v)	[maŋgusts]
chinchilla	šinšilla (s)	[ʃinʃilla]
skunk	skunkss (v)	[skunks]
porcupine	dzeloņcūka (s)	[dzelɔntsu:ka]

89. Domestic animals

cat	kaķis (v)	[katʲis]
tomcat	runcis (v)	[runtsis]
dog	suns (v)	[suns]

horse	zirgs (v)	[zirgs]
stallion (male horse)	ērzelis (v)	[e:rzelis]
mare	ķēve (s)	[tʲɛ:ve]
cow	govs (s)	[gɔvs]
bull	bullis (v)	[bullis]
ox	vērsis (v)	[vɛ:rsis]
sheep (ewe)	aita (s)	[aita]
ram	auns (v)	[auns]
goat	kaza (s)	[kaza]
billy goat, he-goat	āzis (v)	[a:zis]
donkey	ēzelis (v)	[ɛ:zelis]
mule	mūlis (v)	[mu:lis]
pig	cūka (s)	[tsu:ka]
piglet	sivēns (v)	[sive:ns]
rabbit	trusis (v)	[trusis]
hen (chicken)	vista (s)	[vista]
cock	gailis (v)	[gailis]
duck	pīle (s)	[pi:le]
drake	pīļtēviņš (v)	[pi:lʲte:viɲʃ]
goose	zoss (s)	[zɔs]
tom turkey, gobbler	tītars (v)	[ti:tars]
turkey (hen)	tītaru mātīte (s)	[ti:taru ma:ti:te]
domestic animals	mājdzīvnieki (v dsk)	[ma:jdzi:vniɛki]
tame (e.g. ~ hamster)	pieradināts	[piɛradina:ts]
to tame (vt)	pieradināt	[piɛradina:t]
to breed (vt)	audzēt	[audze:t]
farm	saimniecība (s)	[saimniɛtsi:ba]
poultry	mājputni (v dsk)	[ma:jputni]
cattle	liellopi (v dsk)	[liɛllopi]
herd (cattle)	ganāmpulks (v)	[gana:mpulks]
stable	zirgu stallis (v)	[zirgu stallis]
pigsty	cūkkūts (s)	[tsu:kku:ts]
cowshed	kūts (s)	[ku:ts]
rabbit hutch	trušu būda (s)	[truʃu bu:da]
hen house	vistu kūts (s)	[vistu ku:ts]

90. Birds

bird	putns (v)	[putns]
pigeon	balodis (v)	[balɔdis]
sparrow	zvirbulis (v)	[zvirbulis]
tit (great tit)	zīlīte (s)	[zi:li:te]
magpie	žagata (s)	[ʒagata]
raven	krauklis (v)	[krauklis]

crow	**vārna** (s)	[va:rna]
jackdaw	**kovārnis** (v)	[kɔva:rnis]
rook	**krauķis** (v)	[krautˡis]

duck	**pīle** (s)	[pi:le]
goose	**zoss** (s)	[zɔs]
pheasant	**fazāns** (v)	[faza:ns]

eagle	**ērglis** (v)	[e:rglis]
hawk	**vanags** (v)	[vanags]
falcon	**piekūns** (v)	[piɛku:ns]
vulture	**grifs** (v)	[grifs]
condor (Andean ~)	**kondors** (v)	[kɔndɔrs]

swan	**gulbis** (v)	[gulbis]
crane	**dzērve** (s)	[dze:rve]
stork	**stārķis** (v)	[sta:rtˡis]

parrot	**papagailis** (v)	[papagailis]
hummingbird	**kolibri** (v)	[kolibri]
peacock	**pāvs** (v)	[pa:vs]

ostrich	**strauss** (v)	[straus]
heron	**gārnis** (v)	[ga:rnis]
flamingo	**flamings** (v)	[flamiŋgs]
pelican	**pelikāns** (v)	[pelika:ns]

nightingale	**lakstīgala** (s)	[laksti:gala]
swallow	**bezdelīga** (s)	[bezdeli:ga]

thrush	**strazds** (v)	[strazds]
song thrush	**dziedātājstrazds** (v)	[dziɛda:ta:jstrazds]
blackbird	**melnais strazds** (v)	[melnais strazds]

swift	**svīre** (s)	[svi:re]
lark	**cīrulis** (v)	[tsi:rulis]
quail	**paipala** (s)	[paipala]

woodpecker	**dzenis** (v)	[dzenis]
cuckoo	**dzeguze** (s)	[dzɛguze]
owl	**pūce** (s)	[pu:tse]
eagle owl	**ūpis** (v)	[u:pis]
wood grouse	**mednis** (v)	[mednis]
black grouse	**rubenis** (v)	[rubenis]
partridge	**irbe** (s)	[irbe]

starling	**mājas strazds** (v)	[ma:jas strazds]
canary	**kanārijputniņš** (v)	[kana:rijputniɲʃ]
hazel grouse	**meža irbe** (s)	[meʒa irbe]

chaffinch	**žubīte** (s)	[ʒubi:te]
bullfinch	**svilpis** (v)	[svilpis]

seagull	**kaija** (s)	[kaija]
albatross	**albatross** (v)	[albatrɔs]
penguin	**pingvīns** (v)	[piŋgvi:ns]

91. Fish. Marine animals

bream	plaudis (v)	[plaudis]
carp	karpa (s)	[karpa]
perch	asaris (v)	[asaris]
catfish	sams (v)	[sams]
pike	līdaka (s)	[li:daka]
salmon	lasis (v)	[lasis]
sturgeon	store (s)	[stɔre]
herring	siļķe (s)	[silʲtʲe]
Atlantic salmon	lasis (v)	[lasis]
mackerel	skumbrija (s)	[skumbrija]
flatfish	bute (s)	[bute]
zander, pike perch	zandarts (v)	[zandarts]
cod	menca (s)	[mentsa]
tuna	tuncis (v)	[tuntsis]
trout	forele (s)	[fɔrɛle]
eel	zutis (v)	[zutis]
electric ray	elektriskā raja (s)	[ɛlektriska: raja]
moray eel	murēna (s)	[murɛ:na]
piranha	piraija (s)	[piraija]
shark	haizivs (s)	[xaizivs]
dolphin	delfīns (v)	[delfi:ns]
whale	valis (v)	[valis]
crab	krabis (v)	[krabis]
jellyfish	medūza (s)	[mɛdu:za]
octopus	astoņkājis (v)	[astɔɲka:jis]
starfish	jūras zvaigzne (s)	[ju:ras zvaigzne]
sea urchin	jūras ezis (v)	[ju:ras ezis]
seahorse	jūras zirdziņš (v)	[ju:ras zirdziɲʃ]
oyster	austere (s)	[austɛre]
prawn	garnele (s)	[garnɛle]
lobster	omārs (v)	[ɔma:rs]
spiny lobster	langusts (v)	[langusts]

92. Amphibians. Reptiles

snake	čūska (s)	[tʃu:ska]
venomous (snake)	indīga	[indi:ga]
viper	odze (s)	[ɔdze]
cobra	kobra (s)	[kɔbra]
python	pitons (v)	[pitɔns]
boa	žņaudzējčūska (s)	[ʒɲaudze:jtʃu:ska]
grass snake	zalktis (v)	[zalktis]

| rattle snake | klaburčūska (s) | [klaburtʃuːska] |
| anaconda | anakonda (s) | [anakɔnda] |

lizard	ķirzaka (s)	[tʲirzaka]
iguana	iguāna (s)	[iguaːna]
monitor lizard	varāns (v)	[varaːns]
salamander	salamandra (s)	[salamandra]
chameleon	hameleons (v)	[xamɛleɔns]
scorpion	skorpions (v)	[skɔrpiɔns]

turtle	bruņurupucis (v)	[bruɲuruputsis]
frog	varde (s)	[varde]
toad	krupis (v)	[krupis]
crocodile	krokodils (v)	[krɔkɔdils]

93. Insects

insect	kukainis (v)	[kukainis]
butterfly	taurenis (v)	[taurenis]
ant	skudra (s)	[skudra]
fly	muša (s)	[muʃa]
mosquito	ods (v)	[ɔds]
beetle	vabole (s)	[vabɔle]

wasp	lapsene (s)	[lapsɛne]
bee	bite (s)	[bite]
bumblebee	kamene (s)	[kamɛne]
gadfly (botfly)	dundurs (v)	[dundurs]

| spider | zirneklis (v) | [zirneklis] |
| spider's web | zirnekļtīkls (v) | [zirneklʲtiːkls] |

dragonfly	spāre (s)	[spaːre]
grasshopper	sienāzis (v)	[siɛnaːzis]
moth (night butterfly)	tauriņš (v)	[tauriɲʃ]

cockroach	prusaks (v)	[prusaks]
tick	ērce (s)	[eːrtse]
flea	blusa (s)	[blusa]
midge	knislis (v)	[knislis]

locust	sisenis (v)	[sisenis]
snail	gliemezis (v)	[gliɛmezis]
cricket	circenis (v)	[tsirtsenis]
firefly	jāņtārpiņš (v)	[jaːɲtaːrpiɲʃ]
ladybird	mārīte (s)	[maːriːte]
cockchafer	maijvabole (s)	[maijvabɔle]

leech	dēle (s)	[dɛːle]
caterpillar	kāpurs (v)	[kaːpurs]
earthworm	tārps (v)	[taːrps]
larva	kāpurs (v)	[kaːpurs]

FLORA

94. Trees

tree	koks (v)	[kɔks]
deciduous (adj)	lapu koks	[lapu kɔks]
coniferous (adj)	skujkoks	[skujkɔks]
evergreen (adj)	mūžzaļš	[muːʒzalʲʃ]
apple tree	ābele (s)	[aːbɛle]
pear tree	bumbiere (s)	[bumbiɛre]
sweet cherry tree	saldais ķirsis (v)	[saldais tʲirsis]
sour cherry tree	skābais ķirsis (v)	[skaːbais tʲirsis]
plum tree	plūme (s)	[pluːme]
birch	bērzs (v)	[beːrzs]
oak	ozols (v)	[ɔzɔls]
linden tree	liepa (s)	[liɛpa]
aspen	apse (s)	[apse]
maple	kļava (s)	[klʲava]
spruce	egle (s)	[egle]
pine	priede (s)	[priɛde]
larch	lapegle (s)	[lapegle]
fir tree	dižegle (s)	[diʒegle]
cedar	ciedrs (v)	[tsiɛdrs]
poplar	papele (s)	[papɛle]
rowan	pīlādzis (v)	[piːlaːdzis]
willow	vītols (v)	[viːtɔls]
alder	alksnis (v)	[alksnis]
beech	dižskābardis (v)	[diʒskaːbardis]
elm	vīksna (s)	[viːksna]
ash (tree)	osis (v)	[ɔsis]
chestnut	kastaņa (s)	[kastaɲa]
magnolia	magnolija (s)	[magnɔlija]
palm tree	palma (s)	[palma]
cypress	ciprese (s)	[tsiprɛse]
mangrove	mango koks (v)	[maŋgɔ kɔks]
baobab	baobabs (v)	[baɔbabs]
eucalyptus	eikalipts (v)	[ɛikalipts]
sequoia	sekvoja (s)	[sekvɔja]

95. Shrubs

bush	Krūms (v)	[kruːms]
shrub	krūmājs (v)	[kruːmaːjs]

grapevine	vīnogas (v)	[vi:nɔgas]
vineyard	vīnogulājs (v)	[vi:nɔgula:js]

raspberry bush	avenājs (v)	[avɛna:js]
blackcurrant bush	upeņu krūms (v)	[upɛɲu kru:ms]
redcurrant bush	sarkano jāņogu krūms (v)	[sarkanɔ ja:ɲɔgu kru:ms]
gooseberry bush	ērkšķogu krūms (v)	[e:rkʃtˡɔgu kru:ms]

acacia	akācija (s)	[aka:tsija]
barberry	bārbele (s)	[ba:rbɛle]
jasmine	jasmīns (v)	[jasmi:ns]

juniper	kadiķis (v)	[kaditˡis]
rosebush	rožu krūms (v)	[rɔʒu kru:ms]
dog rose	mežroze (s)	[meʒrɔze]

96. Fruits. Berries

fruit	auglis (v)	[auglis]
fruits	augļi (v dsk)	[auglˡi]
apple	ābols (v)	[a:bɔls]
pear	bumbieris (v)	[bumbiɛris]
plum	plūme (s)	[plu:me]

strawberry (garden ~)	zemene (s)	[zɛmɛne]
sour cherry	skābais ķirsis (v)	[ska:bais tˡirsis]
sweet cherry	saldais ķirsis (v)	[saldais tˡirsis]
grape	vīnoga (s)	[vi:nɔga]

raspberry	avene (s)	[avɛne]
blackcurrant	upene (s)	[upɛne]
redcurrant	sarkanā jāņoga (s)	[sarkana: ja:ɲɔga]
gooseberry	ērkšķoga (s)	[e:rkʃtˡɔga]
cranberry	dzērvene (s)	[dze:rvɛne]

orange	apelsīns (v)	[apɛlsi:ns]
tangerine	mandarīns (v)	[mandari:ns]
pineapple	ananāss (v)	[anana:s]

banana	banāns (v)	[bana:ns]
date	datele (s)	[datɛle]

lemon	citrons (v)	[tsitrɔns]
apricot	aprikoze (s)	[aprikɔze]
peach	persiks (v)	[pɛrsiks]

kiwi	kivi (v)	[kivi]
grapefruit	greipfrūts (v)	[grɛipfru:ts]

berry	oga (s)	[ɔga]
berries	ogas (s dsk)	[ɔgas]
cowberry	brūklene (s)	[bru:klɛne]
wild strawberry	meža zemene (s)	[meʒa zɛmɛne]
bilberry	mellene (s)	[mellɛne]

97. Flowers. Plants

flower	zieds (v)	[ziɛds]
bouquet (of flowers)	ziedu pušķis (v)	[ziɛdu puʃtʲis]
rose (flower)	roze (s)	[rɔze]
tulip	tulpe (s)	[tulpe]
carnation	neļķe (s)	[nelʲtʲe]
gladiolus	gladiola (s)	[gladiɔla]
cornflower	rudzupuķīte (s)	[rudzuputʲi:te]
harebell	pulkstenīte (s)	[pulksteni:te]
dandelion	pienenīte (s)	[piɛneni:te]
camomile	kumelīte (s)	[kumeli:te]
aloe	alveja (s)	[alveja]
cactus	kaktuss (v)	[kaktus]
rubber plant, ficus	gumijkoks (v)	[gumijkɔks]
lily	lilija (s)	[lilija]
geranium	ģerānija (s)	[dʲɛra:nija]
hyacinth	hiacinte (s)	[xiatsinte]
mimosa	mimoza (s)	[mimɔza]
narcissus	narcise (s)	[nartsise]
nasturtium	krese (s)	[krɛse]
orchid	orhideja (s)	[ɔrxideja]
peony	pujene (s)	[pujene]
violet	vijolīte (s)	[vijɔli:te]
pansy	atraitnītes (s dsk)	[atraitni:tes]
forget-me-not	neaizmirstule (s)	[neaizmirstule]
daisy	margrietiņa (s)	[margriɛtiɲa]
poppy	magone (s)	[magɔne]
hemp	kaņepe (s)	[kaɲɛpe]
mint	mētra (s)	[me:tra]
lily of the valley	maijpuķīte (s)	[maijputʲi:te]
snowdrop	sniegpulkstenīte (s)	[sniɛgpulksteni:te]
nettle	nātre (s)	[na:tre]
sorrel	skābene (s)	[ska:bɛne]
water lily	ūdensroze (s)	[u:densrɔze]
fern	paparde (s)	[paparde]
lichen	ķērpis (v)	[tʲe:rpis]
greenhouse (tropical ~)	oranžērija (s)	[ɔranʒe:rija]
lawn	zālājs (v)	[za:la:js]
flowerbed	puķu dobe (s)	[putʲu dɔbe]
plant	augs (v)	[augs]
grass	zāle (s)	[za:le]
blade of grass	zālīte (s)	[za:li:te]

leaf	lapa (s)	[lapa]
petal	lapiņa (s)	[lapiɲa]
stem	stiebrs (v)	[stiɛbrs]
tuber	bumbulis (v)	[bumbulis]

young plant (shoot)	dīglis (v)	[diːglis]
thorn	ērkšķis (v)	[eːrkʃtʲis]

to blossom (vi)	ziedēt	[ziɛdeːt]
to fade, to wither	novīt	[nɔviːt]
smell (odour)	smarža (s)	[smarʒa]
to cut (flowers)	nogriezt	[nɔgriɛzt]
to pick (a flower)	noplūkt	[nɔpluːkt]

98. Cereals, grains

grain	graudi (v dsk)	[graudi]
cereal crops	graudaugi (v dsk)	[graudaugi]
ear (of barley, etc.)	vārpa (s)	[vaːrpa]

wheat	kvieši (v dsk)	[kviɛʃi]
rye	rudzi (v dsk)	[rudzi]
oats	auzas (s dsk)	[auzas]
millet	prosa (s)	[prɔsa]
barley	mieži (v dsk)	[miɛʒi]

maize	kukurūza (s)	[kukuruːza]
rice	rīsi (v dsk)	[riːsi]
buckwheat	griķi (v dsk)	[gritʲi]

pea plant	zirnis (v)	[zirnis]
kidney bean	pupiņas (s dsk)	[pupiɲas]
soya	soja (s)	[sɔja]
lentil	lēcas (s dsk)	[leːtsas]
beans (pulse crops)	pupas (s dsk)	[pupas]

COUNTRIES OF THE WORLD

99. Countries. Part 1

Afghanistan	Afganistāna (s)	[afganista:na]
Albania	Albānija (s)	[alba:nija]
Argentina	Argentīna (s)	[argenti:na]
Armenia	Armēnija (s)	[arme:nija]
Australia	Austrālija (s)	[austra:lija]
Austria	Austrija (s)	[austrija]
Azerbaijan	Azerbaidžāna (s)	[azerbaidʒa:na]

The Bahamas	Bahamu salas (s dsk)	[baxamu salas]
Bangladesh	Bangladeša (s)	[baŋgladeʃa]
Belarus	Baltkrievija (s)	[baltkriɛvija]
Belgium	Beļģija (s)	[belʲdʲija]
Bolivia	Bolīvija (s)	[boli:vija]
Bosnia and Herzegovina	Bosnija un Hercegovina (s)	[bosnija un xertsegɔvina]
Brazil	Brazīlija (s)	[brazi:lija]
Bulgaria	Bulgārija (s)	[bulga:rija]

Cambodia	Kambodža (s)	[kambɔdʒa]
Canada	Kanāda (s)	[kana:da]
Chile	Čīle (s)	[tʃi:le]
China	Ķīna (s)	[tʲi:na]
Colombia	Kolumbija (s)	[kɔlumbija]
Croatia	Horvātija (s)	[xɔrva:tija]
Cuba	Kuba (s)	[kuba]

| Cyprus | Kipra (s) | [kipra] |
| Czech Republic | Čehija (s) | [tʃexija] |

Denmark	Dānija (s)	[da:nija]
Dominican Republic	Dominikas Republika (s)	[dɔminikas rɛpublika]
Ecuador	Ekvadora (s)	[ekvadɔra]
Egypt	Ēģipte (s)	[e:dʲipte]
England	Anglija (s)	[aŋglija]
Estonia	Igaunija (s)	[igaunija]
Finland	Somija (s)	[sɔmija]

| France | Francija (s) | [frantsija] |
| French Polynesia | Frančū Polinēzija (s) | [frantʃu poline:zija] |

Georgia	Gruzija (s)	[gruzija]
Germany	Vācija (s)	[va:tsija]
Ghana	Gana (s)	[gana]
Great Britain	Lielbritānija (s)	[liɛlbrita:nija]
Greece	Grieķija (s)	[griɛtʲija]
Haiti	Haiti (v)	[xaiti]
Hungary	Ungārija (s)	[uŋga:rija]

100. Countries. Part 2

Iceland	Īslande (s)	[i:slande]
India	Indija (s)	[indija]
Indonesia	Indonēzija (s)	[indone:zija]
Iran	Irāna (s)	[ira:na]
Iraq	Irāka (s)	[ira:ka]
Ireland	Īrija (s)	[i:rija]
Israel	Izraēla (s)	[izraɛ:la]
Italy	Itālija (s)	[ita:lija]

Jamaica	Jamaika (s)	[jamaika]
Japan	Japāna (s)	[japa:na]
Jordan	Jordānija (s)	[jorda:nija]
Kazakhstan	Kazahstāna (s)	[kazaxsta:na]
Kenya	Kenija (s)	[kenija]
Kirghizia	Kirgizstāna (s)	[kirgizsta:na]
Kuwait	Kuveita (s)	[kuvɛita]

Laos	Laosa (s)	[laosa]
Latvia	Latvija (s)	[latvija]
Lebanon	Libāna (s)	[liba:na]
Libya	Lībija (s)	[li:bija]
Liechtenstein	Lihtenšteina (s)	[lixtenʃtɛina]
Lithuania	Lietuva (s)	[liɛtuva]
Luxembourg	Luksemburga (s)	[luksemburga]

Macedonia (Republic of ~)	Maķedonija (s)	[matˈedonija]
Madagascar	Madagaskara (s)	[madagaskara]
Malaysia	Malaizija (s)	[malaizija]
Malta	Malta (s)	[malta]
Mexico	Meksika (s)	[meksika]

Moldova, Moldavia	Moldova (s)	[moldova]
Monaco	Monako (s)	[monako]
Mongolia	Mongolija (s)	[moŋgolija]
Montenegro	Melnkalne (s)	[melnkalne]
Morocco	Maroka (s)	[maroka]
Myanmar	Mjanma (s)	[mjanma]

Namibia	Namībija (s)	[nami:bija]
Nepal	Nepāla (s)	[nɛpa:la]
Netherlands	Nīderlande (s)	[ni:derlande]
New Zealand	Jaunzēlande (s)	[jaunzɛ:lande]
North Korea	Ziemeļkoreja (s)	[ziɛmelˈkoreja]
Norway	Norvēģija (s)	[norve:dˈija]

101. Countries. Part 3

Pakistan	Pakistāna (s)	[pakista:na]
Palestine	Palestīna (s)	[palesti:na]
Panama	Panama (s)	[panama]
Paraguay	Paragvaja (s)	[paragvaja]

Peru	Peru (v)	[pɛru]
Poland	Polija (s)	[polija]
Portugal	Portugāle (s)	[portuga:le]
Romania	Rumānija (s)	[ruma:nija]
Russia	Krievija (s)	[kriɛvija]

Saudi Arabia	Saūda Arābija (s)	[sau:da ara:bija]
Scotland	Skotija (s)	[skotija]
Senegal	Senegāla (s)	[senɛga:la]
Serbia	Serbija (s)	[serbija]
Slovakia	Slovākija (s)	[slova:kija]
Slovenia	Slovēnija (s)	[slove:nija]

South Africa	Dienvidāfrikas Republika (s)	[diɛnvida:frikas rɛpublika]
South Korea	Dienvidkoreja (s)	[diɛnvidkoreja]
Spain	Spānija (s)	[spa:nija]
Suriname	Surinama (s)	[surinama]
Sweden	Zviedrija (s)	[zviɛdrija]
Switzerland	Šveice (s)	[ʃvɛitse]
Syria	Sīrija (s)	[si:rija]

Taiwan	Taivāna (s)	[taiva:na]
Tajikistan	Tadžikistāna (s)	[tadʒikista:na]
Tanzania	Tanzānija (s)	[tanza:nija]
Tasmania	Tasmānija (s)	[tasma:nija]
Thailand	Taizeme (s)	[taizɛme]
Tunisia	Tunisija (s)	[tunisija]
Turkey	Turcija (s)	[turtsija]
Turkmenistan	Turkmenistāna (s)	[turkmenista:na]

Ukraine	Ukraina (s)	[ukraina]
United Arab Emirates	Apvienotie Arābu Emirāti (v dsk)	[apviɛnotiɛ ara:bu emira:ti]
United States of America	Amerikas Savienotās Valstis (s dsk)	[amerikas saviɛnota:s valstis]
Uruguay	Urugvaja (s)	[urugvaja]
Uzbekistan	Uzbekistāna (s)	[uzbekista:na]

Vatican	Vatikāns (v)	[vatika:ns]
Venezuela	Venecuēla (s)	[vɛnetsuɛ:la]
Vietnam	Vjetnama (s)	[vjetnama]
Zanzibar	Zanzibāra (s)	[zanziba:ra]